JONATHAN & JESSE
KELLERMAN
THE INTERNATIONAL BESTSELLING AUTHORS

lost
souls

C
CENTURY

1 3 5 7 9 10 8 6 4 2

Century
20 Vauxhall Bridge Road
London SW1V 2SA

Century is part of the Penguin Random House group of companies
whose addresses can be found at global.penguinrandomhouse.com.

Copyright © Jonathan and Jesse Kellerman 2020

Jonathan Kellerman & Jesse Kellerman have asserted their right to be identified as the
authors of this Work in accordance with the Copyright, Designs and Patents Act 1988.

First published in Great Britain by Century in 2020

www.penguin.co.uk

A CIP catalogue record for this book is available from the British Library.

Hardback ISBN 9781780899077
Trade Paperback ISBN 9781780899084

Printed and bound in Great Britain by Clays Ltd, Elcograf S.p.A.

Penguin Random House is committed to a sustainable future
for our business, our readers and our planet. This book is made
from Forest Stewardship Council® certified paper.

lost
souls

CHAPTER 1

O n a damp Saturday, just last year, the sixties finally died in Berkeley.

On Sunday, I came for the bones.

THE END BEGAN the day after Christmas, at dawn. With a wrecking crew standing by, a team of University of California police officers entered People's Park to rouse the two dozen bodies curled limp in the bushes, pressed against tree trunks, atop and under benches, ordering them to vacate the premises.

The third sweep in as many days.

Each time, the park residents who'd been kicked out at six a.m. came back at ten p.m. to bed down, as though returning from a long day at the office.

A week prior, the university had installed a chain-link fence around the perimeter. It had been scaled, sheared open, knocked down.

A month before that, campus cops had circulated through the neighborhood, handing out flyers giving notice of the demolition and verbally notifying those who refused the paper or threw it back, in one instance using it first to wipe an ass.

The previous year, the architecture firm contracted for the project had erected large multicolored signs along Dwight Way and

Haste Street depicting a pristine six-story dormitory alongside detached ground-floor units of supportive housing for the homeless.

Modern. Clean. Green. The drawings showed faceless humanoids gliding through streak-free glass doors. It was impossible to tell the students from the homeless. Everyone was wearing a backpack.

Within days, Berkeley Fire found the signs ablaze in a dumpster.

Articles about the closure of the park and op-eds either lamenting or celebrating its demise had been a fixture of local media for four years running. There'd been a public hearing, two lawsuits, multiple town halls, and city council meetings too numerous to count.

Nobody could claim they hadn't been warned.

The run-up to Demolition Day was a continuation of a fifty-year tug-of-war, begun when a group of hippies wielding gardening implements converged on a muddy, disused lot owned by the university and claimed it in the name of The People.

As far as sacred spaces go, it ain't much to look at.

Three scrubby acres, few natural features, murals flaking, vegetation in perpetual decline, the province of drifters, addicts, and the mentally ill. An average day sees the cops summoned five times. There's a playground, but not one you'd knowingly take a child to. Not long ago, a nanny short on context, common sense, or both brought a two-year-old boy to the swings. A parkie sauntered up and shoved a "Tootsie Roll" into his mouth. It turned out to be meth.

Nobody who cares about Berkeley looks at the park and sees the existing reality. They see what it represents.

Love Not War. Food Not Bombs. Freedom of Speech. Respect Mother Earth. Heritage. Progress. Hope.

The housing crisis. The mental health crisis. The opioid epidemic. Crime. Corruption. Waste.

On that damp December morning, what remained of The People stood behind sawhorses at the corner of Bowditch and Haste: nine aging Boomers waving cardboard signs. They looked invigorated, passing around a joint between chants.

Whose Park?

Our Park.

A bulldozer started up, drowning them out.

One protester began to weep. Others cast about in search of the cavalry. Nobody was coming. It was too chilly. Too early. Undergrads had decamped for winter break. And to them, People's Park meant nothing but a chronic shortage of dorm beds and an inconvenient detour walking home from the library at night.

The construction foreman unlocked the fence gate and spread it wide.

The first bulldozer rolled over the sidewalk and lumbered toward the western side of the park, lowering its blade as it advanced on the Free Speech Stage. Mist clung to the lawns. Over the growl of the diesel engine rose a wet, mealy crunch, steel teeth chewing plywood and paint. Depending on whom you asked, it was either a dagger through the heart of a dream, or a stake driven into a corpse.

DON'T COUNT THE People out just yet.

By late the next morning, the crowd behind the sawhorses had swelled to over a hundred. Demolition noise still outpowered the chants, but not by much.

U-C police!

We see fascists!

The People 2.0 were environmental activists, housing activists, transit activists, vegans, freegans, black-bloc types in Guy Fawkes masks. Plus the one-offs: A trance-dancing nudist with nipples erect in the cold. An emaciated man with a skull-like face who let out a bloodcurdling shriek whenever the tree trimmers lopped off a branch.

At the other end of the site was a smaller counterprotest, fifteen strong. They'd driven in from Alamo and Santa Clara, bringing American flags, coolers, a charcoal grill.

Na na na na they sang.

Na na na na.

Hey heeeeey—goodbye!

Smack between them, the media.

Under the operations tent, a UC police lieutenant named Florence Sibley was keyed up and pacing. This was her show, an unwelcome chance at stardom. For every professional reporter or cameraman on hand, she assumed, three amateurs were livestreaming.

So far, so good. Minimal resistance from the parkies. No violence from the protesters. The mood was taut but not incendiary. How long could she keep it that way?

She had Alameda County Sheriff's on standby if things got out of hand. But her superiors had made it clear that asking for help would constitute an embarrassment for the department.

Put on your big-boy pants.

Sibley looked at the protesters. The nudist twirled in ecstatic circles. Purple body paint on her back spelled out L O V E.

In the counterprotester camp, lots of taunts and burger chomping. One man had stripped off his shirt and was slapping his bare belly.

Who said the two sides couldn't find common ground?

One of Sibley's sergeants, Brodie Ford, jogged up. "You need to come see something."

"What something?"

Ford didn't reply.

Sibley thought: *Not part of the plan.*

THE FOREMAN WAS a man in his midfifties named Nestor Arriola. He wore a hard hat, a reflective vest, and a black polo shirt emblazoned with the construction firm logo of a derrick. He'd been up since six a.m., just like every morning of his working life since age fifteen. He met Sibley and Ford at the southwest pedestrian gate, handed them each a hard hat and a reflective vest, and led them to the vicinity of the former Free Speech Stage, now a hexagonal pit.

Debris had been cleared, and the excavator operator had begun peeling back Mother Earth in layers. The driver was a young white guy with sunken cheeks and a tall brow wearing his hat crookedly, like a mushroom cap.

"It sort of caught the sun, you know?" he said. He glanced apprehensively at his boss, as if to apologize for being observant. "Got my attention."

"It" was an eyeball. Nestled in a mound of rich dark soil, about ten feet from the pit's edge, it stood out like a boil.

Sibley said, "You did right."

Nestor Arriola told the driver, "Go take ten," and the guy hustled off.

Arriola turned to Sibley. "Looks fake to me."

He was probably right. The stage had stood on that spot for decades. No way an eyeball wouldn't decompose. But probably wasn't for sure.

Sibley scooted down into the pit and walked over, stooping to examine the eyeball. It was cartoonishly large, with a bright-blue iris. She had never married or had kids, but she did have nephews. She'd bought them tons of gifts over the years, before they hit adolescence and morphed into—her sister's words—"uber-assholes."

Point being, Sibley knew a doll eye when she saw one.

She flashed a thumbs-up at Arriola. "Fake."

He turned to fetch Mushroom.

It was then that Florence Sibley made the first of two consequential decisions.

She said, "Hang on a sec."

Arriola, impatient to get back on schedule, said, "What for?"

Sibley didn't have a ready answer. She didn't know what she

expected to find. More fake eyes? Who cared? But she was having second thoughts, and she motioned Brodie Ford into the pit. He looked as skeptical as Arriola.

Sibley said, "We'll just do a quick sift."

The two of them knelt, pawing with their bare hands, cold hard rock and the moist squish of earthworms and beetles, digging elbow-deep. Sibley began to feel foolish.

Ford said, "Hold up."

Surfacing in the dirt, another speck of blue, the same garish shade as the fake iris.

He worked his fingers in and tugged out the corner of a blanket.

Grimy, edged in satin. Sibley could picture the matching teddy bear. The items would have come as a set. Maybe monogrammed, initials or a first name.

Brodie Ford continued to scrape away at the ground, revealing more of the blanket, bundled up and packed down.

"Ah, shit," he said.

His breathing had gone fast and shallow.

He reached.

Sibley grabbed his wrist. "Leave it."

The bundle of blankets had become disturbed.

From one end protruded the sharp tip of a broken bone.

Cradled in a fold was a tiny, dirt-smeared tooth.

The noonday sun fell frigid on Sibley's neck.

Nestor Arriola stood at the pit edge, wearing the defeated sag of a man who answers the door to find an unloved relative toting suit-cases.

Florence Sibley stood up, knees cricking, and made her second consequential decision of the day.

CHAPTER 2

I didn't know anything yet. I wasn't at the bureau.

I was trapped in a chair, being held hostage.

"Please," I said.

Pitiless eyes stared back.

"Please," I repeated, my voice breaking. "I can't do this any longer."

The eyes scrutinized me. *Are you truly this weak.*

"It's been two hours," I said. "I can't feel my arms."

The eyes blinked lethargically. They were getting bored of me and my pleading.

"Thank God," I whispered.

The eyes blinked once more, fluttered, then closed.

Slowly—I'd never known I was capable of moving so slowly—I rose from the glider, carried the baby to the crib, and set her down.

I tiptoed out.

I shut the door.

I ran.

I MADE IT to the kitchenette, seizing an abandoned tuna fish sandwich from the counter before pivoting sharply toward the futon—the kind of elegant, ankle-straining maneuver that, back in the day, would've thrown a defender off balance and gotten the crowd going.

Ooooh lookit! That right there is dis-re-speck-ful.

I stretched out, groping for the remote, bringing the sandwich to my mouth.

My right pocket vibrated.

A text from Amy.

everything ok

Before I could thumb a reply, more bubbles started popping up.

how many oz did she take

did she seem gassy

remember to mark the bag after u sterilize nipples

don't you have patients I managed to write.

in 5 min

we're fine don't worry

it's hard I miss her I'm thinking about her and my milk is letting down

I'm sorry. she misses you too

should I come home

The baby began to wail.

we're totally fine I wrote, except that what I actually wrote was *were totally fone,* which my phone changed to *we're totally done.*

done with what Amy wrote.

fine we're 100% done

what's going on is everything ok

fine fine duck this ducking shirt

The crying built steadily.

we are fine I wrote. *promise*

can u send me a pic

she's in her crib I wrote, not lying.

when she wakes up

The crying filled the universe, blotted it out.

remember Amy wrote *dr said we need to avoid day/night confusion*

ok

expose her to sunlight

ok

don't let her nap more than two hours at a stretch

not a problem I wrote.

I left the sandwich and the phone on the coffee table and went to Charlotte's room.

She'd worked herself free of the swaddle, knocked the pacifier out of her mouth, and was now whacking herself in the head like a crazed penitent.

"My love," I said. "Why must you do this to yourself?"

She went quiet and looked up at me.

I read somewhere that all babies start out resembling their fathers—a trick of evolution, meant to curtail paternal abandonment or infanticide. Almost certainly it's apocryphal, and I was suffering from infatuation.

But.

The dark, floppy hair: mine.

The light-brown eyes, flecked with gold: mine.

Through the baby fat you could see the contours of her face, and they were mine, slightly feminized.

The way she liked to lie, curled up on her left side—that's how I sleep. When I stood her in my lap I could feel her not merely bearing weight, but actively trying to jump, and I pictured her long body, drawn out like molten glass, reaching to haul in a rebound.

Her resting expression, studious and steady, fixing on a point of interest with unnerving tenacity. It's the face I use to wait out a suspect withholding information.

When she smiles, though, it's pure Amy. Starting on the right and working its way across, a slow-rolling wave of joy. All aboard the happiness train. That includes you.

Charlotte smiled.

I smiled back.

"Very funny," I said. "You know what this is, right?"

"Ooh," she said.

"That's right. It's Stockholm syndrome."

"Ooh."

"I agree." I lifted her out of the crib. "Coffee sounds great."

THE DISCOVERY OF potential human remains sets a protocol in motion.

The first call goes to local law enforcement. Not necessary: Sibley was already there.

The next step depends on the competence of the officers at the scene. Ideally, they touch nothing, back away, and secure the area. Bored or creative or stupid types have been known to poke around. I've had uniforms move a body for no other reason than to remove a bothersome sight.

We don't like that.

Thankfully, Sibley was diligent by nature. Even her impulse to rummage in the dirt stemmed from a more fundamental desire not to fuck up.

Flo Sibley knew protocol.

The second call goes to the Alameda County Sheriff's Office, Coroner's Bureau. That Sunday, there were four deputy coroners on duty, none of whom were me. I was home, mixing formula.

On any other day, under any other circumstances, with any other officer running the show, I never would have gotten the case. But shrewd, diligent Florence Sibley—desperate to not be the person responsible for bringing a ninety-eight-million-dollar project to a standstill—did something that was, for her, unprecedented.

She broke protocol.

Instead of calling the Coroner's Bureau, she phoned her boss, Captain Albert Yang.

He said, "Goddammit, Sibley."

Not wanting to be that person, either, he called *his* boss, Donald Vogel, the chief of UCPD ("Goddammit, Al"), who called the UC Berkeley chancellor.

She didn't pick up. She was at a conference in Zurich, serving on a panel about the changing nature of standardized testing. Nice timing.

The chief then called the executive vice chancellor, who said, "Oy vey."

With no one to punt to, the chief hurried to reassure the vice chancellor that in all likelihood the bones would turn out to be non-human. And if they were human, that didn't necessarily portend a lengthy hiatus. There might be a completely innocuous explanation.

"For God's sake, Donny," the vice chancellor said. "Beneath the *stage?*"

Vogel agreed the optics weren't great. Still, after an initial in situ analysis, any investigation would take place offsite, at which point they could authorize work to resume.

The vice chancellor said, "Give me worst-case scenario."

Vogel said, "Well, say the remains were Native American. You know."

"I don't. What happens then?"

"There's a group takes care of it. They repatriate to whatever tribal land's closest."

"And then?"

"And then we get right back to work."

"I asked for worst case."

"In theory, they could ask to inspect the rest of the site. But—but, look, around here, it's not uncommon to find bones. Happens all the time."

"Exactly." The vice chancellor was thinking of the myriad local development projects drowning in litigation. He was envisioning his brand-spanking-new mixed-use dormitory, smothered in crime scene tape.

"Native versus non-Native," he said. "Who makes that determination?"

It dawned on the chief that there *was* someone he could punt to.

"The Coroner," he said.

"Not an anthropologist?"

"They have people they work with."

"Have they been informed yet?"

"I was going to call them next. I wanted to give you a heads-up."

"I appreciate that," the vice chancellor said. "You are aware that we happen to have an *outstanding* anthropology department right here on campus. Number two, worldwide."

"That high? I didn't realize."

"Top five, at least, for the last several years. I'm confident this is a question they're more than capable of answering."

"Right." The chief hesitated. "In my experience, the Coroner's Bureau has individuals they prefer to use."

"Of course. Of course. By all means, do what you need to do. I'm not suggesting otherwise. I'm saying from an *informational* standpoint. So that I—we—can know what to reasonably expect. You can understand, given everything at stake—people, and jobs— that it's essential for us to stay a step or two ahead."

"I understand."

"It can't hurt, either, to have our own expert on hand. As a supplement. To provide the scholarly perspective. You don't mind if I make a quick call."

"Sure," the chief said. "How long will it take?"

"Not long at all, I should think."

"What do you want me to tell the foreman?"

"Tell him," the vice chancellor said, opening his contacts, "to enjoy his lunch."

AMY SAID, "How do people do this?"

At four p.m., I was dressing for work. She was getting ready to shower. Steam billowed over the curtain.

The logic behind my transfer to night shift was that, by trading off with the baby, we could both return to work relatively quickly. The pregnancy was unplanned, which meant I'd banked precious little leave. Amy had more flexibility. She's a psychologist, and the clinic where she works has a decent maternity policy. But she felt a duty toward her patients, caught in the throes of addiction and crisis.

She had a PhD from Yale. She refused to be mommy-shamed into submission.

With at least one of us at home round the clock with Charlotte, we could avoid paying for daycare.

That was the plan. Its success assumed that Charlotte would sleep at some point in every twenty-four-hour cycle.

So far, that had proven a piss-poor premise.

Most days Amy and I saw each other awake for five to ten minutes, purely to exchange information: How many ounces? Diapers? Burps? Naps?

"I don't get it," she said. Her blouse hung unbuttoned, nursing pads peeking up from her bra. Her face was puffy and her eyes half-closed and I loved her. "How does anybody function?"

I wrung out a smile, bent to lace my boots. "Do they? Function."

"Somebody must. Planes aren't crashing. The power's on."

"Most of the time."

"True. But there must be at least a few people out there capable of doing their jobs."

"They don't have kids."

Amy laughed. This was the most substantive conversation we'd had in weeks, and it took me a moment to realize she was also crying.

I stumbled over to embrace her.

She rested her forehead against my chest. "I feel like I'm failing at everything."

"You're not."

"It's like, rather than be a good mother or a good doctor, why not be shitty at both?"

"Honey. Stop. You're doing great. I'm so proud of you."

"I feel like a dairy cow."

"You're the most beautiful cow west of the Mississippi. Blue ribbon."

She wiped her nose on her sleeve. "Today in session, I caught a patient staring at my chest. I've been working with him for a year, and he's never been anything other than appropriate. But all of a sudden he's gawking. He's not even bothering to hide it. I'm trying to decide whether to say something when I feel something wet, and I look down and there's this *huge* stain on my blouse. I put the pad in wrong, I'm leaking everywhere."

"Oh no. What did you do?"

"I said, 'I'm so sorry, please excuse me,' then I ran into the bathroom and changed into my spare shirt."

"Good for you, having a spare shirt."

She shook her head. "It was dirty. I spent the whole day smelling bad."

"I like how you smell."

"You work at a morgue. I'm so tired, Clay."

"I know."

"We're never going to sleep again, for the rest of our lives."

"Possibly."

She looked up, a brilliant woman terrified by a wisecrack. "You really think so?"

"No, I don't."

"It's true, though. She's never going to learn to sleep."

"She'll learn."

"How can you say that?"

"Because everybody does. And she does sleep."

"For ten minutes. In the car seat."

"Proof she can. It's just a matter of stretching it out."

"What if she only ever sleeps in car seats? What if we have to keep buying her a series of bigger and bigger car seats?"

"Then we'll send her off to college in a giant custom-made car seat."

"Can we afford that?"

"College, or the car seat?"

"Either. Both."

"Probably not."

"Why is everything so fucking expensive?"

"She can go to trade school." I kissed the top of Amy's head. "Learn to weld."

"I want her to be able to do whatever she wants."

"She will."

"I want her to be happy."

"She is."

"Every time I leave I think *She hates me.*"

"She doesn't hate you. Are you kidding? To her, you're God."

"Plenty of people hate God."

"She loves you."

"How do you know?"

"Because—"

The monitor flared. We didn't need a monitor. We lived in a four-hundred-forty-square-foot mother-in-law cottage. You could stand in the kitchenette and play catch with someone in the bathroom.

Charlotte could not yet sit up, let alone walk. But we'd put plugs in the outlets and latches on the cabinets; padded the corners of the coffee table with foam.

To enter the cottage, you climbed two bricked steps. I had installed a gate at the top to prevent our daughter—who had only recently discovered her feet—from somehow opening the door, strolling outside, and tumbling down to the garden pavers to receive a fatal head injury.

Shields on the stove knobs. Safety tassels on the blind cords. The number for Poison Control, taped to the fridge in forty-eight-point font.

I kept my unloaded Sig Sauer at the back of the highest kitchen cabinet. I'm six-foot-three, with a seventy-eight-inch wingspan, and

I had to stretch to get it. Ammunition lived inside the bread machine we'd gotten as a wedding present and never once used.

Now our unneeded monitor crackled and flashed. Amy shuddered against me, wiped her face again, and trudged to the bedroom.

Hello, honey pie.

A lull, before the baby smelled her and resumed howling with a vengeance.

I'm so happy to see you.

I finished getting ready and stuck my head in the bedroom.

Amy smiled and put a finger to her lips. The baby had passed out on the nursing pillow.

Many cops make sure to always kiss their loved ones goodbye. Just in case. Sometimes it devolves to superstition. Forget and drive off, you need to turn the car around.

I don't do any of that. It might seem odd, given how we'd transformed our home into a temple of parental neuroses. But there's the risk to my daughter and the risk to me, and they don't compare, either statistically or emotionally. It's not even close.

Each year, two hundred cops die in the line of duty. That includes shootings, stabbings, vehicular crashes, aircraft mishaps, environmental toxin exposure, animal-related incidents, and heart attacks during physical fitness assessment.

Each year, six thousand children under the age of one die in accidents.

Two-thirds of them by suffocation.

One in seven in a motor vehicle accident. One in fourteen due to drowning.

Of all the jobs in law enforcement, mine is among the safest. I can't do it properly if I'm walking around burdened by fear.

If we're going to worry about remote possibilities, everyone leaving for work should kiss their loved ones goodbye.

You can die merging onto the freeway. You can choke on your take-out salad.

I've seen it all.

Either live in thrall to statistics or make them your friends.

Standing in the doorway, watching my wife and daughter, I marveled at how vibrant they appeared, and I engraved their image in my mind, an icon to clutch close as I left them behind and descended to the realm of the dead.

CHAPTER 3

"**C**oroner's Bureau."

"Yes, hi. This is Lieutenant Florence Sibley, University of California PD, badge twenty-eight."

I said, "Hey, Lieutenant. Deputy Edison. What can I do for you?"

"I'm over at People's Park. We got what looks like some remains dug up."

I slid an intake sheet to the center of my desk. "Go ahead."

In describing the scene, she had to compete with several other voices talking nearby.

"Beg pardon," I said. "You said an eyeball?"

"No. Yeah, but—it's bones that are the issue."

"How many bones are we talking about?"

"I don't know. A tooth, too, I think."

Off in the distance, I heard a piercing shriek.

"Cripes," Sibley muttered.

"Everything okay?"

"If you could get over here."

"Couple more questions, then sure. When were the remains found?"

"Noon. Give or take."

A delay of one to two hours is normal. Three or four, if the scene is especially chaotic. More than five and you can bet somebody dropped the ball.

The top of my computer screen read six fifty-six p.m.

"Can you narrow the time frame down some?" I asked. "More give? Or more take?"

A male voice said *Lieutenant.*

"We've got everything under control," Sibley said brightly.

"There's people there and you can't discuss this right now."

"That's correct."

I said, "On my way."

KAT DAVENPORT AND I loaded up the van with the bone kit and drove to Berkeley.

Traffic was subdued, sidewalks desolate. The December outrush of students had created a citywide vacuum, leaving the solitude of a winter night without much holiday cheer to compensate. At the corner of College and Derby, someone had added a sticker to the stop sign, creating a new message:

I could sense the disturbance in the air from blocks away. It came pulsing through the windshield, less sound than vibration, the warning rumble of a system gone wrong.

We made the turn onto Haste and the protesters exploded into view, a convulsive stew of rage, filling the intersection.

A handful of UCPD uniforms kept a wary vigil.

Chain-link twelve feet high and double-thick plastic fence weave surrounded the park, obscuring its interior. Banners for Siefkin Brothers, Builders, pouched in the breeze. I could see the tops of construction trailers and vehicles but not much else. A weird glow oozed up from within, like a cauldron bubbling with ghoulish potential.

Davenport pulled to the curb. I called Sibley's cell. "We're here."

She directed us to a pedestrian gate. I got out carrying the bone kit, and we skirted around the back of the crowd. Nobody paid attention to us. They were too busy channeling their anger toward the other protesters at the far end of Bowditch.

Up ahead, a white woman in UCPD blues emerged through the fence and quickly shut the gate behind, as if to prevent something from escaping.

Florence Sibley was tall, with hair pulled tight into a pompom of red curls. Freckles softened whittled facial features; a high sheer forehead seemed to tug her eyebrows upward, giving her a look of permanent astonishment.

She held out an evidence bag containing an eyeball, made of glass or plastic, roughly an inch in diameter. The iris was iridescent blue; on the reverse was a little attachment loop.

"I didn't want it to get lost," she said. "Otherwise we tried not to mess with anything. That's why I couldn't give you a good count on the bones."

"Gotcha. Thanks."

I expected her to stand aside, but she continued to block the entrance, tugging at the fence wire with two hooked fingers.

"Everyone's here," she said.

Kat Davenport frowned. "Who's everyone?"

The zeal of youth. Sibley seemed at a loss for words.

I said, "Anything else you want to tell us while we have the chance?"

Sibley paused. "I'm sorry."

I STEPPED THROUGH the gate and stopped short.

It wasn't accurate to call People's Park my old stomping grounds.

I'd spent my undergraduate years on the practice courts or in the athletes' dining hall. But I had walked or driven past the park hundreds of times. Its grunginess was, if not inviting, at least familiar.

It was gone.

In its place: a bombscape. Banks of industrial work lights blew out the darkness, flooding the cratered lawns with an icy, nauseating glare. I could pick out individual blades of grass from twenty yards away—an eerie, unpleasant sensation, contrast and sharpness dialed up to the max.

The trellises were gone. The flower beds and vegetable gardens were gone. Benches, lampposts, picnic tables: gone. They hadn't yet gotten to the bathrooms, but the basketball hoops had been felled and the concrete court smashed to chunks. Everywhere heavy machinery brooded over the carnage.

"Holy shit," I said.

"I know, right?" Davenport said. "*So* much better."

From beyond the fence, the disembodied voices of the protesters continued to ring out, like battlefield ghosts.

A group of people congregated by a ragged, asymmetrical pit roughly thirty feet long by forty feet wide. Its depth varied between six feet in some places and inches below surface level in others. It took me a moment to realize I was looking at the site of the Free Speech Stage.

"Everyone" consisted of two men in slacks and coats, a woman in a pantsuit, and a thickset guy in work clothes. All wore hard hats and reflective vests.

Nice of Sibley to apologize. No big deal, though. We were used to working with a live studio audience.

Then I noticed movement in the pit, and I came forward to discover two more people crouched down in the dirt, murmuring over a lump of electric blue.

Before I could ask who they were and what they were doing in my scene, one of the guys in slacks intercepted me with his hand out.

"Thanks so much for coming," he said.

He introduced himself as George Greenspan, UC Berkeley executive vice chancellor. Straight gray hair, combed back and sprayed, hardly moved as he pumped our arms. He was *delighted* to meet us.

Likewise UCPD chief Vogel and Dana Simon, VP of operations for Siefkin Brothers, Builders: delighted, just delighted.

The less-than-delighted guy in cargo pants was the foreman, Arriola. He nodded curtly and trudged off to the trailers to fetch us protective gear.

Dana Simon flashed an apologetic smile. "Liability."

Meanwhile the pair in the pit had stood up: first, a handsome man in his late thirties; man-bun, trail shoes, gray Irish fisherman's sweater, gray wide-wale corduroys. He came to the edge of the pit and rested on his elbows on the grass, like a swimmer taking a break from laps.

Greenspan said, "Professor Kai MacLeod, one of our rising stars. He won't tell you that, so I will. And his grad student—eh?"

"Chloe Bellara," MacLeod said. "One of *my* stars."

The elfin young woman behind him gazed shyly at the ground, her hands retracted into the sleeves of an oversized flannel shirt.

"I hope you don't mind," Greenspan said. "I invited them because, frankly, I know nothing about this. It's Kai's area of expertise. This way we all get to learn something."

Sibley squirmed helplessly.

"Your area of expertise is People's Park?" I said to MacLeod.

"Classical Mesoamerica," he said, scratching three days' worth of blond beard.

"Okay," I said. "First, I need you to tell me if you touched anything."

"Oh no, no, no."

"Then we'll take it from here."

MacLeod said, "We're happy to stay and pitch in."

"That won't be necessary, Professor."

"I've done my fair share of fieldwork. You can use my kit, if you'd like. The brushes are badger hair. Handmade in Italy."

"Ours are nylon," I said. "Machine-made in China."

MacLeod gave a good-natured chuckle. He hoisted himself out of the pit, then turned to offer his grad student a hand up.

"Kai?" Greenspan asked. "Thoughts?"

MacLeod dusted off his pants. "You're fine. Whatever's in there is clearly modern."

"Excellent. When do we think we'll be able to start work again?"

Chief Vogel said, "Typically no more than a day or two."

Davenport said, "With respect, sir, this is a Coroner's case now. Nobody's doing anything until further notice."

MacLeod said, "I'm reasonably certain the Ohlone didn't use polyester."

The foreman returned with our protective gear slung over his shoulder.

"I hear that you're eager to get back on track," I said, struggling to get my vest on. It was a normal-sized vest, for normal-sized people. "The sooner we start, the quicker it goes."

Greenspan gestured grandly. "As you will."

Davenport and I hopped into the pit. She began taking pictures, and I crouched to examine the blanket.

Under the work lights, it seemed a gaudy, unreal thing, fibers matted with mud and exuding a swamp mustiness, the decorative satin edging fever-sheened.

A splinter of bone, dull and yellow as old ivory, shot free of the cocoon.

Examination of skeletal remains begins with three questions.

Are they human?

If so, how many individuals are represented?

How long ago did death occur?

The tooth was small. I was impressed that Sibley had recognized it as such. Most people would take it for a pebble.

If human in origin, it hadn't come from an adult.

The fuzzy blanket pointed in the same direction.

I reminded myself that we were at the epicenter of People's Park, which is the epicenter of Berkeley, world capital of Impassioned Causes. This is a town that loves its rituals—the more solemn or shocking, the better. When I was a sophomore, an animal rights group staged a funeral procession for a piglet. Dressed in black, to the whomp of a New Orleans jazz band, they marched the corpse, snuggled inside a tiny, purpose-built coffin, through Sather Gate and across campus to Memorial Glade, where they interred it in the turf.

Maybe that's what we had here. The remains of a dearly beloved pet.

Davenport joined me, and we began to undo the bundle. It had been elaborately tucked and knotted, and the damp pressure of the earth heaped upon it had caused the layers to laminate. Each unfolding required that we pause to brush away soil; take pictures; bag fragments that, like the tooth, had worked themselves loose and come to settle in crevices and pockets.

Kat Davenport had been with the Coroner's less than a year. On the ride over she'd confessed that this was her first skeletal remains call. At her request, I tried to point out a thing or two. Sub-adult remains are often mistaken for those of rodents, and vice versa. Long bones in isolation aren't as helpful as species-specific features.

That? Could be a chip. Could be a stone. Take it anyway. Take everything, take no chances. How old? Hard to say. Newer bones give off an oily funk. They're dense. Ancient bones feel plasticky, artificial, their fragility and dryness palpable through gloves. You have to consider soil composition, acidity, weather, what's growing nearby.

The wind had died. The work lights poured down without mercy.

We proceeded methodically, the gruesome opposite of tearing into gift wrap. Feeling the eyes of the onlookers on us, I shifted my body to obstruct their view.

The innermost layer came away.

Species-specific features.

A bowl-shaped pelvis, adapted for single-leg balance when striding upright.

A disproportionately large cranium, evolved to allow room for speech, memory, complex calculation, impossible ideas, hopes, dreams, plans; love and hate; good and evil.

In absolute terms, the hip bones were four inches wide.

The skull would fit comfortably in my palm.

Not quite walking.

Not yet talking.

Davenport said, "Clay."

I looked at her.

"You good?" she asked.

She knew I had a newborn at home. She was imagining what she would've felt in my position.

You can't predict how having children will change you. You don't get to choose, any more than you get to choose the child. Parenthood lays bare your instincts, from the noblest to the most shameful, and at the risk of sounding smug, I'll venture that Kat Davenport—twenty-five years old, steady girlfriend, no kids—could not have guessed what I was really feeling.

It was the same feeling I had when, in some public place, I heard a stranger's baby starting to cry.

Relief.

Not mine.

"You guys doing okay down there?" Professor Kai MacLeod stood at the pit's edge, sliding his hips easily. "Want me to come have a look?"

What I wanted was to punch him in the balls.

I smiled. "We're good."

MacLeod gave a peace sign.

We gave him our backs and continued working.

To my eye the skeleton appeared remarkably complete. The tight wrapping—*swaddling* I thought—had helped to contain everything. Still, I didn't want to risk leaving pieces behind.

Davenport began unpacking the sifters. I waited for MacLeod to move out of earshot, then called Sergeant Brad Moffett at the bureau to apprise him and request assistance. He said he'd do his best, though he cautioned me not to expect anything anytime soon; a shooting over by Acorn had everyone tied up.

I climbed out of the pit and asked Sibley and Chief Vogel to step aside with me.

Greenspan followed right along behind.

"If you wouldn't mind, sir," I said.

"Yes, of course, sorry." He retreated, poking at his phone.

I asked Vogel, "Is your detective coming?"

"I haven't called him yet."

"You might want to. Although there's no rush. We're going to be here awhile."

Vogel worked, not successfully, to suppress his alarm. "Really. You think?"

"Yes, sir, I do."

"Looked like you got what you needed."

"There's the rest of the pit we have to search," I said. "The displacement pile."

Vogel chewed his lip. "Is that truly necessary?"

"In my opinion, sir, it is. If you disagree, though, feel free to call my sergeant."

Vogel blinked and thought and said to Sibley, "Get Tom over here."

The tiniest hitch before she said, "Yes, sir," and walked off.

Chants carried across the ravaged lawns.

Vogel said, "You realize we're facing a unique situation."

"I do, sir. Sooner we finish, sooner work can resume."

"What do you need from me?"

"Ask everyone to clear out, please."

"Will do. Sibley can stay on as your point person."

And to babysit us. "Thank you, sir."

I rejoined Davenport in the pit, and the chief went to speak to the civilians.

Not long after, Greenspan came over to announce that they'd leave things in our capable hands. He looked forward to hearing from us once we'd reached our conclusions.

"You know, we used to have a basketball player named Edison on our squad. Pretty good point guard, if I recall."

I nodded and continued sifting.

With exaggerated surprise, he said, "*No.* That was *you?*"

"That was me."

"What are the *odds.* Small *world.*"

I said, "Anything else I can help you with?"

"By all means, carry on. Soon as you have news to share, I'd be grateful to hear it. One Cal man to another."

Davenport rolled her eyes.

"We'll be in touch," I said.

"Terrific. Well." He saluted. "Go Bears."

Before leaving, Kai MacLeod offered us his card.

"You can put it right there," I said.

He tucked it in the grass and left, Chloe Bellara trailing dreamily in his wake.

Davenport said, "Those two are fucking, right?"

"That would violate the University Code of Conduct."

"Definitely fucking."

I DIDN'T MIND Sibley as a babysitter. I could tell she felt bad about the circus, and she let us alone, departing at nine fifty to oversee the dispersal of the protesters. I heard her through a bullhorn: *This is a residential neighborhood. People are sleeping. Please go home.*

Voices continued to reverberate in the brittle air.

At ten ten a slack-jawed guy in khakis and a black UCPD fleece shambled up.

"Tom Nieminen," he said. "Investigations."

I took off my gloves and went to confer. "Looking like it might be human. Juvenile."

Nieminen said, "Wow. Kinda weird, huh."

I waited for him to ask questions. He didn't.

"We'll know more after the autopsy," I said.

He didn't ask when the autopsy would be, either.

"Okey dokey," Nieminen said and sauntered away.

Behind his back, Davenport made a jerking-off motion.

At ten thirty the cops again asked the protesters to please disperse.

They repeated their request at eleven, eleven fifteen, eleven thirty.

The noise persisted until one thirty in the morning.

At two a.m. Sibley returned.

"The detective came by," I said. "Nieminen."

"Okay." She sat down cross-legged and began plucking grass.

The next time I looked, she was flat on her back, snoring.

AT TWO TWENTY, a pair of CSIs showed up. Even with the extra hands, it took until three fifteen to finish searching the pit. We completed our search of the displacement pile at half-past six. We were filthy and exhausted and clammy with perspiration. My eyes were dry and I had a hellacious tension headache. We'd uncovered a few more potential fragments, but nothing as impressive as the initial haul.

Dawn broke, sluicing the neighborhood with light the color of sour milk. Flo Sibley struggled up on her elbows. Gigantic black bags hung under her eyes. "D'you find the bear?"

"Bear?" Davenport asked.

"A teddy bear," Sibley said. "The eye?"

"No bear," I said.

Sibley looked like she might burst into tears. "There has to be."

The door to the office trailer opened, and foreman Arriola emerged, wearing slept-in clothes. Thermos in hand, he approached the pit. "We good to go?"

"I'll let you know within forty-eight hours," I said.

He snatched up the vests and hard hats, pivoted, and headed back toward the office.

A DOZEN OR so protesters had spent the night camped out behind the sawhorses, spreading out on the sidewalk in sleeping bags—a human pilot light for the flames of resistance. Now their replacements began showing up, bringing breakfast and fresh throats. On my way to the van I paused to watch the changing of the guard. One young man raking words on a poster board noticed me staring. He smiled, capped his marker, and raised his middle fingers to the sky.

CHAPTER 4

The anthropologist said, "Showboating prick."

Monday afternoon, I'd arrived early at the bureau to attend the autopsy.

"Where does he get off?" Professor Ralph Szabla taught at Chico State, consulting for our office as needed. Suspenders held up drab baggy pants; beneath a stained white short-sleeved polo shirt he wore a second polo, maroon and long-sleeved. For several minutes he'd been holding forth about his distaste for Kai MacLeod, whom he'd met, once, at a symposium.

Rumors had MacLeod flying to Los Angeles to meet with a TV development company about creating his own reality show. The working title was *Can You Dig It?!*

"He's not even tenured," Szabla said. "He's a goddamn *assistant.*"

Atop the slab, the recovered bones lay arranged in standard anatomical position, flattened, like the victim of a Looney Tunes steamroller. The blanket and glass eye had been sent out for analysis.

The pathologist, Judy Bronson, straightened a vertebra and said, "We can't all be purists like you, Ralph."

"Fuck *that*," Szabla said. The suspenders had a pattern of llamas wearing sunglasses. "I just feel bad for my friend here who has to put up with him."

He nudged me. "You all right there, Deputy? You look a little green."

"How's the baby?" Dr. Bronson asked. "Getting any sleep?"

"Hey now," Szabla said. "You had a kid? Boy or girl?"

"Girl. Fourteen weeks."

Szabla guffawed. "'Fourteen weeks.' You realize nobody talks like that except new parents. 'Fourteen weeks . . .' How many milliseconds? Well, no shit. Congratulations. I take a sabbatical and next thing you know, *bang*, there's more people."

"We're trying to decide whether to sleep-train her," I said. "Or—Amy is. I'm for it."

"You gotta let em cry," Szabla said. "It's the only way."

"That's what you did?"

"Fuck no. Six years my wife didn't sleep. That's why she left me."

Judy reached up for the spotlight, panning it slowly over the table while she and Szabla pointed out features. The skeleton of a human infant contains around two hundred seventy bones, more than an adult's because sections fuse together and the count drops. What we'd pulled from the ground included most of the major structures, including three teeth. Missing were the miniature puzzle pieces: hands, feet, ear bones.

The decedent was human.

There was one individual represented.

As to the third question—how long ago did death occur?—I figured Szabla's rotten mood came in part from having to concede to Kai MacLeod: The skeleton was modern in origin. We all regarded as far-fetched the idea that someone would dig up ancient remains, wrap them in a twentieth-century material, and rebury them. More tellingly, the bones lacked the characteristic reddish tinge that comes from prolonged exposure to soil.

Even so, the window for date of death remained wide.

"When was the stage built?" Szabla asked. "Gotta be before then."

"I spoke to a guy at Berkeley parks department," I said. "They replaced all the wood in '98, but apparently they didn't disturb the earth. The original structure went in sometime in the early seventies. He was a little hazy on the exact date."

"Early seventies, bet your ass he's hazy."

Based on the extent of cranial suture fusion, ossification, and dentition, Szabla estimated the age at death to be between six and eighteen months. More than that he hesitated to say.

"At this stage of development, you can't determine sex from skeletal morphology," he said. "Changes to the pelvis don't kick in till puberty. Same goes for ancestry: big-ass can of theoretical worms. I'm not going to tell you there's no such thing as race, but given the degree of variability in kids, I'd be bullshitting you if I got specific. 'Hey, this here sucker's eleven percent Lithuanian.'"

The right clavicle had been snapped in half. The sternum and ribs showed stress fractures. I wondered about child abuse, but Szabla and Judy agreed that the damage was more consistent with the trauma of disinterment. Infant bones are delicate, and an excavator shovel is not a precision instrument. The same bundling that had kept the bones together would have also caused them to bash into one another.

There were no previously healed fractures. No unambiguous blade marks. No crushed hyoid to suggest throttling; no hyoid, period. The structure starts out as three pieces of cartilage, and complete ossification can take until puberty. Along with all the other soft tissue, it had melted away.

Common methods of infanticide such as smothering leave no skeletal trace.

While the presumption of foul play felt reasonable—why bury a body in a public place, other than to hide it?—none of us was ready to come out and say homicide.

Imagine a mother who hasn't slept in weeks, tripping on the rug and losing her grip.

A father, nerves frayed, rocking his child at four in the morning, praying *please go to sleep*, rocking harder, *please*, harder, *just go to sleep already*, harder, too hard; then looking down and realizing, with sudden wakefulness, what hell his impatience has bought him.

Think like a parent driven mad with panic and grief.

Or think like a parkie. Say the baby had been conceived there. Could be the spot was chosen for its symbolism: a return to innocence. Crazy, yet kind of beautiful.

Berkeley.

For the last twenty-four hours, construction at People's Park had been suspended. In that time, the protest had tripled in size, spilling through the sawhorses to occupy the entirety of Bowditch between Haste and Dwight. The counterprotesters had wisely abandoned ship. Our office had fielded calls from media outlets, the mayor of Berkeley, and the chief of Berkeley PD. The university chancellor had reached out from her hotel in Zurich. The sheriff himself had emailed to ask how things were moving along.

Whatever future you envisioned for the park, all could agree on one thing: It would *really* help to know who this person was.

The crime lab was quoting me a two-week turnaround for dental DNA. By law, I had less than a day left to rule on origin.

I said, "But we're comfortable going with non-Native."

Bronson nodded. "I think so."

"Cheer up," Szabla said. "You're gonna make people happy with that answer. Piss off some others, too. Evens out in the end."

"I'm not keeping score," I said.

"Atta boy."

OUR OFFICE PUT out a press release. Demolition at People's Park had uncovered human remains of modern, non-Native origin. The decedent, a juvenile, had yet to be identified, and the cause of death remained undetermined. Anyone with information was encouraged to come forward. Effective Wednesday, work was cleared to resume.

Maybe I should've been keeping score.

On Wednesday morning I was at home, lying on the floor, doing tummy time with Charlotte, our noses touching as she bellowed her displeasure.

"Hands and knees," I said, slapping the carpet. "You can do it. Head in the game."

She spit up and face-planted in the puddle.

"Way to fight." I wiped her down. Amy called from the car. "Hey," I said.

"Is she there?"

"She is. You're on speaker. Say hi to Mommy."

"*Hi honey,*" Amy cooed.

Charlotte smiled.

"You never use that voice with me," I said.

"I will if you want."

"Don't. It's creepy. What's up?"

"I just drove by campus. Is something going on? There's cop cars everywhere."

"I don't know," I said. "Hang on."

I carried the baby to the futon, jogging her in my lap as I switched on the early local news. Tail end of the Warriors recap. Then:

Back to our developing story in Berkeley, where a protest over the discovery of human remains in People's Park has been growing since late yesterday afternoon. KRON-4's Danika Shih reports. Danika?

Thanks, Susan. Yeah, as you can see behind me, people are climbing the fence, and if we come around you can get a look . . . They've formed human chains around the bulldozers. Now, the police have repeatedly warned the protesters to vacate, but they haven't made any arrests, and so far nobody appears to be listening. Earlier I spoke with one woman who described herself as an activist. She compared the situation to Tiananmen Square.

The screen cut to a prerecorded interview. A gaunt young woman in an oversized sweater said *It's well documented that the area of the park overlaps with sacred Ohlone burial grounds.*

The chyron identified her as Chloe Bellara, UC Berkeley Department of Anthropology. It did not mention that she was a graduate student, rather than faculty, or that Associate Professor Kai MacLeod regarded her as his star pupil, or that they might or might not be definitely fucking.

"Oh boy," I said.

"Clay?" Amy said.

"One sec."

Bellara was still talking. *The university knows that if they admit that, they'll be forced to give up their false claim to the territory.*

What about the Coroner's report that said the remains aren't Native American?

I was there when the Coroner removed the bones. I interacted with them directly.

"You are so full of shit," I said.

"Clay," Amy said. "She's going to learn that."

So you're saying the report is false? the reporter asked.

I'm saying a lot of powerful individuals stand to lose a lot of money. Everybody knows what happens then.

For Executive Vice Chancellor George Greenwald and the university, the issue had been resolved. Whoever the child may have been, regardless of what his or her death meant, he or she did not currently constitute a legal impediment. Cue the wrecking crew.

My duty is to the decedent and the next of kin, and I was nowhere near resolution.

The National Missing and Unidentified Persons System had three open files for Alameda County children under the age of two. None fit the bill. The dates of last contact were 2008, 2005, and 2002, well after the construction of the Free Speech Stage.

I widened the search radius, one county at a time: Contra Costa, Santa Clara, San Francisco, Marin; up to Napa and Sonoma and out toward the Central Valley.

The case notes made me ineffably sad, far more than the bones had. When I sorted the results by age, children who'd gone missing younger than twelve months appeared as "0 years," as though they'd never existed. Their physical characteristics were likewise jarring and full of heartbreak.

Height: 1'9" (21 inches)
Weight: 9 pounds
Hair: Unknown or completely bald

Most were alleged parental abductions. Most of the alleged abductors were fathers.

Sometimes there were older siblings, also missing.

Sometimes a mother's body had been found, without her child.

Computerized age progressions showed the victims at ten years old, fifteen, twenty-six, forty-two. Every update applied a fresh coat of desperation. The subject was always depicted with a smile, as though he or she had carried on living happily, reaching milestones, maturing, thriving.

A parallel reality where nothing bad ever happened.

By week's end, I'd winnowed the candidates down to five.

Elizabeth Turney. Citrus Heights, Sacramento County. Date of birth, June 11, 1961. Date of last contact, May 14, 1963. Her mother had left her outside a grocery store to buy a loaf of bread, coming back to find the stroller overturned on the sidewalk. At the time of her disappearance Elizabeth was wearing a yellow floral dress.

John David Ortega. Tahoe, Placer County. Date of birth, August 26, 1963. Date of last contact, July 4, 1965. The Ortega family had spent the holiday weekend camping by the lake. A thorough search of the water and surrounding woods failed to turn up any sign of the boy. He was barefoot, wearing dungarees and a red T-shirt. It was presumed he had wandered off or been abducted.

Michael Ewing. City of Merced, County of Merced. Date of birth, September 3, 1964. Date of last contact, April 19, 1966. His hair was black. No more information given.

Sybil Vine. Tracy, San Joaquin County. Date of birth, November 6, 1968. Date of last contact, August 8, 1970. Federal warrant issued for her father, Warren. The alleged abductor had family in Los Angeles and Las Vegas; possibly he had fled there. He had a scar on his forehead. The child's height and weight were an approximation.

Olive Rheinholtz. Crows Landing, Stanislaus County. Date of birth, April 30, 1970. On January 7, 1972, baby Olive, along with her mother, Edith, and nine-year-old sister, Anne-Louise, were reported missing from the family farm. The next day their station wagon was located by the side of the road, five miles south down Highway 33, doors open, keys in the ignition. From an adjacent field police recovered a single girl's shoe, brown leather, strap broken. The three had never been found.

Even as I compiled the list, I recognized its arbitrary nature. I'd chosen cutoff dates of 1/1/1960 and 12/31/1975, restricting the search to the northern half of the state. Not every missing persons case finds its way into the database. The older the file, the more likely it is to languish in a steel cabinet, crumbling, waiting for some retired cop or devoted amateur to take up the cause and drag it into the new millennium.

Geography alone made these five cases a stretch. The missing children came from relatively rural areas, far from People's Park, communities with no connection to Berkeley or any of the values and stereotypes and behaviors that typified the Bay Area during the Age of Aquarius. I'd been to Merced. I could guess what it was like in 1966.

Would an abductor drive for hours, to a city with far greater population density, and start digging at random?

Unless that was the goal: Pin it on the hippies.

"Nikki left this for you." Sergeant Brad Moffett stuck a Post-it to the back of my neck.

I peeled it off. There was a phone number with a San Francisco area code and a truncated note scribbled in Deputy Nikki Kennedy's loopy hand. Basically a text in ink.

Peter Franchette
got ur name
wants 2 talk abt PPI

PPI stood for "People's Park Infant"—our quasi-official short-hand.

I called Kennedy, catching her in the middle of rehearsal. "What's this guy about?"

"Not sure," she said. "He was pretty clear he'd only speak to you."

In the background, the distorted screech of a detuned violin. Nikki Kennedy fronted a thrash-bluegrass Everly Brothers cover band called Die, Die Love.

I thanked her, then dialed the number on the Post-it.

"Hello?"

The voice was diffident, mildly suspicious.

"This is Deputy Edison at the Alameda County Coroner's Bureau. I'm looking for Peter Franchette."

"Yes." Eager, now. "Sorry, it came up as a blocked number. Clay Edison."

"Do we know each other?"

"I know of you. Delilah Nwodo suggested I get in touch."

Nwodo was an Oakland homicide cop. We'd collaborated on a case, and she'd sent congratulations after Charlotte's birth, but otherwise we hadn't been in regular contact for some time.

"How do you know Detective Nwodo?"

"She's a family friend. Her father. But her, too."

"What can I help you with?"

"To be honest, I'm not sure."

"Your message mentioned an ongoing investigation."

"Yes. The child. In People's Park."

"Did you have information to share?"

"I'm not sure," Franchette said again. "I think it might be my sister."

CHAPTER 5

His call wasn't the first. Anytime you solicit the public for tips—even when you don't—you're bound to hear from folks nursing conspiracy theories or personal grievances.

Dead kid? You need to talk to my ex-husband.

We'd also become a target for protesters seeking to vent their spleen about the park with hang-ups and profane tirades.

Peter Franchette didn't sound disgruntled. Maybe he was working his way up to crazy.

I said, "What makes you think that?"

"I had a sister who—she died, I think."

"You don't know if she died."

"It's a little complicated," he said. "I believe she's still considered missing. Although I'm not a hundred percent sure about that, either. Look, this would be a lot easier in person. I've some material I'd be happy to show you."

Here we go: crazy. Hadn't even taken that long. "What material would that be?"

"Photographs. Newspaper articles. At one point I hired a private investigator to do a public records search for me. There's interviews, I have the audio files. I mean, I've only gotten so far. I wouldn't be calling you otherwise."

"If you'd like, you can send the material to me."

"It's a lot of stuff."

"How about you pick one or two items that you think are informative?"

"I was really hoping we could meet."

Only his mention of Nwodo had kept me on the line this long. "Can I ask your sister's name?"

"I don't know."

"Uh-huh."

"I understand how this must come across," he said.

"Is there anything you *can* tell me?"

"My best guess is that she was about three when she disappeared."

"In that case, it's doubtful she's the individual whose remains we recovered."

"Why?"

"I'm sorry. It's an active investigation. I can't discuss details."

"She might be older," Franchette said, "or younger. There's a lot that's unclear."

"As I said, feel free to send me a couple of items."

"I can pay you. I'm happy to pay."

I said, "That's not how it works."

A silence.

"I apologize," he said. "It wasn't my intention . . . I apologize."

"It's fine, sir. No harm done."

"I . . ." A short, crestfallen laugh. "I think I've been building you up in my mind. The way Delilah spoke about you, I had this idea . . . I'm sorry."

I felt a twinge of pity.

"The offer stands," I said. "Send me something to look at. I can't promise I'll get to it right away, but I'll do my best."

"Thank you."

"No problem. Take care, Mr. Franchette."

"You too."

I hung up and called Nwodo.

"The great Clay Edison," she said. "To what do I owe the pleasure?"

We spent a few minutes catching up. She'd recently transferred to sex crimes.

"I asked myself, 'How can you make your life more depressing? There *must* be a way . . .' How's that baby of yours? Balling yet?"

"I got her a little basket, attaches to the side of the crib. Amy made me take it down. Apparently it's a quote-unquote 'strangulation hazard.' "

Nwodo clucked her tongue. "That woman, where are her priorities? You know, I got a present for you sitting in my trunk. I went by your place. Some dude answered the door."

"We moved to Berkeley a little while ago."

"Nice."

"Cheaper."

"Since when is Berkeley cheaper than anywhere?"

"We're renting from a friend of Amy's parents. She's giving us a deal. Saving up for a down payment."

"Aw, my boy's growing up."

"Yeah, well, I'm starting to wonder if we'll survive that long. There's one bedroom where the baby sleeps. Amy and I are on a futon next to the kitchenette."

"You can't stay with family?"

"Tried that. After two weeks it became a quote-unquote 'strangulation hazard.' "

Nwodo laughed. "Invite me over for dinner. I'll give you the present then."

"Sounds good. Hey, so: I just got off the phone with Peter Franchette."

"No kidding."

"He called me up wanting to know about this body at People's Park. He had an idea it might be his long-lost sister."

"Is it?"

"Doubtful. Wrong age. He sounded wound up, though. Said you sent him my way."

"Hold up," she said. "That's not what happened."

She'd last seen Franchette back in March, at her father's seventieth birthday party. Royal Nwodo had built his first fortune bringing internet service to Ghana, and with that money, several subsequent fortunes. It was a running joke that Delilah's job was just for fun.

"You know how your GPS reroutes you around traffic?" she said. "Franchette wrote the software that finds the new route. My dad was an early backer."

At the party, she and Franchette got to schmoozing. She told him about the murder she'd recently wrapped, a case I helped out on. By that point in the evening everyone had a few glasses of wine in them. Franchette, whom Nwodo thought of as a buttoned-up sort of guy, started opening up to her about his own personal mystery, a sibling he'd never met.

"How'd I come into it?"

"Man, I don't know. I was listening with half an ear. He's going on about how he keeps getting stuck, the cops won't take him seriously."

"Can't imagine where he'd get that impression."

"You know how it is," she said. "People are always dropping their baggage on me. Either that, or they freeze up like I'm going to pull out a warrant. It's like: I truly do not care if you shoplifted in sixth grade . . . Anyway, I probably said something along the lines of, 'You should meet my friend Clay, this is right up his alley.' "

"Thanks so much."

"Like I said, wine. I didn't think he'd follow up. It was months ago, I figured he forgot about it."

"I guess hearing about the park reminded him."

"You say it's unrelated, though."

"Unless we're off the mark on age. Or he is. Either way, I ain't about to get his hopes up."

"Too bad. He's a decent guy."

"He offered me money."

Nwodo started to laugh again. "No he did not. How much?"

"We didn't get that far. To be fair, I don't think he meant it as a bribe. More an honest mistake. Like he's used to solving problems with a credit card."

"Don't tell me you wouldn't do the same if you could."

"*If* of the century," I said. "Good to hear your voice, Delilah."

"You too. Text me your address so I can bring you that present."

"Will do."

"Seriously, though," she said. "You might want to talk to Peter, get his story. It's actually pretty interesting."

"I thought you were listening with half an ear."

"Half of mine," she said, "beats two of yours."

THE CRIME LAB report on DNA from the infant's tooth stated that the donor was two point nine trillion times more likely to have been Caucasian than black or Asian. Not that we needed additional proof, but it felt good to have science in our corner.

The report also stated that the individual was male. As a courtesy to Nwodo, I briefly flirted with calling Peter Franchette to give him the bad news. I didn't think it would help. Either he'd taken me at my word, in which case I'd be rubbing in his disappointment. Or he hadn't, in which case a piece of paper would do little to change his mind.

What about lab error he'd say. *What about sample contamination? I'll pay for a retest.*

I sent a note to the UCPD detective, Nieminen, and forwarded the profile for entry into the various state and national DNA databases.

With no reason to go to People's Park, I'd stopped monitoring the situation there, assuming that the protest had gone the way of most causes in our short-attention-span age: out with a whimper.

I was surprised, then, to pass by a few days later, en route to my in-laws' to drop off the baby, and notice the site quiet. No chugging machinery, no swarms of men in hard hats and reflective vests. The closest thing to a sign of life was a line of people sitting cross-legged on the sidewalk along Haste, holding cardboard signs.

$HAME ON UC

PROTECT NATIVE LANDS — SAVE OUR PARK

GREEDY DEVELOPERS OUT OF BERKELEY

They weren't chanting, just staring into the distance, stolid and grave, as though they'd fused to the concrete.

The next surprise met me in the squad room that evening: the unit captain, waiting at my cubicle.

"Deputy," she said. "Can I steal you for a minute?"

Rarely did Noreen Bakke leave her perch on the fourth floor, and never for a grunt such as myself. I managed to shoot a look at Moffett, who gave a micro-shrug and put his head down. "Yes, ma'am."

In the elevator she said, "How are you adjusting to fatherhood?"

"Just fine, ma'am. Thank you."

"You don't have to put on a brave face for me, Deputy. I know how it is."

"We're hanging in there," I said.

A small frown. She seemed to want an admission of weakness.

"Tired, no doubt about it," I added.

"Lieutenant Hambrick tells me you weren't able to piece together much time off."

"I appreciated his flexibility, ma'am."

"Night shift's working out."

"Yes, ma'am."

"I'm not interrupting you, am I?"

"No, ma'am. Not at all."

"It'll be quick," she said. "Quick as you make it."

Waiting in her office was the day's third surprise.

Sitting half-twisted—one arm thrown carelessly back—in all his coiffed, glen plaid glory, was University of California, Berkeley, executive vice chancellor George Greenspan.

He stood to pump my hand.

"Clay. Good to see you again."

"Have a seat," Captain Bakke said.

I took the remaining chair.

"I went and checked out your stats," Greenspan said. "Either I was being forgetful, or you were being modest. You were one *hell* of a point guard."

"Thank you, sir."

"How'd you—" he began.

End up here.

"—choose this path," he settled on.

"I wanted to serve my community," I said. "The best way I knew how."

Greenspan smacked his thighs. "That is *wonderful*. Let me tell you: I've been at this game for thirty years, and that kind of attitude is something we could do with more of. A *lot* more. Not to take anything away from our kids. We need our doctors and our lawyers and our entrepreneurs. I don't begrudge anyone that. You're the first in your family to go to college? Go ahead. Spread your wings. We support you, one hundred percent. That is a core part of our mission."

He paused expectantly.

"Yes, sir."

"At the same time, when I came up, there was this feeling— I realize how corny it must sound to the contemporary ear—but we had a certain sense of *togetherness*. It was in the air. We understood that we would sink or swim as one, and that each of us was going to have to work a little, and give a little."

"'Ask not what your country can do for you,'" Captain Bakke said.

"That's right," he said. "Although you're not old enough to know that."

She smiled obligingly.

"Anyway," Greenspan said, "take it from a geezer. I look around today—not just at our kids, but at the wider society—I can't escape the feeling that something's missing. A national shortage of . . . I don't know. Call it civic duty. Between you and me, I find the prevailing attitude to be a little selfish, and more than a bit frightening. So I'm glad to hear we're on the same page, you and I."

I said, "Thank you, sir."

It was the prudent thing to say. Same question at a party? I'm going to give a very different answer.

"Which is why"—his pensiveness curdled into annoyance—"it *pains* me, in a way that these self-proclaimed 'community activists' cannot begin to understand, to be accused of attempting to take advantage of that community. Our sole aim in building is to increase the housing stock and alleviate the strain on our students, and by extension on the city as a whole. It's basic supply and demand. Three thousand dollars for a studio? Not when you're the first in your family to go to college. They're hurting the very groups they claim to protect. But."

He sighed. "Neither here nor there. Point is, there's a lot of emotional steam built up around this issue that needs to be vented off. The chancellor also feels it's important to amplify that the status of the remains is not, ultimately, UC's decision. We're merely accepting your ruling."

I wasn't sure if he meant the Coroner's Bureau or me personally.

"The idea came up to hold a panel," Greenspan said. "Allow the public to air concerns and ask questions in a venue that's safe and constructive."

"Pardon my saying so, sir," I said. "It's within your rights to go ahead. I'd think you'd be concerned about legitimizing the opposition."

"That's a fair point, an excellent point." Greenspan grinned at the captain. "You can see why I thought of him." To me: "What's on my mind is the history, and what we can learn from it. We don't need a repeat of the stadium fiasco."

Said fiasco was a two-year-long tree sit-in. "No, sir, I'm sure you don't."

"What was missing from that process was transparency. Since day one I've been adamant that we need to be open, in order to get public opinion on our side. In point of fact they're on our side already, they just need to be made aware of it. There's this notion floating around that the same support exists for keeping the park as did twenty-five years ago. But that's mistaken. We've done extensive polling. Overwhelmingly folks want it gone. But they also don't want to feel like we've sneaked in in the middle of the night and stolen the socks off their feet. You see what I mean? From an informational standpoint, we need to put this to bed. Include a multiplicity of perspectives— legal, academic, medical, tribal, policy-oriented. A united front, so that everyone can see how deeply in the minority the opposition is."

The captain said, "The sheriff has asked us to send a representative."

Why me.

"I'm flattered, ma'am. Thank you."

"See," Greenspan said. "This is a guy who plays ball."

I said, "Wouldn't you prefer someone more qualified, though?"

"On the contrary, I think you bring a unique point of view. You're a Cal alum, and a prominent one at that."

"Nobody remembers me, sir."

He turned to Bakke. "There he goes, being modest again. You said it yourself, Clay: You've chosen to serve the community in this . . . unique way. You've got expertise. You're used to performing under the microscope. Plus the captain tells me you have experience with educational programming."

Confused, I looked at Bakke.

"The school group visits," she said. "You used to help out with those, didn't you?"

"Those were tenth graders, ma'am."

"These folks waving signs," Greenspan said, "they're basically kids, too."

"All I did was set up the classroom. The sergeant did the talking."

"You won't be up there alone," Bakke said. "Dr. Bronson has agreed to participate."

"What about Professor Szabla?"

"I don't think we can rely on Ralph to play nice," Bakke said. "I appreciate it, Clay. The sheriff wanted me to let you know that he appreciates it, too. He'd do it himself if he could. We discussed it with Media Relations, and everyone agrees you're the best fit."

Greenspan said, "Of course they do. We're shooting for a balance of authority and accessibility."

And expendability.

Captain Bakke said, "I know you've got a lot on your plate. We should find some ways to accommodate you, going forward."

Behold, a carrot for the Sacrificial Lamb.

I could see now why she preferred me exhausted and needy.

"When is this happening?" I asked.

"Splendid," Greenspan said, smacking his thighs again. "One week from yesterday. You'll meet with our team and be given ample time to prepare. Although the longer we wait, the more entrenched falsehoods get. Already some joker's filed for an injunction. Misinformation travels fast."

The captain gave a weary nod.

"So." Greenspan smiled. "Are we feeling good about this?"

I said, "Go Bears."

CHAPTER 6

The email came to my work address.

Dear Deputy Edison,

Per our recent conversation, I am sending you something to look at.

Best,
Peter Franchette

Two PDFs attached.

First, a scanned snapshot, the oversaturated palette of old Kodachrome. A young woman stood outside a house, smiling and clutching a baby to her chest. She wore mint-green slacks; a sleeveless blouse, paler green, called attention to rail-thin upper arms. The outfit set off the olive of her complexion, a crescent of paler skin peeking through at her waist, hemline riding up as she bent back for better leverage.

Her hair was tied up with a kerchief. Black flyaways jutted like television aerials.

The smile was wry. Stretched a bit wide: She'd been holding the pose for too long while the photographer fiddled with the focus. Urging through her teeth.

Hurry up, please.

But she wanted to look happy. She knew she ought to be. A familiar expression, one I saw every day. On my wife; and sometimes in the mirror.

The infant was wrapped in a blanket, its face hidden. You might mistake it for a pillow, if not for a chubby leg protruding and ending in a tiny foot sheathed in a yellow bootie.

The blanket was white, not electric blue.

Franchette had also scanned the photo's reverse. Dated in ink: 5-10-69.

The second PDF was the opening pages of a newspaper I'd never heard of, the *Berkeley Trip*. "Newspaper" is a generous description. Top left, pinholes and a reddish dent commemorated a rusty staple. The nameplate was hand-drawn, puffy letters and a goofy character with his eyes spinning in their sockets. The text was typewritten and crowded and smudged. Date of issue, March 16–20, 1970. You didn't need it to know what era had given rise to the *Trip*. The headlines sufficed.

Charlie Manson's Great Big Hassle
Slumlord Fuckers!
The Wilting of the American Cock

Pseudonyms made up the bylines. Mike Rotch, Cheez Louise, Derrière Payne.

At the bottom, Peter Franchette—or someone—had circled an article.

Nuke Prof Gets Roasted

BY PUTTA HURTON

Hot time in Berkeley Town!

Last Friday the thirteenth's four-alarmer up on Vista Linda Way in them thar hills was one hell of a far-out scene. Flames were jumping higher than yer gramma barefoot on a camp stove. *(cont'd 2)*

I scrolled down.

It wasn't just anybody's domicile getting the infernal treatment, but none other than that inhabited (or shall we say infested?) by Notorious Sonuvabitch Warmonger Gene Franchette. In case you have your head lodged someplace sans sunshine, that be the selfsame Professor Franchette responsible for making sure that when we finally do get around to dropping the Bomb on Hanoi, we damn well get em all.

Gee but it's poetic, ain't it, to imagine ol' Gene watching the smoke twirl into the sky?

At first blush, not much linked the photo to the article, other than the time period.

Franchette was counting on me to find the connection.

Piquing my curiosity. Testing me at the same time.

What had Nwodo told him about me?

You should talk to him, though, get his story. It's actually pretty interesting.

She was right. I was curious.

I reexamined the snapshot, shifting my attention from the woman in the foreground to the house. Pink concrete walkway, flanked by mod geometric topiaries. Brown shingle exterior, a shallow porch overhung by an American flag. Nailed to the railing, four blurry numerals: 1028.

Vista Linda Way turned out to be a short road amid the steep and twisting neighborhood at the western foot of Tilden Regional Park. Google Street View showed a low wooden fence, topped by a cloud of overgrowth that obscured the façade of 1028.

I opened a real estate website. The transaction history described 1028 Vista Linda Way as a two-bedroom, two-bath, sixteen-hundred-square-foot home built in 1947. It had last changed hands in 2006 for $1.265 million. Kitchens and baths fully updated.

I clicked through the photo gallery, trying to match the exteriors to the house in the snapshot. Topiaries chopped down. A porch, but different design and no flag. Brown shingles replaced by clean white siding.

Proof of a bad fire?

Or just a routine renovation?

Or they were totally different houses.

"You guys looking to move?"

I craned around in my chair.

Moffett stood behind me, gnawing an apple. "I thought you had a sweet deal."

"Doesn't hurt to know what's out there," I said.

He winked, ripped off a chunk, and lumbered to his desk.

PICTURE A GROWN man, six-foot-three, unshaven, shuffling up the sidewalk in sweatpants and slippers with holes, eyelids at half-mast, humming tunelessly to himself.

That's a guy to avoid. Wide berth. Cross the street.

Now strap a baby to that guy's chest.

Now that guy is a goddamn American hero.

He's Father of the Year.

"Aww. How old?"

"Fifteen and a ha—about four months."

"Aww. So *cute*."

With a smile, the woman who'd stopped to look charged up the hill, ponytail flouncing.

I looked down at Charlotte, zipped inside my hoodie, her head bent back and pink lips blossomed in a pout. "You're better than a puppy."

She slept on, and I resumed walking, leaning into the slope, keeping time against her bottom. Marin is one of the steepest streets in the city, and one block along I was already breathing hard.

The thought had been *exercise, fresh air, vitamin D.*

The slippers were unintentional. I'd left the house in them.

At the intersection with Euclid I passed a stop sign to which someone had added a sticker, red background and square white lettering, so that the message became—

By the time I reached Vista Linda Way, my quads burned and my back ached and I could feel Charlotte squirming against my sweat-soaked shirt.

"Sorry, little lady."

I tugged down the zipper and took in the view. Fog cascaded downhill, twining through the California redwoods that rose from backyards, faceless sentinels presiding over the restless sprawl of Berkeley, Albany, Richmond. I marveled that a person could own one of those trees; own one of those backyards, and this panorama.

Over the water, white traceries knit together into a turgid gray mass that enshrouded Treasure Island and threatened to crush like an anvil the few boats battling through chop. The Golden Gate was nearly erased, only the peaks of its towers and shifting orange slashes visible.

Vista Linda indeed. It justified the million-dollar price tags. Compared with farther west, the homes here were older, shabbier, with cramped or nonexistent front yards and carports instead of garages. Running out for diapers would take effort.

Quiet, though. I could hear Charlotte's breathing; feel its lacy flutter on my throat.

I negotiated a buckling sidewalk blocked by garbage cans and parked cars, two wheels up on the curb to accommodate the narrowness of the road. Gasping winter sun stirred eddies of warmth that broke the chill before vanishing.

The overgrowth outside 1028 had since been pruned back. I compared it with the snapshot Franchette had sent me.

"What do we think?" I asked. "Same house?"

Charlotte had no opinion. I rotated ninety degrees to show her the front door.

"I think it might be."

I unlatched the gate, mounted the porch, and rang the bell. Nobody home.

Had I been there on official business I would've left my card.

Today I was a regular guy, taking his daughter for a walk.

Exiting the gate I heard a startled *oh*. A woman in pajamas stood at the mouth of the adjacent driveway, poised to take in her trash can. Gray-haired, with soft, guileless cheeks, she drew tight her bathrobe, assessing me and the danger I presented.

Deranged hair? Check.

Mismatched clothing? Check.

Baby?

Baby.

She relaxed. "Good morning."

"Morning. I had a question for the homeowner. Any sense of when they're usually around?"

"It's unoccupied at the moment," she said. "What's your question?"

"History, I guess you'd call it. I was reading about a fire that took place here a while back. I was wondering if this was the right spot."

She nodded. "It is."

"You know the one I mean?"

"I do. I was fifteen at the time."

"Were you living next door when it happened?"

"All my life." She indicated her own house. "It was my parents', then."

I held up the snapshot. "Mind having a look at this?"

She came over and took it from me. "That's Bev."

"Bev . . . Franchette?"

"Poor woman. She had it hard."

"Because of the fire?"

No answer. She stared at the photo, thrust it back.

"I have no idea what became of her," she said.

A strange thing to volunteer. "Do you happen to know the baby's name?"

"Sorry, I can't stay out here, it's freezing."

"May I ask your name?"

She hurried inside, forgetting her trash can at the curb.

I moved it to the bottom of the pitched driveway for her. Charlotte woke up and began to mewl. From my hoodie pocket I took a bottle of formula, feeding her as I hiked back down to the car. All hail the Father of the Year.

THE NEIGHBOR'S NAME was Diane Olsen. She was sixty-five years old, divorced, with a daughter in San Francisco. Handful of prior addresses around Berkeley; she'd resided at 1024 Vista Linda Way since the midnineties. I assumed she'd spoken loosely, rather than lied, when she said she'd been there all her life. Maybe that was how it had felt to move back into her childhood home—as though she'd never gone anywhere or made any meaningful progress. Maybe she'd returned after the end of her marriage or to care for an aging parent.

She had no criminal record.

Neither did Bev, Gene, or Peter Franchette.

The Electronic Death Registration System came up blank for Bev and Gene or any Franchette. That didn't rule out much: Our search permissions are limited to Alameda County. I can't even check neighboring counties, let alone out of state. It's a major source of frustration. You have to get on the phone and pray someone accommodating picks up.

A death notice for Beverly Franchette appeared in the online edition of the *Albuquerque Journal,* May 1, 2014. Time and location of the funeral. No obituary.

Gene Franchette, on the other hand, presented a different challenge: thousands upon thousands of hits to sort through, the bulk of them academic citations. He'd spent his career at Los Alamos National Laboratory, in New Mexico. No mention of Berkeley. An in-house lab newsletter celebrated his retirement in 2009, noting his contributions to the fields of high-energy physics and optics. The final paragraph quoted him as saying that he would continue to come into the office twice a week. *They'll have to carry me out in a pine box.*

I pulled a current address in an Albuquerque suburb.

It appeared that he was still alive, at the age of ninety-eight.

I called Peter Franchette.

"All right," I said. "I'll bite."

He laughed. "Thank you."

If he owed thanks to anyone, it was Diane Olsen. Her weird reaction had nudged me from curious to intrigued.

"We need to set a few ground rules. First, you can't offer me money."

"Yes. I got that."

"My job takes priority. I can't use county resources, either." Bit of a fudge on my part. I already had. You'd be hard-pressed to find a cop who hasn't, at one time or another, checked up on a daughter's or niece's new boyfriend. But I had to set boundaries going forward, for his sake and for mine.

"I understand," he said.

"And you understand that that makes me not much better off than you, vis-à-vis access. A private investigator can probably get more."

"I told you, I've tried that. I've come to realize there are more important qualities."

"Such as?"

"Giving a damn."

"No guarantees there, either."

"You called," Peter Franchette said. "That's good enough for me."

CHAPTER 7

D r. Judy Bronson said, "This was a terrible idea."

In the basement green room of Zellerbach Hall, we hunched around a CCTV monitor, watching the auditorium fill to capacity.

Gary Lopez, Jr., elder of the Muwekma Ohlone tribe and local liaison to the Native American Heritage Commission, said, "You didn't realize that before?"

"It's seeing them," Bronson said. "How many there are."

The fourth panel member—Dana Simon, VP of operations for Siefkin Brothers, Builders—sat in an armchair, sipping tea and tweeting.

Leticia Stroh, Berkeley city councilmember for District 8, would moderate.

The assistant to UC Berkeley executive vice chancellor George Greenspan, whose name was Denali, and who had a shaved head and a bushy beard, as though he'd gotten up that morning and accidentally put his hair on upside down, said, "Everyone's been checked for contraband on the way in."

Greenspan himself was not present. After greeting and thanking us, he'd left to take his seat, up in the light booth.

Denali touched his headset. "Copy, two minutes. Shall we?"

We filed out.

You're used to performing under the microscope Greenspan had said, and it was true that I could run, pass, and shoot in front of five thousand people without choking. I could kneel in the street to examine a body and not become distracted by hecklers.

Answering questions—prescreened or not—was another matter.

I felt worse for Judy. Pathologists tend not to be the most social creatures. As we neared the wings, and the rumbling grew louder, she began to murmur, "Oh, oh, oh."

We stepped into the light and found our seats.

Stroh welcomed everyone, briefly introduced us, and laid out the format. Each panelist would be allotted five minutes before the floor was opened to questions. Topics had been chosen to cover as many of the issues as possible. If you had not submitted your question in advance, you could do so now. Use the slips of paper provided. Hand it to one of the ushers. Q&A would be limited to sixty minutes. Be aware we might not get to yours.

"Dr. Bronson," she said. "Let's begin with you."

The blood drained from Judy's face. "Yes. Yes. The—uh—process of—uh—dating human remains is, uh." She pushed up her glasses with shaking hands. "Multifactorial . . ."

Soon enough she stopped stammering and found her groove. Perhaps too well: She failed to notice Denali cuing *one minute left,* and eventually Stroh had to cut her off, leaving me less than three minutes to explain what a coroner's judgment of origin means. Dana Simon's talking points stressed that Siefkin Brothers, Builders, had always prided itself on working with the community and responding to user input. They were committed to honoring the historical presence of indigenous peoples. To that end, their award-winning design team had drawn up new plans for the lobby interior that incorporated traditional Native elements.

Gary Lopez, Jr., did not react to this announcement. When his turn came he said simply that the tribe did not have sufficient grounds to object. To be sure, they regarded the park the same way they did the East Bay as a whole: as Ohlone land. But be practical.

People dug everywhere, constantly, and with three permanent staff members, the Heritage Commission was already struggling to keep up. They had to focus on the locations where scholarly consensus fell on their side, such as the West Berkeley Shellmound.

I scanned the audience for Chloe Bellara.

"Thank you, everyone," Leticia Stroh said. "We'll move on to Q and A. Microphones have been set up in each seating section. If I call your name, please come up. State who you are and who your question is for. Sam Thiele."

A gangly kid loped down the balcony aisle. "Uh, I'm Sam Thiele."

"Your affiliation, I mean," Stroh said.

"Oh. Yeah, okay. I'm a sophomore. My question is for the construction company. How are the dorm rooms going to be connected to the supportive housing, and will people in supportive housing have access to the dorm?"

Dana Simon smiled. "Great question, Sam. Thank you. If you look closely at the plan, which is available for download at our website . . ."

The next few were softballs as well. Small local business owner Arvind Singh ran a restaurant on Telegraph Avenue. He wanted to thank the university for finally moving the process forward and doing what it could to keep the neighborhood livable and safe. Gayle Boyarin, a professor at the UC Berkeley School of Public Health, asked what was being done to identify the deceased child. I told her the investigation was ongoing.

"We encourage anyone with information to get in touch with our office," I said.

Speaking of the West Berkeley Shellmound, what was its status? Was there going to be an apartment building put up? Larissa Dupree, massage therapist, wanted to know.

Gary Lopez, Jr., was pleased to announce that the city council had rejected yet another attempt to ram the approval through. But the fight wasn't over. Already the developer was preparing an appeal. Over his dead body, Lopez said, would condos stand on sacred land.

"When there's something worth protecting, you can bet we're ready to go to bat."

I wondered if the hall was packed with confederates—a Potemkin audience.

"Trevor Whitman," Stroh said.

A man in his midtwenties approached the mezzanine mike. Khakis, a blue button-down, hair in a sharp side part. He looked like the president of the local Junior Rotarians. With a flourish he drew a piece of paper from his breast pocket.

"I have in my hand a copy of a map showing the locations of known Native burial grounds," he said. "You can clearly see that these areas fully encompass the current park boundaries."

From that distance I couldn't clearly see anything. Nobody could, except for the people sitting within a five-foot radius of the microphone. He could have been waving a take-out menu.

"Did you have a question, Mr. Whitman?" Stroh asked.

"I do," Trevor Whitman said. "It's for Mr. Lopez. And it is this, sir: Are you aware of the existence of this map?"

"Am I aware?" Gary Lopez, Jr., said. "What am I supposed to be aware of?"

"You're saying you're not aware."

"I'm saying I don't know what that is."

"In that case—"

"Mr. Whitman," Stroh said.

"I haven't gotten to my main question yet."

"Okay, well, please move it along."

"My question, sir, is this: If you are not in fact aware of the existence of this map, how can you claim to knowledgeably represent the interests of the tribe? And, as a follow-up, if you *are* aware, and you're ignoring this evidence—"

"I told you," Lopez said.

"—excuse me. Excuse me, I'm not done. If you are aware, then does it not bother you, sir, to sit up there and lie to our faces?"

"Mr. Whitman," Stroh said.

"How much did the university have to pay you to do that? Or maybe—"

"Excuse me. Mr. Whitman."

"—since you're basically a political puppet, you did it for free."

"Listen, asshole," Lopez said.

"And, as a follow-up, was it worth it, sir—"

"That's enough," Stroh said.

"—to sell not just *your* soul—"

Two ushers began hurrying up the mezzanine aisle.

"—but the souls of your *ancestors,* your *people,* and—"

I could barely hear the end of his sentence—*generations to come*—because, for one thing, the audience had begun to cheer and clap and hoot and shout, and also because at that moment the booth operator cut sound to the mike. Trevor Whitman spun around, slapped back the hand of an usher, and strode toward the exit.

Gary Lopez, Jr., clawed at his armrests, ready to jump from the stage and give chase. Judy Bronson's forehead glistened with flop sweat. VP of operations for Siefkin Brothers, Builders, Dana Simon refused to stop smiling.

Stroh rapped the lectern, calling for quiet, please.

"I am going to ask that individuals please stick to the questions that were submitted," she said. "Please refrain from using inflammatory language. This is a dialogue."

Bullshit someone yelled.

"Excuse me. Excuse me. The next . . . Desmond Poland. Is there a . . . Okay. Thank you. Can we turn the micr—thank you. All right, Mr. Poland. Who's your question for."

"For you, actually, Councilmember."

"All right, go ahead, please."

"So, I live near the park, and first what I want to know is, is that your district?"

Stroh appeared momentarily befuddled. "You're asking if the park falls within my district?"

"That's correct."

"Not technically, no. That would be District Four."

"Right, yeah. So that's Councilmember Davies."

"I'm sorry, Mr. Poland, but I have to ask you to stick to the topic."

"This is the topic," he said. "What I want to know is, if you don't represent me or the people who live in the neighborhood that's being affected by this, how come you're up there, instead of her? Where's she in all this?"

"It's true that we represent individual districts, but when it comes to issues facing the city as a whole—"

"Well, but hang on a second, cause what matters to me isn't the same as what matters to your constituents. You work for rich people."

"I think we can all agree that People's Park—"

"I don't know that we can," Desmond Poland said. "I voted for Jodi Davies, and one of the reasons I did is she promised to take the pulse of the people before making major decisions. I want her to know, I don't support this decision, and I don't remember her asking my opinion."

"If you'd like to communicate that to Councilmember Davies, you can go to her office hours—"

"I tried that and she didn't show up. I also sent her an email. So I'm challenging her here to keep her word, or else I think we need to start talking about impeachment: her, and you, and all of you."

The room once again erupted. It took Stroh a good three minutes to regain control.

"Ladies and gentlemen—"

What about the rest of us someone yelled.

"And *everyone*," Stroh said. "Now, I value your perspective, Mr. Poland, and I'm glad that we're getting to hear a diverse range of opinions. Obviously I can't speak on behalf of Councilmember Davies—"

Then get her someone yelled.

"What I can tell you is that part of our job, every one of us, is to listen to a lot of different voices, because we have a lot of stakeholders, and as a community we need to ensure that everyone feels heard."

Answer the question.

"And, and, speaking for myself, let me add that I have consistently supported the rights of Berkeleyans to demonstrate their values, and my voting record reflects that."

Answer the fucking question.

"When we had white supremacists parading in front of City Hall, I was the one—"

Boos and cheers and general rumpus.

"I have consistently called for greater police accountability, and—"

You could almost see her digging the hole.

"Excuse me. Please. Let's remember, this is not a referendum on—if we can't adhere to the format . . . Sarah Whelan," Stroh bellowed. "Sarah, please come up."

A woman in her early forties slid out of the back row of the orchestra section. She approached the mike, yanked it off the stand, and gripped it in two hands.

"My name is Sarah Whelan," she said. "I'm a proud Berkeley resident for twenty-six years. I have one question, and it's for the audience."

She faced the crowd. "Whose park?"

The response was instantaneous, but dim: scattered voices, awaiting this moment.

Our park.

Had she stopped there, the gesture would have read as sad and tepid. But of course she didn't stop there. The first stab was just that—meant to puncture the inertia, to kick-start the mechanism lying dormant in the hearts and minds of so many present.

"Whose park!" Sarah Whelan yelled.

Now dozens of voices came echoing.

Our park!

"Excuse me—" Stroh said.

"Whose park!!"

Our park!!!

"Ms. Whelan—"

"Whose park!!!!!"

Our park!!!!!!

Sarah Whelan climbed onto a seat, and the others began rising, too, fists pumping and feet stamping, drowning out Leticia Stroh's pleas for order.

Whose park, our park, whose park, our park.

The mike had once again been turned off. It didn't matter. Someone handed Sarah Whelan a megaphone.

So much for confiscating contraband.

Whose park! Our park!

Crumpled question slips rained from the upper sections. The floor shook. To my eye, the shouters and clappers were a minority, but their fervor dominated the room, becoming the only relevant factor as the rest of the audience began filing toward the exits.

To my left, an ashen Judy Bronson was pinned back in her chair.

Dana Simon, VP of operations for Siefkin Brothers, Builders, got up and ducked through the curtains.

Gary Lopez, Jr., crossed his legs, grinning angrily and shaking his head.

"Ladies and gentlemen—" Stroh yelled.

Her mike cut out, too, as someone disconnected the cord.

Whose park!

Our park!

Sarah Whelan swung an invisible lasso. *"Let's take it back!"*

Within seconds, the trickle erupted into a full-on stampede, elbows and screams and bodies clambering backward over seats. I was sure someone would get killed. Small local business owner Arvind Singh had his palms up, mouthing *pardon me, pardon me* over and over again as he flailed, unable to escape his row.

I stood, ready to dive into the fray. I felt the peacekeeper's instinct as well as the rubbernecker's. And in fact I did start toward the stage right steps.

Amy's voice in my ear: *Don't even think about it.*

I turned to ask Stroh what we were supposed to do now. She was gone. I caught a glimpse of Gary Lopez, Jr.'s broad shoulders as he swished through the curtain, leaving Dr. Bronson frozen up there like a character out of Beckett.

I went back to my seat and joined her, and we watched the room clear, the roar growing muffled and fading as, outside, the mass of protesters—led by Sarah Whelan and Trevor Whitman, co-founders of a direct action group later identified as "Defenders of the Park"—spilled into Lower Sproul Plaza. There they rendezvoused with the third member of the Defenders' triumvirate, Chloe Bellara, along with a hundred-fifty-person flash mob. Everyone had been instructed to bring along a heavy object. Bats, pipes, hockey sticks, two-by-fours. There were reports of a man toting a broadsword. The two crowds merged and began marching south down Telegraph.

Take our park. Take our park.

Along the way they broke the windows of Walgreens and Bank of America. The smell of spray paint filled the air. Trash bins were overturned, hydrants opened, newspaper dispensers torched, windshields obliterated. Fortunately for Arvind Singh, Mumbai Kitchen survived relatively unscathed but for a few streaks of graffiti above the door. Everyone liked to support small local businesses, and besides, the restaurant was known for having the best potato dosas in town.

Rounding the corner at Haste, the crowd rushed toward People's Park, smashing through the fence and sweeping across the lawn, attacking construction vehicles, slashing tires and seat cushions, knocking out glass. Down came the work lights. They kicked in the door to Nestor Arriola's trailer and ransacked it. They scaled the remaining trees to take up residence.

I didn't witness any of it.

I was sitting onstage in the silent auditorium, squinting in the direction of the light booth. The glare made it impossible to tell if UC Berkeley executive vice chancellor George Greenspan was in there. Just in case, I waved and gave him a thumbs-up.

Judy Bronson shifted to face me. The creak of her chair leather carried clear to the back of the room. Zellerbach Hall has world-class acoustics.

She said, "What just happened."

I said, "Berkeley."

CHAPTER 8

Amy said, "When you heard my voice, warning you not to go, how did I sound?"

Tuesday morning marked day five of the Re-Occupation of People's Park. We had the TV on mute, watching the live coverage while enjoying a rare breakfast together.

"What do you mean? You sounded like you."

"Was I begging? Scolding? This imaginary version of me, I'm trying to get a sense of how shrewish she is. That way I have something to aim for in real life."

On-screen, a tree-sitter raised a gallon jug of water up to his branch using a rope. He had a bucket up there, too. Input/output.

I said, "Every part of me wanted to get in there. Pure instinct."

"For your daughter's sake, it might be time to revise your instincts."

Several protesters had chained themselves to a backhoe.

"The real question," Amy said, "is will Bakke keep her word and give you credit for participating."

"No chance. Every time she looks at me, she's going to be reminded how idiotic it was. I'll be lucky if she doesn't find some excuse to demote me."

Chloe Bellara's face filled the screen. The chyron identified her as PROTEST LEADER.

I switched the TV off and took our plates to the sink.

"What time are you meeting this guy?" Amy asked. "I'd like to take a run, if possible."

"I'll be back in a couple hours. Love you."

"You too."

The monitor crackled, and the baby began to make noise. I kissed Amy on the head and hustled out.

PETER FRANCHETTE'S OFFICE was on the eighth floor of a building in downtown Oakland. My conversation with Nwodo and the background I'd done on him had led me to expect a lavish setup, with tech-sector quirks and perks.

I once took a removal call at a start-up near Jack London Square. The head of sales had dressed down an underperforming rep, who left the conference room and crossed the open floor plan to the gym, where it was assumed he intended to sweat out his stress. Thirty minutes later, co-workers found him hanging from a noose fashioned out of a jump rope and affixed to a hook meant for a heavy bag. The CEO, I was told, was really into boxing as a metaphor for business. A second heavy bag swayed gently next to the body, twin columns of leather. We rolled the body out on the gurney, past the other employees, baby-faced and tearstained as they huddled atop the common-area furniture: rich-hued fabric blobs meant to invite lounging, chance collaboration, divergent thinking, productive play.

Franchette Strategic Ventures had a more modest setup. A small reception area fronted two offices. White walls, generic chairs, potted dracaenas. No air hockey table or milkshake dispenser. In place of a logo, a mosaic of headshots hung behind the reception desk, women and men in smart attire, each tagged with a name and the name of a company.

A young woman at work in one of the offices stood from her computer to shut her door, pausing first to smile at me and nod.

The receptionist, a husky guy in Banana Republic, sent me through.

Franchette's own office had a south-facing picture window but was similarly austere.

"Nice to meet you," he said, extending a hand.

I knew the basics. Born in Albuquerque, a graduate of New Mexico Tech. Married, three children, home address in Piedmont and a second in Bolinas. He'd come to Silicon Valley straight out of college, right before the first dot-com bubble began to inflate. His street-routing software, Straight Shot, was acquired by a larger GPS firm for one hundred ninety million dollars. In the intervening decades he'd retreated from public life, enough so that a tech blogger had included him on a Whatever Happened to Them? listicle.

He wore jeans and flannel, a reddish-brown goatee, fashionable in his heyday and unchanged save a minor incursion of gray on the left flank. Hair the same rusty color, utilitarian cut. He looked delivered from the womb straight into middle age, except for the eyes, an unexpected cobalt blue nestled amid stellate, impish creases.

He toed an overstuffed cardboard box tucked against the side of the desk. "This is everything."

"A few questions, first."

"Be my guest."

We sat. I placed a printout of the snapshot on his desktop. "Beverly's your mother."

He appeared pleased that I'd ferreted out her name. "Yes."

"And you think the baby is your sister."

"That's how it started, the photo. After my mom died, I went home to clean out her things and found that in her vanity. At first I thought it was me. I didn't recognize the house, and when I saw the date I knew it couldn't be. I was born in seventy-four. So I did the logical thing, went and showed it to my dad. He claimed not to remember, but I could tell from his reaction that there was something wrong."

I said, "He's getting up there, age-wise. Could he be reacting to something he can't remember?"

"I see where you're coming from. He'll be ninety-nine in April.

Assuming he makes it till then. Which—I see no reason to believe he won't. I know: Everyone dies. But he still lives on his own. He has a nurse who comes over during the day, but for the most part he's self-sufficient. He could be a hundred and ten, and I'd still be surprised to get the call."

"I applaud your optimism."

"Oh, it's not that," Franchette said. "He's an unbreakable bastard. Put it this way: His senility kicks in at convenient moments. He has no trouble remembering when the Cubs are playing. I've asked him about the photo multiple times. At any point he could've said, 'No, that's so-and-so, nothing to do with us.' He's never denied she existed, he just refuses to talk."

"And you know it's a she because . . . ?"

"He slipped, once. I was down there, visiting him, and I said, 'Did the baby die? Tell me where it's buried, at least, so I can put flowers.' I'd been pestering him about it, and he finally lost his temper and started shouting at me. 'It's over. She's not coming back.' I don't understand why he'd use those words, unless he thought she might still be alive. If he knew she was dead, why not come out and say that?"

"Too painful for him to talk about?"

Franchette shook his head. "Anyone else, I'd agree. But everything with him is calibrated. There's no room for sentiment. Unlike my mother, who was emotional to a fault."

He shifted in his chair and looked to the side. "I can't explain it. It's like he wants me to keep asking, but has no intention of answering."

"Do you think he'd be willing to talk to me?"

"You're welcome to try."

"Let him know I'll be calling."

"That won't necessarily improve your odds. But I will."

I said, "What makes you so certain the baby in the photo doesn't belong to someone else? Say a friend of your mother's."

"The way she hid it—it was obviously deliberate. It was at the back of a drawer, buried in lipsticks and whatnot."

"She might've forgotten about it."

"She wasn't the type to hang on to material possessions. When I was a teenager, she'd go into my closet and purge it without my consent. Take my word for it: The photo was there because she wanted it there. I'm not coming to these conclusions based on nothing. How you interpret the data depends on how well you understand my parents."

"Let's back up, and you can help me understand. Start by giving me a sense of your family as a whole. Any other siblings?"

"Just me."

"Grandparents, uncles, cousins."

"My father's the youngest of four. The rest are dead, one before I was born, and the others when I was young. My mom had one sister. She's in a home, outside Philadelphia."

"Have you asked her about the photo?"

"Yes. I recorded the calls; the audio files are in the box, on a thumb drive. It's pointless. She's had several strokes. You can hear for yourself, she's impossible to follow. The rest of the extended family is back east. We didn't have much to do with them. Anything, really."

"Where are your parents from originally?"

"My dad was born in Chicago. He came out during the war, or a little before, to join the lab at Berkeley."

"The article you sent me about the fire said he worked on the bomb."

"That's what he did at Los Alamos, too."

"That paper's really something else, by the way. Where'd you find it?"

"The public library, believe it or not. They have a historical collection. Some of it's searchable online."

"Whoever wrote the piece didn't seem too upset by what happened."

"I doubt 'weapons scientist' was a popular calling card around Berkeley back then."

Or now. Signs posted at the city line continued to declare it a nuclear-free zone.

Franchette said, "He liked to play it up. He always drove Lincolns, and he'd keep a little plastic mushroom cloud stuck to the dash."

I asked about the newsletter I'd found celebrating Gene's career at Los Alamos.

He nodded. "I've seen that. 'High-energy physics' is a euphemism. I knew what he did. Everyone did, it was common knowledge. Growing up, all my friends' fathers worked at the lab. That's who we socialized with. My parents used to argue about it, because my mom couldn't stand the other women. She called them Stepford wives. They'd throw potlucks, and her Jell-O mold always came out lopsided or whatever, and he'd accuse her of doing it on purpose, to embarrass him . . . Anyway. The photo's not the first time I've asked him something and not gotten an answer. He has plenty of practice being tight-lipped."

"And your mother? What's her story?"

"She was a housewife. Grew up in New Jersey."

I waited for him to add more, but his gaze had wandered to the snapshot. Beverly Franchette was frail where her son was fleshy, her throat sunken and dark from sun exposure. Nobody wore sunscreen in those days. In contrast, the backs of Peter's hands glowed a watery blue, a lifetime of computer monitor light soaked into his skin.

"You don't much resemble her," I said.

"I'm all Gene." He smiled. "Gene's genes."

"Do you know when your mom came to California?"

"In her twenties, I think."

"How did they meet?"

"At a party? I'm not sure." A beat. "It must seem—I don't know. Deficient. To be missing such elementary facts."

"You'd be surprised. People don't always think to ask."

"For me it came from understanding, early on, that I didn't have permission to ask. There was a lot of silence in our house. Then one day you turn around and realize you know nothing about yourself, or where you come from. By then it's too late."

"Your father was a good deal older than her."

"About twenty years."

"Was it his first marriage?"

"That's another thing they didn't bother to tell me about," he said, rifling in the box.

He tugged out a marriage certificate. Eugene Franchette and Beverly Rice had wed before the Alameda County clerk on May 8, 1964. The groom listed one previous marriage, ended by dissolution.

"I couldn't get any further than that," Peter Franchette said. "The courthouse doesn't seem to have any record of the divorce, and I can't submit online records requests without both parties' names, which of course he won't tell me. So I still don't know who this first woman was. It's the same for other records: The age of the file means it hasn't been scanned, or I'm missing some piece of essential information. I can't search for a birth certificate with my parents' names alone. I need the baby's name, or the date and the city of birth."

His tone remained even, but the pale hands had balled. As if discovering he'd given something away, he opened them quickly and offered a joyless smile. "First-world problems."

Behind the irony lay genuine sorrow. His parents had locked him outside the house, so to speak, ignoring him as he pounded and pleaded to be let in.

I said, "Let's run with the idea that she is your sister and that she's not dead. Have you considered that she might've been put up for adoption?"

"I did. That's why I hired the private investigator. He claimed he could find that out for me. He took a whole year and came back with nothing."

"That doesn't mean there's nothing to find. Adoption records are tricky." Or the PI realized who he was working for and decided to treat him like an ATM.

"I thought about it," Franchette said. "It just doesn't make sense to me. My mom . . . she was a helicopter parent before the term existed. She never let me out of her sight. I got accepted into MIT and she wouldn't let me go. She and my father had a huge fight about it. Usually, he pushed her around, but on that she wore him down. Me, too."

"Maybe she felt guilty for having given up a previous child."

"But she felt fine with it a few years prior? What could have changed so drastically, between the baby's birth and mine, to make her do a one eighty?"

I said, "The experience of giving up a child."

He waved, conceding. "*Something* happened to make her that anxious and overprotective. And whatever it was, I have no doubt she decided it was her fault."

"Twice now you've mentioned your parents arguing. Was it that kind of marriage?"

". . . no."

I cocked an eyebrow at him.

"As long as she did what he wanted," he said, "they were fine."

"Did she?"

"Most of the time. The incidents I cited stand out because they're exceptional."

I wasn't wholly convinced. "Aside from your father's slip-up, do you have any reason to believe the baby *isn't* deceased?"

"Well," he said, reaching over and mousing, "it's a little difficult, trying to prove a negative. I must've called every cemetery in the Southwest. Nobody has her."

He turned his monitor around to show a spreadsheet of addresses and phone numbers.

"Lot of work," I said.

"My wife thinks I'm crazy. 'Why can't you find a normal hobby?' Golf, or wine."

He eyed the file box like a prizefighter sizing up an opponent. "I had no idea what this would become. If I did, I might never have started."

I said, "You mind if I ask what it is you do here?"

"Socially conscious VC. We search out and develop CEOs we believe in."

"The headshots on the wall out there are your mentees."

"Yes."

"Any exciting prospects?"

"A few. We're young. Soon I'll need to take on more staff. For the moment it's me and Radhika, plus Nat and a support team in Belarus. It's not about money, though."

"With due respect, only rich people say that."

For the first time he laughed: a thin, metallic sound. "Look, I'll never turn down an opportunity, but I'm far more concerned with supporting missions we can get behind. Big ideas that create social value."

I have a low tolerance for Silicon Valley's sense of noblesse oblige. More often than not "Big Idea" translates to on-demand pudding delivery, and the "social value" created takes the form of increasingly unmanageable rents and scooters cluttering the sidewalk. It's like the rapture came and God decided the scooter riders alone were worthy of salvation.

At the same time, who was I to judge? Maybe a few years down the line I'd fall into my own existential crisis. With less capital to prop it up.

"Let's talk about the fire for a second. I take it your father won't discuss that, either."

Franchette shook his head.

"Given the nature of his work, arson had to be a consideration."

"The PI looked for a police report but couldn't find one."

"The fire department report?"

"I didn't ask him to check for that."

An avenue. I said, "Did the PI speak with Diane Olsen?"

"I've never heard that name."

"The next-door neighbor on Vista Linda. I met her. She was a teenager when it happened."

He leaned forward, charged up by the prospect of a lead. "What did she say?"

"She wasn't in a chatty mood. I'll try again. How'd you find this guy? The PI."

Franchette hesitated. "Yelp."

I started to laugh.

"He had five stars," he said.

"Of course he did."

"What can I say? I have faith in technology."

"Sure," I said. "It's been all upside for you."

He allowed a boyish grin, and I found myself starting to warm to him. Wild success at a young age can have a distorting effect. You get used to people telling you what you want to hear, you start to believe the universe is tailor-made for you. It can make you cruelly jaded or blindingly naïve, sometimes both at once.

Peter Franchette seemed to have fared moderately better.

"Just to keep the timeline straight," I said. "The fire occurred in 1970. Your parents left California for New Mexico when?"

"I'm not totally sure. I think it was a year or two later. One thing I do have is a copy of the deed to the Albuquerque house." He searched in the box, came up with a page. "'July 27, 1972,'" he read. "So around two years later. But it's an approximation at best."

"I asked you how old your sister was when she died. You said about three."

"That's right."

"Did you arrive at that based on the moving date?"

"I suppose so."

"She could have gone with them."

A beat. His lips twisted. "It never really occurred to me. How could I miss that?"

I said, "There's a lot of information to deal with. If we're being strict, why assume she was gone before you were born?"

He blinked, startled anew. "You think we could have overlapped?"

"If you were a baby, why not?"

He'd divided his parents' lives into two parts, giving himself sole possession of the latter. Now the bright-blue eyes got active. Revising his assumptions.

"I guess I figured that if she'd lived there, I would have seen . . . clothes, or . . . I don't know," he said. "But you're right."

"She could have been older than three," I said. "She could have been younger. Your parents could have moved before buying a house. They could have rented. They could've bought but not moved for six months. She died. She was adopted. Or you never had a sister and the baby was someone else's. You see what I'm saying?"

"That I don't know anything."

"No more or less than anyone would in your position. But you should ask yourself if you can handle rehashing all of this."

"I can. I want to."

"You don't know what I might find. It could be upsetting."

"I understand. Whatever it is, I'd rather know."

But I could sense an ambivalence beginning to emerge, a return to his previous moodiness that increased as I continued to question him, poking at the edges of his ignorance. He told me, for instance, that he'd uploaded his DNA profile to various ancestry sites. He showed me pages of distant relatives. But when I asked if he'd attempted to contact any of them, he got defensive.

He'd meant to. He had other things on his plate. His CEOs needed him. He was about to fly to Austin for a three-week deep dive. He could only afford to think about his sister's case in fits and starts. Sometimes he got so busy that he had to abandon the search for months on end.

His attitude reminded me of how he'd described his own father: *It's like he wants me to keep asking, but has no intention of answering.* But where Gene was cagey and manipulative, Peter sounded simply exhausted.

"It's been draining," he said, slumping in his executive chair. "Every time I hit a wall, I promise myself I'm going to stop. That's where I was, mentally, when I spoke to Delilah. I swore I wouldn't call you. Then I heard about the, the thing in the park and thought, 'Let's get the answer and be done with it.' "

We'd been talking for an hour and a half. I needed to leave.

I said, "There may not be an answer."

"I accept that."

"Do you?"

He didn't answer me right away. He picked up the box and walked me out to the elevator.

"Delilah says you're the best," he said. "If I'm lucky, the question will bother you as much as it bothers me."

CHAPTER 9

Back at the office, doing what the county paid me to do, I got some good news.

A DNA hit on the tooth.

A parental match, to the state criminal database. Given the child's fate, I wasn't surprised to learn he came from less-than-sterling stock.

The severity of the rot, however, took me aback.

The matching profile belonged to one Frederick Dormer, aka Fritz, aka Frizzy. Sixty-seven years old, he was a founding member of the Nordic Knights, a violent white supremacist gang active up and down the West Coast. At present he was serving a double consecutive life sentence plus seventy years for racketeering, kidnapping, attempted murder, and murder.

Dormer's catalog of sins made for stomach-turning reading. The murders were particularly ugly, because they had nothing to do with the business side of crime—disputes over money or territory, suppression of rivals.

What had landed him behind bars for good was plain, old-fashioned hate, married to unadulterated psychopathy.

On St. Patrick's Day, 1994, Fritz Dormer and his fellow Knights were at their clubhouse in San Francisco's Tenderloin, drinking and smoking meth. It was late on an unusually sultry night, and conver-

sation turned, as it so often did, to the impending race war. The bulk
of the Knights' income derived from drugs, giving rise to conun-
drums: Who would be their target customers, after the niggers and
the spics were gone? Once the kikes had been eliminated and the
banks all shuttered, where would they keep their money?

Fuckin shitbrain, you don't have to be a kike to run a bank.

The opinion of Loren "Eejit" Sykes.

Gimme a goddamn calculator Sykes said. *I'll do it for you.*

Vigorous debate ensued as to whether Eejit Sykes could work a
calculator.

Gregg "Ape" Redding didn't think so, seeing's how Eejit could
barely keep count of his own balls.

You all Fritz Dormer said *are missing the fuckin point.*

The room went quiet. When Dormer talked, everyone listened.

Did they really think, he wanted to know, that banks started
with Jews?

No one answered. Apparently, many of them did think that.

Dormer corrected them: Banks, like sports or music or television
or anything of enduring worth, were a white creation.

*By rights they belong to us. So why's it Goldberg, sitting behind
the desk? Who put him there?*

Silence.

We did.

What happened, Dormer explained, is that the mud races hid
out, lying in wait for us to turn our backs so they could seize control. That was how they operated. Deceit was part of their nature.

*It's what they're doing, right now, while we argue amongst our-
selves like a bunch of fuckin pissants.*

He stepped to the window, peering out at the straggling holiday
revelers.

Saint Patrick was a white man. A fucking martyr. *So tell me why,
right now, right this instant, there's a million fags struttin around in
green hats.*

Russell "Razor" Towne said *Cause they stole it.*

Cause we let *them steal it.*

Outside on the sidewalk, a man stopped to light a cigarette. He was black, wearing a white tank top with a rainbow-colored shamrock and gold hoop earrings, his hair in a picked-out Afro. He rested his foot on the bottommost step of the clubhouse entrance and took a drag.

Dormer smiled. He gestured at the man. *I rest my case.*

Eejit Sykes wobbled up off the couch. *Fuck that.*

Go on then Dormer said.

Eejit Sykes did not move. His compatriots attributed his lack of response to stupidity—Sykes being too dense to perceive the challenge thrown at his feet. They were wrong. Eejit Sykes was calculating on the fly. Eejit Sykes's real name was Benny Palmieri, and he was an undercover agent for the California Bureau of Investigation. It had taken him a year and a half to infiltrate the Nordic Knights, and now he worked feverishly to determine a course of action that would cement his standing in Fritz Dormer's eyes, short of beating the shit out of the poor doomed motherfucker enjoying a valedictory smoke, who continued to unknowingly worsen his situation by ashing against the metal clubhouse banister.

Dormer said *This fuckin monkey.*

Giving up on Eejit, he looked around pointedly for someone, anyone, to sack up.

Gregg "Ape" Redding humped to the clubhouse door and threw it open.

Hey faggot.

The man raised his head. *The fuck you say?*

Redding said *Private property. Fuck off.*

The man's name was Anthony Wax. He was twenty-three years old, studying to become a dental technician. Now he stood up straight and stared back at Redding through tongues of smoke. *The fuck did you say to me.*

You heard him Dormer said, stepping to the threshold.

Behind Dormer and Redding gathered the silhouettes of ten more men.

Possessed of enough common sense to fold, Anthony Wax took one last drag and flicked the butt into the gutter.

You pick that up Dormer said.

Wax turned and walked away.

Faggot.

Wax kept walking.

Ape Redding bit first, jumping down the steps and catching up to Anthony Wax near a fire hydrant. He tackled Wax to the pavement, and the two men rolled around, throwing punches. Despite Redding's three-inch, fifty-pound advantage, he appeared to be losing the fight. Wax managed to get on top of him and began hammering away at Redding's face and arms, while Redding hollered at him through blood to *get the fuck out of here.* He said this not to protect himself, but because he knew that Dormer and the rest of the Knights would be coming shortly. Redding did not want to be responsible for what happened to Anthony Wax when they did.

Ape Redding's real name was James Finch. He was an agent with the Federal Bureau of Investigation. As part of an interstate operation aimed at dismantling the West Coast narcotics supply chain, he had spent the last two years undercover, infiltrating the Nordic Knights. The FBI had kept the operation a secret from state law enforcement, including the California Bureau of Investigation. The CBI had done the same to the FBI.

Accordingly, neither Agent Finch nor Agent Palmieri knew about each other.

Run Finch said to Wax. *Please.*

That last word, "please," had the desired effect. With his fist drawn back, Wax balked. On the stand Finch would describe Wax's expression as confused—chagrined, almost, as if he resented being made to recognize Finch's humanity.

Before Wax could reply, Fritz Dormer stabbed him in the back.

Razor Towne threw Wax to the ground, and together with Dormer joined in kicking and stomping and stabbing.

Agent Palmieri, in character as Eejit Sykes, stumbled from the clubhouse. In an effort to disrupt the altercation, he charged forward, "mistakenly" lurching into Towne and Dormer.

Dormer, mistaking Palmieri's mistake for what it was—deliberate interference—whirled around. His attorneys would contend that Dormer thought he was being attacked by a bystander, and therefore was acting in self-defense when he plunged the knife into Palmieri's chest.

The blade, an eight-inch bowie engraved with swastikas, pierced Palmieri's breastbone, severing his aorta.

Agent Palmieri sank to his knees.

Agent Finch struggled up, attempting to restrain Towne from beating Wax to death.

Towne punched Finch in the throat.

Sirens began to approach.

Benny Palmieri was pronounced dead at the scene.

The next day, Anthony Wax died of his injuries at Saint Francis Memorial.

After the facts emerged, there was some bickering between the California attorney general and the US attorney about who should prosecute. On one hand, the feds took precedence. On the other hand, Jim Finch had gotten away comparatively light, with black eyes and a ruptured trachea. A state cop had died. The compromise was to divvy up the offenders.

The jury rejected Dormer's self-defense claim.

Russell Towne was dispatched to the United States Penitentiary, Marion, Illinois.

Fritz Dormer settled into retirement at San Quentin State Prison.

I HADN'T HEARD from the UCPD detective, Tom Nieminen, so I called him. "Nice news about the match."

He had no idea what I was talking about.

He hadn't seen the DNA report, let alone read Dormer's file.

I forwarded him both.

Three days went by before I got tired of waiting and called him again.

"Oh yeah," he said. "Sorry, I meant to . . . Little busy around here, you know?"

I assumed he meant the occupation of the park, now entering its second week and showing no signs of abating. The momentum had picked up, more protesters arriving every day, some from out of state, in response to calls put out on social media by the Defenders of the Park. There was a run on poster board and marker. While there'd always been a certain number of sidewalk tents in the neighborhood, more sprang up along Hillegass and Dwight, clusters that swelled, touched, and finally united into a bona fide, hundred-person encampment. Traffic around campus locked in a permanent snarl. Amy and I had begun allotting an extra fifteen minutes to get to work. Many of the stores along Telegraph had yet to reopen, and some of those that had, such as the bank, had been vandalized again.

Why any of that concerned Nieminen, I couldn't say. With the unrest spilling off university property and spreading into the surrounding city streets, an overwhelmed UCPD had ceded control of the park perimeter to Berkeley PD. Plus Nieminen was an investigator, not a patrol cop.

"Did you get a second to look at the stuff I sent you?" I asked.

A beat. "Yeah, some. I mean, wow. You imagine having a fella like that for your pops? Guess I should head up there and ask old Fritzy what's what."

"Before we go," I said, "we should make a game plan."

"Oh. Yeah?"

Thrown. With good reason. Coroners don't often tag along during interviews.

I had my own reasons for wanting to be in the room.

Fritz Dormer was the infant's father—the baby's sole family, so far. I had a duty to inform him of the death of his son. I could have shunted the task to Nieminen. But the guy didn't inspire confidence.

"Dormer's next of kin," I said. "I'm required to notify him."

"Oh yeah. Okay. Yeah."

We arranged to meet at the prison in a few days' time.

ON THE MORNING of, I came back from a walk, ready to hand the baby off and hit the road. A roasty smell wafted from the bathroom. I found Amy ironing her hair.

"Are you going somewhere?" I asked.

"Work."

"You're not working today."

"Yes, I am. I'm covering for Melissa. She had her baby. It's on the calendar."

"I didn't see it."

"It's there. Check if you don't believe me."

"I believe you," I said. "I have an appointment today."

"Did you put it on there?"

"I thought I did." I tugged out my phone, thumbed through our shared calendar.

Sure enough, the day had but a single event blocked out: *Amy at work.*

"I definitely put it on," I said. "I *remember* putting it on."

"Maybe there's a bug in the app," she said charitably. "What's your appointment?"

"Notification visit. It's important. Can you reschedule?"

"Wish I could. I really can't do that to Melissa. She covered for me the whole time I was out."

"Right." I was irritated with myself for coming to the negotiation unarmed, having squandered all my brownie points on the meeting with Peter Franchette.

Amy set the iron down. "I can see if my mom's available."

"Would you, please?"

Theresa Sandek had to teach. So did Amy's dad.

I called my mom and left a voicemail.

Neither of us suggested my father. He was at work, his phone turned off. He kept it off at home, too. Nobody could understand why he bothered to pay for one.

I leaned against the kitchenette counter, Charlotte wriggling in my arms, while Amy assembled her handbag.

"I'm sorry, honey," she said. "Any other day I'd do what I can."

"Don't be. It's my fault for not checking the calendar."

"Where are you headed? Could you take her with you?"

A title screen flashed in my head. *Lockup: Diaper Rash.*

"Go," I said. "I'll figure it out."

She kissed us both, shouldered her bag, hesitated. "You're sure you'll be okay."

Wavering, her soft heart.

One tiny push; that's all it would take to spring the trip wire of maternal guilt. I'd have my freedom, and she'd have a day to devote wholly to her daughter.

Win–win.

I feel like I'm failing at everything.

"Of course we will." I waved Charlotte's arm. She was making her patented skeptical face: eyebrows raised, mouth aslant.

I let Amy's footsteps fade before dialing my brother.

"DUDE. WHAT IS *happening*. Long time. It's like you died. How's shawty?"

Already I could see my mistake.

"She's good," I said, lifting Charlotte to burp. "That's actually why I'm calling. I'm kinda stuck here."

Luke couldn't babysit, either. "Love to, but I got business down the Peninsula. We developed a strain for intense focus. Sour Diesel bred in with some highly specialized Nepalese shit. It's called Lazer Beam. With a 'Z.' These coders, man, can't get enough of it."

My brother worked for Bay Area Therapeutics, a cannabis and

lifestyle company founded by a high school buddy of his. While I thought it a questionable career for an ex-con and drug addict, it seemed to make him happy. Certainly my mom made sure to inform me, whenever we spoke, of how well Luke was doing; how he'd really managed to build a new life for himself.

He said, "Scott gave some to a friend who's C-suite at—I mean, I can't share the name, at the present moment, but trust me when I say you use their products every day. She loves it, goes wild, starts talking about bringing us on as wellness consultants. Everyone's psyched: whole new revenue stream, total blue ocean. We're presenting to the head of HR next week, so me and my team got to powwow about the deck and get that bitch ship*shape*."

By now you'd think I would've gotten used to the corporatese, but it still sounded bizarre coming out of his mouth, like he was speaking in tongues. "Gotcha. Thanks anyway."

"Hey, you know what, though? Andrea might be free."

"That's all right." Charlotte spit up down my neck. "I'll manage."

Luke shouted, "*Baby?* Baby, are you . . . Oh shitballs," he whispered. "She's meditating. I'm supposed to be quiet. I can have her call you back."

"It's fine."

"Hey, though, I really have been wanting to see you guys. I mean, she's my niece, right? She's got my DNA and everything."

"Some of it."

"Hmm. Man, *fuck* it. Gimme twenty minutes to get over there."

Amy's voice in my ear: *No.*

"What about your meeting?" I asked.

"I can push. Blood be blood, fam. Sit tight, I'ma Mr. Mom you the fuck *up.*"

I heard Amy's voice again, something she'd said to me a few years back, when my brother was fresh out of prison and I was struggling with how to be around him.

Believe him when you can.

I was pretty certain the advice didn't apply in this context.

Next time, my darling, choose your words more carefully.

"Park on the street," I said. "Don't block the driveway."

TWENTY MINUTES ENDED up being closer to sixty—ample time for buyer's remorse. Assuming Luke had bailed, I started composing an email to Nieminen, explaining that I'd gotten caught up. A loud knock came at the door.

I opened it with my finger over my lips.

"Whoops," Luke said. "Sorry, dude. She's asleep?"

"Probably for another half hour. There's a bottle on the counter with formula premeasured. Add six ounces of filtered water. *Six* ounces. *Filtered* only."

"Roger."

"Mix it slowly so it doesn't get air bubbles. You don't need to warm it up. Room temperature is fine. In fact, definitely do *not* warm it up. I don't want her to get burned. Once she's eaten you need to burp and change her. Do you know how to do all of that?"

"I mean." He scratched at a burly arm. Since his release he'd become fanatical about lifting weights. Every time I saw him, he seemed to have expanded. "Is it more complicated than that?"

"Yes. She—you have to—*yes*. Sit down."

I walked him through the entire process: what angle to hold the baby at, how to take breaks so she didn't spit up, regular versus overnight diapers, butt cream. His attention began to drift, and for an instant I saw what he was seeing, my hair greasy and my eyes like pits. Sitting amid dried-out baby wipes and stray socks, the unmade futon, mug rings crusting the coffee table. I am, if not quite a neat freak, then a dedicated neat enthusiast. Always have been. Growing up, Luke and I shared a bedroom, and you could draw a line up the middle of the carpet, entropy on one side, alphabetized books on the other.

It must have gratified him to find me at wit's end.

"Are you getting this? Do you want to write it down?"

He recited the information back to me, verbatim. He's smarter than he appears.

The problem has never been a lack of intelligence.

I said, "*Any* questions, call me. If you're not sure whether something is a question—"

"Call you."

"I'll be back before Amy gets home. If for some reason she gets here first—"

"I'm visiting," he said. "You were with me the entire time. You ran out to pick up diapers."

I felt bad. For asking him to lie; for the implied insult.

He said, "Don't worry, man, we're good to go."

"Thanks."

"No stress. One thing: Does she prefer indica? Or is she more of a sativa lady?"

"That's not fucking funny."

Luke patted my arm. "Go on, bro. Do justice."

DESPITE MY EAGERNESS to get on the road, I paused briefly outside to look at Luke's car. You couldn't *not* look at it: a metallic green Camaro, kitted out with snarling custom grillwork, twenty-four-inch rims, a spoiler. Parked beneath a birch, it shone with fresh wax, standing out amid the neighborhood Subarus and Priuses like a grenade in a gumball machine. My own car, a mid-aughts import, appeared positively anemic in comparison.

My brother has always been a motorhead, with a particular weakness for muscle cars. It was just such a vehicle that landed him in prison, when he capped off a multiday crack-and-vodka binge by hotwiring a Mustang and careering through the streets of Oakland. The joyride came to a quick end. He blew threw a red light, colliding with a compact Kia and taking the lives of two young women.

A little over two years had passed since his release. In that time he'd already bought and sold several cars. He worked on them at home, at night and on weekends, steadily trading up. The Camaro

I'd never seen before. What did it say that the stolen Mustang had also been bright green? The cynic in me detected an attempt to re-write history. Riding around in this echo of the past, making full stops and signaling every lane change, he became a responsible citizen; not Luke Edison, convicted felon, but a stand-up, hardworking guy in his midthirties with a wife, a mortgage, and a cool car. A hardworking guy in his midthirties deserved at least that much. He had a job, albeit a legally nebulous one. He made our mother proud.

In her defense, I don't think she meant to gloat about his new-found success or to denigrate my choices. More that she had to boost him up in order to stave off her own guilt. She'd invested a great deal of hope in his rebirth. They both had.

Maybe I was being too harsh on him. I had a tendency to do that. Maybe he just liked the color. The Bay Area Therapeutics logo was a snippet of DNA with leaves budding at the edges, rendered in marijuana green. Maybe Luke was showing company pride.

I had to wonder, though: If the family of his victims spotted him idling at a busy intersection, waiting obediently for the light to change, how would they feel?

I peered down the driveway toward the guest cottage. The view was obstructed, so that I couldn't quite make it out from where I stood on the sidewalk. I lingered, listening for the sound of my daughter's cries, hearing nothing but the rasp of dry leaves.

CHAPTER 10

The road to San Quentin State Prison runs through a village of the same name. Main Street, post office, snug clapboard houses originally built for prison staff and their families. Today the homes are privately owned. If you can get comfortable with having four thousand of California's most dangerous offenders for neighbors, it's a lovely place to live.

Picturesque cove. Stunning views. Easy access to wine country. The upscale mall a few miles down the freeway offers high-thread-count linens and artisanal salumi.

I passed a FOR SALE sign.

It's a testament to the lunacy of the East Bay real estate market that I found myself asking how bad, really, my commute would be.

We couldn't afford it, anyway.

Through the fog, the prison's blocky shoulders shifted and rolled. I entered the lobby a few minutes late. Nieminen was nowhere to be seen. At twenty past he came tripping in, crimson and winded, as though he'd arrived on foot.

"Traffic," he said. I'd taken the same route. Nothing exceptional.

A correctional sergeant named Blake Tipton led us along cinder-block corridors painted khaki and reeking of locker room. Over that, the acrid coating of bleach, fruitlessly applied. What noise I could hear was stifled and unsettling, like the tick of a faulty water heater, hinting at a violence scarcely contained.

"Fritz'll be happy to see you," Tipton said. "He doesn't get a lot of visitors. I checked the log. Last one was his son, couple of years ago."

"He has a son?" Nieminen asked.

"Three of them," I said.

"Make that four, right?" Nieminen said. Winking.

I ignored him. Fritz Dormer was a monster, but he still had minimal rights, one of which was to learn about the death of his child before strangers did.

Nieminen must've interpreted my silence as a factual objection, because he corrected himself: "Well, sure. Now it's back to three."

PRISON UNIFORMS RUN on the baggy side. You're not being fitted for the runway. Fritz Dormer's was the pale blue of a lifer. Pushing seventy, he filled it out, knots of muscle bulging under crepey skin covered in a dense network of tattoos.

Elaborate scrollwork and gothic lettering, Norse and Nazi iconography, sheathing his arms and crawling out from under his collar. The irony seemed lost on him: In the effort to prove his own whiteness, he'd dyed himself black, square inch by square inch. The eagle-and-swastika spanned his throat. He rubbed at it, smoothing down a nicotine-stained horseshoe mustache as he took us in from across the steel table.

He smiled. "Oh goody."

A voice like a lawnmower.

We introduced ourselves. I was in uniform, Nieminen in jacket and slacks, and it was to him—the More Important Person—that Dormer directed his attention.

"University police," he said.

"That's right," Nieminen said.

"You come to enroll me, forget it. I already got my degree. Associate of arts in general education. Not from Berkeley, though. I ain't sure I got the grades for that."

"Don't sell yourself short," Nieminen said. "Always more to learn. You know what they say. Knowledge is power."

"That so? Way I see it, power is power." Dormer turned to me. "What's your deal, sweetheart?"

The best way to break bad news is to do just that: break it. Fast.

I said, "Mr. Dormer, we recently discovered some human remains. The DNA came back a match to you. The decedent is your child. My condolences."

No reaction—in itself a reaction, and what you might expect from the likes of Fritz Dormer. It takes a lot to get a psychopath revved up.

It was also possible he was stalling; or in shock; or he hadn't heard me right.

Wait and watch his next move.

He leaned back in his chair, laced his fingers behind his head, and said nothing.

"Right now we're still gathering information," I said. "We don't know the decedent's name or the circumstances surrounding the death. We haven't been able to identify the mother, either. I was hoping you'd be able to help us out."

"Nope."

"No, not willing, or no, not able?"

"Neither."

"I understand that this must be hard for you."

"It would be, if it wasn't a bunch of bullshit. But it is. So, no. Not hard."

"Which part do you think is bullshit?"

"My boys are alive and well. They send me Christmas cards."

"They don't visit, though," Nieminen said.

Dormer stared at him. "Come again?"

I said, "The individual whose remains we found—"

"What's that mean, 'remains'? Found where?"

Wanting to preserve Nieminen's line of questioning, I hesitated.

Dormer snorted. "Yeah. What I thought. Bullshit."

"You want to see the lab report?" Nieminen said, feeling in his pockets.

Hard to say what he meant to accomplish. The report ran to half a page and contained nothing more descriptive than a pair of ID codes and a relationship probability.

"This here's you," Nieminen said. "And that's the baby."

To that point I hadn't specified the age of the decedent.

At the word "baby" Dormer's face registered a trace of—interest? Pity? Fear?

Nieminen didn't notice, too busy reading upside down. "'The probability of paternity is ninety-nine point nine nine percent.' See? They didn't have room for any more nines."

"All I see's words," Dormer said.

The emotion—if that's what it was—had evaporated.

"Anyone with a computer makes that in ten seconds," he said. "Don't mean shit."

"We have no reason to lie to you," Nieminen said. "Why would we?"

"Oh, I dunno. Prolly cause you're a lying sack of squirrel turds."

I thought of Luke's comment—*blood be blood*—and asked myself what would matter to a man like Dormer, for whom racial purity was a cardinal value. "Genetically, this child is no different than your living children."

Dormer shrugged. "So."

"So, if it were mine, I'd want to understand what happened."

"All right, what happened."

"I'd want the mother to know. I'd want to provide a proper burial."

"Gimme a shovel," he said.

"More along the lines of covering costs."

"I look like I got money to spare?"

"If you're not willing to contribute," I said, "I have a responsibility to search for next of kin who might be. Is there anyone you can think of who I should talk to?"

No answer.

"Your sons, maybe?"

"I don't think so."

"The decedent is their sibling."

Another snort.

I glanced at Nieminen. He leaned on his palm, spectating.

"You have two sisters," I said to Dormer.

"I got one. The other married a spic so I count her dead."

"They might want to chip in."

"Ask them. Do whatever the hell you want. I told you, doesn't concern me."

You could read his indifference through several different lenses.

The first, and simplest, was guilt. He'd been party to the child's death, and the obvious strategy was denial.

Even if he was innocent, playing defense was the way to go. He had to assume that the child had not passed peacefully. Why else would I be speaking to him about discovered human remains? And why would a detective be present?

Or he was telling the truth and had no knowledge of the baby. That, in turn, could lead to paranoia: We'd cooked the whole thing up to incriminate him. Or not paranoia. Rational fear. He was in prison partly because he'd been fooled by not one but two cops.

I said, "You used to hang around Berkeley. Back in the day."

"Did I?"

"You got arrested there a couple of times."

"I got arrested everywhere. I couldn't buy a gallon of milk without you motherfuckers crawling up my ass."

"Wild scene, back then."

Silence.

I said, "Late sixties, seventies."

Dormer's lips moved as if to spit. Whatever was welling up got swallowed. The swastika on his neck bulged briefly. "Shit. I was just a kid, then."

"Come on now," I said. "We both know you haven't been a kid since you were about nine years old."

Dormer laughed. "I got growed up, if that's what you mean."

"Where'd you hang out? Who'd you hang out with?"

"Don't remember."

"Big blank."

"Living in a cage does funny things to your brain."

"Drugs?"

"Aw gee, I wouldn't know about that."

"Girls?"

A faint smile. He couldn't resist. "Here and there."

"Anyone who you remember fondly?" I asked.

"Well, shit. The harvest was, how you say? *Bountiful.* Great big blur of pussy."

"Start with a few names, maybe."

Dormer nodded soberly, then peered at the ceiling, stroking his mustache, pondering. "Lemme see. There was your mother." To Nieminen: "Followed by yours. *Her* pussy was big as a freeway lane."

Finally the detective opened his mouth. "Hey ho. Unnecessary roughness."

"Followed by both your sisters. At the same time," Dormer said.

"We'll be sure and check with them," I said. "Anyone else?"

"I didn't keep a diary. Tween you and me I never did go in for hippie chicks don't shave their legs or pits. Make an effort, wouldja? Bush, that's nice. These young fellas all want em smooth." He sighed. *Kids these days.* "They're pedos down deep. Where did this bullshit allegedly go down?"

I said, "You get any of these girls pregnant?"

"Nope."

"You're sure about that."

"Knock a bitch up, she's bound to come crying with her hand out."

"And that never happened."

"No, sir."

"What about asking for money for an abortion?"

He iced over. "I don't truck with that."

"Not saying you would. But someone could ask—"

"That shit's for coons. Let them wipe themselves out. Saves me a bullet."

Revolted, I kept my poker face. "Look, obviously it didn't end that way. The baby was born. What I'm wondering is if the mother could have approached you for money, then changed her mind."

"Any cunt dumb enough to ask, I'd change her mind for her."

"You think it's possible there was a pregnancy but she didn't mention it?"

"I think you make babies by fucking. I think I fucked a lot. You didn't answer my question."

"Which question would that be."

"Where'd it happen? You kept on talking like you didn't hear me."

Reluctantly, I looked to Nieminen.

"People's Park," Nieminen said. "In Berkeley? That mean anything to you?"

"The fuck's that shithole got to do with anything?"

"They're doing construction. The body came up in the dirt."

Dormer stared at him. "*In* the park? How the fuck did it get there?"

"Right now that's unclear," Nieminen said.

"How did it die?"

"Also unclear."

"Go fuck yourself, unclear."

The lab report lay on the table. Dormer pressed his fingers to the page. "Boy or girl?"

"A boy," I said.

Dormer nodded. He lifted the page up to the light, as if to peer into its depths.

Slowly, neatly, he tore it in half.

Twice more.

He gathered the pieces into a deck and set it in the center of the table. "I'm done talking to you clowns."

NIEMINEN SAID, "NICE work."

I looked at him. No sarcasm; he meant it.

We stood in the parking lot by the trunk of his Crown Vic, buffeted by gusts cutting off the water. An unlit cigarette dangled from the corner of his mouth.

"That thing about him getting arrested in Berkeley?" he said. He turned out his pant pockets. "I like how you came up with that."

All I'd done was read the file. "Thanks."

"It rattled his cage. And that thing about having two sisters? Now he knows you know more than you're letting on."

I'd been trying to give Nieminen the benefit of the doubt. Now I accepted that his limp-noodle style wasn't some sort of clever psychological long game, just habitual apathy.

I thought back to the night of the bones: UCPD chief Vogel chewing on his lip, trying to decide which detective to give the case to. He had to give it to someone. But at that point, pre-DNA-test, Vogel had no way of knowing if the remains were Native American or not. The best strategy, then, was to stall.

Call the one guy you could count on not to do shit.

Get Tom over here.

Florence Sibley had hesitated before obeying.

By the time Tom Nieminen got it in gear, the lawyers would have done their thing. People's Park would be a distant memory, and the dorm would be halfway up.

The only question was if Vogel had ordered him directly not to do shit or was relying upon the detective's innate sloth.

"Damn," Nieminen said, patting himself. "You got a light?"

"Sorry."

"Ah. Ah. Ah. Hang on." He fished a squashed book of matches from an inner pocket. I watched as he struggled to keep one lit in the wind. Finally he succeeded, sucked hard, rubbed his forehead with the heel of his hand. "So. What's our play?"

I'd made my list before leaving the building.

Item one: Dormer's sons.

"Not sure," I said. "Why don't I think it over and give you a call?"

"Sounds good. No rush."

AMY'S CAR WAS still gone when I arrived home. Maryanne, our landlady, a sweet woman and an avid gardener, was in her front yard making use of the dregs of daylight, kneeling by a planter box sprouting with the rough arms of winter vegetables.

She tugged off her gloves and rose to greet me.

"I met your brother," she said.

"Sorry. I should've warned you he'd be around."

"No, no, not at all. He's a sweetheart. Playing so nicely outside with the baby. We got to chatting. He gave me some wonderful pointers about soil restoration. He really knows his stuff."

"That he does."

"My kale's looking good. I'll bring you some."

I thanked her and headed down the driveway.

Inside the guest cottage, Luke lay on the futon, watching a documentary about bodybuilders. His shovel feet dangled off the mattress edge. By tenth grade he wore a size fourteen. His friends used to call him El Roachkiller.

Charlotte snoozed on his chest.

"Yo, Captain America," he murmured.

Formula powder on the kitchenette counter, wipes by the sink.

Not much worse than if it'd been me in charge. Better, possibly.

He reached for the remote and shut the TV off.

"She nailed me a little," he said, indicating a spit-up stain near his shoulder. "I forgot the burp cloth."

"Rookie mistake," I said. "Can you hang out for ten more minutes so I can shower?"

"Yeah, man, have at it. I was right about to move her to the crib."

"Don't bother. She won't transfer. I'll get her from you when I'm done."

He nodded.

But when I came out, wrapped in a towel, Luke was standing in the hallway, peering into the darkened nursery. He grinned at me and curtseyed.

"Kazaam," he whispered.

Through the bars of the crib I could make out Charlotte's still, small form. My first thought was that he'd put her down on her stomach or done something else equally dangerous. I barged into the room, heroic, ready to snatch her up out of harm's way.

She was on her back. Eyes closed, lids fluttering, breathing slowly and smoothly.

I tiptoed out and shut the door. "How'd you do that?"

"Do what?"

"Move her without waking her up."

"I mean. I waited till she was ready."

"But how did you know when she was ready?"

"I don't know. She felt ready." He laughed. "You're welcome."

He went to collect his things.

Trailing him, I said, "Luke."

"Mm?"

"Thank you."

"Sure."

"I also wanted to . . . I'm sorry."

He paused with his fleece halfway on. "What for?"

"You saved my ass today."

"Yeah, bro. Anytime. She's a great kid."

"And I apologize if I suggested that you—I apologize."

He fished out his key ring, twirling it on a long finger. "Nah, man."

"I saw the new car. Looks great."

"I know, right? Already I got two offers, but she's so sweet I'm thinking I might keep her for a little."

I nodded. "When you were away."

He stopped twirling and looked at me.

"I should've come to see you more," I said.

He stared at me. An awful sadness stole over him, and he seemed to age before my eyes, the decade he'd forfeited coming due. Shoulders caved, head bowed, the healthy tissue he'd worked so hard to rebuild shrinking back from the bone.

Then: whiplash: he straightened, swelling up like a rude totem made of eyes and mouth and fists. I saw the process reversing itself, saw him race backward through time. Twenty-two years old, eighteen, sixteen, stoking chaos, toppling my parents' breakfront, igniting outmatched fistfights on the Siempre Verde courts.

Plowing a green Mustang through an intersection at seventy miles an hour, drunk, high, laughing.

He laughed. His laugh is my laugh, his smile, my smile, toothy and broad.

He clapped me on the shoulder. It stung. "All is blessed, bro. Say hi to Amy for me."

CHAPTER 11

Many of the items in Peter Franchette's file box were redundant or immaterial, reflective of a collector's impulse for completeness. Also evident was a preference for quantifiable data over human intelligence.

A surplus of lists, maps, photos of buildings, public records.

A scattering of interviews or any other narratives.

For all Franchette's insistence that I needed to understand the personalities involved, he didn't seem to want to get close to anyone.

Afraid of what he'd learn? Or was the act of collection itself the source of his pleasure? The unexpectedly wealthy can feel like undeserving impostors. Did Peter Franchette want to complicate a luxe existence, balance out his privilege? If so, resolution might be a letdown.

If so, he'd recruited the wrong person to help.

For the next several days, working while Charlotte napped or did tummy time, I sorted.

The Gene Franchette stack ran to four inches thick.

Beverly Franchette had thirty pages, all related to her death and burial.

Midcentury housewives didn't have Facebook or Instagram to document their daily travails. Few would've considered domestic stress worth writing about. Whereas Gene conducted exotic science and lived to publish.

Even so, the disparity was striking.

A manila envelope contained snapshots and Polaroids spanning several decades. Lots of Gene. Bare-chested in too-short swim trunks. On a ladder, screwing in a plant hanger. At his desk, absorbed in writing. He had a large square head, his features all straight edges welded at efficient, ninety-degree angles. Like something that had come off an assembly line, individual components replaceable in case of damage.

A shot taken in old age transferred him to a suede La-Z-Boy, blanket on his lap, goat-horn tufts of white hair poking over the stems of steel eyeglasses. Bristling pocket protector. Long brownish smirk, as if he was delighted to inform you your fly was unzipped.

An unbreakable bastard.

Gene's genes.

Far fewer pictures of Beverly. Every one had her ducking the camera or seeking shelter behind a blurry hand.

The incredible shrinking woman.

It must seem—I don't know. Deficient. To be missing such basic facts.

Go to the source.

I called Gene Franchette's home phone.

"WHAT."

"Good afternoon, Mr. Franchette, my name is Clay Edison—"

"Not interested."

Click.

I hit REDIAL. "Mr. Franchette, I'm not selling anything."

Click.

The third time he didn't answer.

I sent Peter Franchette an email, asking him again to make the introduction, and turned to the recordings of his phone calls to his aunt.

Aunt Edie. It's Peter Franchette.

Who?

Your nephew, Peter. Beverly's son? Silence. *We met a long time ago. Do you remember me?*

I . . . I don't have any.

I'd like to talk to you and ask you some questions. Do you feel up for that?

I don't . . . What?

He tried to explain.

Her voice clogged with agitation, she said *I didn't have a baby. Not you. My mother. Your sister. Her baby.*

What?

A baby. Before me.

She wasn't any good.

Did she tell you about the baby?

What do you want? I can't do that.

He'd tried four more times with even less success.

I switched to the most detailed item on Beverly Franchette: her death certificate.

Born Beverly Rice, February 27, 1940, in Paramus, New Jersey, to father Samuel and mother Victoria. Died May 3, 2014, Presbyterian Hospital, Albuquerque, New Mexico. Cause of death: acute respiratory failure secondary to metastatic cancer of the lungs.

Blank space for OCCUPATION.

You never know what people will deem worth preserving. A pair of Paramus High School alums had taken it upon themselves to scan and upload yearbooks going back to 1952.

I scrolled through the graduating classes of 1958 and 1959. Girls in scoop necks and pearls. Boys in white dinner jackets and black bowties. A zippy paragraph noted each student's accomplishments and aspirations.

No Beverly Rice.

Thinking she might've skipped a grade, I checked 1957.

Nothing.

On a whim I checked 1956.

There she was.

She hadn't skipped a grade. She'd skipped two.

For her senior portrait, she'd plucked her eyebrows thin and high, gotten an Audrey Hepburn pixie cut. Heavy makeup. Stabs at sophistication, intended to erase the age gap between her and her classmates, they ended up having the opposite effect, exaggerating her large, child-like eyes. She had fixed her expression as women do when walking in rough areas or riding BART: a warning smile, gaze slid three degrees off center, denying eye contact while keeping you within her awareness.

Call her pretty at your own risk.

Beverly Eileen Rice. 295 Winders Road. French Club 2, 3; Library Council 2; Band 1, 2; Math Club 1, 2, 3, Vice President 4; Physics Club 1, Secretary 2, Vice President 3, President 4.

Everybody knows Baby Bev has a big brain! She plans to attend Brooklyn College and study the mysteries of the universe. Wherever she goes, she'll be a success.

In the Math Club photo, she stood a head shorter than everyone else. One of two girls.

In the Physics Club photo, she posed front and center, befitting her presidency. The sole girl.

The City University of New York system maintained an online archive of yearbooks.

In 1960, aged twenty, Beverly Rice had graduated summa cum laude from Brooklyn College with a joint BA in applied mathematics and physics. By then, she'd grown her hair out and teased it into a bouffant. A Phi Beta Kappa inductee, she had served for two years as co-president of the Society of Physics Students and intended to pursue graduate studies.

The yearbook didn't offer a portrait of said society, but I hazarded its membership as predominantly male.

Lots more to Beverly Franchette than being Peter's mother and Gene's wife.

I phoned the UC Berkeley Physics Department. The man who answered couldn't tell me offhand whether they'd ever had a graduate student named Beverly Rice or Beverly Franchette. The computerized roster went back only to 1997.

He said, "The information is probably somewhere." *But I'm not looking for it.*

I hung up and called my father-in-law.

"Clay, my boy."

Paul Sandek and I first met when I took his class in social psychology. A former basketball player himself, he was a fixture at Cal home games, whooping encouragement from the bleachers while I ran the point. After a knee injury ended my hopes of going pro, he and Theresa became guiding lights to me, which made for a weird and lucky set of circumstances: Well before I fell in love with my wife, I adored her parents.

"Hey, Paul. How are you?"

"How am *I*? How are *you*."

"Every day is a new opportunity for growth."

"That is a fabulous attitude. Is the baby there? Can we Face-Time?"

"She's asleep. She'll be up in a little while."

"Well then call me back in a little while."

"Good to know I'm still a person worth talking to."

"Why in the world would I want to talk to you? You've served your function, amigo."

We caught up a bit. I sketched my conversation with Peter Franchette. "I'm wondering if anyone in the physics department might remember Gene or Beverly."

"That's a heck of a long time ago. Most everyone's gone, I'd assume."

"Could you ask around?"

"Sure. Don't hold your breath."

But I could tell that he was excited. He always got a kick out of playing detective.

Early Saturday evening, as Kat Davenport and I were returning to the bureau with a body, my cellphone buzzed in the cup holder, a familiar number flashing. I let it go, finished the intake, and headed out to the parking lot for the callback.

Paul said, "I have a name for you. Delia Moskowitz. Professor emerita."

"How'd you track her down?"

"Be impressed, my boy." He chuckled. "Not really. I have a friend in the physics department—Antonio Stokes, from the Old Fart Pickup Game? Speaking of which, everyone keeps asking me when you'll be back."

"In thirty years."

"Oh, unkind, unkind . . . As I was saying, I asked Antonio, who asked a colleague, and so forth. *Et voilà.*"

"Terrific. *And* impressive. Thanks so much. So she taught at Cal?"

"She started off as a physicist, right around the period you're interested in, but somehow ended up in history of science. I've got her email address. You can have it on one condition."

"What's that?"

"Bring me that baby."

Dear Mr. Edison,

Thank you for your email. I read it with great interest. Yes, I remember Bev, and Gene, too. I'll gladly answer any questions you may have. I go twice a week to the Faculty Club for lunch. They make a superlative turkey club. Wednesday's soup is split pea. Perhaps you would care to join me?

Sincerely,
Delia Moskowitz

CHAPTER 12

Situated in a quiet pocket of campus, behind a glade edged with oaks and Japanese maples, the Faculty Club comprises several structures knitted together by dim hallways. I hadn't been inside since my playing days, when the athletics department would book it for grip-and-grins with team boosters.

Climbing the steps, I heard the rush of nearby Strawberry Creek, dry most months, hectic as winter barreled toward spring. Muted sun yielded to gloom as I stepped inside.

Carved pillars, stained glass, antlers over the fireplace—the chummy, thready elegance that belies professional jealousy. At eleven twenty-five a.m., the bar was doing brisk business, white hair predominating.

The hostess responded to the name Delia Moskowitz with a vacant smile. There was no such member, she assured me. Perhaps I wanted the Women's Faculty Club?

She showed me out through a rear exit, directing me up the road toward a more demure brown-shingle building landscaped with hydrangeas and dogwoods.

The lobby of the women's club was a sprucer, softer, more compact version of its male counterpart—whitewashed plaster in place of knotty paneling, cream upholstery rather than tobacco leather. From the library came the sound of a lecture; I glimpsed chairs arrayed in a circle and a young woman gesturing toward a Power-Point headed CLEAN WATER: THE COMING GLOBAL CRISIS.

Obeying a sort of cosmic equity, a male host stood behind the desk. Delia Moskowitz's name made him nod readily.

He led me to a corner of the dining room overlooking the patio. At a table laid with white cloth and china sat a plump woman dressed head to toe in lavender: tweed skirt, silk jacket, lavender crocodile-skin pumps. She looked younger than her eighty-two years, streaks of undyed brown at her hairline, a quick, mischievous pucker gracing full lips.

"Let me guess," Delia Moskowitz said. "You went to the other one."

I laughed.

She clapped her hands. "Happens every time."

"I must've walked past this place a thousand times." I pulled out a chair. "I'm a little embarrassed to admit that I never knew what it was."

"That's the point. Drink?"

"No, thanks. I have to drive home."

"As do I." She waggled her wineglass. "I find this makes it much more fun."

We ordered sandwiches and soup.

"Thanks for agreeing to meet," I said.

"You're welcome. I don't mind telling you that your letter gave me a kick in the pants. Bev Franchette . . . Now, there's a name I haven't thought about in ages."

"How well did you know her?"

"Reasonably well, I'd say. For a brief period we were quite close."

Delia Moskowitz had enrolled in 1962 to begin a PhD in physics. The following year, Beverly arrived from Columbia University—not as a grad student, but as a postdoc.

"You're sure about the date? Nineteen sixty-three?"

"Unless I'm misremembering," Delia said, smiling in a way that indicated she was constitutionally incapable of misremembering.

"She graduated from college in 1960."

"If you say so."

"That means she would've had to complete her PhD in three years. Less."

"I confess it's been a while since I've done such advanced math. But I suppose so."

"It can't be typical to finish that fast."

"Not for most people," Delia Moskowitz said. "For Bev it sounds about right."

"She must have been brilliant."

"Oh yes. I detested her."

"I thought you were friends."

"I said we were close."

"Is there a difference?"

"Have you ever seen planet earth?" she asked.

"Beg pardon?"

"It's a TV series. *Planet Earth.*"

"Oh. Yes, I have."

"There's one part—I believe it's the very first episode—about emperor penguins."

"Remind me."

"Emperor penguins," she repeated, savoring the concept. "After they mate, they spend several months in the middle of an ice plain in Antarctica, incubating their eggs, huddled together for warmth. Each penguin depends on the insulation his neighbors provide in order to make it through the winter. If they don't stick close to-gether, they'll die. But the outermost ring of penguins has nothing at their backs to protect them from the elements. So they start shoving their way to the center of the circle. No sooner have they made it there, however, than the next incoming wave of penguins pushes in, followed by the next wave, and the next, so that eventually that first penguin gets forced back to the outside, and has to start shoving in all over again."

She took a long swig of wine, leaving lavender lipstick on the rim.

"Do you see how it works?" she said. "What appears as a noble sacrifice made for the betterment of the group, is nothing of the sort. Quite the opposite: It's the continual struggle between individuals that keeps them alive, by forcibly spreading the suffering around."

I said, "That was your relationship to Beverly."

"It's not a perfect analogy. The penguins are males. The females have gone off to find food. Of course. With Bev and me, it was just the two of us, not a large, engulfing mass. The fact of the matter is that we were both exposed at all times. In essence, though, yes. We were partners in hardship."

I thought of Beverly Franchette's yearbook.

Sole female member of the Math Club.

The *don't-mess-with-me* expression.

Our food arrived. Delia Moskowitz picked up her turkey club and went at it with gusto, pausing occasionally to dab at the corners of her mouth with her napkin.

I said, "You ended up leaving the program."

"She left first," she said, chewing. "I hung on for a while before it got to be too much to handle on my own. What was I supposed to do? If you'll forgive the mixed metaphor, I was a gazelle among lions."

She put the sandwich down and reached for more wine. "I suppose you could accuse me of weakness, not wanting to endure who-knew-how-many more years of professors sticking their grubby, chalk-covered hands up my skirt."

"When you say Bev left, where did she go?"

"That was another thing. Not only did she abandon me, she took the easy way out and married the teacher."

"Gene."

"Don't look so disappointed. Way of the world."

Chloe Bellara and Kai MacLeod. *Definitely fucking.*

I said, "When did their relationship start?"

"Well now, my dear, I wasn't in the room to witness it."

"Approximately."

"Approximately? As soon as she got off the bus. He was her adviser."

"Business as usual."

"Quite. Though their particular business did cause a bit of a brouhaha."

"Why?"

"The surprise factor. Some of the men were notorious lechers, you learned to steer clear. Gene wasn't one of them. He had a reputation as a family man, which made it ever so much juicier. Academics are awful gossips, you know. What we lack in dollars we make up for in schadenfreude."

I recalled the date on Gene and Bev's marriage certificate: 1964. The groom had one previous marriage, ended by dissolution. "Must've been a whirlwind romance."

Delia Moskowitz said, "Bear in mind, those days you couldn't get divorced by filling out a form. You had to show cause. Either that or you spent a few weeks living in Reno. That's what Gene did, if memory serves. Off to Nevada. *Quel scandale.*"

One reason, perhaps, that Peter Franchette had been unable to find a record of the divorce.

"Naturally, Beverly bore the brunt of the shame," Delia said.

"Forced out of the program?"

"That depends what you mean by 'forced.' Doubtless she was made to feel excruciatingly unwelcome. Whether she was gifted or not was immaterial. She was now a homewrecker. Everyone who was friends with Gene and Helen had to pick a side."

"Helen was his first wife."

Delia Moskowitz nodded.

"Any chance you remember her maiden name?"

"She was always Helen Franchette to me."

"You called him a family man. I take it they had children."

"A girl and a boy. You'll want their names . . . Let me think, it'll come back to me. One thing I can tell you is that the young man took it quite hard. He was a teenager when the whole sordid business came out. The stigma of a broken home? Then Helen goes and sticks her head in the oven—"

"Wait wait wait," I said. "She committed suicide?"

"She tried. It didn't work. People—it sounds hideous to joke, but—they said, 'Helen, poor creature, she can't even get that right.' Looking back I wonder if she intended to go through with it, or if it was a ploy to bait Gene into staying. Regardless, she failed."

"The poor kids."

"Their unhappiness must've been chronic. Before the scandal—having parents like that."

"Like what?"

She paused. "Gene could be . . . severe. He brooked no fools. If he didn't care for what you were saying, or if it was something he already knew, he'd turn on his heel and walk away, right in the middle of your sentence. And Helen. Not very bright. Obviously, she had a dramatic streak. She liked to drink."

"You knew her."

"Insofar as whenever there was a social gathering for the lab, I ended up talking with the wives, rather than my alleged colleagues."

I repeated Peter's description of Beverly and the Albuquerque Stepford wives.

"That's it exactly," Delia Moskowitz said. "Here I am, up to my elbows in quantum theory, and they're asking me, do I have a good recipe for meatloaf."

"He also called her emotional to a fault."

"I suppose relative to Gene, she was."

"Did she drink?"

"Not noticeably more or less than the rest of us. Everyone smoked and drank. On that note." She waved her wineglass at the waiter: *Another.*

I was about to ask about Gene and Bev having children of their own when Delia rapped the table. "Norman. That was the son's name. Norman Franchette. Troubled boy."

"Define 'troubled.' "

"He beat Gene up."

"That's pretty troubled. How bad?"

"I don't think he was seriously hurt. More like shaken up. And talk about *scandale:* It happened at the lab."

"It's funny," I said. "I haven't been able to find a record of Gene working at Berkeley."

"Well, they've probably written him out of the lab history. There's a sort of rivalry between us and Los Alamos. Not a feud, but they're always competing for funding and talent. It had to be a coup for Los Alamos when he transferred."

"Which was his site? Here or Livermore?"

"At that time they were one and the same. They didn't formally split Livermore off till later. Gene worked at both. He kept an office up the hill, a few doors down from where a few of the other grad students and I shared space. We'd be schvitzing over the page, chipping away at the next great discovery, five of us crammed into a room ten by twelve. We had to leave the door and windows open or else we'd suffocate . . ." She shook her head at the memory. "Anyhow, I heard this ghastly commotion out in the hall. I stick my head out, and there's the boy, kicking and thrashing while guards drag him out. Gene's following along behind, holding his broken glasses. 'No, no, let him go, it's a family matter.' One of the more thrilling days I had in my brief career as a research scientist. I'll add that I was gratified not to feel like the most ogled person in the building for once."

"After Bev left academia, what did she do?"

Delia Moskowitz shrugged. "Became Mrs. Gene Franchette."

"Did they have children?"

"I thought it was their son that put you up to this."

"Other than him, I mean. An older child."

"I assume I would've heard about it if it happened while I was still around the department. Nobody invited me to any baby shower."

I showed her the snapshot of Beverly and the child; the date on the back.

Delia smiled. "Madonna and child. Good for her. No, we'd fallen out of touch by then. 'Sixty-nine, I was no longer in Berkeley. Although it reminds me of the last time I did see her. This must've been late '65 or early '66, because I'd made up my mind to drop out. I was adrift, at a loss for what to do next. I went to the library and began wandering the stacks, picking up books at random. I thought I might find one that called out to me. Wouldn't you know, there's Bev, alone in a carrel."

"Doing what."

"Nothing. Just sitting there. I meant to leave her in peace, but she spotted me and waved me over. My goodness, but was she happy to see me. As I told you, our friendship was built on common interest. Enemy of my enemy, et cetera. It had been a long time since we'd had reason to speak. But she looked at me like I was salvation itself. She started asking about my work. She was hungry for information. When I told her I was quitting, she got very upset. 'You can't do that. You'll regret it.' "

"She wanted to save you from making the same mistake she had."

"Perhaps. I wasn't about to take advice from her. She'd made her choices and had to live with them."

No harshness, just the perspective of someone who'd made her own hard decisions.

If Peter Franchette was right, and the child in the snapshot was his sister, Gene and Beverly had been married for four or five years before having her. I said so to Delia, wondering out loud if they'd had difficulty conceiving.

She said, "Who knows? Or they didn't want a child to begin with. Accidents happen."

"Or people change their minds."

She smiled. "A universe of possibility."

"I'm guessing you didn't hear about the fire, either."

"What fire?"

I told her.

"Goodness," she said. "Norman was madder than I realized."

"He's who comes to mind?"

"Oh, now, I was speaking facetiously. I didn't know the kid from Adam, except for what I witnessed at the lab, and what I heard through the grapevine. Problem child."

The waiter brought her a fresh Chardonnay. Delia sipped at it, gazing out a window on the opposite side of the dining room. "Those were brutal days, downright barbaric. Your generation is clueless. You think things are nasty today . . . We didn't have the luxury of insulting each other from behind a keyboard. If you wanted to effect change, you had to get up, go out into the streets, and crack heads. This nonsense? It's child's play."

I realized she was staring in the direction of People's Park.

"Don't I sound like a relic," she said.

"You sound nostalgic."

"Well, perhaps I am."

"You could always get out there now," I said. "Crack some heads. I won't tell."

A wicked gleam. "Pardon my skepticism, pig."

I KNOCKED AT my father-in-law's office door and entered. Paul had the baby propped on his lap and was making googly faces at her.

"Hey there," I said. "Everything go okay?"

"It went perfect. *You*," he said to Charlotte, "are perfect."

She gurgled happily.

"You see that?" Paul said. "She knows when she's being complimented. Don't you?"

"Gah."

"Yes. Grandpa."

"Gah."

"Are you hearing this? She's saying 'Grandpa.'"

"I'm hearing it."

"Don't mind him, Charlotte. Grandpa understands you. How'd your lunch go?"

"I hope my memory's half as good as hers when I'm her age. What about you guys? What'd you do?"

"Oh, a bit of everything. We played. We talked. I explained why correlation doesn't equal causation. She got it faster than most adults. Most adults don't ever understand, do they, Charlotte? It'll be your job to help spread awareness. The burden of perfection."

"You know, you're not supposed to tell them that."

"Tell them what."

"That they're perfect," I said.

"Says who."

"All the parenting manuals."

"What, pray tell, is the problem?"

"It establishes unrealistic expectations."

"It would for children who aren't actually perfect. Fortunately for you," he said, lifting her up and nuzzling her stomach, "you are."

I glanced at the car seat insert. "Did she sleep?"

"Not a wink. Who can sleep, with so much ground to cover? I wasn't about to waste our precious time together *sleeping*." He held her out to me. "Let that be Daddy's problem."

CHAPTER 13

I blasted the radio and opened the windows to let in cool air, trying to keep Charlotte awake until we'd gotten home and I could move her to the crib. She fell asleep regardless. I carried the insert to the nursery, turned on the white noise, and crept out.

That morning's coffee had gone tepid. I added milk straight to the carafe, gulping it while leaning over the kitchenette counter with my laptop and notepad.

A 1994 obituary in the *East Bay Times* noted the peaceful passing of Helen Franchette, aged sixty-seven, of Walnut Creek. She was survived by son Norman Franchette and daughter Claudia (Darren) Aldrich, as well as grandchildren Alexis and Hannah.

I found it interesting that Helen had kept her married name.

Conventions of the era?

Unable to let go?

Norman, too, despite his animosity toward his father.

Perhaps they'd reconciled.

Peter Franchette had asked me to find him a sibling. I'd gone one better and found two. Half siblings, yes. But a pair of those seemed preferable to one full sister who might not be real.

I decided to wait to tell him until I'd spoken to them first. While Peter had never known about Norman and Claudia, the reverse wasn't necessarily true. Per Delia Moskowitz, Norman was an angry teenager during the divorce, putting him in his early to midtwenties by 1974, when Peter came along. I expected Claudia to be in the same ballpark. Old enough to be aware of the birth of a half brother. And to resent him: He was the incarnation of their childhood unhappiness.

Unless Helen and the children had cut ties with Gene after the divorce. Or Gene had managed to conceal Peter's existence from them.

Keeping secrets did appear to be a family trait.

I began looking for Claudia and Norman Franchette.

IT'S HARD TO hide these days.

The information was always there. Lurking in property tax rolls, collecting dust at the local recorder's office. But you had to know where to look and how to ask.

You drove to a grungy civic center, in a dispossessed county seat, with crappy parking. You stood in line and smiled at the petty bureaucrat who rejected your form because you'd forgotten to check box 7b.

You slunk to the back of the line again. Learned that another request required a different office. Three blocks away.

Don't forget to feed the meter.

Arms overflowing with red tape and paper, you learned how to assemble that paper into the shape of a human being, gleaning desire and intention and sin from the hieroglyphics of bureaucracy.

Now kick back and let the internet do the work for you. A few clicks bring an alarmingly intimate smorgasbord: current and prior addresses, landline, cell, warrants, traffic records, liens, judgments, bankruptcies, foreclosures, gun licenses, family and associates.

A tidy report with easy-to-read graphics is available instantly for $9.99. Or subscribe monthly for *unlimited access*. All you need is a credit card.

If, like me, you work someplace that subscribes to the right databases, you don't even need that.

The casual destruction of privacy is one of the most momentous and least visible social revolutions of our time, and the safeguards to anonymity that remain are largely a function of numbers—what I call the Big World Problem.

It's a Big World, inhabited by hordes of John Aguilars and Sarah Kims.

Fewer Reginald Beards or Desiree Ameses, but even they can number in the dozens.

Only one Pondicherri Sauvage that I'd ever encountered.

Suicide; pills.

I'm not blaming her name. I'm also not *not* blaming her name.

Other variables that muddy the waters include age, geography, and socioeconomic status. An impoverished ninety-year-old shut-in wasting away in Queens leaves a lighter trace than a duck-faced, wannabe-influencer tween posting every frame of her *aymayzing* life keepin it classy in Biloxi.

Too often database results turn out to be incomplete or misleading or overly inclusive. Scraper algorithms indiscriminately suck up every available byte. They upgrade forgotten acquaintances to blood relatives. Frequently I'm looking for people at the margins of society. Getting to them is still more art than science, requiring a human touch and abundant patience.

There was, or had been, a woman named Claudia Aldrich who taught economics at Emory. Her CV testified to a long, distinguished career. Bachelor's from Columbia. Doctorate from the University of Chicago by the age of twenty-four. Beverly's spiritual child, though not her biological one.

Her name brought up scores of publications in academic journals, the earliest of which attributed authorship to Franchette, C. Then Franchette-Aldrich, C. At some point she must've tired of writing out a seventeen-letter surname, because she dropped Franchette.

A notice in *The Atlanta Journal-Constitution,* dated last August, mourned her death at sixty-seven—the same age Helen had been when she passed. She was survived by her husband, Darren; her daughters Alexis and Hannah; and one granddaughter, Isabella.

A picture accompanied the text. As with Peter, Gene's genes carried the day. Lantern jaw; hard stare, ripe with judgment. It spoke volumes that this was the most flattering photo her family could come up with.

I was down to Norman.

At first blush, he didn't seem like a very sociable fellow. Other than Helen's obituary, I found nothing but reams of autogenerated garbage.

Claudia's obit made no mention of him.

Bad blood with her as well as Dad?

Time to shift gears. Yearbooks had been good to me, and I went back to the well, finding Norman in the Berkeley High graduating class of 1966. He looked miserable: unshaven and cowlicked, head an inverted gumdrop wobbling at the end of a too-long neck. Cheeks bunched as if bracing for impact.

Not much resemblance to Peter, Gene, or Claudia. Maybe he took after Helen.

No extracurriculars.

Troubled boy.

How troubled?

I wanted to know more about him. More about this fire.

The following morning, with Amy on baby duty, I drove to downtown Berkeley, hoping to answer both questions.

THE PUBLIC SAFETY Building sat opposite the Peace Wall, conflicting principles fashioned from the same municipal concrete. I started upstairs, at the fire department, where I spoke to a man with incredible hair. I've never met a firefighter who doesn't have great hair.

The guy was a captain named Jason Oblischer. In addition to his crown of platinum, he sported the physique of someone who fills idle moments with push-ups. He walked with a slight limp, adding to his charm, as you imagined the valiant cause of his injury.

"Nice to meet you," he said, meaning it.

That's another thing about firefighters. They're happy to see people, because people are happy to see them. You can be on the meanest street in Oakland, guys shooting at each other from behind garbage cans, and they'll break to let a fire engine through.

Hold up. Hold up.

Cause, who knows where that truck is headed? Their cousin's house, maybe.

Besides, whose heart is so cold that he doesn't enjoy a nice, shiny fire truck?

I showed Oblischer my badge but added that I was on my own time.

He scratched a well-formed chin. "Nineteen seventy, the file's gonna be in storage. Yeah. See?" He showed me on his monitor: The search form wouldn't accept a date prior to January 1991. "I can email them and ask to send it over."

"That would be great. Thanks."

"My pleasure," Oblischer said.

Meaning it. Firefighters.

I DESCENDED ONE flight to the police department. The shift in mood was palpable, like jumping out of a warm bath, only to discover you have no towels. Same result, though. I gave the desk sergeant my spiel and was told: "Not in the computer."

He didn't offer to email storage. He handed me a form.

I filled it out, then watched him stick it at the bottom of the inbox tray and begin excavating his ear canal.

Eager to speed things along, I asked if Nate Schickman was around.

"Why?"

"Buddy of mine."

He hollered over his shoulder: "Anybody seen Schickman?"

The answer drifted back: *People's Park.*

"What's he doing there?" I asked.

The sergeant extracted an orange gob from his ear, gazed at it contemplatively. "With any luck, not getting pissed on."

I PARKED ON Channing and continued on foot, paddling upstream against students in yoga pants and North Face, lost in their earbuds and sipping boba tea. It had been a month since the debacle at Zellerbach Hall. Life had resumed on Telegraph Avenue, windows reglazed, graffiti scoured off or vanquished by new graffiti. Allow for the neighborhood's baseline grunginess and you could be forgiven for thinking nothing out of the ordinary had occurred.

But as I got closer, I felt it again: the subsonic growl Davenport and I had picked up the night we came for the bones.

Subtler, now. The pot brought down to a simmer.

With numerous lawsuits pending, Alameda County Superior Court judge Sharon Feeley had issued a temporary injunction prohibiting construction at People's Park until such time as she could get the claims sorted out and consolidated. Together with the other groups aiming to preserve the status quo, the Defenders of the Park, led by Chloe Bellara, Sarah Whelan, and Trevor Whitman, had declared the ruling a victory.

The University of California had immediately filed a motion to vacate the injunction. But the administration had been set back on their heels. To prevent further damage to their equipment, Siefkin Brothers, Builders, had retreated.

I turned the corner for the park, made a slow tour of the perimeter.

The trailers were gone. The fence was gone. The heavy machinery had been evacuated, save a hamstrung front-end loader missing three tires and repurposed as a jungle gym. The basketball court lay in rubble, like the aftermath of a drone strike. In place of the Free Speech Stage gaped the pit.

The mess had done little to discourage attendance. To the contrary: Galvanized by crisis, The People had shown up in force, creating a morbidly festive atmosphere. On a normal day you'd have fifty bodies dotting the acreage. Now I estimated five times that.

A team of volunteers in gloves and kneepads toiled to rebuild the demolished garden. Beneath a gazebo fashioned from tarp and PVC pipe, a pair of women ran a rudimentary woodshop, churning out planter boxes and plank benches.

Restoration of the lawns had also begun, mounds leveled out and holes partway filled, gentling the landscape so that it evoked less a war zone and more an inadequately maintained mini-golf course. Parkies smoked, swigged, orated, bartered; either underdressed for the weather or swollen by fifteen sweat-soaked layers. Hip-hop pulsed. Malnourished dogs scrounged. A grizzled man wearing a FACEBOOK T-shirt pushed a shopping cart brimming with recyclables in a tight, determined circle.

Outside the bathrooms, a group squatted at the curb, shooting dice. Murals and mottoes scaled the building exterior.

We didn't ask permission we just got busy.

The homeless encampment stretched clear to College Avenue.

Stationed at each corner, twiddling his or her thumbs, was a Berkeley city cop.

Bowditch proved the liveliest stretch, home to the tree-sitters. A man in a pig mask perched high in the branches of an American elm, reciting Marx through a megaphone.

What the bourgeoisie, therefore, produces, above all, are its own gravediggers.

On the pavement below, a man pushed a shopping cart back and forth, mirror image of the guy with the Facebook shirt, except this guy's hat said GOOGLE.

At the corner of Dwight, someone had added a sticker to the stop sign, creating a new message.

Nate Schickman leaned against the pole, staring sourly at the pavement. He tensed at my approach, then recognized me and broke into a relieved smile, bounding forward to give me a bro hug.

"What's up, man?" The Kevlar beneath his uniform made it feel like I was embracing a refrigerator. "Been a minute. What brings you to this neck of the woods?"

"Just taking a stroll."

"At your friendly neighborhood civil disobedience zone."

"I was down at the PD. They told me you'd be here."

"Oh, I'm here all right."

"What happened to homicide?"

"Done-zo. City policy: four-year rotation, back on the street. So we 'stay grounded in the community.'"

Our conversation had attracted the attention of the man in the pig mask. Raising the megaphone to his snout, he began to chant in our direction.

All. Cops. Are. Bastards.

I said, "Is there an endgame?"

Nate looked at me like I was insane to even ask.

"Fair enough," I said. "Rules of engagement?"

He recited drearily: Stand down. Expect to be tested, insulted, recorded. Remain calm. Remain polite. Do not intimidate, harass, or threaten. Regard arrest as a measure of absolute last resort.

No helmets. No shields.

Direct orders from City Hall.

I got the intent. A horde of Blue Meanies in riot gear recalled, in all the wrong ways, those iconic photographs from 1969.

National Guardsmen squaring off with flower children. A helicopter spewing tear gas; a daisy jammed in the barrel of a rifle.

Still, it seemed a bit much to demand of the front line. I'd taken the desk sergeant's comment about getting pissed on as sarcasm. But Schickman told me he'd had a bucket tossed at him two days ago.

"Aw, man, I'm sorry."

"No big deal, he barely got me. Smelled weird, though. Probably vegan or keto or whatever."

The chant had been taken up by other voices.

All cops, are bastards.

Middle fingers sprouted in the canopy, like wrathful, fleshy fruit.

He said, "What can I do for you?"

"Does there have to be something?"

He laughed.

I said, "Old arson. I put a file request in but I'm not sure it's gonna see the light of day."

"Who'd you give it to."

"Sergeant Kalb."

"You're right to worry," he said. "You want me to follow up?"

"If you don't mind."

"Not a thing."

"Thanks, brother. I'll send you details."

All. Cops. Are. Bastards.

Schickman started for his post. "Send me a poncho."

ON THE WAY back to my car I stopped along Dwight to watch the gardeners at work. They were a multigenerational group: elderly hippies and their modern-day equivalents in muddy overalls. They'd made progress, laying out paths of crushed stone and cutting new beds. I had to admit that it was a vast improvement on the demolished garden, which I'd only ever seen in disrepair.

Pot smoke rose in mini-thermals. Inside the Free Speech Pit, something fluttered.

I crossed the lawn to have a look.

Down in the dirt was a weather-beaten jumble of flowers, pictures, trinkets, and toys: a shrine to the dead child.

Notes tucked inside sandwich bags, ink bleeding as condensation beaded up.

never forget u

justice for all

Dead votive candles in glass cups.

Mylar balloons, collapsed and tossing listlessly.

A score of stuffed animals, including several teddy bears.

One of which had electric-blue fur.

I stared at it.

How many teddy bears in the world?

How many blue ones?

It's a Big World.

Blue is everyone's favorite color.

I glanced around.

The gardeners were gardening.

The parkies were swapping sandwiches and spit.

I hopped into the pit.

The blue bear lay on its side, behind a pink giraffe.

I eased it free with a pen.

Eight inches high, in good condition. Fur clean and soft and bright. It might've come out of the package that morning, save a single blemish.

The left eye was missing.

CHAPTER 14

Loose blue threads marked the spot of the missing eye. The right eye was bulbous, with a bright-blue iris and an attachment loop on the reverse. Those threads, too, were loose, only a couple left to keep the eye from falling off.

In every respect, it appeared identical to the eye Flo Sibley had found, currently sitting in an evidence locker.

A paper tag, yellow and brittle, gave a clue to the doll's age.

Marjorie's Menagerie
Kuwagong Happiness Co. (H.K.) Ltd.
Kowloon, Hong Kong
Reg No. PA-2739 (HK)

Faded logo, an owl hovering over its young.

I took photographs, climbed out of the pit, and began making the rounds.

The gardeners had more important things to do than answer my questions. They were reconsecrating a temple. No, they couldn't tell me who had created the shrine in the pit or how long it had been there, let alone the provenance of a specific teddy bear. It's not like there was a guest book. These things happened organically.

Ditto the picnickers and the dice players and everyone else I approached. They denied knowing anything or flat-out ignored me.

The patrol cop at the southwest corner hadn't observed anyone go near the pit.

I jogged back to Schickman.

"Fuck's sake," he said. "Give me a little time. I'd said I'd follow up."

I brought him over and showed him the bear.

"Huh," he said. "I mean, I don't know. I can find out who's been on shift, see if they saw anything." He glanced at me. "What do you want to do with it?"

Leaving it behind was not an option. What if the donor had second thoughts and came back for it? What if someone else swiped it? By time-honored tradition, items deposited in People's Park became free for the taking.

The rules said I should call Tom Nieminen. His scene. His responsibility.

But Nieminen was *my* responsibility. Didn't that make the scene, and the bear, mine by transitive property?

Schickman watched me uneasily.

I said, "I'll call the detective."

He relaxed and nodded.

TOM NIEMINEN ANSWERED with his mouth full. "Early lunch," he mumbled.

He could be there by noon. I told him I'd wait.

As insurance, I texted a photo of the bear to Flo Sibley, along with the words *found it.*

Ten seconds later she texted back for my location.

Twenty minutes later she came jogging up to the pit and put her hands on her hips.

"Dang," she said.

She climbed in to examine the bear. Then she climbed out and proceeded to do what I'd done: turn in a circle, clocking everyone within a hundred yards.

"I tried," I said. "Nobody saw shit."

"Do you believe them?"

I shrugged.

Sibley addressed Schickman. "How's it going?"

He acknowledged her with a nod. UCPD and city cops have a lukewarm relationship, with the latter regarding the former as bush league, and the former regarding the latter as arrogant. Ordinarily they each mind their own business, but that moment highlighted everything uncomfortable about the dynamic. The operation had started out under UC's authority—specifically Sibley's. She out-ranked Schickman. Yet here he was, juggling the consequences and dodging bodily fluids.

To his credit, he stepped away, promising to ping me.

After he'd gone, Sibley said, "Thanks for the call."

"Called Nieminen, too, but figured you'd want to know."

"It's been driving me up the wall. I go to sleep and dream about teddy bears. I wake up and it's more teddy bears."

"The tag's old," I said. "Like it's been in a closet for forty years."

Sibley nodded. "I'm trying to imagine what's going through her head."

I didn't have to ask whose head she meant. "Not a place I'd want to be."

"The kid gets dumped, and all this time she's been hanging on to it? I mean, this is guilt we're seeing, right?"

"As opposed to."

"Psycho killer taunting."

"I don't see it that way," I said. "When I got here the bear was hidden behind another doll. No effort to call attention to it."

"What I'd really like to do is set up a camera, in case she comes back."

"You think they'll go for that?"

"I dunno. Maybe I can get Tom to sit out all night on surveillance." She checked her phone. "The heck is he?"

"Did he tell you about our talk with Fritz Dormer?"

She shook her head.

I recounted.

"Sounds like a peach," she said.

"Maybe the bear will jog his memory."

The sun pried through the clouds, flushing the air with warmth.

"Honestly," Sibley said, scanning the lawns, "I almost prefer they keep it like this. Don't get me wrong. It's a toilet. But take everything away and what's left?"

"One fewer toilet?"

"What this place is," she said, "is your asshole cousin. He's an asshole. But he's also your cousin. All of a sudden he starts acting nice, it makes you nervous. Well looky here, the noble explorer has reached shore."

I followed her gaze to the opposite end of the park. Tom Nieminen wandered among the tree stumps, shading his eyes with his hand. Sibley waved, and whistled, and—when that didn't get his attention—phoned him.

"Hey, Tom. Here. At the park. Yeah. I know, he's with me. Over here. Not—*other side.*"

He finally spotted us.

She put her phone away. "Never ceases to amaze."

"Really?" I said. "Cause you don't sound that amazed."

Sibley smiled.

Nieminen came up, wheezing, a mustard stain on his tie. "What's this about a bear?"

CHAPTER 15

The stereotypes that typify the Bay Area flourish alongside their opposites. Sixty miles separate San Francisco from the Central Valley, with Alameda County functioning as a buffer between them. Our electoral map mirrors the country as a whole: densely populated coastal areas bleeding blue and a vast, sparse tract of hillside, farmland, and unincorporated wilderness, red to the core.

All of it's my jurisdiction.

Fewer people means fewer dead people. We don't often get out to the eastern fringes, where Dale, Gunnar, and Kelly Dormer made their home. When I called Nieminen to let him know I intended to pay them a visit, he said, "They're where?"

"Rip's Gulch."

"Never heard of it."

I hadn't, either. "About eight miles southeast of Livermore."

"Huh. What's anyone doing out there?"

Living under the radar. Making and disseminating their very own white power podcast. Staying out of trouble, except for when they were causing trouble.

The Dormer brothers' exploits paled in comparison with their father's. With a name like Gunnar, you'd think he'd be the hardest core, but only Dale had done real time, eighteen months for aggravated assault, after he shot at a station wagon that cut him off on the freeway. Smaller potatoes for the other two: petty theft, malicious mischief, trespassing, DUI, public intoxication. Pulling donuts in the Walmart parking lot appeared to be a cherished pastime.

I wondered if Fritz felt disappointed in or proud of his brood.

I told Nieminen I was headed out on Saturday afternoon.

"Ah, geez . . . My daughter's got a soccer game, and then— weekend's stacking up kinda busy, know what I mean?"

"Why don't I talk to them and report back to you?"

"You don't mind, do you."

"Not in the least. Any news on the bear?"

"Flo sent it to the crime lab."

Good on you, Sibley.

A FEW DAYS later, with the sun falling at my back, I rolled through the bedroom communities of Dublin and Pleasanton. Auto plaza, outlet mall, warehouses: bland matte piles blending into the sapped terrain. A sign noted the exit for Lawrence Livermore National Laboratory, where Gene Franchette had spent a portion of his working life designing bigger and better bombs. On my GPS it registered as a village-sized blank.

I'd never been inside. Either no one died there, or the feds had their own way of dealing with it. The closest I'd come was the removal of a bicyclist, a chemist struck down by a van as he exited the parking lot and turned toward the Vasco Road BART station. The impact threw his backpack thirty feet down the shoulder. When I unzipped it, it appeared full of vomit, and a powerful, earthy smell bloomed out at me. His fiancée would tell me that he made his own hummus, bringing deli containers to work to share with his colleagues.

Today's high-speed tour continued past Altamont, site of the concert where the Rolling Stones had hired the Hells Angels as security with predictably deadly results. Ahead loomed the county line and the city of Tracy. One of the missing persons cases I'd browsed had gone down in Tracy. A little girl taken by her father, Sybil Vine.

As I wondered how she was doing—if she was alive—the freeway split, and I was heading south.

The second off-ramp coughed me out into low crumbly hills, unsuitable for agriculture but tailor-made for hiding. The asphalt skinnied and deteriorated until it had become a single fissured lane, unlit and bounded by flaccid telephone lines. On my left ran a chalky berm; on my right, an endless stretch of barbed wire.

The GPS began counting down—five hundred feet, two hundred, one—until it announced, absurdly, that I had arrived. Nothing about that spot differentiated it from the preceding half mile. No sign for Carlos Canyon Road; no address marker or mailbox. Way off in the distance, an angular smudge indicated the presence of human beings, but I couldn't see how to reach it, short of plowing through the fence.

The sun sent up a death knell flare.

I crept along.

In three hundred feet, make a legal U-turn.

I made an illegal one.

You have arrived at your destination.

I shut the GPS off.

On my third pass I spotted a subtle variant in the fence line: a doubled post, one of which could be wiggled loose, allowing the wire to be folded back. A pale strip of hard-baked dirt ran toward the encroaching dusk.

I bounced along the track, wheels spitting gravel. Slowly the smudge began to resolve, like a body surfacing in swamp water. Structures, then vehicles, then living things: gaunt dogs and children chasing one another, their roles as hunter or prey in constant flux. Bare feet raised a dusty haze.

I counted three half-ton trucks, two motorcycles, four ATVs, and a riding mower. Half a dozen single-wide trailers with steps made of hammered planks formed a semicircle. The leftmost sported a satellite dish on its roof.

Here and there and in between rose hillocks of junk: buckets, lumber, spare parts, cinder blocks and bricks, orphaned furniture, mutilated toys.

Amid a weedy patch, a woman slouched in a lawn chair. Pustulant acne ravaged her face; she could have been eighteen or forty. A slack-limbed toddler slept on her chest. She was managing to keep the child balanced while also doing her nails. Bothered by the glare from my headlamps, she squinted, then blew quickly on the wet polish, recapped the bottle, and heaved up, shifting the child to her hip.

She headed for the middle trailer, dress billowing behind.

I stopped the Explorer and got out.

The air carried woodsmoke. Cicadas droned.

From behind me came the beady click of a racked shotgun.

A man's voice said, "Hands up."

I said, "County Coroner."

"I don't care if you're Luke fuckin Skywalker. You're trespassing. Hands."

I raised them.

"Turn around slow."

I did, recognizing Dale Dormer from his mugshot. He was a sinewy, shrink-wrapped version of his father, Willie Nelson braids and a sheepskin coat. The shotgun was ancient, with a chewed-up stock, like he threw it to the dogs to gnaw on when not in use.

I said, "I'm just here to talk."

"Didn't you see the sign? Private property."

I remembered a similar warning made to Anthony Wax, right before Fritz Dormer and company murdered him. "Must've missed it."

"Yeah, well, I dunno about that. Plain as day."

"I've been trying to call," I said. "Your phone's off."

"What phone?" he said. "I'll need you to surrender your firearm."

"You understand I can't do that."

"Then looks like we're at uh *impasse.*"

The children ranged in age from a two-year-old in a low-hanging diaper, her belly as distended as a July peach, up to twin adolescent boys. In my periphery I saw them gathering; saw the glint of the dogs' eyes, mutts with a strong streak of German shepherd, stalking, licking their chops. Rectangles of yellow light yawned, doors creaking and blinds whipping up, narrow-shouldered silhouettes leaning out.

The woman in the dress stood on the threshold of her trailer, withdrawing to allow by a second man, who came thunking down the steps in jeans and cowboy boots and a John Deere shirt.

The youngest son, Kelly Dormer. Taller than Dale, rough-hewn, he wore a glassy, dissolute stare: the Marlboro man on a weekend bender.

He scratched his neck and spat, and with a rolling gait went to join his brother.

My position—surrounded on all sides by property, pets, womenfolk, and offspring—was somewhat reassuring. Nobody could shoot at me without fear of collateral damage.

Nobody sane.

My own wife and daughter were far from my mind. I did not run the slow-motion film of Amy answering the phone and falling to her knees, or the time-lapse of Charlotte growing into a girl and a woman and a mother, her image of me growing more faded and idealized every day. I did not feel the futility of being unable to explain myself, to tell them it was Tom Nieminen's fault I'd gone out there alone.

Instead I examined the angle of the shotgun barrel and the height of the Ka-Bar knife sheathed on Kelly Dormer's belt; the yardage between them and me; numbers expressed as a multiple of the distance from my own hand to my service weapon.

What could Nieminen have done, anyway? I hoped his daughter had won her soccer game.

"Gentlemen," I began, bringing a smile to Dale Dormer's face.

"Hear that, Kel? We're gentlemen now."

Kelly Dormer's reply was to hook his thumbs in his belt loops and shove his hips out. One scabby finger tapped the knife sheath.

"Nossir," Dale said. "You're looking for gentlemen, you came to the wrong place."

"I'm not here to cause problems for you, or to accuse you of anything. It's a courtesy call. I think you and your brothers will want to hear me out."

"*Courtesy* call. All right, then. Let's have it."

"In private."

"Anything you got to say you can say in front of all of us."

"Here's the deal," I said. "I'll leave my card, and if you change your mind, you can get in touch. The card's in my jacket. I'm going to take it out. Okay?"

Dale had allowed the shotgun to dip; he flung it back up. "I'll advise you to refrain from doing that."

Buzz-saw quiet; gnats frantic in the columns of light that lay like felled timber.

Nobody sane would fire a shotgun toward a backdrop of his loved ones.

Nobody sane would chase down a man and beat and stab him for being black and discarding a cigarette butt.

The knife concerned me most. A majority of gunshots miss. But a blade, at close quarters, doesn't have to be accurate to do serious damage.

"I'm leaving," I said.

I took one step backward and a door banged open. I jumped, Dale Dormer jumped, the shotgun twitched in his palms; the dogs began to leap and prance and yelp hoarsely, and I realized that their vocal cords had been cut.

From the trailer with the satellite dish stepped Gunnar Dormer. He was the biggest of the trio, forearms straining the rolled sleeves of a lumberjack shirt, thighs like grain sacks. A forked brown beard draped his gut.

He descended the steps. The children parted to allow him into the circle.

He frowned at me, frowned at his brothers. "Is there a problem."

"The *gentleman*," Dale Dormer said, "was just leaving."

"Put that away," Gunnar said.

A beat, then Dale lowered the gun.

Gunnar said to me, "What do you want?"

"To speak with you concerning a family member."

"He won't say what it is," Dale said.

Gunnar stroked his beard. "Let's get acquainted."

DALE AND KELLY closed ranks behind me as I followed Gunnar into the trailer. The interior had been reconfigured as a recording studio, foam baffling on the walls and the fold-down table set with a laptop, two USB microphones, two sets of over-ear headphones, a pair of black swivel chairs, broad and plush enough to accommodate a two-hundred-seventy-pound host and that week's special guest.

The Dormer brothers' podcast was called *Tide of Fire*. To access it, you had to join their mailing list, which I hadn't been willing to do, because I wasn't interested in receiving Nazi-themed spam. Keep your swastika pillowcases. White sale be damned.

I stood by the sink, hemmed in by Dale and his hot, panicky aura. Kelly shrank into the shadows by the door.

Beneath a flyblown light fixture, Gunnar pulled out one of the swivel chairs and sat, flapping his beard. "Speak."

His expression didn't change as I explained who I was and why I'd come.

Dale, on the other hand, grew noticeably flustered, sputtering in incredulity when I raised the issue of defraying funeral costs.

"No fuckin way," he said. "You think we're idiots?"

Gunnar clucked his tongue. "Our father doesn't know about any child."

"That's what he told me."

"You saying he's a liar?" Dale said.

"I'm saying it's possible the mother never informed him she was pregnant. There's no doubt it's his son. I can show you the test results, if that matters."

Dale waved peevishly. "Give it."

I handed him the sheet, watched him blink without comprehension.

"I don't see nothing about me or any of us."

"You could have the sample tested against your own."

"Right, so you shitbirds can steal our DNA. Nice try. I seen *CSI*."

"Why would you expect us to know who the birth mother is?" Gunnar asked.

"I don't," I said. "By all means, tell me if you do. My primary concern is giving the decedent a proper burial, and I'm running out of options."

"You want us to pony up," Gunnar said.

"I'm giving you the option of contributing."

"How thoughtful of you. Say we decline, as well."

"The remains will be disposed of by the county."

Gunnar's smile was stubby and gray, set far back in the sprouting cliffside of his face. "Somebody *did* dispose of them. Feels like a waste of taxpayer money to do it twice."

He spoke with a kind of calm sadism. It was as though Fritz had divvied himself up and handed out heirlooms: the hotheadedness to Dale, to Gunnar the guile.

As for Kelly, he had yet to say a word.

Someone had to inherit the taste for blood.

Outside, a child was squalling.

"You're not interested, that's fine," I said. "There's no legal obligation."

"Put that way," Gunnar said, "it makes me think you think there's a moral obligation."

"I have no opinion. I'm relaying facts. Your brother's body was left in a public park. Nobody deserves that."

"Ah. Ah. That's an opinion, not a fact."

"You're free to head over and have a look yourself. I think you'll come to the same conclusion. There are people, perfect strangers, leaving flowers and notes. It doesn't bother you that they care more than you do?"

Gunnar chuckled. "You know what I hate most about cops? How judgmental you guys are. You take one look at a person and decide you know everything there is to know about them, including what their life's worth. Same attitude lets you feel entitled to go around shooting unarmed niggers in the back."

"I would've thought you'd consider that a net positive."

"Fine, till you come for us, too. That's what you don't under-stand. What matters to me is the liberty of the individual, and of individual races, to pursue their sovereign destiny. Once that's achieved, the rest'll sort itself out according to the laws of nature. I'm not worried. Strength is strength. But I'll need interfering pricks like you to get out of the way first."

I was getting tired of this. "Right. You change your mind, any of you, let me know, soon as possible. And, by the way, your dad misses you. You might want to do more than send him a Christmas card."

I started forward.

With the shotgun in his hands, Dale stepped out to block me. His eyes bugged, and I thought: *Well, this is it, this is how it happens for me, in a water-stained trailer, in my thirty-sixth year.*

Sorry, Amy.

Sorry, kiddo.

"Excuse me, please," I said.

"Say it again."

"Move," I said. "Now."

Silence.

Gunnar said, "Kelly will escort you off the property."

The murk stirred and the door whined open, admitting a gush of moonlight.

"Dale," Gunnar said.

Dale remained in place, gripping the shotgun, grinding his jaw.

Gunnar said, "Not today."

Shriveled, trembling, Dale stood aside. I sidled past, hand near my holster, backing out into the coarse air, fixed on the shotgun's snout. As it slipped from view, I caught a single word, Gunnar Dormer's parting utterance, faint and flat: *tomorrow.*

KELLY DORMER RODE lead, cutting a line through the blackness and preventing me from straying off the road and blowing a tire. A hundred yards shy of the fence, he roared ahead, then swung the bike ninety degrees, spraying dirt.

I jammed on the brake.

He set the kickstand, dismounted, and began ambling toward me.

I checked the locks and took the safety off my gun.

He motioned for me to roll the window down. When I didn't, he cupped his mouth.

"How much's it cost?"

His voice was high and reedy. Kelly Dormer had been nine years old when his father shipped off to San Quentin. His decision to worship the same gods was in one sense forgivable, and at the same time incoherent.

Whatever sympathy I could muster for him was dwarfed by my concern for the baby in the pit.

I cracked the window a few inches. "That's up to you. Cremation runs seven, eight hundred bucks. Plot and a stone, sky's the limit."

Even the lower figure had him grimacing. "Do they, like, offer financing?"

"Some places do. Read the fine print before agreeing to anything."

He ran his tongue over chapped lips. "I don't want my brothers to find out."

"They don't have to."

"What do I do?"

"First thing is to call a mortuary or funeral home."

"I don't know any."

"You have the internet."

He toed the ground morosely, like a big, unshaven toddler.

"I'm not permitted to recommend a specific funeral home," I said. "Most are fine. One thing to bear in mind is the location of the cemetery. You don't want to be driving three hours to visit the grave. I mention it because people don't always think about that. Once you decide, tell them the remains are with us. They'll take it from there."

I lowered the window a bit more, just enough to hand him my card.

He raked at one edge with a blackened nail. "I always wanted someone littler'n me to kick around."

I did not point out that, had the baby survived, it would be roughly twenty years his senior. "Let me know what you decide."

He went to roll his bike out of the road.

CHAPTER 16

Berkeley Fire had no incident report on 1028 Vista Linda Way. Jason Oblischer said, "Not sure what to tell you. I had them double-check, and there's other reports from that month and year, so it's not like they destroyed the whole batch. But the system's returning a blank for that address."

"The cops say they don't have anything, either."

"They wouldn't, necessarily. They don't have a dedicated arson investigator. We send our own guy out to every significant fire. PD might get involved if there's deaths, but usually they're happy for us to field it."

"Less paperwork for them."

"You know it. Made to guess, I'd say it got misfiled."

"Shit. Well. Thanks for looking."

"Anytime, brother. I'm sorry I can't help you more."

He sounded like he meant it.

Firefighters.

WITH ITS SOARING ceilings and oily oaken tables, the central branch of the Berkeley Public Library harks back to a grander, more civic-minded era. No other local building embodies more starkly the gulf between 1900s idealism and twenty-first-century reality.

I climbed a wide marble staircase, bullnosed by thousands of feet, to reach the crowded main reading room. Some folks still came seeking knowledge and self-betterment. Many just wanted a place to rest their heads and get out of the rain. The scent of unwashed skin stewed with those of paper and glue to create a smothering atmosphere.

Official report or not, I tended to believe a fire had taken place on Vista Linda. I'd asked the neighbor, Diane Olsen, to confirm the story, and she'd done so without a moment's hesitation. Not until I'd showed her the snapshot did she get jumpy.

Gee but it's poetic, ain't it, to imagine ol' Gene watching the smoke twirl into the sky?

I showed the reference librarian my printout of the *Berkeley Trip,* the image of the goofy guy with the spinning eyeballs.

She said, "You need Jack," and directed me to a back corner of the second floor. A sign above locked double doors read BERKELEY HISTORY ROOM.

My knock drew a white man in a pink bow tie and brown nubuck waistcoat. Early fifties, with a meringue twist of gray hair and multiple piercings in his ears. As if Orville Redenbacher had taken to plundering the high seas.

He braced himself behind the door to interrogate me. What did I want? Who told me to come? Why hadn't I made an appointment?

Satisfied I wasn't there to purloin his mother-of-pearl desk set, he admitted me grudgingly, locked us inside, and took my driver's license for safekeeping.

A man for whom solitude had become an entitlement.

He grumbled and handed over an engraved card.

Jack, it emerged, was JAC: J. Artemis Cole, director of special collections and guardian of Berkeley's printed legacy. The history room was his fiefdom, a dignified space clad in golden maple and lit with low-wattage bulbs. Vellum maps and photographs of city forefathers and -mothers hung on plumb. Blurry tintypes showed the western end of town in the 1860s, when it was still a separate municipality called Ocean View. There was a large central reading table and a microfiche machine and a glass display case containing a balsa wood model of the Campanile clock tower.

I gave him the *Trip* and explained I was trying to corroborate its story on the fire.

"Did you check the *Daily Gazette*?"

"The online archive stops after 1957."

"They continued publishing into the seventies." He retrieved a microfiche cartridge from the cabinet. "As I recall, they printed a regular fire report."

For the week of March 8–14, 1970, Berkeley Fire had answered nineteen calls, including a pan left in the oven on Virginia Street, an overheated engine on Third and Jones, a false alarm on Shattuck, and four cats stuck in trees.

Nothing on Vista Linda Way; nothing the week before or after.

The *Gazette* likely got its information from the fire department. If the department's record keeping had gone awry, the paper would have no source.

How then would an obscure, copy-shop outfit like the *Trip* find out?

JAC shrugged. "The counterculture had its ear to the ground."

I pointed to the byline, *Putta Hurton*. "Any way to find out this person's real name?"

"There's no index. One assumes that they wrote pseudonymously for a reason."

"I didn't see any other issues besides this one on your website."

"That's because they're not *on* the website."

He strode to a wall of shelving packed with journal boxes. GOURMET GHETTO. CIVIL RIGHTS. URBAN PLANNING 1910–1939. Two boxes devoted to People's Park.

He pulled down EAST BAY UNDERGROUND PRESS. "I intended to digitize the entire collection. We ran out of server space, so in most instances I've had to limit myself to a single representative item. Are your hands clean?"

"I think so."

"Mm." He set the box down, pulled a pair of white cotton gloves from a desk drawer. "Put these on."

The box contained several dozen file folders, each tabbed with the name of a publication I'd never heard of. The *Berkeley Bang*. *Cosmic Traveler*. *End of the Rainbow*.

"Thrice I've applied for a grant," JAC said, riffling folders, "only to be told there are 'higher priorities.' What could be more important than making these documents available to the public, I cannot fathom. Ours is an intellectual community, and these are its lifeblood."

The documents *were* available to the public. You just had to visit the library. But by replicating the history room's contents in virtual reality, JAC could avoid having to admit actual people, with actual sweaty hands, to the actual history room.

"Here we are," he said.

He tugged out the *Trip* folder and began laying out its contents.

No gloves for him. Apparently his own sweat was acid-free.

The inaugural issue of *Berkeley Trip* had come out in November 1969. Five more followed, on no particular schedule. The issue Peter Franchette had found, featuring the story about the fire, was the sixth and final one, as though the paper had ceased to exist immediately thereafter. While I didn't want to wring causation from correlation—my infant daughter knew better—I did find the timing peculiar.

"Is this the complete print run?" I asked.

"I've made every effort to be thorough, but it's impossible to know for certain. These have come to us in dribs and drabs. I can't afford to be choosy."

Curious if other counterculture papers had picked up the story, I asked to check for issues on or around March 13, 1970. One by one JAC took them out.

The *Berkeley Pipe*. The *Groovy NewZ*. *Blastoff!*

"You have to envy their sense of possibility," he said lovingly, as we perused the *Berkeley National Spotlight*. "Who puts the word 'national' in a local paper? It seems so *whimsical* by today's standards. Issue a manifesto. Change the world."

"It's still true. Everything in Berkeley's political."

"Except politics," JAC said. "That's personal."

Grandiose name notwithstanding, the *National Spotlight* was little different from the *Zinger* or the *Truthteller* or any of the others: printed on the cheap; festooned with hokey graphics, excitable prose, and occasional grainy nudity. Authorship unattributed or pseudonymous.

Only the *Trip* mentioned the fire at the Franchette home.

While paging through the *Weakly Freekout*, I stopped on the comix page, peering at a strip titled *The Tao of Mortimer Q. Nutsack*. Over four panels, its protagonist waxed philosophical, concluding that the meaning of life was "a nice pickle sandwich."

It wasn't Nutsack's insight that had drawn my attention. It was his exploding hair, the spirals he had for eyes.

They matched the character from the *Trip* nameplate.

The author of the strip was *F. Henkin*.

I pointed out the similarities to JAC, who shrugged, unimpressed. "A relatively small circle of people created these. Run out of money, get shut down, regroup, start over."

The clock on the wall chimed two. I noticed JAC appraising me sidelong. I had yet to identify myself as law enforcement. It also helps that I have a lot of experience appearing trustworthy. It's a skill, like any other.

I said, "Any suggestions?"

"Frank might know more."

"Frank . . ."

"Henkin."

I'd taken it for a pseudonym. "That's his real name."

"It's the one he goes by. He was active in the scene."

"He must have some stories."

"No doubt."

"Do you know if he might be around?"

JAC hesitated, as if on the verge of divulging the nuclear launch codes. He slicked up the front of his hair, then said, "He runs a record shop in Temescal."

I thanked him, which made him grimace. He waved me off when I offered to help clean up the papers. He didn't want things getting out of order, so if that was all . . .

In exchange for the gloves, he returned my driver's license. As the door closed behind me, the dead bolt punched home.

TEMESCAL IS WHAT realtors call a transitional neighborhood. In truth, the transition is well under way, and if you have to ask, you can't afford it.

Telegraph and Shattuck avenues boast several record shops, hipster-owned and -operated. Striking out there, I found myself pacing a stubbornly grungy block of Forty-Seventh near the freeway. Wayback Vinyl had a two-star rating on Yelp and was supposed to be around here somewhere. All I saw was an abandoned bank no one had yet converted to a beer garden.

A lull in traffic allowed the faintest whine to eke out. I followed it, crunching over puddles of safety glass, to the rear of the building, where I discovered an unmarked door wedged open with one purple Croc.

I parted a bead curtain—the electronic eye made a sci-fi ray gun sound—and stepped into a cloud: the sweetish, chemical odor put out by two tons of decomposing celluloid. Black mold caked the ceiling, which was surprisingly high, giving not a sense of lightness and lift but of peering up from the bottom of a well. The walls had been painted a nauseating green, then plastered over with decals and concert posters drawn in the same style as Mortimer Q. Nutsack. They touted weeknight billings at the Freight & Salvage; beins and protests; a festival in Golden Gate Park, Jefferson Airplane headlining. The effect was dizzying, like a rabid mob of angels adorning some gonzo cathedral.

I crabbed sideways, through racks set disagreeably close, to reach the register.

A pasty man with long, curly hair the color of pigeon excrement sat on a high stool, paging through a robotics magazine, hands warmed by a countertop space heater. Bluegrass warbled on the turntable. The singer recounted a litany of misfortunes. His crops had failed, his mule had died, and his woman had left him. I couldn't blame her.

"Frank Henkin?"

The man sighed. Gappy teeth, too-small head. He wore a fraying cable-knit sweater, and his fingers were white and agile and slender, drumming as he waited for my question, which was obviously going to be an utter waste of his time.

I put my copy of the *Trip* on the counter. "Am I right in thinking this is your work?"

"Huh." He centered the pages. "Blast from the past."

He regarded me with newfound interest. *A fan!* "What can I do for you?"

"I wondered if maybe you'd kept in touch with some of the other people who wrote for the paper. This person, for instance—"

"Yeah, sure."

He hadn't even glanced at the page.

"You know him," I said.

"Yup."

"Putta Hurton."

He smirked.

I said, "You're him."

The smirk became a jagged, *what-can-I-say* grin.

"The whole paper was you."

"Shit don't write itself."

"This one story, who was the source?"

"Same source I always used. Middle third of a joint."

I smiled.

Henkin issued a put-upon grunt and felt around for his reading glasses, finding them tangled in his hair. He balanced them on the end of his nose and murmured:

" 'Nuke prof gets roasted.' "

The grin faded; the small muscles of his face began to twitch, and his chin tilted up and back, as though he was recoiling from a punch. The paper wrinkled in his tightening grasp. Thinking he might actually take a swing at me, I shifted my feet in anticipation.

Instead he slid off the stool.

He had nowhere to hide—the area behind the counter was about five by five—but he made a game effort to shut me out, fiddling with the turntable, knocking the tonearm out of the groove and bringing the banjo break to a screeching halt. In the scraped silence he began seizing other records lying nearby, pretending to scan the track listings.

"Mr. Henkin—"

"We're closed for lunch," he said.

"It's three thirty."

"Closed." His hands were trembling. "Leave."

"Yours is the only paper that covered the fire," I said. "How'd you learn about it?"

No reply.

"Did you know Gene Franchette?"

The trembling intensified. He shook a Bob Marley album from its sleeve. It slipped out of his hands and bounced on the concrete.

"Mr. Henkin."

He picked up the record, blew it clean, and set it on the platter, reaching for the tonearm, his lips moving soundlessly.

I said, "Norman."

CHAPTER 17

At once the pressure flooded out of him. He dropped the tone-arm; dropped his head so low it seemed to retract into his torso, keeping his back to me as he spoke.

"Gimme one reason why I shouldn't call the cops on you."

I am the cops. But I wasn't a cop, not then.

"You have a half brother. His name is Peter. Beverly's son. I'm here on his behalf."

"That doesn't sound like any kind of reason to me."

"He's asked me to search for relatives."

"Still not a reason."

"To be clear, it wasn't you he asked me to find, but his sister."

Norman Franchette snorted. "Claudia? Good luck with that."

"Not her. This would be your half sister."

I set out a printed copy of the snapshot. "We think this is her."

A beat. He turned, corkscrews of hair swinging. Spread his fine white fingers on the countertop, bracketing the photo to hold it at bay. "Where'd you get this?"

"Beverly had it hidden. Peter found it after she passed away."

"Jesus . . . Look at her. She was one skinny-ass bitch, wasn't she?"

That's who Beverly was to him: always and forever the skinny-ass bitch who'd split his nuclear family. Though his flat tone made the contempt come across as rote rather than active.

"What'd she die of," he asked.

"Cancer."

"Whaddaya know, that's what got my mom, too. Maybe Gene has a type, huh? Nose em out, like one of those cancer-sniffing dogs."

"I take it you're not in touch with him."

"Gene? He's alive?"

"He was, as of a few weeks ago. I called him to ask about the baby."

"Holy hell . . . Fuckin engine that don't quit. Did he cuss you out?"

"He hung up on me."

"Losing your edge, Genie."

"What can you tell me about the baby?"

"Nothing. I never met her."

"Her name?"

Norman frowned. "This guy's her brother and he doesn't know her name?"

"He never met her, either. We can't locate her. Gene and Bev kept her a secret from him."

"Figures."

I waited for him to continue, but he said no more. "Do you know it?"

"You're asking if I know her name."

I nodded.

He eyed the photo, as if afraid he might conjure her into the flesh by speaking. "Mary."

The sound of one word: a key turning. I had to restrain myself from pumping a fist. "Mary Franchette."

"Yup."

"Any idea what happened to her? Peter thinks she may have died young."

"Died . . . ? I never heard anything like that. I gotta think my mom would've said something if the kid died."

"Or been adopted."

"I mean. I don't know. I told you, I had nothing to do with her. Any of them."

"Your mother kept tabs on Gene."

"Oh yeah."

"Is that how you heard about the baby in the first place? From her?"

"I guess so. I can't think who else would've told me."

"It must have upset her, when the baby was born."

"My mom? Fuck, yeah. She never got over it. Him, on the other hand: He made up his mind to leave, *zhup*." He slashed at the air. "Me and Claudia, we didn't fit the theoretical model no more. He just stuffed us in the trash."

If he didn't care for what you were saying, or if it was something he already knew, he'd turn on his heel and walk away, right in the middle of your sentence.

"Truth be told I didn't mind Bev. Little I knew her, she was wallpaper. I mean, it doesn't excuse what she did, but she's what, twenty years old? Talk about predatory. You try pulling that shit today? *Psssh.* Out on your ass. I always wondered if they had an S-and-M-type thing going, you know? Like he tied her up." He snickered. "Or the opposite, they get into the bedroom, she's whips and chains and he's begging her to stomp on his balls. Makes you think."

"What about Claudia?" I asked. "Did she ever meet the baby?"

"Not on your life. She didn't have any love lost. Couldn't wait to skip town, the first opportunity she had, she took it. Me, I'm cursed with the fatal flaw of a warm, beating heart. Now that you mention it, adoption'd be a real Gene Franchette way to solve the problem."

"Problem?"

"Getting rid of a kid."

"What makes you think he would want to get rid of her?"

"He had his fill with us. He was old. You think he wanted to start changing diapers? Not that he ever did that."

He picked up the snapshot. "This is really her, huh? You can't see her face."

"It's the best we have."

He stared at it, set it aside. "I actually wanted to meet her. I tried to. Rode my bike up to their house. Shit," he said, raking his scalp, bewildered. "That was a weird goddamn day."

"Weird how?"

"I rang the bell and some chick answers, real hot. I figured Gene went and ditched Bev, found himself an even younger piece. I had to hand it to him. It'd only been a couple of years since he'd walked out on my mom."

"When was this?"

"Well, lemme see. Jupiter was in Capricorn, and it was a balmy eighty-three degrees . . . I have no clue." He glared at me. "You're making me lose my train of thought."

"Sorry. Go on."

"This chick, I go to her, Who're you? Where's Beverly? She goes, Beverly's not home. She's the babysitter. I tell her I'm Gene's son, and she gets real huffy. 'Gene never said anything about a son.' Well, that pissed me off."

"I bet."

"Right? I'm putting out a damn olive branch, and you're treating me like a leper? What I shoulda told her is Gene never said anything to *me* about a *babysitter*."

"I went up to the house the other day," I said. "I ran into the next-door neighbor, Diane Olsen. Back then she lived with her parents. You think it could've been her?"

"Maybe. Is she smoking hot? Cause if not, then no. I tell you, man. This chick."

A dreaminess took hold of him.

"Blond, down to here, and . . . How girls used to dress, with the mini-skirts, the tight shirts? It's summertime, I just rode uphill five hundred miles, I'm standing there sweating like a pig. She's got almost—I mean, she's not holding much back . . ."

His description didn't match my mental image of a younger Diane Olsen. People change, of course. But she was fifteen at the time of the fire.

"You didn't happen to get her name," I said.

"I was just trying not to come in my pants. I go, 'Long as I'm here, can I see the baby,' and she slammed the door in my face."

"Then what?"

"Then nothing. What am I gonna do, break in? They want to shut me out, that's on them. I have to live my life."

"So you knew about the birth, you tried to make contact, but nothing after that."

"That's right."

"What about the fire?" I asked. "How'd you hear about that?"

The downshift in his mood was sudden. "What's that got to do with the baby?"

"Nothing, necessarily. What made you decide to write about it?"

"It's a newspaper. You put in news."

"Nobody else picked it up."

"Yeah. I'm Clark Kent, okay? Look, pal, I don't know what you think I'm going to say. I was stoned ninety-eight percent of the time. I had an idea, I wrote it down."

His attempt at nonchalance didn't quite get there.

I said, "I could be wrong, but it seems like you stopped publishing right after this article came out."

"I don't know. Maybe. Probably, yeah. They were hounding the shit out of me."

"The cops?"

He pried his hands open and raised them to the sky. The sole graceful component of a graceless man. "Love of God, how many times do I have to say it? It wasn't me."

"They questioned you about the fire."

"They couldn't do anything to me," he said. "Based on what? My 'tone'?"

"Angry article."

"Course I was angry. I had a reason to be. So I wrote about it. That's *all* I did. *Write.* That was enough to summon the jackboots."

"I heard about a fight with your father."

"What fight?"

"At the lab."

He appeared startled that I would know such a thing. "Who told you that?"

"One of your father's former colleagues. It was pretty much public knowledge."

"That happened way before. It was completely overblown. And, and, and," he said, tapping the counter, "I tried to make it up with him. That's why I went to the house. He wanted nothing to do with me. With us. I don't know where you get off. You come in here all friendly, telling me I have a brother, then you start accusing me."

"No accusation."

"You know what I think, I don't think there is any brother. I think it's some bullshit you made up so I'd talk to you."

"Not at all. I've been straight with you."

"Says you. I know what this is."

"What is it?"

"You're a cop. Huh? That's what."

"I'm working for Peter."

"Yeah. Sure. Okay, then, what's he like?"

"He's about fifty. He works in tech. Five-nine, reddish-brown hair—"

"I'm not looking to date him," Norman said. "I mean what's he *like.*"

"As a person."

"No, as a raccoon. Yeah, as a person."

"Analytical. Smart. He seems a tiny bit uncomfortable with personal interaction."

"Oh well, in that case, he's definitely my brother. Where's he live?"

"His office isn't too far from here."

"Nicer than mine, I bet."

"It doesn't have nearly the same amount of character."

He fought smiling but gave up. "This isn't the half of it. Sole proprietor of the truth."

"I was at the Berkeley library. They have a bunch of your stuff."

"They can have it all when I die. Historical value."

His ire had dissipated, flushed out by ego.

He pointed to the Jefferson Airplane poster. "That was my masterwork. They paid me a hundred bucks, plus an eighth."

"Not bad."

"Oh yeah. I thought I was Gustav goddamn Klimt."

I asked if he was still politically active.

"Hell no. What's the point? Nothing gets better. These trust-fund pricks buying up the neighborhood got Bernie bumper stickers. They're Gordon Gekko in skinny jeans. So what're you gonna tell this guy? You found his long-lost brother, who's not really long lost?"

"He doesn't know about you yet. I wanted to sound you out first before I told him."

"Yeah, well. Gimme his phone number and I'll think about it."

I gave him my email address instead.

"My advice," he said, "don't waste your time with Claudia. She'll never talk to you, she was always a tight-ass."

I assumed he was making a macabre joke. Likewise when I'd talked about finding his sister, and he'd said *Good luck with that.*

But his expression was serious.

He wasn't listed in her obituary.

He didn't even know she was dead.

The fragments of this family lay strewn far and wide.

"Look," he said, "I don't want to be rude, but I don't want to talk about this anymore. I'm hungry and I got to take a shit. Figure that one out. Godspeed."

He started to turn away, pausing to regard the snapshot of Beverly and the child. "Can I keep this?"

I nodded.

He folded it up, tucked it into his breast pocket, and began again to pick through the 33s.

As I hit the sidewalk, I heard music. The Airplane's "Somebody to Love."

AT HOME, I found Amy in pjs, kneeling beside the play mat, grinning ear to ear.

"Check out your amazing daughter."

Charlotte was sitting up on her own.

"Wow." I dropped my bag and got down on my stomach to be close to them. "When did this happen?"

"Literally two minutes before you walked in. I'm keeping my hands here in case she takes a header but so far we're going strong."

"Wow. Look at you, lady."

"Hnnnng," Charlotte said.

"She's trying so hard to talk," Amy said. "She's been doing that all day."

"Hnnnng."

"Is that so?" I said. "Tell me more, Grunty the Clown."

"*Hnnnngg.*"

"Can you imagine how frustrating it must be?" I asked. "All these thoughts and no way to get them across."

"Oh my God. It's so, so sad."

Charlotte's lip began to quiver.

"Oh no, honey. We're not laughing at you."

"Gzzzhh," Charlotte said dolefully.

I said, "You're the shrink. What's she thinking?"

"'These people are idiots.'"

"'I like her more than him.'"

"'Mommy, why don't your socks match?'"

"Gimme some dat titty."

"No way. I fed her like thirty minutes ago."

"I was speaking for myself."

Amy smiled. "How was your day?"

"Good. Thanks for being flexible."

"Of course."

"What about you guys? What did you do?"

"The usual. Eating. Barfing. Crushing milestones. Liz brought Jonas for a playdate."

"Oh yeah? Did he and Charlotte get along?"

"They lay next to each other and drooled. I will say, she's clearly more advanced. He can't even grasp a rattle."

"Sometimes I forget how competitive you are."

"She brings it out in me." She touched Charlotte's cheek. "You kicked his little ass, didn't you, honey pie? Yes, you did. Kicked it right off the growth chart."

Charlotte squealed with delight, and the three of us just sat there. I felt a fierce urge to grab hold of the moment, to enshrine that exact configuration of our bodies in the amber light; the moist tickle on my knuckles from my daughter's breathing; the totality of her, tiny and unstoppable as a bullet; the frenzied thrum of growth in real time, cells sprinting off in new directions; my wife's contented *hm* when she shifted on her hip and her ankle brushed the back of my calf.

Only then, in silence and peace, days after the fact, did I remember facing down a shotgun.

I stared at the play mat, pressure mounting behind my eyes. I wondered if I'd always have to lie to the two most important people in my life. Where I'd hide these shards of sadness and fear.

"Whoa there," Amy said.

Charlotte's head had begun to gyrate.

"She's getting tired."

I cleared my throat of its dull ache. "Hard work, sitting up."

"I have this theory: The way a baby acts when she's tired, that's how she's going to be as an adult when she's drunk. Like, are you the angry drunk, throwing chairs through windows? Or are you a fun drunk who gets loopy and starts kissing everyone."

"What kind of baby do we have?"

"Fun for sure."

I said, "You're totally right. It's like having a roommate who never sobers up."

"Laugh a little. Cry a little. Poop yourself."

Charlotte pitched toward the floor, bursting into tears as Amy caught her.

"Aaaand we're *done.*"

"You want me to put her down?" I asked.

"I was hoping to stretch her for another half hour."

I hauled myself to my feet and grabbed the baby carrier. "I'll take her for a walk."

"Is it cold out?"

"I'll put a blanket on her. Don't worry. I got it."

"I know."

Wrestling with the straps, hunching and contorting. "I hate these things. Why don't they make them bigger?"

"Clay. Did you hear what I said?"

I stopped and looked at her. "Sorry. What?"

"You're a great dad," she said. "I want you to know that."

AT THE MOUTH of the driveway, I paused to adjust the blanket over Charlotte's head. My fingers grazed the soft spot in her skull, parchment skin drawn drum-tight, pulsing like the vulnerable heart of a bird.

CHAPTER 18

Flo Sibley called to let me know the bear was a bust, forensically.

"But it's not all bad news."

"Hit me."

"Last year they earmarked a chunk of money to cover overtime during the demolition. Too much, as it turned out. There's some cash sitting around. Whatever we don't spend by the end of the fiscal year goes back into the pool. Use it or lose it. My captain, he's a guy, likes gadgets. I went to him: 'Don't you think we could use a new camera? If I set it up to watch the pit, that makes it a park-related expense.'"

"Genius."

"Yes and no. Because we're supposed to be treading water. He can't have it look like we're being overly aggressive. He agreed, but there's strings. First is we get it for no more than a month. For three hours a day."

I could only laugh at such pristine bureaucratic logic.

"On the other hand," Sibley said, "we are talking a brand-new camera. Tom's real excited."

"He's our cameraman?"

"Another string."

"What's that going to achieve, three hours a day? We can't schedule when the mother's going to come back."

"We don't know *if* she's going to come back. This is a shot in the dark at best. Be grateful. Originally it was two weeks. I had to negotiate him up."

"What happens after a month?"

"I'm not going to worry about that now. So what'd the Dormer boys have to say?"

I described my visit to the homestead.

"Good grief," she said. "Are you okay?"

"Yeah, fine."

"So Kelly has some kind of soul."

"Maybe," I said. "I'll be shocked if he comes through with the money. I'll wait awhile, but sooner or later I'm going to have to cremate. I did hear from Tipton, the CO at San Quentin. I emailed him a photo of the bear and asked him to show it to Fritz."

"And?"

"What do you think? He's never seen it in his life."

"Right. Well, maybe the video will work out."

"You're an optimist, Florence Sibley."

"A girl can dream," she said.

I'M NOT AN optimist. Would you be, after you've carried the body of a man stabbed in the groin for bringing his girlfriend a box of Valentine's Day chocolates, because what was he trying to say? Huh? That she was fat?

She didn't mean to kill him. Just teach him a lesson in sensitivity.

His bad luck she hit the femoral artery.

Nor am I a pessimist. I've also seen neighbors rally to pay funeral costs for a man found in a tent on the side of the Claremont Avenue off-ramp.

My sister-in-law Andrea would say that I try to accept things as they are, dispassionately.

While I hoped Mary Franchette's name would yield a wealth of new information, I expected little. And got less.

No death certificate. No obituary.

No news item in the *Gazette* or any of the local papers.

The Mary Franchettes who popped up on family tree sites or Find A Grave were the wrong age, either too young or having died in the 1890s.

I wrote to Nate Schickman and asked him to search again, then called Peter Franchette to provide a status report. I could confirm his sister's existence at a reasonable level of confidence, and I felt I had to give him advance notice, on the off chance that Norman tried to contact him.

He was in Aspen, at a thought leadership conference. I caught him between sessions and laid it out: Helen, his half siblings, the baby.

"I'm not sure how I'm supposed to react," he said.

"I don't think there's a right or wrong way."

"I mean, everything's changed. And nothing has."

"I understand."

In the background came the swift chatter of bright young people.

"About the affair," he said. "I can't say I'm surprised."

"You knew already."

"On some level, yes, I think so. Obviously they weren't going to tell me outright. It's a lot harder for me to understand why they would've hidden the baby. Unless it's like you said, it was too painful for them to talk about. I'm trying to see the situation through my mom's eyes. I feel like I ought to have a clearer picture of her, based on what you've told me. But it's fuzzy. I grieved for her, and I was grieving for a completely different person."

He paused. "I'm sorry for rambling. I'm having to rethink a lot of things. It's like you showed me a color I've never seen before. So you don't know where she is. Mary."

"Not yet. I'll keep looking. Having her name helps."

"It's not what I would've predicted. It's so . . . biblical."

"They named you Peter."

"Mm. I never thought of it like that, but . . . And you said Claudia had children?"

"Two. One grandchild."

"I'd like to know more about her."

"You can try reaching out to them."

"Would you do it?"

Not challenging. Scared to make the approach.

"Sure," I said.

"Thank you."

"No guarantees they'll respond."

"Of course. Thank you, Clay. You've already done far more than I could ask for. What about Norman? Frankly he sounds a little unstable."

"He's a bit of an odd duck."

"He's the only one left, though."

"I'm not saying you shouldn't meet with him," I said. "But I'm still not certain what his role is in all of this."

"You think you can find out more?"

"Hard to say. I have a few irons left in the fire. Unless you want me to stop."

"Say I did," he said. "Would you?"

Before I could answer, he said, "Keep going."

CLAUDIA ALDRICH'S WIDOWER, Darren, was a pediatrician on staff at Children's Healthcare of Atlanta. His daughters appeared to have left the city, Hannah settling in Los Angeles, Alexis in New York. I worked up the best email addresses I could find for each of them and sent notes off into the ether, keeping in mind that they were recently bereaved.

It's a position I find myself in often: having to intrude upon a family's pain and ask personal questions about their loved one. You can easily become a proxy for the indifference of the world.

On the other hand, grief does sometimes give rise to radical hon-

168 / JONATHAN KELLERMAN and JESSE KELLERMAN

esty, and a stranger's exactly who you need. Spouses and children have volunteered unimaginably intimate details simply because I happened to be standing nearby. There's no way to predict how an individual will react.

When no response was forthcoming from Darren Aldrich or his daughters, I let it lie.

Then a different iron came out of the fire.

Captain Jason Oblischer called me. "Yo, sorry to bother you."

Firefighters.

"No bother at all. What's up, man?"

"I felt pretty lame I couldn't help you out. I started thinking about it some more, and it occurred to me, from when I was on active duty, we had these old logbooks. What these things are, they're basically a summary of the day's events, separate from the incident reports. Sort of like a backup copy, but they're handwritten, in these great big old albums. We don't keep em anymore, cause now everything's computerized. I always liked reading em. Little snapshot of history, you know? That address you gave me, Engine Seven's the current response district, but they didn't open till 2000. It used to be Engine Four, down on Marin. I called them and the captain's like, 'Yeah, we got em. Tell him to come on by.'"

"Amazing. Thanks so much."

"Don't get too excited," Oblischer said. "The logs are pretty bare bones compared with a full report. At most you're gonna get a paragraph or two. But at least you'd be able to know if the station responded to the address on that date."

"I'll take it. I really appreciate it, Jason."

"Of course. Totally my pleasure."

I WAS AWARE of Fire Station Four as a circular, UFO-like structure planted in the triangle of land created by the intersection of three streets. The house Amy grew up in and where her parents still live is a few blocks away. I shared a cup of coffee with my mother-in-law, left Charlotte with her, and walked over.

I'd called ahead, but the nature of the job was such that I couldn't schedule an appointment. I arrived at the station to find it unstaffed save a statuesque African American woman with a Grace Jones flat-top.

Introducing herself as Lieutenant Beadle, she led me to the lounge.

The logbooks took up a whole cabinet, tucked behind the foosball table. They were as Oblischer had described: tall leather-bound tomes with cracked spines and flaking gilt trim. The final one was from 1977. Beadle tugged out 1970, and we sat on a swaybacked couch.

Each entry began with roll call, followed by a cryptic string of abbreviations and numbers. The color of the ink would switch from blue to black without warning, suggesting that the writer had been interrupted midsentence and returned hours later to find his pen gone. Which, I supposed, was what happened at a firehouse.

Beadle paged to Friday, March 13.

"Let's see if I can decode some of this for you," she said. "That day, Lieutenant Davidson is on the engine. Boyle's the Engineer. He drives and runs the pump panel. Budenholz, O'Meara, and Vietri are your Hos, which is short for 'Hoseman,' neither of which is a term we use anymore, for obvious reasons."

I laughed.

She pointed and continued. "Singleton, he's your captain on the truck, and these other guys are Hosemen, too. 'Watch' means who's monitoring the tape. The way it used to work, before cellphones, every corner had a pull box."

"I've seen those."

"Yeah, there's a few left. San Francisco still uses them as a fail-safe. You see smoke, you run to a box and pull the handle, it sends a signal to the nearest stations. There's a ticker-tape machine that spits out the box number. Somebody has to sit there round the clock, watching the tape. The new guy, probably, cause he gets the shit duties."

"That's what these are. Box numbers and call times."

"Right. The old-timers knew the location of every box. They could look at the tape and be like, 'Box Two Ninety-Six, that's Shattuck and University,' or whatever. Usually it's nothing: A kid pulled the handle for fun. When that happens, they just record the box and the time."

She flipped the page. "You said Vista Linda?"

At ten nineteen p.m., Box 1392 came over the tape.

Engine and truck dispatched two minutes later to 1028 Vista Linda Way.

While more elaborate than the preceding entries, the description of the job was clipped, almost curt. Beadle walked me through.

Total job time, from tone out to return, four hours. One-story residential, fifty percent involved. Four hundred feet of two-and-three-quarter-inch hose and a hundred feet of one-and-a-half-inch.

Practically the entire station had responded, hook-and-ladder, truck, hose wagon. Structure fire in the hills, adjacent to Tilden Park; would've been a big deal, she said.

I pictured the tortuous street, wooden houses shouldering together.

Nowhere did Gene, Beverly, or Mary Franchette appear, except by omission.

The person making the entry had noted no casualties.

Penciled in the margin, dashed off in a different hand: *Hopewell FBI 451-9782*

"Is that what I think it is?" I asked.

"Hunh. Must be."

"It couldn't stand for something else."

"Like what?"

"I don't know. 'Fuel based ignition.' 'Fresh brewed iced tea.'"

Beadle smiled. "Not to my knowledge."

Norman Franchette had griped: *They were hounding the shit out of me.*

The cops?

He hadn't answered directly.

Love of God, how many times do I have to say it? It wasn't me.

I said, "That can't be typical, for the Feds to get involved."

"In eighteen years I've never seen it."

"Only thing I can think of is the homeowner worked at Lawrence Berkeley. It's a national lab."

"Fine, but this is his residence. Why are they showing up?"

I said, "I'll ask them."

BOTH THE FBI resident agency in Oakland and the main field office in San Francisco put me off. They didn't have or wouldn't give me information on an agent named Hopewell. When it came to accessing files, I heard a familiar line: 1991 onward had been digitized; anything older would've been destroyed or off-loaded to Washington, DC.

The most straightforward way to find out, I was told, was to submit a Freedom of Information Act request, which I did.

Straightforward, but not quick. I got an email acknowledging receipt and promising a response—not necessarily an approval—within thirty business days.

Knowing that our bomb squad ran joint exercises with the FBI, I called a colleague there. He linked me to an agent named Tracy Golden, who offered to order the files on my behalf, with the caveat that she might not do much better than the general FOIA process.

"Maybe I'll get them a little sooner, cause they won't have to redact." A fretful beat; then she hedged: "Honestly, I'm not sure what the requirements are for giving them to you."

"I don't want to make problems for you."

"Let me think it over."

"What about this person, Hopewell? You ever cross paths? If he's alive he's probably in his eighties by now."

"Sorry, no. There's a group, AFIO, the Association of Former

Intelligence Officers. Someone might know him there. I can try their listserv, if you'd like. Now that I think about it—yeah, that's definitely your best bet."

Overselling to make up for reneging.

I thanked her and waited.

ON MARCH 29, Judge Sharon Feeley of the Alameda County Superior Court denied UC's bid to lift the injunction banning construction at People's Park. In the suit against the university, she designated as lead plaintiff the Defenders of the Park, whose application for tax-exempt 501(c)(3) status was pending, and whose financial infrastructure consisted of a GoFundMe page and a card table set up on Telegraph Avenue with a sawn-off watercooler bottle into which sympathetic pedestrians occasionally dumped loose change.

The next day, the Defenders announced that a San Francisco law firm had agreed to represent them pro bono. Money donated up to now would be redirected toward other projects raising awareness about the issue of appropriation of Native lands.

With the reconstruction of the park vegetable garden nearing completion, volunteers began readying the beds for warm-weather planting.

Berkeley PD didn't have so many officers that they could devote resources to what increasingly seemed a stalemate. Quietly they began drawing down their presence at the park, reducing it to a single uniform stationed at Dwight and Bowditch.

On March 31, Amy took Charlotte for her six-month checkup, where the pediatrician declared her "ninety-ninth percentile for cute."

On April 1, a young woman named Veronique Lujan stepped off a thirty-hour, three-stop flight from visiting her grandma in Guam. She got in a rideshare and texted a friend to meet her at the New-Park Mall Starbucks. She needed to get back on California time. Plus she was hella hungry. She hadn't eaten anything on the plane, she said, and airport food was so nasty. She ordered a latte and a maple scone and excused herself to pee, leaving the friend to pick up their coffees. Fifteen minutes later Veronique had yet to reemerge, and the line for the bathroom stretched past the milk and sugar station. People groused about April Fools'. Knocking brought no response; nor did the friend's frantic texts. The manager unlocked the door to find Veronique Lujan dead on the smeary tiles.

The friend wept as she spoke to me. Yes, Veronique had seemed groggy. But wasn't that normal, after such a long trip? But she should have known better; she should have known something was wrong.

Autopsy would reveal the cause of death as respiratory failure, caused by hypoglycemic shock, followed by diabetic seizure.

Veronique Lujan was twenty-five.

Jurow and I loaded her onto the gurney van, drove her back to the morgue, and did the intake. While he began looking for her parents, I checked a missed call.

Deputy Edison: Ross Spitz responding to your question on the AFIO list. I worked for Buddy Hopewell at the Bureau. Feel free to give me a ring.

I reached Spitz at his home in Eugene, Oregon, where he'd settled after leaving the FBI. At present he ran a one-man security consulting firm.

"Mostly I fish," he said.

He spoke warmly of Hopewell, under whom he'd spent a couple of years as a junior agent in San Francisco during the 1980s.

I said, "You must've been close, to keep in touch this long."

"He was a mentor to me," Spitz said. "I was fresh out of law school, I didn't know what the hell I was doing."

"You're not familiar with the name Franchette, or the fire."

"Unfortunately not. Before my time. When you start out they throw a variety of things at you, so you get the experience, and they can see what you're good at. When I worked for Buddy, he was on the financial crimes desk."

"You think he'll remember?"

"I'd be surprised if he didn't. He's got a mind like a steel trap."

Spitz gave me the name and number of an assisted living facility in Millbrae.

"Be forewarned: He's all there, but he is stone-deaf. It can be hard communicating with him over the phone. He'll appreciate the visit. His wife died a while back, and I don't think his kids see him that often. I used to have a client in Palo Alto, and whenever I was down I'd try to pop in on him. It's been a while, though."

"I'll send your regards."

"Please do. There's not many like him left."

CHAPTER 19

The regrettably named Hanging Gardens Senior Living Center was a split-level ecru box situated beneath the departure corridor for San Francisco International Airport.

I climbed the entrance ramp with ears plugged against the shriek of a 747 rising toward the Pacific. Talking to the desk nurse I heard the same plane return, eastbound, having made a U-turn over the water. The lobby windows shivered and the faux-brass pendant light began to sway like an admonishing finger.

I wondered if Buddy Hopewell had been deaf before he moved in.

I found him in the dayroom, ensconced in a wicker rocker, Weejuns three inches shy of the linoleum. Round as a turnip, in a denim shirt and jeans one shade lighter, silver belt buckle stamped with Navajo motifs. A high white mustache climbed up into his nostrils. Scant hair had been slicked to the side, spread for maximum coverage, and clamped in place with a headset.

"And that's when I knew," he said. "It was either *him* . . . or *me*."

His audience consisted of four women, hanging on his words to the neglect of a television droning *The Price Is Right*. Buddy was the real entertainment. He might be old; he might be squat; but he had a pulse and was compos mentis.

The headset was black and chunky, like a halo that had rotted off. From one ear trailed a wire terminating in a microphone the size of a lipstick tube. Buddy paused his tale of derring-do to jab it in my direction. "Yes, young man."

"I'm Ross Spitz's friend," I said.

A plane barreled low above.

Buddy shimmied down from his throne. "Don't fret, gals, I won't be two jiffs."

We went to the dining room, all torn pleather and pressboard wainscoting that smelled of ketchup. I fetched water from the dispenser.

"Didn't mean to break up the party," I said.

"Ah, they're not going anywhere."

"Him or you, I'm assuming you won."

"I'm here, aren't I?" He raised his Dixie Cup to me.

Another departing plane shook the building. Throughout our conversation it kept happening, every few minutes. Buddy would lower the headset volume, wait five seconds, then dial it up again to continue talking.

He asked after Ross. I had to confess that I didn't really know him.

"Good man," Buddy said. "Fast learner."

"He thought you'd remember the case."

"Like it was yesterday. It's yesterday I can't remember for the life of me. How's a coroner come to be involved?"

I told him about Peter. His face briefly lost its shine.

"That's a damned shame. Here I thought you were going to tell me they finally found the girl's body."

"Mary Franchette."

"Margaret. Not Mary. They called her Peggy. Where'd you get Mary from?"

"Her half brother, Norman."

"Boy oh boy. That fella."

"He's my only source. Gene won't talk. There's nothing in the papers. We have no clue what happened to her."

"What happened was she was kidnapped," Buddy said. "Grabbed

right out in the open. Family never got a ransom request, never heard nothing at all. She just up and vanished. This long, you tend to assume she's dead. That's what I thought you were going to tell me."

"I couldn't find records at the local level, either about her or about the fire."

"Yeah. Cause we took em all."

"Took them?"

"Fire. PD. Whole kit and caboodle."

"Why would you do that?"

"Well, listen. You need to—"

A plane chundered overhead. Buddy waited for the noise to fade, then settled into his raconteur's pose. "Listen and learn, son."

HE'D COME OUT of Abilene, Texas, starting at the Bureau in June of '69.

"Hell of a time to cut your teeth. I was making ten thousand four hundred dollars a year, and I didn't have this big gut. I did have a full head of hair and a royal blue Barracuda with racing stripes. I loved that car. Girls loved it, too. I'd cruise around and pick up coeds from San Francisco State. They didn't like me cause I was the Man, but they sure as sugar liked that car."

I pictured him tooling through the Haight, honking his horn and winking.

Once a ladies' man, always a ladies' man.

"Those days the Bureau was still Hoover's kingdom. Out here on the West Coast, he couldn't keep as close an eye on us, or do like he did in New York, drop in unannounced and scare the pants off the ASACs. What it amounted to was he harbored a degree of mistrust. He thought the hippie culture had a corrupting influence. Needless to say, everyone was pretty keen to demonstrate the opposite.

"My first boss, Francis Ingles—he was a Hoover man. Shameless suck-up. He'd show up for work in a trench coat and fedora, like some G-man out of central casting. All he did, all day long, was draft memos to SOG."

I said, "Don't know that one."

"Seat of Government. That's what they call the headquarters in DC. Any damn thing required a memo. Make a phone call, write a memo. Tie your shoes, scratch your balls, write a memo. First week I'm on the job, Ingles calls one of the agents into his office and starts laying into him for failing to complete a form in triplicate. Left his door open, so the rest of us would hear. 'You've embarrassed the Bureau.' No worse sin than that. I joined up to do police work, and here I am, watching a grown man grovel for using the wrong carbon paper. Meanwhile Ingles gets lost leaving the bathroom."

I smiled.

"You know the kind of guy I'm talking about," he said.

"I've met a couple."

"Tiny dicks . . . The other thing to understand is context. You've got riots at the Democratic National Convention. You've got Abbie Hoffman and SDS, the Weathermen blowing crap up. Everyone's on edge. Early 1970 is when it really started to heat up, because they blew up some police cars in Berkeley, and then they bombed the police station in Golden Gate Park."

I'd read about the San Francisco bombing, but not the one in Berkeley.

"It didn't get as much attention, because nobody died, but that's dumb luck. Golden Gate, they killed a cop."

Not long after, Gene Franchette's house went up in flames.

"On its own, it's not of interest to us. Private citizen, we wouldn't necessarily have jurisdiction. But in light of recent events, it starts to look like part of a pattern."

"Bomb the bomb-maker."

"Bingo. Ingles got a giant hard-on." He grinned. "Mebbe a medium one."

"Why didn't the Oakland office take it?"

"Ingles went over them. Technically they answer to San Francisco. He wanted guys he could control, so he threw it to me and another junior agent, Phil Shumway."

"Seems like it would warrant more than a two-person opera-tion."

"We didn't have a specialized response team like they do now. A case was high-profile enough or DC was in a generous mood, they might send out someone handy with forensics. They did that for Golden Gate. That's where the bulk of the manpower was being concentrated. With Franchette, we had a situation that might be related, might not be. Ingles tapped us to do recon."

"What'd you find?"

"Not much. We didn't make it to the scene till a couple of days after the fact. The place was an unholy mess by then. You ever try to collect evidence from a fire?"

"A few times."

"That's right, y'all had that awful business at the nightclub."

"The Ghost Ship."

"I read about it. Ugly."

"It was."

"Firemen . . ." He pursed his lips. "Lemme think how I can put this. Cause I have the utmost respect for what they do. Hell, you couldn't pay me enough to run into a burning building. When it comes to preserving evidence, though, they are the absolute pits. Not their fault. They're trying to put the damned thing out, spraying water and running around, trampling the place to bits. They're not thinking about the consequences for an investigator.

"Me and Phil show up, there's cinders shoveled onto the lawn, animals running every which way. Best we could tell, based on the char, the point of origin was inside the garage. We couldn't find any sign of an incendiary device. The Weathermen liked to use timers. They'd set it to go off at night and stick it in a vent. We didn't have much in the way of training, mind you. But we didn't see anything like that. No fuses, no wiring."

"Doesn't rule out something lower-tech."

"Or a regular old pyro playing with matches."

"What about an accelerant?"

"Not that we could detect. The science wasn't what it is today, send in a pinprick and they tell you what brand it is and what the perpetrator had for lunch."

"Forced entry into the garage?"

"No way to know. Anything that might prove it got destroyed. Dr. Franchette told us he'd leave the windows open at night on occasion, air it out from the stink of varnish. He kept a workshop in the corner. Lumber, a soldering iron, wood stain, paint thinner, the works."

"That's a lot of ways for a fire to start."

"You bet. And once it caught, it went hell-for-leather. It's a miracle the whole place didn't burn down to the foundation."

"How much of the house was destroyed?"

"I reckon half at least."

"Did the Franchettes file an insurance claim?"

"It didn't belong to them. The lab owns it, or did. They used it to put up visiting scholars. That's how we got our foot in the door, by calling it an attack on federal property. As I recall, Dr. Franchette and his family had only been there a short while, while they looked for something more permanent."

"To me that suggests the attack might not have been aimed at them specifically."

Buddy nodded. "The place sat vacant a lot of the time. If it was arson, it's possible whoever started it didn't realize anyone was inside. Fact of the matter is, we never could be certain it wasn't a pure accident."

"The Franchettes got out okay."

"They caught some smoke. Mrs. Franchette smelled it and woke up. She got Peggy and her husband, and they climbed out the bedroom window."

Canvass hadn't yielded any witnesses.

"Folks were in bed. You didn't have ten thousand TV channels to keep you up."

"When I went by the house, I ran into the neighbor. Diane Olsen. Ring any bells?"

Buddy shook his head.

"She's lived next door most of her life. She was fifteen then. I asked her about it and showed her the picture of Beverly, and she clammed up and walked away."

"Well," he said. "I don't know. Must've been a scary thing for a kid."

His discomfort was evident. Talking to cops about their unsolved cases is always fraught. In theory, everyone recognizes the value of a fresh pair of eyes. Harder to accept that it's your eyes that have staled.

A detective once charged me in a drunken fit. I've learned to tread lightly.

I asked Buddy if anyone had claimed responsibility for the fire.

"No. They didn't, always. The Golden Gate bombing, for instance—nobody came out and said 'We did it,' but we knew who we wanted."

"Was that your understanding here? A political gesture?"

"Ingles thought so. That's why he had us jump on it and grab the files. He didn't want anything getting out to the public. He was terrified of leaks."

Days after Golden Gate, the San Francisco field office had received a tip that several of the Weathermen were hiding out on a boat up in Sausalito.

"Turns out someone'd tipped them off, too. Our guys got there prolly ten minutes too late. They found a cup of tea on the counter, hot, with the bag in it. When Hoover heard about that, he went bananas. He telexed the SAC, reaming him out."

"And shit rolls downhill."

"Law of nature."

"At the risk of being rude," I said, "if the boss was afraid of leaks, first place I'd look would be your office."

Buddy chuckled. "Well, he couldn't very well admit it might've been one of our guys. It was a big joint operation, remember. SFPD, state police. Could be anyone's big mouth."

"Except the FBI's."

"You're a fast learner, too," Buddy said. "From then on, everything had to be airtight, or look it. Ingles had me approach the firemen and the Berkeley cops. 'Can we borrow your files? We need to make secure copies.'"

"They just handed them over."

"Course they did. We're the goddamned FBI."

"What happened to them?"

"Hell if I know. I think Ingles had us stick em in a closet."

This decision—and the casual air with which Buddy described it—brought to mind the Nordic Knights case: agencies hoarding secrets, with disastrous consequences.

"Nobody ever asked for them back," I said.

"Maybe at first. Pretty soon they stopped. You ever met a cop who begged for more work?" He paused, a hint of wariness in his grin. "Aside from yourself."

With the physical evidence inconclusive, Buddy and Phil had turned to motive.

"Ingles was pushing the political angle, so we ran down the local radicals."

"Must've taken a while."

"You betcha. You couldn't walk down the street without tripping over a revolutionary. I couldn't tell you everyone we spoke to. We whittled it down to a short list. The one I liked was this gal, Janice Little. She and her boyfriend lived in a co-op, baking bread and weaving baskets outta armpit hair. They weren't part of the Weathermen, but they ran in some of the same circles, and she'd been picked up on a couple of occasions trespassing near the lab. Once they caught her fooling around by the fence with matches and lighter fluid. She claimed she was having a picnic. She didn't have any food on her, though. What's on the menu? Barbecued lizard? We brought her in, boyfriend, too, and put em through the wringer. We didn't have anything to hold them."

"What about personal motives? Norman Franchette, or Claudia or Helen."

"We talked to Norman, sure. Matter of fact he came to us. He was practically begging us to arrest him."

"Why would he do that?"

"He liked to bluster. Maybe he thought it'd get him laid, saying he was wanted by the FBI. We interviewed him a bunch. For a little bit we even put a tail on him. Worst thing he ever did was buy skin mags. It was clear he was puffing his chest out. But that was when we were asking about the fire. Then Peggy went missing and his tune changed real quick."

That surprised me; Norman had denied knowing the baby's fate.

"Horseshit," Buddy said. "Of course he knew."

My mind raced back through the conversation in the record store. "Makes me think he was bullshitting when he got her name wrong. Putting distance between him and her."

"Could be. On the other hand, he did smoke a lot of dope. I didn't like his attitude, but we had nothing that would stand up."

I mentioned the incident at the lab and Norman's attempt to visit his half sister.

Again I saw Buddy squirm. "News to me."

"The fight happened a few years prior, and I'm thinking Gene declined to press charges, which is why you never heard about it. Norman's not going to volunteer information that puts him in a bad light."

"Well, fine. But I interviewed Chrissy a whole bunch of times and she never said anything to me about him coming to the house, either."

A new name. "Chrissy's the babysitter."

"Nanny. Chrissy Klausen."

"Norman sounded a little in love with her."

"She was a nice-looking gal, no two ways about it."

"What about her? Was she a suspect?"

"She alibied out for the fire, out of town. The kidnapping, she was our primary witness."

On July 25, 1970—the eleventh anniversary of the Cuban Revolution, and approximately four months after the fire at the Franchette house—the Bay Area's third bombing of the year took place, at the US Army installation in the Presidio.

Three days later, Chrissy Klausen took Peggy Franchette out for a walk. The family had since rented a new house in a neighborhood farther south. Chrissy headed for a nearby park, the name of which escaped Buddy.

"It had a big slide made of concrete," he said, snapping his fingers.

"Codornices."

"That's the one. What fool uses concrete for a slide?"

"My wife grew up going there. It's a Berkeley institution."

"Institution of what? Brain damage? Mebbe that's the reason they're soft in the head. No offense to your wife."

It was a chilly, foggy Bay Area summer morning. At seven a.m. the park was deserted. Chrissy and Peggy had made several trips down the slide and were climbing up the hill for another round.

"She notices these two guys, one white and the other black, following them. They reach the top, where there's sort of a platform, and the men rush them. The black guy wraps her up. The other guy grabs Peggy, sticks her under his arm like a football, and takes off. The black guy tries to leave, too, but Chrissy grabs his leg and hangs on, and he starts whaling on her till she has to let go. Meanwhile the first guy jumps into a car with the girl."

"Did she get a plate?"

"It was too far away to read. All she could say is that it was a sedan, navy blue or black. Bear in mind, she's getting the tar beat out of her. The guy shoves her off the platform, she goes tumbling, crashes into a tree, and breaks her leg."

Her screams attracted the attention of a man walking his dog. By the time he had gotten to a pay phone, and made the call, and a squad car had arrived, and the patrolman had taken a statement and called a detective and notified highway patrol; by the time the news had made it to Buddy's desk—

"We didn't stand a chance."

Twenty-four hours ticked by.

"Today you've got Amber Alert, traffic cameras, the computer. Her face'd be everywhere. Ingles didn't even want her name in the papers."

"Because of leaks?"

"In part. The rule we followed was you keep a tight lid, cause you don't want to encourage the kidnappers and lend credence to their cause, or spook em so bad they panic and kill the victim to be rid of her. The thinking started to change with Patty Hearst, due to who she was. Me and Phil called the editors, and they agreed to hold the story back. You could do that. Trouble is, now we've got a barrel of nothing to go on."

Two days. Three. A week.

"We kept waiting on a phone call," Buddy said. "Ransom note, letter to the press."

A month.

"We brought in the same people we talked to after the fire. Norman included. We talked to sex maniacs, guys with priors, guys on parole, on probation. Matching vehicles. Everything moved slower then."

After two months and still no word from the kidnappers, the decision was made to appeal to the papers. But they'd waited too long. The story was stale.

"They stuck it on the back pages. I wanted to try and drum up some interest but Ingles kiboshed it. He didn't want the angle to become how we'd screwed up."

Three months. Six.

"Bev'd phone me up and ask if there had been any progress. She never raised her voice, like folks do. Almost wish she had. She was so quiet, it felt like a feather in my ear. Made my skin crawl." Hastening to add: "Not her. Just what she reminded me of."

By the one-year mark, they no longer expected a note or a letter, just a body.

"It bothered the hell out of me we couldn't give them even that much. Then they left town, she called less. Some point she stopped altogether. I reckon she got busy with her new kid. I don't suppose it makes up for the loss, but . . . I'm glad they were able to have another."

"She didn't tell you when Peter was born."

"It wasn't that way. We didn't have a personal . . . I tried to do right by her. I always tried to do right. I never did get a great read on her. She was doped up most of the time."

"On what?"

"Mother's little helpers. All the ladies did them. I remember we asked her if she had any enemies. That's where you start, right? What you ask anyone. Most folks go, 'Oh no, not me, I get along with everyone.' They think too highly of themselves to consider anyone'd want to hurt them. Funny thing about Bev, she goes: How could she have enemies if she didn't have any friends? And you know what, I believed her. She was just lonesome as hell."

Beverly Franchette, crying in the library stacks.

"What about Gene? Did he ever call you?"

"Not much. Men of that generation, it wasn't their way to get hysterical."

"I understand he could be abrasive."

"He was never anything but polite to me."

"And cooperative."

"Fully."

"You didn't have reason to suspect either he or Bev were involved in some way."

"Absolutely not."

"Norman said Gene didn't want to start dealing with a baby at his age."

"Baloney. They had another, didn't they? You can't believe a word that moron says."

"If I'm understanding you, the premise from the outset was that the two cases were connected."

"That's correct."

"You also said the fire might've been an accident."

Buddy bristled. "I said we couldn't come down firm on either side. But come on, now. You got to use common sense. The fire's a month after the Golden Gate bomb. Then you get the Presidio bombing and the kidnapping three *days* apart. What's the alternative?"

"Bad luck."

"I've never heard of luck that bad."

I had. Most coroners would say the same. But we draw on a biased sample.

"Look," he said, "you ever been to that park?"

"A few times."

"You ought to know, then. The slide's back from the street a hundred fifty yards. They didn't just wander in and grab the first kid they saw. It was planned. They went right after them. That sound to you like a crime of opportunity?"

He waved his cup at me. "You mind?"

I brought a refill from the dispenser. He gulped it down.

"Shit," he said, wiping his mouth, "it's a sore subject. Don't tell me you ain't got one of those."

"More than one."

"I'm not saying we didn't make mistakes, either."

"I get you. And really, I'm just spitballing. I'm here to learn."

He nodded abstractedly.

I said, "Besides race, could Chrissy describe the men?"

"Nothing we could work with. Her memory was in pieces—what you expect from a woman fighting for her life. I went to see her in the hospital. Her ribs're broke, her leg's broke, her face is a bloody mess, she can hardly breathe from the pain, and she keeps on apologizing, over and over."

"For what?"

"She was burning up with guilt. She loved that girl. One thing I've learned over the years," he said, "it's the decent folks can't stop blaming themselves, while the bad ones go around with a spring in their step. Later we sat her down with a sketch artist. We even had her hypnotized, if you can believe that."

"Any other eyewitnesses?"

"It was too early in the day for most folks to be out. The guy walking his dog, he saw a dark sedan go by in a hurry. But he couldn't be sure, and he couldn't give us a plate, either."

Within a few years Buddy had shifted his focus to white-collar crime. Phil Shumway transferred to Boston. Periodically they'd get on the phone to revisit the case.

"Sort of a ritual we had."

"Are you in touch with him?"

"Phil? No. He passed on."

"When was that?"

"Early nineties, I think. I don't rightly recall. Maybe it was '89."

As statutes of limitations began to run out, some of the radicals who'd been living underground began to resurface. Time makes the best truth serum, but everyone Buddy had ever spoken to was adamant in their denial, regardless of what else they admitted to.

Peggy Franchette's case went to pending inactive status.

"It didn't mean much, practically. We'd dried up long before."

He slumped in his chair, stray hairs stuck to his damp forehead. We had ventured onto a portion of the map he did not possess, waters churning with hindsight and regret.

A band of light slanted on the wall. Suddenly it began to tremble; the foam ceiling tiles danced in their frames and shed tiny particles that descended like ash. From an unseen sky, the shriek came crescendo. As it reached its punishing apex, I noticed Buddy's hands clenched in his lap. He kept them there, not bothering to lower the volume, and I could only guess how loud and terrible was the clamor in his head.

CHAPTER 20

That afternoon, I put Charlotte down for a nap and sat to review my notes.

The depth of Buddy's recall impressed me. At the same time, I was perplexed by a number of things he'd said and more so by things unspoken.

I'd mentioned Claudia and Helen as suspects with personal motives, but Buddy had brushed that off, wanting only to talk about Norman, whom he obviously loathed. Yet he'd missed Norman's visit to Linda Vista. Had never heard of Diane Olsen, the literal girl-next-door.

Had the other members of the Franchette family been questioned at all? Or did Buddy and his partner assume no involvement? If so, why? They had to know that most serious crimes against children are committed by relatives or close friends.

He'd spent much of our conversation harping on fugitive radicals. I could understand why. The era was tumultuous, and the bombings did appear to line up with the Franchette family's misfortunes. But I could see another advantage to the political angle: Focusing on it distracted from the investigation's shortcomings.

I knew better than to let hindsight make me smug. Every cop has had to let someone go for lack of evidence.

But we're people, too. We bring our own quirks to investigations, and Buddy was a performer, with a need to be admired. So much of success in life boils down to acting like you know what you're talking about, even when you don't.

Especially when you don't.

I needed to see that file.

I got out my laptop to follow up with Tracy Golden, my initial point of contact at the FBI. I hadn't finished the email when Nate Schickman's name appeared on my cell. I figured he was calling to let me know he'd been unable to find information on Mary Franchette.

Now I could tell him why: Mary was Peggy, and the records had been confiscated and lost.

I picked up. "Yo."

My ear filled with noise.

"Clay? Are you there? Can you hear me?"

"Yeah. What's going on?"

"I'm at People's Park. We got sort of a situation. There's a guy— fuck, hang on."

Shouting in the background. Raw anger.

Nate came back on. "There's a guy here stirring shit up, claims you sent him."

"What?"

"That's what he says."

"What guy?"

"Big dude. Nazi tats. He has your card."

I said, "On my way."

I HURRIED OUTSIDE to find Maryanne kneeling by her planter boxes.

"Hello there," she said. "Lovely day."

"I'm so sorry to do this," I said. "But would you mind listening for the baby? Amy's at work, and something's come up and I have to run out."

"Not at all."

I thanked her profusely, handed her the monitor, and told her I'd try to be back before Charlotte woke up.

She laughed. "I can hear her fine without that."

No time to argue. I ran to my car.

ENTERING THE PARK on Haste, I hustled toward a massing crowd.

The shrine inside the Free Speech Pit had exploded since my last visit, expanding to fill its entirety and taking on the feel of an art installation. In addition to bouquets and signs were an altar table, edges dripping with candle-wax stalactites; two ratty, full-sized couches; a ratty chaise longue; meditation pillows and yoga mats; a bamboo teepee, lashed with twine and strung with Tibetan prayer flags. The stuffed animals had been raked into a single heap, like an offering. Amid the jumble of furry heads and limbs, a familiar patch of neon blue.

Letters of tribute to the "Child of the Earth" had been pinned to a huge corkboard and propped on an easel. A second corkboard displayed a gallery of other dead or missing children, along with people killed by law enforcement throughout the country, titled with the catchall VOICES OF THE VOICELESS. A map outlined the original territorial boundaries of Bay Area tribes. Posters divulged THE TRUTH ABOUT COAL. MEAT. GMOS.

The gardeners had stopped work and were giving a statement to a Berkeley city cop, who kept saying *One at a time, please.* Three more cops formed a porous boundary to contain some fifty onlookers, many of them waving phones and chanting anti-Nazi slogans.

I slipped on my neck badge and worked my way to the front, where a hand shot out to take me by the arm.

Nate Schickman, dagger-eyed, steered me to the sidewalk. "That's him."

Kelly Dormer sat on the curb, boots in the gutter, hands cuffed behind his back. He wore a leather motorcycle vest, and his left shirtsleeve dangled by a scrap of flannel, exposing the swastika on his shoulder. The knife sheath hung on his belt. The knife itself was missing. Blood trailed from his nose and ran fang-like over mouth and chin to dry in jagged brown bolts down his stubbled neck.

Two city officers kept watch over him.

Across Dwight stood a pair of men in soiled jeans, gloves, and kneepads. They appeared in similarly rough shape, one with a bloody T-shirt pressed to his face and the other flexing a sore elbow. They were uncuffed, talking to a single cop.

That it took four times as many people, numerically, to control Kelly gave me a hint of what had occurred.

"He says you told him the baby's his brother," Schickman said.

"It is."

Nate blinked.

I said, "Really."

"And that he had to come down here."

You're free to head over and have a look yourself.

I think you'll come to the same conclusion.

There are people, perfect strangers, leaving flowers and notes.

It doesn't bother you that they care more than you do?

I said, "I was trying to get him to pay for burial."

"Whatever," Schickman said. "He didn't like what he saw, cause he jumped into the pit and started ripping the other pictures down. The gardeners are like, 'Cut that out.' He gets mad and starts knocking shit over. Those guys"—the injured men—"decide they're gonna be heroes."

Each side claimed the other had thrown the first punch.

"I don't give a shit," Schickman said. "I'm trying to avoid an international incident."

Translation: Your mess. Get a mop.

I left him on crowd control and went over to Kelly. The city cops stood back.

He eyed me groggily, said nothing.

I said, "Why are you messing with the stuff in the pit?"

"They turned it into a goddamn circus. That's *my* brother died in there. All that other shit don't belong."

"It's a public park."

"I'm supposed to let them disrespect my family?"

"They're not. That's how this place works. It's what it's known for. People are free to express their opinions."

"Cept me."

"There's expression and there's destruction."

He hawked and spat into the street, in the direction of the two men. They flipped him off.

"Fuck you," Kelly yelled.

"Hey," I said.

"Fuck *you*, Nazi scum."

"Little bitch," Kelly yelled, trying to stand.

"*Hey.*" I clamped a hand on his shoulder, pressed him down to the curb. "Knock it off."

The crowd jeered.

Fuck you, Nazi.

Clap, clap, clap-clap-clap.

Fuck you, Nazi.

Schickman stared at me imploringly. *Get him out of here.*

"They attacked me," Kelly said.

"They say the same about you."

"Self-defense."

"Arrest them, they gotta arrest you. Is that what you want?"

"Fucking bullshit."

"Go home, Kelly."

"I'm still cuffed."

"I can tell them to let you go, but then you got to clear out."

He didn't respond.

"You hear me?" I asked.

"Yeah, fine."

I nodded to one of the uniforms, who uncuffed him. "Where are you parked?"

"Over that way."

"Let's go."

Kelly sat rubbing his wrists and banging his boot heel against the asphalt. "My fuckin foot's asleep."

"Come on. I don't have time for this."

"Those cops took my knife."

"That's for the best."

"I want it back."

"We'll FedEx it to you," I said, reaching to haul him up.

I guess his foot really was asleep. He stumbled as he rose, head-butting me lightly in the chest. To prevent us both from toppling over, I grabbed him—a reflex—and we ended up performing an awkward little waltz, drawing ire from the crowd.

Nazi lover.

"Pussy-ass bitches," Kelly yelled.

"Go," I growled.

I frog-marched him toward Telegraph. He kept trying to turn around and confront the crowd; I kept shoving him forward.

"Gunnar was right about you," he whined. "You want my money, but you won't do shit to protect my rights."

"One has nothing to do with the other. Get this straight: The money's not for me. It's to give your brother a proper burial. And you haven't spent a dime, yet."

We rounded the corner, the heat of the crowd diminishing.

"I won't pay for something before I've seen proof," Kelly said.

"The remains aren't here. You want to see them, you can come to the morgue."

"I ain't gonna do that," he said quickly.

"Then I need to know what you intend to do. Pretty soon I'm going to have to act, with or without you."

He sulked, and we walked on, passing a stop sign someone had updated with a sticker.

He'd left his bike outside a ramen shop.

"End of the week," I said. "Let me know what you decide."

HE DIDN'T CALL, not by the end of that week or the end of the next. Left without an option, and with Sergeant Brad Moffett growing impatient, I sent the bones of the People's Park Infant for cremation. The proper course of action, but that didn't make it less disappointing.

Flo Sibley said, "It's just so freakin sad. Poor, poor kid."

"It sucks, but what can I do. How's the camera going?"

"You had to ask, huh? Our privileges are about to run out. So far nothing."

"Per Tom?"

"I've reviewed the footage," she said. "There's a few people who show up more than once, but for the most part it's the same faces you get in the park during the day."

"So we're SOL."

"With the surveillance, yeah. I had another idea, though. My sister in Bakersfield, she's got three boys. The youngest got in with a bad crowd when he started high school. My brother-in-law decided to stick a tracking device in his backpack to see where he was going after school."

"Did it help?"

"Nope. It was crap. It beeped when the battery was low, so Matty found it on the second day and dropped it in the trash. But this was a couple of years ago. We live in the greatest country on earth, right? They're constantly coming up with new and exciting products."

She directed me to the website of a company called EyeKnow.

Their deeply creepy motto was *Always Watching*.

The GPS tracker Florence Sibley had requisitioned was the size of a deck of cards.

"I sewed it inside the bear," she said.

I burst out laughing.

"No big deal," she said. "I had to take out some of the stuffing so it weighs a little more. But it's not that noticeable unless you squeeze hard. It's back in the pit as we speak."

"Damn, Sibley. You're like if James Bond and Martha Stewart had a baby."

Rather than put out a steady signal, the tracker updated its location at twenty-four-hour intervals. The spec page claimed the battery lasted last up to a year on a single charge.

"You believe that?" I said.

"Yeah, well, the pit's not going to be there in a year, one way or the other."

I wasn't so sure. "What'd you tell Nieminen?"

"I didn't tell him anything. I don't need him bugging me to share."

FOR A SHORT while, Amy and I had been making progress, the baby managing as many as five hours at a stretch. Then sleep regression kicked in. Four to three to two. Then a host of dreadful ninety-minute swings.

The previous night had been particularly rocky, and while Amy rushed through her morning routine, I paced around the cottage, yawning, Charlotte chewing on my neck and sobbing.

"Did you give her Orajel?" Amy called from the bathroom.

"Yes."

"There's a teether in the freezer."

198 / JONATHAN KELLERMAN and JESSE KELLERMAN

"She doesn't want it. Can I give her Tylenol yet?"

"Not for another hour."

"Then I'm going to put her down."

Eyeliner in hand, Amy leaned out to stare at me in horror, as though I'd suggested deep-frying our daughter. "Do *not* do that."

"You don't think she sounds tired?"

"She's barely been up for an hour."

"She's exhausted."

"Because she was awake all night. That's why we have to keep her up during the day. Did you read the book I gave you?"

"Which book."

"*Zombie Baby.* There's a chapter on circadian rhythm. Did you read it?"

"I think so. Mostly what you highlighted."

"Jenna said Riley learned to sleep in two weeks. But you have to follow the rules. It's a system. We both need to be on board or it's never going to work."

"I'm on board."

"Promise me: Under no circumstances will you put her down before nine thirty."

"I'll try."

"No. Clay. Promise."

"I promise."

"And you can't let her sleep for more than two hours. Any longer and we're completely fu—screwed. Please. Two hours in the morning, one in the afternoon."

"Understood."

"Thank you. What time is it?"

"Eight twenty-five."

"Shit." She ran to grab her bag, pecked me on the cheek. "I'll pick up dinner."

THE REMAINDER OF the morning can only be described as baby Guantánamo. I tickled Charlotte, bounced her, blasted Tupac. I took her outside to show her Maryanne's asparagus standing proud. I made repeated lead-footed circuits of our block, passing the same stop sign, defaced with a pair of stickers.

"Stay awake, please. You have to stay awake."

Charlotte moaned and drooped and lowed mournfully.

"You sound like Chewbacca."

"Gaaahh. Gaaaahh."

"That's right, lady. You're Wookiee of the Year."

At nine seventeen a.m., she shut her eyes and her little body relaxed. I held her for another thirteen minutes, at which point I could tell Amy truthfully that I had not put her down before nine thirty.

Collapsing onto the futon, I flipped on the TV.

When I opened my eyes it was four fifty-two in the afternoon.

I lurched to the nursery. Charlotte was sitting up in her crib, babbling. She looked perky and content. Which made sense. She'd taken a seven-and-a-half-hour nap.

"Mommy's going to murder me."

She giggled.

I fed her and changed her and bathed her and changed her again. At six fifteen Amy returned toting take-out bags. I caught a whiff of Thai.

"How'd it go?" she asked.

My reply was cut short, as from outside came a peal of shattering glass, followed by a woman's scream.

CHAPTER 21

I gave the baby to Amy, telling her to stay inside and lock the door. I didn't stop to get down the Sig Sauer, let alone take the ammo out of the bread machine. Jumping the child safety gate, I ran up the driveway, toward the sound of Maryanne's cries.

Maryanne Reece had spent her career in the nonprofit sector, most recently as director of an organization working to reduce the high school dropout rate in urban areas. Her friendship with Amy's parents had begun in grad school and spanned forty years.

She was in her sixties now, widowed and retired, with one son living in Los Angeles and another in Munich. In the past she'd rented the guest cottage out to strangers, but the arrangement always felt impersonal and sometimes adversarial. The risk of a tenant refusing to leave was so high—the cost of eviction so prohibitive—that she'd let the unit sit unoccupied for several years prior to our moving in. She told Amy and me we were doing her a favor. Having a baby around kept her young.

I'm almost ashamed to charge you.

By the time I reached the front lawn, the screaming had stopped. The house is a well-preserved Craftsman with original leaded-glass windows. One window's center left panel was gone. Through the gap I saw the living room, cozily lit. Etta James played on the stereo.

Maryanne cowered by a bookcase, fumbling with her cell.

I called her name. Startled, she dropped the phone, snatched it up, squinted out fearfully into the darkness.

"It's Clay," I said. "Meet me at the front door."

Pale and shaking, she cracked the door, then widened it to admit me.

"Are you hurt?"

"I don't think so."

"Your arm is bleeding."

She looked down at it. "I didn't feel anything."

It wasn't a bad cut. I fetched a box of tissues from the powder room and she pressed a wad to her wrist.

"What happened?"

"I don't know. I came in to get a book and . . ."

She waved toward the living room.

I edged into the doorway.

Glass flickered viciously on the carpet, splintering the moon-light, lurking in the nooks of an easy chair. In the window frame, broken strands of leading dangled, like a cobweb annihilated by one thoughtless stroke.

The weapon was a brick. A divot in the quarter-sawn oak marked where it had struck and bounced before settling, surreally, on edge. Painted on its broad side, in half-inch strokes, was a red swastika, glossy in the lamplight against the duller red of the clay.

I work for you baby Etta sang. *Work my hands to the bone.*

Care for you, baby, till the cows come home.

I shut off the music, retrieved a toppled wineglass, and returned to Maryanne in the foyer. "Come with me."

We exited the house via the rear porch and crossed the yard to the guest cottage. Before entering I announced myself in a loud voice.

Amy sheltered in the bathroom, an irate Charlotte pressed close to her chest. "What's going on."

"Probably nothing more. Don't worry. I'm going to call the police. Stay here, please."

The women stared as I put on my windbreaker, dark blue with

ACSO CORONER in yellow lettering. I didn't want the cops to show up and draw on me.

In the kitchenette I got down the Sig Sauer and the bread machine.

"Clay," Amy said.

"It's going to be fine," I said, loading the magazine. "Sit tight."

After clearing the back and front yards, and calling the cops, I circled the block, peering into parked cars and bushes. It's a pretty neighborhood, straddling the southern city limits. Handsome birches and brown shingle homes line rumpled streets. Our block alone enjoys no fewer than three Little Free Libraries, birdhouse-like cabinets, set on four-by-fours, that invite passersby to take or leave used books. A recent uptick in temperature had excited the wisteria, causing their gnarled branches to throw out purple clumps.

With the initial shock wearing off, fear began trickling in, infusing everyday objects with menace. I holstered my gun, leery of firing at someone's pet or garden gnome.

I'd walked this exact route that morning, carrying my daughter.

Had they been watching me then?

The responding officer was named Young. She was perplexed to be greeted by a coroner. Dispatch hadn't mentioned anything about a body. How had I gotten there so fast?

I gave her the thirty-second summary.

"Did you see a vehicle?" she asked.

"No. I didn't hear tires, either, although I wasn't paying a hundred percent attention. They could've been on foot or on a bike. Maybe Maryanne saw."

Young called for a second car, and we walked back to the cottage.

Along with a thrashing, wailing Charlotte, the two women huddled on the futon. A box of Band-Aids and a tube of antiseptic sat on the coffee table.

Officer Young asked if Maryanne would accompany her to review the damage and give a statement.

Maryanne stood. "Yes, of course."

The door shut.

Amy put Charlotte on the play mat and faced me. "Are we safe?"

"Whoever did it is gone."

"They might come back."

"Not with the cops here."

"The cops aren't going to stay forever."

I shook my head. "No."

Amy chewed her lip. The baby rolled around, mewling with delight, her misery of one minute prior forgotten. I envied her.

"I'm going to spend the night at my parents' house," Amy said.

"Okay."

"You think I need to."

I realized that her first statement, *I'm going,* had been a question, probing for danger. "I don't think it's necessary. But if it'll make you feel safer."

Together we packed an overnight bag; a second, larger bag with baby supplies.

"What are you going to do?" she asked.

"Deal with the cops."

"Are you coming with us?"

"Depends what time we wrap up."

"You should stay here with Maryanne. She's scared to death."

Amy didn't sound frightened. But I knew she was. Foolish not to be.

"It's you they wanted," she said. "Right? Not her."

"I don't know," I said.

She accepted my words for what they were, a comforting lie.

I'm a sheriff. My wife is a psychologist. It doesn't matter that I work primarily with the bereaved or that the overwhelming majority of her clients are benign.

We try to be careful. Our mail comes to a PO box. We've taken steps to reduce our online footprint. But it's hard to hide these days. All it takes is one disgruntled lunatic with a credit card and an internet connection to gain *unlimited access.*

I shouldered the bags to the curb, snapped the car seat into its base, and bent close to Charlotte. "Be good for Mommy."

She seized me by the nose, digging in with her tiny talons. She didn't look remotely tired. Why would she? She'd taken a seven-and-a-half-hour nap.

I freed myself, kissed her, and turned to embrace Amy. "Say hi to your folks for me."

"Call me, honey. Please."

"I don't want to wake you up."

"I'll turn the ringer off if I go to sleep."

Her turn for a comforting lie. She'd be up all night.

We held each other for a while.

Behind us, the second squad car pulled up.

"I love you," I said.

We kissed, and she climbed into the driver's seat and I watched them leave.

The arriving officer came over. His nametag read ANZA. He gave a confused smile. "Coroner?"

MARYANNE APOLOGIZED. SHE'D had her back to the window, hadn't seen the perpetrator.

"I don't understand. I have no issues with anyone. Why would they do this to me?"

"It's not you," I said.

Outside, I showed the officers the trellises scaling the side of the main house, wisteria and bougainvillea and white pinpricks of star jasmine. Along with the poor angle, the profusion of new growth completely hid the guest cottage from the street.

"Her address is 3130. We're 3130A. It's a smash-and-go. No way are they taking the time to go prowling in search of a subunit. If they even noticed the A."

They looked skeptical. But the swastika and the potential threat to a fellow peace officer were enough for them to call a detective.

Officer Anza went off to cruise the neighborhood. Many a bad guy has been nabbed simply because he was running, in street clothes, for no apparent reason.

Young and I sat with Maryanne in her kitchen over cups of tea. From the living room seeped a low, steady draft, the open window frame a wound refusing to clot.

"I'm so sorry," I said.

"There's no need to apologize."

"We'll pay for the repair."

"Don't be silly. We don't know that it has anything to do with you."

It was a night for comforting lies.

"It's just glass," she said bravely.

The detective turned up around eight. His name was Billy Watts. I knew him, or of him, through Delilah Nwodo. When he learned who I was he broke into a shit-eating grin.

"The man, the legend," he said.

I was glad Amy wasn't around to hear him chuckling.

"Anybody you think I should talk to?" he asked.

I told him of my visit to the Dormer brothers' compound.

Bricks lying on the ground.

A young woman painting her nails blood red.

Gunnar's mild drawl. *Tomorrow.*

I described my recent run-in with Kelly Dormer.

He said, "Makes sense. We'll drop in on them. Anyone else you've pissed off?"

"What do you think?"

"Yeah, huh?" Watts arched his back. "Everyone's a critic."

BY NINE FORTY-FIVE the cops were gone, taking the brick in an evidence bag. I helped Maryanne sweep up the glass and patch the hole with cardboard.

She declined my offer to sleep in the main house.

"That's what they want, isn't it? To cause panic. Thank you, though."

"I'm here if you need me."

"I didn't realize you kept a gun on hand," she said. "I suppose I should have."

"I apologize if that upsets you."

"I assume you know how to use it safely."

"I do. It's part of our training. I practice regularly."

"And you keep it far out of reach from Charlotte."

"Yes."

She nodded. "Well, then. Have a good night."

THE BAGS OF Thai sagged on the kitchenette counter, ice-cold and untouched. I hadn't heard from Amy in hours, not since she'd texted to let me know she'd arrived.

I wolfed peanut noodles from the carton, typing. *Are you awake*

We both are

I winced. Before I could figure out a reply she wrote again:

What's happening there

Everything ok. Cops are gone

Maryanne?

Upset but sturdy

My parents are worried. They think we're fighting

What did you tell them

We had a gas leak and you're fixing it

I can come over

No stay I don't want her to be alone

Ok

When can we come home

That's my girl.

Whenever you want I wrote.

Ok. I'm not planning to go in to work tomorrow

Sounds good. I'll probably be out when you get back. I need to take care of a few things

There was a pause.

Please don't do anything dangerous she wrote.

I frowned.

The cops were on it. Why would she think I would do anything at all?

She was right, though.

I did want to do something.

Very much. Right now.

I'm not sure if her words created the urge, or if she anticipated me, laying her finger on a blemish in my character that I preferred not to acknowledge.

I won't I wrote. *See you tomorrow. I love you*

You too

I stretched out on the futon, listening to the life cycle of the night. I wasn't tired, either. I'd taken a daylong nap.

Eventually the walls began to smolder, a fragile rose-gold, indecisive, like a childhood incident remembered only from photographs.

I got up. I put on my vest. I took my knife and gun and car keys.

The lights were on in Maryanne's kitchen. Dressed in yesterday's clothes, she stood at the sink, filling the kettle, oblivious to me as I passed in the shadows.

I MADE IT to Carlos Canyon Road in under an hour.

Sunlight flooded the open plain between the barbed-wire fence and the trailers. Columns of dust would signal my approach. Presumably that was one reason for setting up so far back: to have advance warning of visitors.

In day I noticed the sign Dale Dormer had referred to, nailed to a fencepost.

NO TRESPASSING
VIOLATORS WILL BE
TAUGHT A LESSON

Small and rust-eaten and baked colorless. Practically illegible. They wanted people to miss it. Good excuse to shoot someone under plausible legal cover.

I swung the car around, doubling back half a mile to the four-way intersection that led out of the hills and toward civilization. I veered onto the shoulder and parked.

Anyone going anywhere—a gas station, Walmart—would have to pass by.

No telling whether that would happen. The Dormer brothers were homebodies. I doubted they ventured out any more than necessary. Probably once a month, to shop in bulk.

If someone did pass by, it might be Kelly or either of his brothers.

A wife.

Those twin boys—they looked old enough to drive.

Could be no one or anyone I was waiting for.

Probably I was wasting my time.

Please don't do anything dangerous.

I tuned to sports talk radio and racked the seat back.

By nine the air felt like a sweat sock and I couldn't keep my eyes open. Rummaging in the pockets and compartments yielded an ancient granola bar. As I started to unwrap it, a shape appeared in my rearview mirror.

I sank down.

A single-cab pickup chugged by. It was primer white, its passenger side door a solid panel of rust.

Its law-abiding driver signaled right.

Dale Dormer.

I dropped the granola bar in the cupholder.

I let him make the turn, counted twenty, and followed.

He didn't go far, just past the wind farm substation and under the freeway, to a liquor store on the outskirts of Tracy. The parking lot was large and, at that hour, empty. I pulled up to see him entering the store, braids swinging.

I parked cater-corner to the truck.

Please don't do anything.

I left one hand on the steering wheel. Moved the other to my knife.

I didn't know Billy Watts. Had no idea if he was a good investigator. Maybe he was humoring me when he asked who I thought he should talk to. Maybe he'd let it slide.

Please don't do

My knife is a Ka-Bar. It's more or less identical to the one Kelly Dormer carries, which is more or less identical to the one first manufactured for the US Marine Corps during World War II. Seven-inch carbon-steel blade, partially serrated near the hilt for ripping. Grooved nonslip handle, well balanced. Mine seldom sees use other than opening packages, so it keeps relatively sharp.

I felt confident it would pierce a truck tire, certainly a bald one.

Please don't

The Dormers had sent me a message.

We can do whatever we want.

To you.

To your family.

I was sending one back.

That's *my* family.

My wife. My daughter.

I reached for the door handle, scorching metal.

The truck's dull surface and single rusty door gave it a strangely two-dimensional aspect, like a colorblock collage made from construction paper.

I imagined Dale coming out to find it disabled.

I imagined the conversation that would take place in Gunnar's trailer.

Escalate. Retaliate.

Please

Time thickened. I left my fingers on the handle.

Dale exited the store carrying two stacked cases of beer. He set them on the ground, opened the truck's passenger door, and transferred the cases to the seat. The clerk brought out another two cases. They belted them in and filled the passenger footwell and went back inside for two more cases apiece.

Eight cases made close to two hundred cans of beer. I wondered how long that would last them. The Dormers drank Schlitz. No fucking Mexican imports for them, thank you very much. Dale and the clerk were having a hard time figuring out how to Tetris the remaining cases into the truck. They'd used up the available interior space. They settled on the truck bed. Dale had a tie-down strap, but the ratchet was busted and kept slipping. They laughed about it. They'd done this before. They were buddies. The clerk didn't care what tattoos or opinions Dale had. He was a good customer, he bought in bulk.

Dammit, Dale, every damn time.

Finally they gave up and tied the strap into a chunky granny knot. I doubted it would hold. He'd have to keep it below fifteen miles an hour or beer would end up flying all over the highway. I doubted, too, that Dale Dormer could exercise that much self-restraint. He eased out of the lot, but I could see him picking up speed as he went, thirsty and ready to be home.

The clerk waved him goodbye, then turned to stare at me across the warped asphalt. He was a heavyset guy, midtwenties but already scalpy up top. Pleated Dickies. Hunter green polo, dark at the underarms and between the breasts.

Maybe he thought I was going to rob him. Liquor stores are high-frequency targets. Many keep a firearm behind the register. One of Amy's great-uncles, on her father's side, owned a liquor store. He was murdered during a robbery. He never managed to get a shot off. The case was never solved.

The clerk raised a fat, quaking hand and pointed to the tin-box security camera fixed askew above the store entrance. There was zero chance it was working.

I took my fingers off the door handle. I picked up my granola bar, started my car, and drove away.

. . .

AMY SAT AT her parents' breakfast table, talking with her mother. Theresa stood to pour me a cup of coffee.

"You're here," Amy said.

"I'm here."

"I thought you had errands."

"Just a quick one. How was your night?"

"Don't ask."

"Go rest," I said. "I'll listen for her."

"Do you mind? I feel like shit on toast."

"Please."

"Thank you. She didn't fall asleep till like four. If she's not up by eleven thirty please wake her. She last ate at seven so she's going to be starving."

I kissed her on the head and she shuffled down the hall to her childhood bedroom. I joined Theresa at the table, folding my legs under and blowing on my coffee.

"Problem solved?" she asked.

I remembered Amy's cover story about the gas leak. "Loose valve."

Theresa nodded. Whatever conflict she imagined between her daughter and me, she wasn't the type to pry. "Sounds like you had a hard night yourself."

"I'm okay."

"Why don't you lie down? I can get you when she wakes up. Or," she said, "I can feed her myself. I know Amy doesn't believe it, but I do know how to feed a baby."

I smiled. "It'll just make me groggy. Thanks, though."

Soon enough we heard Charlotte starting to stir.

I brought a bottle to the guest room and lifted her, bawling, out of the portacrib.

"It's okay, lady. Daddy's here."

I draped her on my shoulder, feeling her body calm. "I'm right here."

CHAPTER 22

Months ago, during my first visit to Vista Linda, I'd spoken to Diane Olsen for three minutes. I didn't know how she'd respond to seeing me again or if she'd even remember me.

She opened the door and her face instantly fell. "Yes?"

She wore drawstring denim capris and a T-shirt that read HUMBOLDT COUNTY in purple script. Flip-flops adhered to her heels as she pedaled her weight back and forth.

I said, "Clay Edison. We met a little while back. I was interested in the Franchettes."

Nothing.

"I had my daughter with me."

More silence. Informed, not surprised. She remembered.

"You said you didn't know what became of Bev—"

"And I still don't."

"Since then I've gotten a little bit more information. She and Gene ended up moving to New Mexico."

"There's your answer, then."

"After Peggy was kidnapped," I said.

She flinched. "Who are you? What's your interest in this?"

"They had another child. A son, Peter. His parents never told him about his sister. I'm helping him piece together his past, was hoping you could fill in some of the blanks."

"You already know more than I do," she said.

"Maybe about certain things. But you were there. It would be helpful to—"

"I was a child."

"Fifteen," I said. "Old enough to notice what's going on."

She shifted unhappily. I prepared for a door slam. But she stayed in place.

"How well did you know the Franchettes?"

"As well as you know any neighbor. They were my parents' generation."

"Did your parents have a relationship with them?"

"They might've come over for dinner a few times. My mom made a point of being friendly."

"I understand the lab uses the house for visiting scholars."

Diane Olsen nodded.

"You must've met some interesting types," I said.

"They're scientists. They keep to themselves."

"Were the Franchettes like that, too?"

"Well, yes, till their house burned down." She hugged herself. "Not that I blame them. They're the ones who suffered most. My dad said it probably had to do with what Dr. Franchette did, with nukes."

"Have there been other incidents over the years?"

"Not like that."

"Anything remotely political. Picketing, graffiti, protests."

"Never."

"What happened to the Franchettes was exceptional."

"I suppose." She brushed back hair. "They were exceptional."

"In what sense?"

"They were locals, for starters. Most of the scientists come from abroad. My mom still put out the welcome mat, like she did for everyone who moved in. She'd bring bread and salt, take the women grocery shopping. Bake cookies for the bachelors. My father would tell her, 'Lil, you're not the official welcoming committee for every weirdo with a suitcase.' She felt bad for the spouses and children. 'Think how you'd feel, being such a long way from home and not knowing a single soul.' She'd invite the kids over to play with me, which I hated, because there was no telling if they'd be my age, or if they'd speak a word of English. I used to be able to count to ten in a dozen different languages."

"Your mom sounds like a nice person."

"She was. Also—I don't mean to take away from her niceness—I think she considered it a form of insurance."

"Against?"

"New neighbors? There's always the possibility of conflict. So she'd preempt and make nice. With the Franchettes, I suppose we interacted with them a bit more than usual, because there was no language barrier. I wouldn't call us close, though."

"The last time we spoke, you said that Bev had it hard."

"She did."

"What did you mean by that?"

"Their house burned down. Then . . . I mean, how much can one family endure?"

"Right. Just that you didn't say *they* had it hard. You said *Bev.*"

"Well, look, I don't know. It's a way of talking. I'm sure it was the same for Gene."

"How long did they live there?"

"A year? Maybe a little more? Longer than the others. Maybe because he was an actual lab employee. Makes you wonder how he finagled it."

"They moved out after the fire."

"There was no choice. The place was a disaster."

"What do you remember from that night?"

"It was terrifying. Everyone was terrified. I was asleep, and my dad ran in and dragged me out of bed and into the street in my nightgown. Up and down the block people started coming out to see what was going on. There I was, standing half-naked. I was mortified. I wanted to go back in and get my robe but the firemen wouldn't let me."

A teenager's priorities. The sting of it seemed as sharp as ever.

"We went down the block to the home of a woman in my mother's reading club. She gave me a blanket and let us wait in her kitchen until they gave us permission to go back inside."

"Was your house damaged?"

"There was scorching on a few roof shingles. One bathroom window faces the property line, the glass broke from the heat. Also water damage, from the hoses. It ruined some wallpaper. It could have been much worse."

"Did the authorities ever interview you about it?"

"Not me."

"Your parents?"

"Maybe. I don't know."

"What about right after the kidnapping? Did anyone talk to you then?"

"No. Why would they? Gene and Bev didn't live here anymore."

"You had a relationship with them—"

"I told you. Not a deep one. It was situational. We didn't . . . We weren't pen pals."

"Okay," I said. "You remember hearing about the kidnapping, though."

"Of course. You don't forget a thing like that."

"How'd you find out?"

"What do you mean?"

"It wasn't in the papers," I said. "Do you recall who told you?"

She had to think. "My mom, probably. That's a guess, I don't remember."

"How would she have found out?"

"I really have no idea. Why are you asking me all this?"

"Just trying to collect information for Peter. Sorry if it's intrusive."

She tapped a foot, but she didn't leave. Maybe she craved human contact of any sort.

I said, "Did you ever meet Gene's children from his first marriage?"

She shook her head.

"He had a son, Norman, and a daughter, Claudia. They would have been a little older than you."

"I just said I never met them."

"What about Chrissy Klausen? Did you know her?"

A seam of dread opened in her face.

She said, "Who's that?"

Bad liar. The will simply wasn't there.

"Chrissy Klausen," I said. "She was the Franchettes' nanny."

The breeze brought a heady gust of jasmine. It grows all over Berkeley, all over California; it's hardy and attractive and inexpensive, and it smells wonderfully exotic, transporting you to a gentle place, a place of repose.

Diane Olsen treadled her flip-flops, as though fleeing in place.

Behind her the house was dim, its rancid breath heightened against the perfume of the jasmine.

I said, "May I come in?"

CHAPTER 23

S he had cats. I didn't need to see them to know; I crossed the threshhold and my eyes began watering.

Coroner's cases can involve some pretty wretched living conditions. Usually I pop an antihistamine before work. On my own time, I hadn't thought to.

I trailed Diane Olsen through the blurry living room and into a galley kitchen, where terra-cotta tile instead of carpeting granted a measure of relief. On the banquette table was a knobby, magenta tumbler and a tablet open to a game of Scrabble. On the floor, bowls of water and kibble. Personalized: URSULA and CALLIOPE.

The countertop radio murmured NPR. She switched it off and took a bottle of pomegranate juice from the fridge, offering me a seat but nothing more.

With her glass refilled, she leaned against the counter. "You didn't bring your daughter along with you this time."

I smiled. "No."

She forced a seasick smile in return.

Relying on me to initiate.

I said, "Tell me about Chrissy."

"What do you want to know?"

"Were you friends?"

"In a manner of speaking." She rubbed her lips. "We weren't on equal footing. She was older. Nineteen or twenty. To me she was this glamorous figure."

"I'm told she was pretty."

"She was a freak. I mean that positively. She had what every girl wanted. Long straight blond hair, gorgeous white teeth, perfect tan. Straight out of *Seventeen* magazine. She didn't even look real. But not stuck-up, like you'd expect. Even to me, with zits, this hair . . . I was amazed she took an interest in me."

"Why did she, do you think?"

Diane Olsen snorted. "Pure pity." She took a deep swallow of juice. "She was bored. I was the closest available source of entertainment."

"She didn't like her job."

"No. She . . . I mean, she loved Peggy. She'd been with her from the very beginning. But it was hard for her, being trapped in the house all day with a baby."

"Trapped."

"Bev wouldn't let them leave."

"At all?"

"They were allowed to go a few blocks. But there's not much to do around here. It's not a walking neighborhood."

"Did Bev give a reason why?"

"Not that I heard. I suppose she was afraid something might happen." She looked straight at me. "And it did."

"Maybe the fire made her nervous."

"No, I told you, they moved after the fire. She already had these rules in place before that."

"Was the family ever threatened?"

"I told you that, too. I never heard of anything. Everything I knew, I got secondhand."

"From Chrissy."

Diane nodded.

Peter had attributed his mother's hovering nature to the emotional scar tissue of losing a child. But maybe the roots ran deeper.

Five years between her marriage to Gene and Peggy's birth.

Miscarriages? A previous death?

More than one tragedy to prime and feed a young mother's nerves?

Diane Olsen drained her glass and began rolling it between her palms. "What it came down to was Chrissy was starved for company. I don't care how bright a child is, there's only so much conversation you can have."

"What about Bev? Chrissy didn't talk to her?"

"The way Chrissy described it, Bev hardly came out of her bedroom."

Mother's little helpers.

All the ladies did them.

I said, "Sounds like depression."

"I'm not a psychiatrist. But I don't know what else you'd call it. She shut herself in. She had Chrissy working unreasonably long hours. Weekends, too."

"Did Chrissy live in?"

"No. She took the bus in the morning and left late at night."

"Do you remember where she lived?"

"I don't know that she ever told me. I want to say somewhere by campus, but I couldn't tell you where I'm getting that from. I certainly never went there. We didn't see each other outside of . . . It was situational."

Given the origins of Gene and Beverly's marriage, no mystery why she wouldn't want an attractive young woman sleeping in the next room.

And yet Bev needed help. Constantly.

So many conflicting anxieties.

Take this baby from me, please.

But not too far.

I asked if anything had ever taken place between Chrissy and Gene.

Diane Olsen sighed. "Right. It's just, the assumptions men make.

Pretty girl, of course there'd have to be hanky-panky. But there wasn't. Chrissy wasn't like that."

"You knew her well enough to say that."

"Like I said, wasn't a peer relationship. Frankly, I kind of worshipped her. They'd drop by after I'd gotten home from school. Or on Saturday morning or Sunday. I wasn't a social butterfly, so to have this magnificent creature wanting to hang out with me—I was thrilled. Anyone would be."

"What about Peggy? You mentioned she was bright."

"Yes. At least I think so. 'Alert' might be more accurate."

"What else can you tell me about her? What kind of child was she?"

"What *kind* . . . ? Cute. Sweet. I wasn't really focused on her."

"How about physically?"

"The first time you were here, you showed me a photo of her."

"Her face isn't visible, and it's the only image we've found."

Diane Olsen sighed again, rubbed her eyes. "Well. She was blond, I remember that. Not that that means much. My daughter was blond as a baby, it turned dark when she was three. They're always changing. You must be familiar with that."

I smiled. "Definitely. Those afternoons and weekends, how did the three of you spend your time?"

"Talking. Listening to music. We'd lie out on a blanket, while Peggy crawled around the yard. Of course I always ended up getting burned to a crisp."

"What did you talk about?"

"Whatever girls talk about. It was mostly a one-sided conversation. I did a lot of blabbering. I told Chrissy about boys I liked, and she'd give me advice. Which I couldn't use, because it assumed you looked like her. Sometimes they'd come over to our house. The Franchettes didn't keep a lot of toys around, and we had a closet full of stuff my parents had never bothered getting rid of. A hobbyhorse, with my name painted on it. It's not normal, is it? Not having toys for a child. Who does that?"

Good question. I said, "Different parenting styles, I guess."

"That's a nice way of putting it. We took short walks. The same four square blocks, over and over, because that's all Bev would allow. It was like a hamster wheel. Chrissy must've felt like she was going bonkers."

"Nineteen years old," I said. "Did she go to school part-time?"

"Not when I knew her. Before she started with the Franchettes, I think she'd done a semester or two and decided it wasn't for her. She talked about having big dreams."

"Of?"

"She was going to be a folk singer, or an actress. She probably could've. She looked a little like—never mind, it's before your time."

"Try me."

"Peggy Lipton? From *The Mod Squad*?"

"Sorry."

"See, I told you. Google her, you'll see what I mean. Anyway, one day it was showbiz, the next it was get married and have ten children of her own. How much can you know about yourself at nineteen?"

"Did she ever mention a boyfriend? Talk about her own family?"

She shook her head.

"Was she from the Bay Area?"

"No idea. She had a certain mystique, which added to her cool. People loved to talk about rejecting the mainstream—'tune in, turn on, drop out.' She actually followed through."

"Speaking of which, any drug use?"

"What she did in her spare time, I don't know. But not around me. She was always responsible with Peggy. Look, I wish I had exciting stories to tell you, but I don't. It was . . . innocent."

She nibbled at the rim of her juice glass.

My nose was running something fierce. I looked around for a box of tissues. The nearest substitute was a roll of paper towels, on the ledge over the sink. But it had taken her long enough to gin up the courage to talk, and I didn't want to disrupt her reverie.

"I don't think she realized what she was getting into," she said. "Taking that job."

"How so?"

"Just what I told you. Bev's depression. Being cooped up."

"Any other issues?"

She stiffened. I thought she might bite the glass in half.

"You're asking the wrong person," she said. "Talk to Chrissy."

"I'd love to. I can't find her. Did she get married and change her name?"

"I don't know. How would I know that?"

"Was Chrissy short for something? Christine, Christina?"

"I called her Chrissy. Please," she said, desperately, "it was fifty years ago."

From the living room crept a pair of longhaired cats, one gray and the other tiger-striped. Ursula and Calliope. They wound figure-eights through Diane Olsen's ankles. She set the glass down and bent to pet them, her spine knuckling through her T-shirt. They purred, luxuriating under her touch, rolling on the cracked tile and blackened grout.

She straightened up. The cats padded to their bowls.

She took a breath and met my eye. "Chrissy was concerned."

"About."

"The general atmosphere. Gene and Bev fought like dogs. My bedroom's on that side of the house, the walls are paper-thin. I could hear them shouting at each other. Hear Gene throwing things."

"Was there physical violence?"

"I only know what Chrissy told me. She thought it was an unhealthy environment for a child. It's common knowledge now what that does to a developing brain. You carry it into adulthood."

"Why didn't she quit?"

"She felt she couldn't abandon Peggy. She was big on positive energy, karma, cosmic vibrations, all that junk. She didn't approve of what Gene did for work. If you'd asked me I would've said I didn't like it, either. But I'd met so many of these scientists over the

years, and to me they came across as harmless. For Chrissy—she
wasn't alone in this—it all tied together: the war, women's rights,
the kind of father he was."

Everything in Berkeley's political.

Except politics. That's personal.

"Then they had the fire, and the whole situation felt much more
urgent. Now we're not just talking about psychological damage, it's
real danger. Chrissy would say—but she was fantasizing. I didn't
give it a second thought. I mean, it would've been ridiculous for me
to . . ."

Outside, a truck rumbled by. Birdsong fell from the redwoods.

I said, "Fantasizing about?"

Diane Olsen turned away to stare at the cats, lazing in a dollop
of sunlight.

"I used to get a ride home from school with a classmate," she
said. "They'd drop me at their house on Spruce, and I'd cut through
on the footpaths the rest of the way. The Franchettes' new house
was over on Keith, and sometimes I made a detour and went past,
just in case I might run into Chrissy. I never knocked, or went in, but
I always hoped I'd catch them in the front yard, or . . . I missed her.
Spending time with her."

I nodded.

"That's what I did, on the day of the kidnapping. I was crossing
at the end of their block, and I saw an ambulance and police cars.
Nobody would tell me anything. I ran home to tell my mom. She
tried to call Bev, but a man answered, not Gene. He wouldn't talk to
her, either."

*We kept waiting on a phone call; a ransom note or a letter to the
press.*

"I was sobbing, I was so worried."

"About Chrissy?"

"About all of them. They already had this terrible thing happen
to them, and now . . . I made my mom call the hospitals. That's how
I learned Chrissy was at Alta Bates. The next day I cut class and

went to see her. I brought her flowers. It broke my heart to see her like that. She had these stitches on her cheeks, I was so afraid for her that they'd scar. They had her on drugs for the pain. It was hard for her to talk. I didn't know what to say. I wanted to be cheerful. She always made me feel good, I wanted to do the same for her. 'Don't worry, they're going to find her.' I didn't believe what I was saying. I just kept talking, and saying things like that. 'Don't worry, they'll get her back.' Chrissy, her beautiful face . . . I started to cry again. Now she's the one consoling me. She squeezed my hand and said, 'It'll be all right.' I thought we were both pretending, trying to radiate good karma or whatever. I didn't want to bum her out. So I went along with it. 'Sure, she'll be fine.' 'She's safe, Diane.' 'Yeah, I know she is.' Then she began tugging on my hand, hard, to get my attention. She was smiling in this very odd way. I can't describe . . . I saw, I thought I saw, this sort of . . . glee. Like she was letting me in on a joke.

"She said, 'She'll be happier now.' "

Diane Olsen fell silent.

I said, "You took that to mean . . ."

"I was confused. It was such a bizarre thing to think, let alone say. Happier than what? I thought maybe she meant Peggy had died and gone to a better place. Or the medication was making her ramble. But she kept squeezing my hand, and then she started giggling, like she expected me to join in."

"And then?"

"She got tired and fell asleep. I sat there for a while and then I left."

"What happened the next time you saw her?"

"There was no next time. I tried to check up on her. I wanted to know how she was doing. And I felt it eating at me, what she'd said. I walked down to the Franchettes' house. Bev answered the door and stared at me. I said, 'I'm Lillian Olsen's daughter. Is Chrissy around?' It was a stupid thing to say. Of course she wasn't around. They didn't need a nanny anymore. I wasn't thinking. I should've asked how they were, or if I could help them. But before I could say anything else, Bev just slapped me."

She reeled a bit, steadying herself against the counter. "Right across the face. I couldn't believe it."

"Did you tell anyone?"

"No. I was ashamed. Of my stupid question."

"Did you tell anyone about what Chrissy said in the hospital?"

"Who would I tell?"

"Your parents. The police."

"Tell them what? That she was doped up and said something strange? No one cared what I thought about anything. I didn't want my dad calling me melodramatic. I didn't want to get Chrissy in trouble. She was a good person. That's all I ever saw, a good person."

Her voice was agonized. The acolyte's undying faith.

"The men who did it, they hurt her so badly." She blinked back tears. "It didn't make any sense for her to . . . And the police were already looking for Peggy, they didn't need me getting in their way. I forgot about it. That's what I did. You can't sit there day after day, questioning reality."

You ever notice, it's decent folks who can't stop blaming themselves, while the bad ones go around with a spring in their step?

She lunged for the window ledge and seized the paper towels. She wrapped a length around her hand, like a medic binding a gash, and ripped it free.

The cats sprang up and darted from the room.

"I don't know," she said. She blew her nose. "I don't know anything."

CHAPTER 24

On my way home I stopped at Codornices Park, site of the kidnapping.

It's a rolling nook, ten acres in the shape of a taco. There's a softball field, a basketball court, a thread-worn play area, and—set into the hillside, snaking beneath the arms of a colossal California live oak—a fifty-foot concrete slide.

Everything about it seemed intended to cause injury. The congested staircase, made of packed earth and pavers, that led to the upper platform. The surface of the concrete, nicked and gouged and studded with pebbles, so rough you had to go down sitting on a piece of cardboard, which in turn made for a ride so slick and harrowing that you could easily spin out, skin an elbow, chip a tooth.

Buddy Hopewell was right. Hard to imagine anyone designing such a thing for children, harder still to understand how it had survived into the age of cushioned tot lots and class-action lawsuits.

Yet as I approached, I saw a long line of kids fidgeting with collapsed Amazon Prime boxes tucked under arms or between knees. Mothers, fathers, and nannies waited at the bottom, bellowing encouragement, iPhones set to record in slo-mo.

A little danger, I thought, was precisely the point. To a modern parent—for whom every substance turned out to be toxic and every misstep threatened permanent damage and nullified a child's chances at college or anything resembling a normal, happy life—willingness to let Avery or Stella or Liam engage in some reckless fun, and then to post that fun on social media, proved: Hey, you're not that uptight, after all.

The slide's very nature as a throwback validated it.

It had been there forever. Nobody had died.

From the foot of the slide I could make out cars crawling along Euclid, hunting for parking. Buddy had estimated the distance to the street at a hundred fifty yards. In reality it was about half that. Still too far away to read a license plate, though. Color and general shape was about the best you could do.

But Chrissy hadn't been here when she saw the sedan.

She'd been up on the platform, getting the tar beaten out of her.

I started for the steps.

The oak tree was an impressive piece of creation, forty feet tall and twice as broad, with coarse grayish skin covered in knotholes and moss. Part elephant, part octopus, it swung its tentacles in search of prey, one thick branch blocking the staircase at chest height. I ducked under and excused myself up through the line of kids, drawing nervous stares. A single man, at the park, taking notes and photos? Charlotte would've provided good cover.

Standing at the top of the slide, I imagined the struggle between Chrissy and the two men. A skimpy safety rail made of welded pipe ran along the platform edge. Not much of a barrier: even an adult could fit through the gaps, and the rail ended several feet shy of the steps. She could have gone through or around it. Below, a series of retaining walls, varying between two and four feet high, terraced the hillside. The oak rooted on the second terrace from the bottom. In Buddy's recollection of Chrissy's recollection, it was there that she'd crash-landed.

The vertical drop to the tree was about twenty feet, enough to break a leg.

I found it more difficult to account for the horizontal distance she'd covered. There were eight terraces in all, each about three feet deep. A person falling off the platform would land atop the nearest one. Maybe, if they'd been pushed very hard, they'd make it as far out as the second terrace.

The idea that a single shove could have resulted in Chrissy hitting the tree was cartoon physics. She would've had to fall and bounce and roll, fall and bounce and roll—six times in all.

Bodies don't behave like that.

I should know. I've handled thousands of them.

Nor did it make sense that her attacker could have picked her up and heaved her through the air.

As to how she'd gotten from point A to point B, I saw two explanations.

One was that she had done the rolling herself.

Or she hadn't fallen at all and had gotten her injuries some other way.

Did descriptions get any more generic than "one black guy" and "one white guy"?

They hurt her so badly.

It didn't make any sense for her to . . .

"Excuse me, mister."

I stood back, allowing a towheaded kid to squeeze by.

The more I thought about it, the quicker the questions popped up, leaching the substance out of Chrissy Klausen's account.

Despite getting the tar beat out of her, she'd managed to witness the white guy getting into a dark sedan with Peggy.

I couldn't see a damn thing. Just like at Maryanne's house. Too much foliage. Bad angle.

Maybe Buddy was misremembering. Maybe Chrissy had spotted the car from below, after she'd already fallen.

I ducked under the safety rail and clambered down to the base of the tree.

I crouched to simulate the position of a woman writhing with a broken leg.

No dice.

Scores of other trees and a severe rise in the terrain created a total blind.

There was simply no way she could have seen the car. Any car.

BILLY WATTS SAID, "Their story: It wasn't them."

We stood together on Maryanne's front lawn. The boarded-up window glared like a rotten tooth. It turned out that while you could replace an ordinary pane that same day, matching a vintage piece of stained glass required a specialty art glazier and a lead time measured in months.

"They didn't come anywhere near here," Watts said. "They don't know where you live. They don't know what you're talking about. They'd never do a thing like that."

"Sure they would. They've done tons of shit precisely like this."

"You don't need to tell me that. I read their sheets. What do you want me to do? There's no prints on the brick. None of your neighbors saw anything. Nobody's got a security camera. The nail polish is nail polish. You want to call Quantico, be my guest."

I already had several unanswered calls and emails in to the FBI. I did not want to call Quantico.

Watts said, "I went out there. I talked to them. Maybe that'll be enough. And—by the way, let's you and I take a moment to acknowledge my doing that, because I am definitely the first person of color to cross that fence and make it out alive."

"Thank you."

"It's the inbreeding Olympics over there," Watts said.

"Appreciate your doing it."

"White Trash Disneyland."

"I deeply appreciate your taking the time."

He grinned. "Brady Brunch on meth. How's your landlady doing?"

"Okay, I think. She was nice enough not to evict us."

"You pay for her window?"

"I keep trying. She won't let me. I asked her what it cost and she quoted me a number that's gotta be a tenth of the real price."

"So write a check for ten times that."

"That's what my wife said."

"How's your wife?"

For the past couple of weeks, I'd been monitoring Amy for signs of disquiet. She was subtle, but I had no doubt she was doing the same for me, both of us working overtime to conceal our distress from each other.

"She's a trouper," I said. "Billy, I really am grateful for what you did."

"Don't even trip. It's my pleasure. You can't do that shit to a cop. Now, about that."

I looked at him.

"You want me to help you out," he said, "you got to do the same."

"Meaning?"

"I spoke to Dale. He was pretty worked up about you paying them a second visit. Hold up. Hold up," he said, putting out his palms. "I'm not saying I'd feel differently in your shoes. It's your family and your home. But you called me. It's my problem now."

"All I did was take a drive."

"Find somewhere else to do that."

"I didn't go on the property."

"Don't go anywhere near them. Okay? Your sake and mine."

"I honestly didn't think he noticed me."

"Oh, he noticed you all right. He said—lemme see, how'd he phrase it." Watts pretended to consult his notes, rubbing his chin comically. "Ahem, yes. 'You let that turd-sniffing piece of shit know he has an open invitation.'"

"Poetry," I said.

Maryanne's bedroom light came on.

I said, "You think I made things worse?"

"I don't think you calmed them down any. Don't underestimate these assholes. But at least they know we're paying attention to them. They'd be real fuckin stupid to move now. So do me and you and everyone a favor and don't throw any more fuel on the fire. I know you got your image to uphold."

"What image."

"The vigilante cowboy thing. Listen, it's action you want, we got tons of openings."

Berkeley PD was in the midst of a staffing crisis that had cut its ranks by a third, as officers fled for other municipalities, the private sector, retirement.

I said, "We could do an exchange program. You become a coroner."

"Disgusting," Watts said. Then he reconsidered. "How's your benefits?"

ALL ACROSS PEOPLE'S Park, the earth coughed up a bumper crop of brambles and weeds. The free food cart was back. You could get free socks on Free Sock Saturday. Concerts had been scheduled. Reggae All-Stars and a Joan Baez tribute. There was still no stage, but the items in the Free Speech Pit had broken loose of their confines, the buildup creeping over the lawn in concentric circles.

Lamps and carpets and rocking chairs; tents, tarps, sleeping bags; an extension cord superhighway.

The blue bear continued to sit there, untouched.

For a second time, Judge Sharon Feeley of the Alameda County Superior Court declined to lift the injunction prohibiting construction. But this time there was a catch, one that provided a glimmer of hope for UC: The judge called for an archaeological site survey to be performed by a qualified and independent expert. Said expert must be chosen by mutual agreement between the university and the Defenders of the Park, with costs split evenly between the two parties. The survey must be completed within six months, or else work would be permitted to resume.

However slowly, she'd set the clock ticking, sowing disorder among the numerous grassroots organizations who had never given consent for Trevor Whitman, Sarah Whelan, or Chloe Bellara to speak on their behalf.

The Defenders announced, via Instagram, the receipt of five thousand dollars toward the expert's fee. Almost immediately they had to give the money back, when it emerged that the anonymous donor was a coalition of NIMBYist property managers who had previously lobbied against construction of the dorm.

Soon after, Chloe Bellara announced on her personal Instagram that, due to irreconcilable visions, she had severed ties with Trevor Whitman and Sarah Whelan and was leaving the Defenders to form a new group, the People's Park Alliance. A number of former Defenders joined the exodus. *Follow us on Instagram.*

The Alliance's first move was to file for a separate injunction in federal court. The second move was to occupy the steps of University House, the chancellor's residence, barricading her front door with sandbags and cinder blocks and playing 24/7 Justin Bieber.

Trevor Whitman posted on his personal Instagram that Chloe had "allowed her ego to wreak immeasurable damage."

An anonymous Redditor revealed that Whitman's uncle worked as an engineer for a petroleum conglomerate. Sarah Whelan, also a child of privilege, had attended Stanford.

The infighting began to erode morale. There had never been a clear leader in the cleanup efforts; no discussion about what a rebuilt People's Park ought to look like. Everyone claimed to prefer a more hands-off approach. These things happened organically. That had been true in 1969, as well. But whatever corny sense of unity had prevailed back then was less attainable for tribes of the digital age.

What arose, organically, was conflict.

A fight broke out between some parkies and a group of volunteers clearing rubble from the basketball courts, ending with one woman being carted off to the hospital with knife wounds. Someone set fire to the flower beds. One of the two remaining tree-sitters slipped and fell to the sidewalk, fracturing his cervical spine and inducing the final tree-sitter to desert her post.

A sixteen-year-old girl attending a summer enrichment program at Cal was groped and had her laptop snatched as she stood by the Maybeck Church, shooting footage of the homeless encampment for Introduction to Documentary Film and Video.

Florence Sibley called me. "The company that manufactured the teddy bear. I found them."

I scrolled through my phone, bringing up the photo I'd taken of the bear's tag. "'Marjorie's Menagerie.'"

"That's the distributor. Look below that."

Kuwagong Happiness Co. (H.K.) Ltd.
Kowloon, Hong Kong
Reg No. PA-2739 (HK)

The owl and owlet logo.

"They're defunct," Sibley said. "However. You ever hear of the Consumer Product Safety Commission? They're the ones who issue product recalls."

"I think my wife has them bookmarked."

"They started operating in '72. 'Seventy-three, there's a press release. One guess who it's about."

"The Kuwagong Happiness Company."

"Gold star for you."

The text of the release was archived on the agency website, way back on the nine hundred forty-fifth page of results. Sibley had come across it while attempting to track down the distributor.

CPSC Warns of Choking Dangers from
Kuwagong Happiness Co. Stuffed Animals

For immediate release

August 28, 1973

Release # 73-038

Washington, D.C. (August 28)—Citing the potential for suffocation hazard, the Consumer Product Safety Commission today warned consumers to discard stuffed animals and dolls manufactured by the Kuwagong Happiness Company, which is based in Hong Kong.

The toys are distributed nationwide by Marjorie's Menagerie, San Francisco, Calif., and Anderson Far East Imported Goods, New Haven, Conn., two mail-order firms.

The toys incorporate glass and plastic elements such as eyes, ears and noses. CPSC Chairman Richard O. Simpson said that shoddy stitching can cause these pieces to come loose, particularly when chewed on by infants, small children, or pets. The shape and size of the pieces create a risk for swallowing or asphyxiation.

In the last year, Simpson said, nine children have been hospitalized due to injuries sustained from the toys. In May, a six-month-old child died after inhaling a plastic eye that became lodged in his airway.

Simpson criticized the manufacturer as well as their United States distributors for failing to withdraw the products, even after numerous warnings and reports of injury. The products, he said, are imminently hazardous.

A complete list of the affected products follows.

"I'm not gonna say, 'There's your cause of death,'" Sibley said. "But."

The mother walking in, finding the baby gray.

Freaking out.

Needing to be rid of it.

Each year, six thousand children under the age of one die in accidents.

"Fantastic work," I said.

"Aw, shucks."

"I'm going to show this to my sergeant," I said. "I'll give you credit."

"Well, whatever. I just feel better knowing. Obviously, it ain't good what she did. But in a way it makes me want to find her even more. All this time she's been living under a cloud. She deserves to know it wasn't her fault."

"How's that going?" I asked. "Any traction?"

"Zip. The bear's still there. Every day I get a text with a map and a pin. Anything changes, you'll be the first to know."

"Thanks." I paused. "I'm trying to decide if I should tell Fritz Dormer. Anything beyond notification would be a courtesy, and I'm not feeling that courteous. On the other hand, once he knows it was an accident, he might stop worrying about being charged with a crime and give up something on the mother."

"Probably a waste of time," Sibley said. "I could send Tom out."

CHAPTER 25

I got a letter—an actual letter—from the FBI.

Regarding my Freedom of Information Act request, a search of the Central Records System maintained at FBI Headquarters had located potentially responsive records. A total of seven hundred ninety-four pages had been declassified and sent to the National Archives and Records Administration facility in College Park, MD, for further processing. If I wished to review these potentially responsive records, I should contact the archive, making reference to case . . .

I bushwhacked NARA's voicemail to reach an archivist named Julie Tallich in the Special Access room. She sounded young and articulate.

And harried. Under the best of circumstances, they had a mile-long backlog, and the recent government shutdown had buried them in unfulfilled requests.

She couldn't simply hand over the file. First someone had to sanitize it, line by line.

"Sanitize it for what? I thought it was declassified."

"All that means is the FBI doesn't object to the release of the information in a general sense. We still have to review it. Anything pertaining to living persons or that discloses protected operational methods has to be removed."

"How long will that take?"

"A file of that length typically takes a couple of weeks, a month at the outside. The issue is that there's a lot of requests ahead of yours. It could take a while before we begin."

"I'm afraid to ask what's 'a while.' "

"At the moment, we're three to five years out."

"Oh man."

"When it's ready we'll let you know. At that point you can either travel to College Park to view the records yourself, or we can send you hard copies. I should warn you that it's eighty cents a page, so it can get expensive."

I didn't think Peter Franchette would object to shelling out a few hundred bucks, assuming he could stomach the delay.

I couldn't. I phoned Special Agent Tracy Golden at the FBI resident agency in Oakland. She'd never responded to any of my attempts to follow up, and when I finally got her on the line she began hemming and hawing.

"I thought I emailed the listserv for you."

"You did. I was able to meet with the original agent. He's super sharp, super helpful. I appreciate the connect."

"Sure thing. Glad to help."

"You know how memories are, though. I'd still like to see the file, if possible."

"Did you try FOIA?"

"By the time it gets to me my daughter will be able to read it."

"How old's your daughter?" she said.

"Eight and a half months. Do me a solid. Please."

Tracy Golden blew out air. "You got some balls, you know that?"

Ten days later, she called to let me know that she had it, all seven hundred ninety-four pages.

I offered to drop by her office.

"Better I come to you," she said.

That evening at the Coroner's Bureau, I went down to the darkened lobby and unlocked the doors. Tracy Golden was in her midthirties, five-foot-one in low pumps, with a deep tan and a dishwater-colored haircut ten years too old. She fizzed with nervous energy, her credentials swinging on a neck lanyard, a turquoise-and-silver pendant playing peekaboo behind.

At her feet sat a huge, shabby cardboard box.

"No copies," she said.

"Understood. Thanks. I'll have it back to you as soon as I can."

She seemed to be wavering: weighing the benefit of helping me against its potential cost, and coming up short.

Before she could change her mind, I picked up the box and gave her my best crowd-pleasing smile. "Thanks again. I owe you two."

She scurried back to her car, continually checking over her shoulder.

YOU CAN TELL a lot about an organization from how it keeps its records. Who's writing? What's preserved? What's not?

I'd never read an FBI case file before. You couldn't knock them for lack of thoroughness. Every move Buddy Hopewell and Phil Shumway made—every thought that crossed their minds—became the basis for a report, in turn touching off a torrent of forms, memoranda, airtels, cablegrams. Each communication dragged along cover letters and administrative pages and daisy-chained reference copies of previous paperwork, much of it out of order, chronologically. Documents documented the issuance of other documents. When in doubt, write it down. Better too much than too little.

It was like watching a person wade through a mud lake, steadily accumulating mass, until he emerges on the other side monstrously ballooned.

In the explosion of paper I saw the hand of Assistant Special Agent in Charge Francis Ingles, the cover-your-ass mentality fear produces. I thought of Tracy Golden's jitters, and I wondered how much the culture had evolved since the days when Buddy watched his boss reduce a man to tears over a clerical error.

A sense of self-importance came through, as well, the desire to preserve everything for posterity, while simultaneously erecting a wall of jargon to keep outsiders out. *We're the goddamn FBI.* Every law enforcement agency—every group of humans—is guilty of this to some extent. We speak in code because it's more efficient and because it infuses bureaucratic drudgery with a bit of esprit de corps.

The FBI house style was formal, heavily seasoned with acronyms and referring to the agents in third person, as though they had a camera crew on them while they worked.

> On April 21, 1970, SAS MILTON W. HOPEWELL and PHILIP J. SHUMWAY established a FISUR of the residence of JANICE LITTLE, 2119 Ward St., Berkeley.

FISUR, I discovered, was physical surveillance—as opposed to MISUR (microphone surveillance) or TESUR (technical surveillance).

> At 11:40 AM JANICE LITTLE was observed to leave her residence. Ms. LITTLE was approached by these agents and asked if she was Ms. LITTLE. She turned away from them and began walking west toward Shattuck Avenue. The agents accompanied her along the sidewalk and identified themselves as Special Agents of the Federal Bureau of Investigation. Ms. LITTLE replied "I know who you are, pigs" and turned north onto Shattuck Avenue. The agents advised Ms. LITTLE that federal statute makes it a crime for anyone to willingly or knowingly make false statements to, or to conceal information material to an investigation from, agents of the United States government. Ms. LITTLE stated in a loud voice "Get fucked." Ms. LITTLE then entered the Ajna Third Eye bookstore located at 2715 Shattuck Avenue. The agents elected not to continue into the bookstore. FISUR was terminated at 11:46 AM.

I laughed, picturing Buddy typing this up about himself.

Milton.

Who'd have guessed?

More isn't always more. Bloat made the file's length deceptive, and once I learned to screen out redundancies, I was able to move quickly, mining snippets of useful information from within the filler.

I found the Berkeley Fire Department report, brief and thin on detail. The narrative alluded to a canvass. But there were no names given, and no follow-up, presumably because Buddy and Phil had swooped in before it could be completed. The local PD reports were likewise stunted. It amazed me to realize that there'd been a time when you could cauterize the flow of information by stealing a stack of paper.

I found Norman Franchette's FD-302 interview form, in which he was described as displaying an aggressive demeanor. Subsequent surveillance observed him purchasing the April and May issues of *Gent* magazine.

I found a list of subversives the agents had questioned—thirty-one in total, all of whom reacted exactly as Janice Little had. Reports bearing Buddy's name at the top dutifully recorded each *fuck* and *cocksucker* and *asshole*. Phil Shumway preferred to write that the subject had "employed profanity."

On April 6, 1970, confidential informant T-9, of known reliability, attested that the fire at the Franchettes' was not the work of Little or her boyfriend, Jake Rosen. *They're too smart for that* the informant said. Buried in that same report was the earliest reference to Chrissy Klausen: A single line noted her Friday-night alibi.

Visiting sister for weekend, confirmed telephonically.

As far as I could see, nobody had ever spoken to Claudia or Helen Franchette.

The initial report on the kidnapping noted Peggy Franchette's date of birth as February 9, 1969. She had straight hair, medium blond to brown, and dark-brown eyes. At the time of abduction, per her most recent pediatric exam, she weighed twenty-two pounds, four ounces, and was twenty-six-and-a-half inches tall. She had five teeth, three upper and two lower. She was last seen wearing a pale yellow dress, white socks, white shoes, and a diaper.

Paper-clipped to the corner was a small snapshot with scalloped edges.

In point of fact it didn't add much to the written description. The color was washed out and the focus barely adequate. She wasn't smiling. I assumed they'd chosen it because it was the most up-to-date.

Simply to see her face, however, took my breath away.

I went through the batch of Franchette family photos Peter Franchette had given me, comparing each of them with Peggy.

Family resemblances are elusive. They evolve over time and draw on our expectations. Recently, while playing with Charlotte, I'd been startled to catch a glimpse of Amy's dad. It's an uncanny sensation, to look down and realize you're tickling your father-in-law.

Made to choose, I would say that Peggy Franchette favored her mother.

No copies.

Nobody said anything about *no pictures.*

Next time, Agent Golden, choose your words more carefully.

I took out my phone and switched to the camera.

MOVING ON, I came upon more photos: thick, creased black-and-whites of Codornices Park, X'd in pen at the site of the struggle between Chrissy and the two men.

I read Buddy's report on his visit with Chrissy in the hospital, where she was being treated for multiple lacerations to the face and hands, three fractured ribs, and a fractured tibia. By and large the story she told him conformed to the one he'd told me. The white guy was older and wore jeans and a baseball cap. The black guy had an Afro. When they ran at her, she misunderstood, thinking they wanted her wallet, or to drag her into the bushes and rape her. She tried to get away, but they cornered her. She put Peggy down behind her and used her body to block the men. She didn't want Peggy to get hurt; she needed to be able to defend herself. But that was a mistake, a horrible mistake. If she'd only held on to Peggy instead, she might've been able to stop the white man from picking her up and running off.

The subject cried as she spoke. After forty minutes she expressed discomfort and fatigue and a desire to rest, and Special Agent Milton W. Hopewell terminated the interview.

There was no mention of a dark sedan.

Maybe it had come up later.

I skimmed back, skimmed ahead.

Buddy and Phil had interviewed Chrissy three more times, once with the sketch artist, once as a follow-up, and the last time with a psychiatrist.

The facial composites Chrissy had helped to create were strikingly old-fashioned, almost romantic, drawn freehand in pencil and pastel.

One nondescript black guy with an Afro. One nondescript white guy in a hat.

The psychiatrist, Dr. James H. Kayman, had written his own report. He spent nine pages delving into Chrissy's childhood. Under hypnosis, the patient had unearthed a history of molestation at the hands of her father, memories henceforth suppressed. The attack had revived the trauma; her response was to suppress that experience, as well. The more recent the memory, Kayman wrote, the more difficult its retrieval. *Consider the ease with which an old scab peels away, as opposed to a fresh wound, still bleeding.*

At no point did Chrissy say anything about a car.

I couldn't see the agents failing to record such an important detail. A lost page seemed more likely. But that's a pitfall of static data: You don't know what you don't know.

The one person who did bring up the car was the second eyewitness—the dog walker, named Floyd Neeley. He told Phil Shumway he'd been climbing Eunice Street when a sedan raced around the corner and tore off downhill, westbound. Navy blue or black. A Pontiac, though he wouldn't raise his hand to that. He wasn't able to describe the driver with any confidence. Nor had he noticed anyone else in the vehicle. He apologized. He hadn't paid it much mind. Only in retrospect, after he got a little closer to the park and heard the lady hollering her lungs out, did it seem to mean anything.

Reading this, I wondered if Buddy had conflated parts of Neeley's story with Chrissy's. If so—if Chrissy had never claimed to see a car—that cast doubts on my doubts about the veracity of her story.

But there was still the problem of the fall from the platform.

In spring 1975, the case went inactive. Francis Ingles signed the form making the change in status. From then on, the paper trail began to dwindle. When Buddy and Phil got on the horn for their annual review, it was Phil who rendered the terse verdict.

No further progress.

The penultimate document was a report dated February 19, 1988, describing an interview between Phil Shumway and Janice Little, at her home in the Oakland hills.

Times had changed. You could see it in the font, ever-so-slightly modernized. According to SA Shumway, the subject was cordial and candid. Gone was the Janice Little who skulked around federal property with lighter fluid and matches; who traveled to Cuba in defiance of a State Department ban, posing for photos with Raúl Castro; who had served fourteen months in federal prison for conspiracy and money laundering.

Now she was part owner of a sandwich shop that employed ex-convicts. She stated that she had always preferred peaceful forms of resistance.

Phil, too, had changed. His writing was freer. At times he lapsed into the first person.

The impetus for their conversation was the publication of Janice Little's autobiography, *Winds of Progress*. Phil had brought his

244 / JONATHAN KELLERMAN and JESSE KELLERMAN

copy with him, and at one point he read a passage aloud to her, which he quoted, unabridged, in the report.

"Around this time the cops really started to put the pressure on. They would hassle us for no good reason, coming to our door before dawn or calling us on the phone in the middle of the night. Jake and I talked it over, and we decided that it was for the best that we withdraw from direct action. We had to find other ways to help the movement, whether that meant writing or recruiting others to take up the reins. Leadership, I learned, means delegating. That lesson was slow to come to me, as I was the type of person who wanted to be on the front lines. But revolutions don't happen because of one or two individuals; they happen because the majority wakes up and realizes that things must change."

Who were the "others," Phil wanted to know. What had they been recruited for?

Janice Little demurred. She wasn't referring to any one person or event, just aiming to capture "the zeitgeist."

The report intrigued me, in part for its content, but more so because it existed in the first place. Shumway had taken the time to buy Janice Little's book and read it. If he wanted her requestioned, it would have been far more sensible to call Buddy in San Francisco and ask him to pop over the bridge.

Instead, Phil Shumway had gotten on a plane.

There was no indication that he'd told Buddy he was coming.

The final document in the file, also by Phil, was an investigative review from November of that same year. He opened with facts. Soon, however, the tone took an intensely personal turn, as Special Agent Philip J. Shumway reflected on nearly twenty years of futility.

In his opinion, they'd gotten it wrong, right from the jump. The need to identify a single perpetrator or group of perpetrators responsible for both the fire and the kidnapping had created a false set of constraints.

Buddy Hopewell had voiced a similar complaint, although not as plainly. More telling was the difference in how the agents evaluated themselves. I'd pressed Buddy about the political angle, and he'd shifted responsibility to Ingles, either to be circumspect or to insulate himself from criticism.

Phil Shumway, on the other hand, was unsparing in grading his own work.

This agent wishes to state for the record that he allowed himself to be led astray. A great deal of time was squandered that might have been spent pursuing other, better leads.

It was a quiet outburst, a career civil servant's cri de coeur.

As for what those better leads were, I caught sight in the final paragraph.

It is the belief of this agent that the investigation to the present moment has ignored the role of Ms. Klausen and that an effort should be made to ascertain her whereabouts with all possible expedience.

CHAPTER 26

"Oh, he hated Buddy."

Elaine Shumway paused. "Scratch that. I shouldn't have said that. It's unfair to Phil, because he didn't truly hate anyone. My husband wasn't a hateful person. I wish I could say the same about myself. He was much nicer than I am. So, no. I won't say hate."

I hadn't been able to find an obituary for Phil Shumway, either in the Boston papers or nationally. What caught my eye instead was an online newsletter put out by the Brookline ward of the Mormon Church, profiling the class of 2016's graduating seniors. Devyn Shumway was soon to depart for her mission in Colombia—an especially meaningful destination, because her grandfather, former FBI agent Philip Shumway, had also served his mission there.

I left a message at the LDS meetinghouse in Weston. By day's end Elaine had called me back. She spoke in measured, elegant beats, her voice nasal and girlish; blond, if voices could be blond.

She said, "How about this: He *disapproved* of Buddy."

"What specifically?"

"You name it. Drinking, smoking, swearing, the merry-go-round of girlfriends. Phil and I came from a different world. I was eighteen when we got married, he was twenty-four. We were living in Virginia at the time while he went to law school. We didn't see ourselves as unusual, because folks tended to get married younger, and anyway all our friends were like us. Next thing the Bureau hands him a letter and we're getting off a plane in San Francisco."

"Must've been a shock."

"Oh yes, yes. We had this tiny apartment in Laurel Heights. Our neighbor to the right played psychedelic music on his hi-fi, and the one to the left played soul music, and they would both keep raising the volume to try and drown each other out. It was like getting caught between two heavyweight boxers. I'd look out my window and be reminded of that painting, the one with all the . . . *The Garden of Earthly Delights*."

I smiled.

"For the first couple of weeks, I was afraid to go outside. Phil was gone at the Bureau morning till night. Our daughter, Hope, our eldest, she was about two then, and I wouldn't do much more than run down to the corner market for milk. Sooner or later I got an awful fit of cabin fever. I made up my mind to be brave and take her out. Somehow I got turned around and ended up wandering through the Haight."

"Wow."

"Wow is right. I'm pushing the carriage, flipping the map this way and that, steering around people sitting naked on the sidewalk. They'd feed drugs to their pets. It was so pathetic, dogs and cats rolling around like they were possessed. Even chickens, all stoned. Ask a person for directions and they'd look you in the eye in complete seriousness and tell you to travel inward."

"Sounds like an education."

"You said it. One month in San Francisco, I learned more than in all my years of schooling combined. I adjusted. We both did. You have to live in the world. That's part of what we believe. Remember, Phil spent two years in Bogotá, knocking on doors and asking strangers to invite him in. Tell the truth, I think he enjoyed mixing it up with the counterculture. It reinforced a sense of confidence in his own convictions. He was fond of Buddy in the beginning. They even went out and shot pool a few times, Buddy with his beer and Phil sipping orange juice." She laughed. "It started to grate, though. Buddy'd turn up for work hung over with lipstick on his shirt."

"I'm surprised the higher-ups tolerated it."

"They had to. The Bureau was trying to bring itself into the twentieth century, hire young agents who could get behind the scenes and not stand out like sore thumbs. Phil was a bit of an anachronism. But he was a wonderful man, and extremely dogged."

"I got that from reading the Franchette file."

"Yes," she said. "It bothered him until the end."

"Did he discuss the case with you? Either aspect, the kidnapping or the fire."

"Not really. He kept his work to himself. They had rules and he stuck to them. And I think he wanted to shield me from the ugliness he saw. He didn't like me to know he was frightened, or hurting, or . . . But I knew, of course. He was my husband."

I thought of my own wife and what she must know about me.

I chased that out of my head, telling Elaine about the final two items in the file, Phil's interview with Janice Little and the confessional case review.

"It ends on an unfinished note," I said. "Like he's leaving it for someone in the future."

"And you're that person?"

"I hope so, Mrs. Shumway."

"November '88, you said?"

"That's right."

"Phil passed that Christmas."

"I'm sorry."

"Thank you. We quarreled about that trip to California. I thought he was too sick to travel on his own. He'd been through so many rounds of radiation, he'd lost a huge amount of weight . . . I wanted to go with him, at least, but he said no, he needed to go by himself. I suppose he meant to clear his conscience. I doubt it worked."

"How sick was he?"

"If you're asking if he knew the end was near, the answer is yes, he did. We'd stopped treatment, and his doctors had told us it was a matter of weeks. That's another reason I didn't want him to go. 'You have a finite amount of time left, and this is how you want to spend it?' As it happened, he ended up hanging on a little longer."

"What did he have?"

"Esophageal cancer. The irony . . . He never touched alcohol or tobacco, he was a fitness fanatic, he ran the Boston Marathon eight times. Now take someone like Buddy, who you're telling me is still alive and kicking. I'm sorry. It's unkind to say. It's not as though there's some heavenly scale, and you can take Phil off one side and swap him out for Buddy. But."

"I understand."

She went quiet for a moment. Then: "Here's something I remember. Phil would always greet me with a smile when he got back from work. But there was one night, right around when the girl went missing, he came home hopping mad. I asked what the matter was, and he said Buddy had gone without him to talk to one of the witnesses."

"Did he say who?"

"I don't think he would've mentioned them by name. I didn't really understand what he was so upset about. He was walking around, pulling off his tie, sort of muttering to himself, and I heard him say—pardon my French—'Fuck her.' I'd never heard him talk like that. That's why it sticks with me, because it was so out of character. I must have looked appalled. Right away he snapped out of it and started apologizing."

I remembered young Buddy Hopewell's report from the hospital.

On July 29, 1970, SA MILTON W. HOPEWELL conducted an interview with CHRISSY KLAUSEN. The interview took place in room 192 of Alta Bates Hospital, 2450 Ashby Avenue, Berkeley. The subject was recovering from a physical assault that had taken place the day prior . . .

Old Buddy Hopewell, ruefully fingering his giant silver belt buckle.

I didn't have this big gut.

I did have a full head of hair and a royal blue Barracuda with racing stripes.

I loved that car. Girls loved it, too.

Nice-looking gal. No two ways about it.

"Do you think," I said, "and I apologize for the language—"

"Oh please. I'm a big girl."

"Any chance it could've been 'He's fucking her'? Something along those lines?"

"I don't know. Maybe. Is that what happened?"

"I don't know, either. Would Buddy do that?"

"I met him a handful of times," she said. "I always thought he was more talk than action."

"Phil didn't come out and accuse Buddy of wrongdoing."

"Not that I know of."

"Other than that, did he mention any other theories?"

"Not that I can recall."

"Did he keep his own private notes?"

"I'm not sure. I could look."

"Would you, please?"

"I'd be glad to."

"Thank you, ma'am. I'm very grateful."

"Of course," she said. "It's nice to talk about him. It brings me back to the kind of man he was. I have seventeen grandchildren, and four great-grandchildren, and none of them ever met him. The oldest was born a few months after he passed. Thirty years, and I'll still read about something that he'd like, and I'll think, 'I should tell Phil that.' "

CHAPTER 27

The remaining leadership of the Defenders of the Park and the University of California issued a joint statement. They had agreed upon an expert to conduct the archaeological site survey: Professor Iliana Marquez Rosales, of the Department of Anthropology, University of Washington.

Getting to that point had required several rounds of heated negotiation.

The Defenders accused UC of stalling.

The UC replied that the Defenders bore responsibility for any delay, having rejected two qualified candidates on grounds of race and gender.

The Defenders replied that those concerns were far from irrelevant. An individual linked to the existing power structure could only perpetuate the overweening privilege that had enabled the theft of the land in the first place.

Judge Feeley stepped in, threatening to fine both parties unless they worked it out.

Professor Marquez Rosales it was, then. BA from UCLA. MA from Oxford. PhD from Harvard. A Rhodes Scholar. A Guggenheim Fellow. Fieldwork in Ecuador, Colombia, Peru. She'd published a monograph on the intergenerational effects of wide-scale violence, which felt apt, given the local mood.

In an interview with *Berkeleyside,* she shared that her team had begun amassing historical maps and documents referring to the park or its environs, collating these materials with modern aerial photography and US Geological Survey data. In order to work freely, she had asked UC and the Defenders to assist in clearing the area of debris and furniture. She expected the excavation to start in July and last three to four weeks, during which time park access would be restricted. It was critical to maintaining the integrity of her findings, even if it meant that, unfortunately, the Joan Baez tribute would have to be postponed.

Everyone went berserk.

Flyers appeared on telephone poles. The bulldozers were coming. This time they wouldn't leave. The site survey was a sham—a Trojan horse to oust The People and undo the rebuilding process. The Defenders of the Park were a fifth column, holding ties not just to UC but to the larger system of oppression.

Meanwhile, citing a lack of jurisdiction, a federal court declined to rule on the injunction filed by Chloe Bellara's breakaway group, the People's Park Alliance. On her Instagram, Bellara uploaded an image of a lit Molotov cocktail. The post got three hundred likes and more than a thousand comments ranging from celebratory GIFs to death threats.

Two days later, in an astonishing coincidence, the UC Berkeley Subcommittee on Academic Standing suspended Bellara's graduate student status for failure to complete required coursework.

New flyers appeared, calling for riots.

Notice went out to UCPD, BPD, and the Sheriff's, placing active-duty personnel in a state of emergency readiness.

Billy Watts called me at work. "There's something you need to see."

FOR THE LAST month, he'd been looking into the knife attack that had taken place near the People's Park bathrooms. The victim was a twenty-seven-year-old woman named Holly Hayes, the on-again, off-again girlfriend of a forty-one-year-old parkie and small-time drug dealer named Malcolm Zane. For the most part Zane sold weed but he was also known to stock the occasional tab of Ecstasy or ketamine.

On the day of the stabbing, Zane and Hayes were hanging out, minding their own business. Hayes went inside to pee. Three men approached from the basketball courts, where they'd been removing rubble. They told Zane it was one thing to smoke, another to deal openly. Attracting the cops caused trouble for everyone. The future of the park hung in the balance. They demanded that Zane vacate the premises.

Zane had no intention of going anywhere. He'd been doing his thing, in peace, since the three of them were still shitting in their pants. Besides, wasn't any cops around. Chill out.

One of the men, a twenty-four-year-old white elementary school teacher named Jeremy Darby, bent down and grabbed the sleeve of Zane's jacket. Later Darby would state that he had done so in self-defense, in response to Zane reaching for his pocket and out of concern that Zane might be armed. Zane would state that he had made no such movement, and that Darby was for real trying to rob him, in broad fucking daylight.

A scuffle ensued. Zane escaped across Haste, where Darby caught up to him on the sidewalk, and, along with a second man, Oliver Ackermann (white, twenty-five years old, aspiring DJ), began removing Zane's jacket to get at the drugs and/or weapons.

Holly Hayes came out of the bathroom. She ran at Darby and Ackermann, screaming at them to let Zane go. Before she could intervene, the third man caught her in a bear hug in the middle of the street. Hayes and the man struggled. She bit him on the shoulder, worked an arm free, and began clawing at the man's eyes and mouth.

By now, the BPD patrol officer stationed at the corner of Bowditch and Dwight had been alerted to the disturbance and was rushing over the lumpy grass. He arrived in time to witness the unidentified man slash Holly Hayes with a knife, twice on the forearm and once more from chin to temple, a sinuous line traversing her left cheek. The man threw her to the ground and fled west on Haste, turning north on Telegraph, at which point the officer lost his visual. He elected not to pursue. He was too busy breaking up the fight between Zane and Darby and Ackermann while also attempting to tend to a shrieking, bloody Holly Hayes.

Jeremy Darby claimed that he did not know the identity of the third man. He'd never met the guy in his life before that day. He, Darby, wasn't in charge. He'd come to the park in response to a tweet.

Oliver Ackermann refused to answer questions. His apparent lack of gainful employment did not prevent him from promptly retaining Palo Alto's top criminal defense attorney.

The woman spearheading the cleanup effort at the court was named Lucinda Eagle Feather. It was she who had put out the call for volunteers. She told Billy Watts she wasn't personally acquainted with everyone who showed up. She didn't ask for names. All she cared about was whether they could lift chunks of concrete.

She adamantly denied sending the men over to confront Malcolm Zane.

Billy Watts assumed everyone was lying to him. But Darby and Ackermann were no longer talking, and neither were the rest of the volunteers. Watts had neither cause to arrest Lucinda Eagle Feather nor means to exert pressure on her. From Zane and Hayes he had obtained a cursory description of the suspect: white or Hispanic male, mid-twenties; medium build; brown hair. Jeans and work boots, black hoodie, gray T-shirt.

No knife, no CCTV footage, no DNA retrievable from the victim's fingernails.

Holly Hayes received seventy-three stitches.

Billy Watts began trawling social media in search of people discussing the attack—the modern-day equivalent of a guy bragging at the bar, except that on the internet new bars opened and closed every ten seconds, and the patrons wore masks, and spoke in false voices, and turned to vapor the instant you struck up a conversation. Watts conceded it was a Hail Mary. He'd checked and re-checked the usual sites and had yet to make any headway.

"I did find that, though," he said.

"That" was a link to a popular image board, just emailed by Watts. I clicked it open.

The image in question had been posted on April 3. It was slightly grainier than you'd expect from a cameraphone, suggesting a still lifted from a video.

I was its subject.

I had just reached down and hauled a gimpy Kelly Dormer to his feet, causing him to pitch forward and me to grab at his shirt. A subtle tilt of the camera created the impression that I was pulling him close, taking him into my arms like a wounded fellow soldier. My neck badge swung free. Kelly's torn sleeve revealed the swastika inked on his shoulder. By chance or by design, the tattoo lay at the picture's focal point, a lurid magnet to the eye.

His forehead rested on my shoulder. His lips were pursed.

As for me, I'd shifted to avoid a head-butt, displaying my own face in three-quarter profile. Eyes scrunched, because—if memory served—Kelly didn't smell too great.

You could also interpret my expression as one of concern. You could, if you wanted, impute to our positioning something like intimacy: an air kiss gone wrong.

That's what the internet had done.

The original poster had captioned the photo *proof berkeley pd loves nazis.*

A spirited discussion—in words, in memes—followed about what punishment I deserved for my embrace of hate, starting with job loss and growing more extreme.

Hitler's head, Photoshopped onto my body.

My head, Photoshopped onto Hitler's body.

Me, but with a neat little toothbrush mustache.

The most industrious individual had flipped me around and

done some creative splicing, so that Kelly Dormer appeared to be penetrating me from behind. I had to applaud the attention to detail: the shading of my naked legs, the silvery line of drool swinging from Kelly's puckered mouth.

"This is insane," I said.

Watts said, "Keep reading."

It was a lengthy thread. The photo had been up for weeks.

A post by user Shitlord5546 upped the ante.

somebody please dox this fascist pos

I scrolled on, my throat dry.

Four posts later, there it was.

My name. Amy's name.

Our home address.

It's hard, so hard, to hide these days.

Watts was talking. I couldn't understand him. My head had filled up with steel wool, a numb effervescence spreading through my skull and scalp, out to the ends of each hair, down my spine and along my extremities. The squad room spun beneath the drill of fluorescents; from ten feet and a thousand miles away came the machine-gun stutter of Rex Jurow typing in his cubicle, Moffett's suffering desk chair emitting a plaintive keen.

"Clay. You there?"

I said nothing.

"Take a couple of deep breaths," Watts said. "Nice and slow . . . Good. That's real good. Give me two more."

My fingers throbbed around the phone. My collar lay cold and damp.

The poster was *Anonymous*.

They'd put our street address, but left off the unit number for the guest cottage.

Poor Maryanne.

"Clay."

"I'm here."

"Are you okay?"

"Not really."

Watts didn't know who Anonymous was or how they'd found me. Possibly they'd been in attendance the night of the community panel at Zellerbach, when I introduced myself to a capacity crowd. Clips from the meeting had been uploaded to various sites. Or it was someone I'd interacted with directly, such as Chloe Bellara.

He'd contacted the site moderators, asking them to remove the thread. He didn't expect them to comply. Better I should have a lawyer write a letter.

"This is so fucked up," I said.

"I'm sorry, but I'm going to say it to you again. Don't do anything rash."

"Do what? How can I do anything when I don't know who they are?"

"I'm asking you not to turn up the temperature any. I'm not done with this, okay? I'll keep looking, both for these motherfuckers and for the guy who cut the girl. Top of my list."

While I appreciated Watts's commitment, I knew—we both did—that it was a lost cause. No one had explicitly called for harm against me. Shitlord5546 had asked a question. Anonymous had delivered, putting the information out and letting human nature run its course. The chance of identifying either of them was remote. If by some miracle we did, they'd claim they were kidding. There for the lulz. Why so serious?

I kept scrolling. Someone else had doxed Kelly Dormer, listing the address of the brothers' compound, naming all three, and linking to their podcast.

"Anyone throw a brick at them?"

"Their website was down as of last week," Watts said.

"Silver lining," I said.

I began aggressively scrolling back up, channeling my agitation into that tiny constricted movement. "The hell am I gonna tell my wife?"

"Do you have to tell her anything?" Watts said.

"It's still up there."

"Nobody's added to the thread in a month. You're old news."

I came to the original photo. My badge, sparkling in the sun. The tattoo, like a beacon.

proof berkeley pd loves nazis

"What pisses me off is it's so dishonest," I said. "You know? It's such a deliberate misread. I don't even work for BPD."

"It appears that their crack team of fact-checkers dropped the ball."

"Nazis? How does that make any sense? Amy's half-Jewish."

Billy Watts roared with laughter.

"Lemme guess," he said. "Some of your best friends are black."

CHAPTER 28

"So I was thinking," I told Amy.

I lay on my side on the living room carpet, my body curved protectively around Charlotte, who was conducting a taste test of various toys.

"Maybe we should start looking for a new place," I said.

She tamped down the lid on her travel mug. "What makes you say that?"

"It just occurred to me, it might be time."

She peered over her shoulder at me. To avoid her gaze, I twisted to retrieve a ball that had rolled out of Charlotte's reach.

"Now that she's crawling, it's starting to feel kinda crowded," I said. "You know?"

Amy continued to study me. "Is that what you want?"

"I'm asking if it's what you want, too."

"I mean," she said. "Eventually, yes."

"Great. I'll check the listings and see what's out there."

"I get notifications a couple of times a week." She took her lunch from the fridge. "I don't think there's much inventory right now."

"Stuff comes on all the time."

"We're supposed to be saving up."

"Sure. At some point we have to bite the bullet, though."

"You know as well as I do that we don't have enough to swing it without asking for help from my parents. We agreed we don't want to do that."

"Right. I'm saying, maybe we should be flexible. It's not like they don't help us a ton already in other ways. They seem fine with it."

"That's different. You're talking about asking for a handout."

"I meant a loan."

"You said you didn't want that, either."

"I know I did. I just don't want to let pride get in the way of our daughter's needs."

"Her needs? She can't walk, yet."

"It's a question of economics," I said. "Prices don't go down here, they go up. It's a treadmill. We can wait and wait and it's never going to happen. Every month that goes by, we're making it harder for ourselves and missing out on value."

"I'm confused. Is the purpose of this to buy, or to get more space?"

"Either. Both. The best-case scenario would be to find a decent-sized rental that allows us to keep putting money aside."

"The best-case scenario is the deal we have now."

"I'm saying if. Let's not rule it out in advance."

"In this neighborhood?"

"It doesn't have to be here."

"I like it here," she said.

"I do, too. But we should be open to expanding the search radius."

"Unless we're expanding it to Arizona," she said, "I don't know what you expect to find."

She canted back at the waist, as if to evaluate me at a critical remove. "What's going on here?"

Clay Edison, Master of Deception.

"I'm just thinking out loud," I said.

"What made you think of it now, specifically?"

"Honey. Come on. It popped into my head. That's it. Please let's not overthink it."

"You're the one who brought it up."

"And now I'm saying let's not worry about it."

"Worry about what?"

"Nothing. There's nothing to worry about."

"Did you hear from the detective? Is that what this is?"

"He's investigating," I said.

"And?"

"He's got nothing concrete."

"Is there something *not* concrete?"

"I told you I'd let you know if there was something worth knowing."

"Yeah. So? Is there?"

"We can't live in fear," I said. "We also agreed on that."

"It's wrong to be controlled by an unwarranted feeling. It's stupid not to take reasonable precautions."

"We have taken them."

"You're telling me we're safe," she said.

"I think so."

She made a frustrated sound. "Why can't you just say it? 'We're safe.' Say that."

"Amy—"

"You can't say it."

"There's no such thing as a hundred percent safe. I could knit sweaters for a living, and I still couldn't make you that promise. We could move to a cave in the middle of the forest and next thing we're wiped out by a meteor."

She said, "You don't knit sweaters."

Her face was wet with tears.

"Honey," I said.

"I worry about you, every day." She plucked tissues from her bag and blotted her cheeks. "Every day you leave and I think, 'He's not coming back.' Uch. Hang on."

She went into the bathroom to fix her makeup. When she re-emerged, she said, "I'm sorry."

"You've never talked about feeling that way."

"It comes and goes. It's not a big deal."

"Big enough for you to say something."

"I shouldn't have."

"I'm glad you did. I am. You look nice, by the way."

"Thanks."

"For what it's worth, I'm as safe as any person in my line of work is. Much safer than if I were on the streets. But some degree of risk is inherent in my job. It's either that or I find something else to do." I paused. "Is that what you want?"

"I would never ask you to do that."

"Fine, but I'm asking you to speak your mind. If you could press a button and make me not a cop, would you?"

"I want you to be happy."

"Amy. Please."

She said, "You're so smart. You could do so many other things, and sometimes it's hard to accept that you've chosen this."

"I made that choice long before we were together."

"I know." She zipped her bag. "Things change."

Charlotte rocked onto her hands and knees and began crawling for the front door.

I crawled after her, offering encouragement. "Someone wants to go to work with Mommy."

Amy knelt beside us. She put a hand on my shoulder, curled a finger under Charlotte's chin. "Someday."

AFTER THE MORNING nap, I drove to Berkeley Bowl. A sense of violation clung to me, humid, leaden; I couldn't shed it; couldn't scrape away the virulence of white letters seared on hollow black.

My name. Amy's name. Our address.

Thank God Charlotte was too young for social media.

I buckled her in the cart and stalked the aisles, vigilant, detached, irate, grabbing food off the shelves and staring down my fellow shoppers and wondering which of them was Shitlord5546.

Middle-aged Asian woman toting an eight-pack of tangerine La Croix.

Hipster couple bickering over fair-trade rice.

Stock clerk tagging canned olives: That you, Anonymous?

The elderly black woman buying swordfish.

The aproned Hispanic man cutting it for her.

Who owned a jar of red nail polish?

"That is *extremely* unsafe."

The woman addressing me was white, in her forties, with a chenille skirt, a sage-green fleece vest, Birkenstocks, and slumping socks.

"Pardon?" I said.

She pointed to Charlotte in the shopping cart. "Those things are death traps. You ought to be ashamed of yourself."

Her own cart contained nothing but dried bananas, fifteen bulk bags' worth, filled to the neck and twist-tied.

I said, "Go fuck yourself, ma'am," and wheeled away, abandoning the groceries by the registers. I was so hacked off that I got Charlotte's leg caught when I lifted her out of the cart. She let out a bleat of pain and began to cry.

The parking lot was the usual honking catastrophe. My pulse was up, my fingertips tingling. While I struggled to buckle in a raging, stiff-limbed Charlotte, a Volvo pulled up to claim my space.

My phone buzzed in my pocket. I tugged it out.

Sibley.

The driver of the Volvo leaned out. "Excuse me. Are you leaving?"

"In a *second*." I picked up the call. "What's up."

The driver mouthed *asshole* and glided off.

"I got a text," Sibley said. "Someone moved the bear."

. . .

THE TRACKER HAD pinged at a location on Oxford Street, three-quarters of a mile from People's Park. I found Sibley standing beneath a stop sign to which someone had added a sticker.

I had Charlotte in the baby carrier, facing out, her feet kicking excitedly at the air.

"Hello you," Sibley said. To me: "Really?"

"What do you want me to do? Day off." I glanced around. "Where's our bear?"

"Here, as of thirty minutes ago."

She showed me the tracking app: a map, marked with a blinking pin. I tapped the pin. A dialogue box popped up with the coordinates and a timestamp.

"Where's it now?" I said.

She shook her head. "We'll find out at noon tomorrow."

"Are you kidding me?"

"Hey. Excuse me for taking into account battery life."

"You do realize," I said, "this could have nothing to do with the baby. Someone took the bear cause it's free."

"That's always been true. What's wrong with you? You look ready to blow a fuse."

I sighed. "It's been a week."

"Yeah, well, chin up, buttercup. This is a positive development. It's a zoo over there. Ever since they announced they're going to excavate, folks are grabbing things and hauling them off. Half the stuff that was there is gone. My hope is the mother caught wind of it, had second thoughts, ran back to get it. You have a better idea, speak up."

I shook my head.

"Fine, then. I'll text you tomorrow."

"It's just, like, the slowest chase in human history," I said.

Sibley leaned toward Charlotte. "You can come, too. You don't even have to bring him."

THE FOLLOWING DAY I headed over to my in-laws' to wait for Sibley's call. Theresa served me homemade biscotti, and we admired the baby as she motored around the kitchen.

"I can't believe how fast she is," Theresa said.

"Future point guard."

She smiled. My mother-in-law is a thoughtful, understated woman, the foil to her gregarious husband. Paul once summed it up this way: *I say ninety percent of the words. She says ninety percent of the words worth listening to.*

"Amy tells me you're thinking about looking for a new place to live."

"In a general sense."

"She said you've been under a lot of pressure."

I shrugged.

"I know you take good care of them," she said.

"I try."

"Paul and I want you to know that we're here to help with whatever you need."

"We do. Thank you."

She nodded again and left it at that.

Charlotte started nosing her way through the service porch entrance. I got up and reset her to the middle of the floor, and she turned around and headed for the same spot.

"She's nothing if not persistent," I said.

"I wonder where she gets that from," Theresa said.

At noon on the dot Sibley texted *MLK @ Berryman*

10 minutes I wrote.

I kissed Charlotte goodbye; kissed Theresa on the cheek and thanked her.

"We'll be fine," she said. "You take care of yourself."

THE BUILDING WAS a triplex of no discernible architectural style, ineffectually screened by a row of black poplars. On the app, the pin sat squarely in the middle of the structure.

"Do we know which unit it is?" I asked.

"The GPS is accurate to fifteen feet," she said.

"So, any of them."

Two doors under the street-side portico, enameled mailboxes labeled GIORDANO and WILLIS. A Post-it, affixed to the wall with clear packing tape, directed delivery people to the end of the driveway for CHEN APT. #3.

Sibley and I sifted through the contents of the mailboxes. *Willis* was Matt Willis. There were also items addressed to his roommates, or perhaps old tenants. Juan Miguel Eisenstein and Matthew Boyarin.

"Attention Target shoppers," Sibley said. "Special on Matts. Two for one."

Giordano was Anita. She appeared to be the sole occupant of apt. #2. Her catalogs skewed older. More promising.

We headed down the driveway to apt. #3. Kevin Chen. Iris Chen. A tower of Amazon packages. Lululemon. Children's apparel. Nobody takes your demographic profile more seriously than a direct-mail marketer.

"Well," I said. "I know who I like."

We rang the bell for Anita Giordano.

No answer.

Middle of the day. At work.

Sibley pressed the bell for Willis.

This time we heard slow, bare feet on hardwood. The peephole dimmed, then the chain went on and the door opened, releasing from within a gust of dude-stink.

"Help you?"

White, early twenties, ectomorphic, bloodshot; black beard segueing into chest hair.

"Mr. Willis?" I asked.

"Yeah."

"I'm Deputy Edison of the County Sheriff's. This is Lieutenant Sibley of UCPD. You mind if we ask you a couple of questions?"

"About what."

"May we come in?" Sibley asked.

"What questions," Willis said.

"It's concerning your neighbor, Ms. Giordano."

A beat. He undid the chain and led us into the living room.

"Have a seat," he said.

We couldn't. Everywhere were pizza boxes, wadded tissues, energy drink cans. A dragon-shaped bong made of green glass leaked tendrils of smoke. Foremost was a massive TV connected to a PlayStation. Half the screen showed a paused video game, the other half a chat module, streaming viewer commentary.

Willis plopped down on the couch and picked up the controller. Donning a large headset with a microphone, he addressed a webcam mounted above the television.

"All right, douchebags, I'm back, and as you can see, I have five-O in the house."

The chat module went wild.

Tears of laughter emojis, weeping emojis, cop emojis, padlock emojis.

LOL SWATTED

Run b4 they beat u

"Mr. Willis, you mind please shutting that off?" I asked.

"I can do this and talk at the same time," he said, unpausing the game.

Sibley and I shared a look. I think we'd both been puzzled by his willingness to let us in. Now we understood: He'd co-opted us into his show.

"But I ain't no snitch," Willis said, smirking.

Snitches get stiches the chat module read.

"What time does Ms. Giordano usually get home?" I asked.

Willis shrugged. His thumbs worked the controller, producing a shower of severed limbs and pixelated gore.

"Do you know where she works?" Sibley said.

"Nope."

"Does she live alone?"

Willis blew a raspberry. "I guess."

"How old would you say Ms. Giordano is?"

"Sixty? Seventy? Older than you guys."

Sibley rolled her shoulders. *Done with this mook.*

We turned to leave.

"Hang on, hang on," Willis said, giggling. "What's the deal? She killed someone?"

"We're looking for a bear," Sibley said.

His eyes unstuck from the screen. "Bear?"

"One's been spotted around this neighborhood."

"You might want to clean up," I said. "They can smell from miles away. Come straight through your window."

Bear emojis flooded the chat stream.

"Wait, what?" Willis said.

"Have a good day, Mr. Willis," Sibley said.

He mashed PAUSE and trailed us to the door. "Like, an actual bear?"

We didn't answer.

Briefly he craned his head out, scanning the street for non-virtual wildlife.

CHAPTER 29

That evening we returned. Anita Giordano answered her door wearing woolen slippers and yoga pants, ash-colored bob damp from the shower.

What's this about?

Normally that's the first thing a person wants to know.

Or: *Is something wrong?*

"Thank you for coming," she said.

Expecting us.

Relieved.

The apartment's layout mirrored that of the adjacent bro-dome. Hers was tidy, Ikea furniture and sun-faded Matisse prints and kitschy souvenirs from South America and Asia. Houseplants nodded. Her television measured a third the size of Matt Willis's and was mounted at a corresponding spot on the wall, as though the monstrosity on the other side had shot roots through the plaster.

A mystery novel with a public library label lay splayed over the sofa arm. Chamomile tea steamed on the end table. She invited us to sit and went to fetch two more mugs.

Uncertain as to the delicacy of her state of mind, we took a little while to circle in, starting with general background questions.

Anita Giordano was sixty-eight years old, a Bay Area native. She'd spent her career as a medical interpreter, Spanish and French.

She'd always had a knack for Romance languages, and after spotting an ad for a training course, she moved to Mexico City. She ended up staying for four years. One was hard-pressed to imagine what the country was like in those days. She was there for the big earthquake, in 1985. Thousands died. Restoring power took months. Her family was beside themselves, calling and writing the American embassy.

Other than that, she had always resided locally. You couldn't beat Northern California for quality of life.

At present she split her time traveling and volunteering at an animal shelter.

I kept waiting for us to hit a nerve.

With utter tranquility she informed us she'd never been married. Never had children.

I said, "Ms. Giordano, you're probably wondering why we're here."

"I assume it has to do with my identity."

Sibley said, "Your identity."

"I did what Officer Deng suggested and froze my credit, but it doesn't seem to be helping. Last night the same collection agency called again at one a.m. I keep telling them that it's not me, someone's got my Social Security number."

"You've been the victim of identity theft," I said.

Confusion began to set in. "Is that not what we're talking about?"

To most people, a uniform is a uniform. Anita Giordano had recently appealed to the cops. We were cops. Forget the UCPD patch on Sibley's shoulder or the Coroner's patch on mine. Probably it gratified her that repairing her credit score had become such a high interagency priority.

Hence her readiness to answer questions about her past.

I found her faith in the system charming.

"I'm sorry to hear about that," I said. "We're here on an unrelated matter, though. I don't know if you've been following what's been going on with the construction at People's Park over the last few months."

"Only a little," she said. Guarded, now. "Why?"

"Back in December, when they first started digging, they uncovered some human remains. Did you hear about that?"

"I don't think so."

"You said you've always lived in Berkeley?" Sibley asked.

"Yes. Here or Oakland."

"Late sixties, early seventies, did you hang around People's Park?"

Anita Giordano spluttered a laugh. "Me? No."

"Did you know a man named Fritz Dormer?"

"I've never heard that name."

I showed her a picture of the bear. "What about this?"

"It's a teddy bear."

"Do you recognize it?"

"I'm sorry, what's going on here?"

"The bear was taken by someone," Sibley said. "We're trying to track it down."

"What's that got to do with me?"

"There's a locator tag inside it. The signal indicates it's coming from in here."

Anita Giordano twisted in her chair, as if we had told her there was a snake crawling up the wall. "Here?"

"Would you object if we had a brief look around?" I asked.

"I . . ." She fretted. "I mean, if you must."

"We'll be quick," I said.

I took the living room and kitchen, leaving the bedrooms and bathroom to Sibley. We went gingerly. No sense in tossing the place. If Anita Giordano was the mother, she was either the most proficient liar I'd ever met, or else mired in deep denial, in which case the truth was better coaxed out.

She laced and unlaced her fingers, her worry lines deepening. "I have to say, I'm finding this a little troubling."

"We'll be out of your hair soon," I said, reaching for the cabinet above the refrigerator.

With a loud scrape, Anita Giordano stood up from her chair. "Hold on."

I looked at her. Her eyes were wild.

"I . . ." she said.

I opened the cabinet.

Inside was a quarter-full bag of CBD/THC gummies.

"I have disc degeneration," she said. She stuck her chin out. "It's the only thing that helps with the pain. They're completely legal. I bought them online."

I shut the cabinet. "Absolutely, ma'am."

Anita Giordano grabbed her teacup and downed it.

Sibley emerged from the bedroom. "We're sorry to have bothered you, ma'am." She left a card on the end table. "If you do see the bear, can you let us know?"

"What do I do about my Social Security number?"

Sibley said, "Follow up with Officer Deng."

OUT ON THE sidewalk, I said, "I believe her."

"I do, too."

Sibley opened the tracking app.

The pin was gone, in its place a red X.

"The crap?" Sibley said.

She tapped the X. A dialogue box appeared.

Device not found (err 4-11)

Sibley smushed the screen with her thumb. "Come on."

"Can you reset it?"

"Hang on." She walked off, fiddling with the interface.

From inside the bro-dome came the strobe of the television.

"No, I do not want to live chat with customer care," Sibley said.

We'd spoken to Matt Willis, instructing him to watch out for a bear. The kind of bizarro disruption to routine you'd mention to buddies at day's end, over pizza and weed.

"Boyarin," I said.

"What?"

"Willis's roommate. The other Matt. His name's on some of the mail."

Sibley stopped pacing and looked at me.

"The night of the panel at Zellerbach," I said. "During the Q and A. There was a woman, a Cal professor, who asked me a question. She wanted to know what we were doing to identify the dead child. That was her name. Boyarin."

MY RECALL FOR names is way above average. I juggle a lot of decedents and families, and it's poor form to refer to someone's loved one incorrectly.

In this case, I'd heard the name once, months prior, while in the throes of stress and exhaustion. That was why, I told Sibley, I'd failed to make the connection sooner.

"Yeah, you're a terrible disappointment," Sibley said.

It didn't matter. Only one Boyarin on the UC Berkeley faculty.

Gayle Boyarin, PhD, MPH, professor of epidemiology, school of public health.

In her department headshot she wore a black blazer and a silk scarf mottled purple and blue. Silver hair, close-cropped; a small, disarming gap between the top two front teeth. She listed several areas of research interest.

Maternal nutrition and perinatal health

Sociology of mothering practices

Infant mortality

We pulled her data. Age seventy-three. Known associates: Adam, thirty-four; Matthew, thirty-two; Richard Blumenfeld, seventy-seven. Address on Francisco Street, near North Berkeley BART, a five-minute drive.

En route, Sibley did a quick and dirty on the rest of them. Adam worked for an alternative energy nonprofit. Matthew was a manager at a rock climbing gym. Richard taught linguistics at San Jose State.

We rolled up to a trim Spanish bungalow. The rest of the block consisted of similarly cute homes, built in the twenties, thirties, and forties to accommodate a growing middle class. Today, battled over like meat scraps.

Drought-tolerant landscaping, ornamental plums. Aspirational vehicles piled in the driveways: BMWs and midsized SUVs, My Cartoon Family decals on rear windows. From behind plantation shutters came the thrum of evening routine, dinnertime and bath time, get your homework done and we'll see about TV.

As a domestic fantasy, it felt far out of reach. No longer could you afford to buy here on an academic salary, even two good ones. Gayle and Richard had likely done it the same way my in-laws had: by getting in early. Now they were accidentally rich.

I thought about my own burgeoning family, filling up every square inch of our space. Despite the beautiful weather, I'd been reluctant to let Charlotte play outside.

I didn't know who was around or what they might do.

A white-haired man in a gingham shirt answered our knock. "Yes?"

"Good evening, sir. Is Gayle Boyarin home?"

He put on his reading glasses to peer at my badge. "Is something wrong?"

"No, sir," Sibley said. "We'd just like a word with her."

He called over his shoulder. "Sweetheart?"

No answer.

"She can't always hear me from her office," he said. "Won't you come in, please."

He left us in the living room. Walnut built-ins were chockablock with books and candids. Gayle Boyarin's transition from dark hair to silver, luxuriant to practical, took place in five-year increments. Richard was absent from the older photos, already gray in his first appearance. The boys had their mother's surname, not his. Second marriage.

Adam and Matthew shared the same pointy chin, one ruddy, the other bronze-skinned. They knelt on a soccer field; flexed with El Capitan in the background; rode camels in the desert. They were close enough in age that I couldn't decide who was who.

People used to have the same trouble with me and my brother. Not anymore.

"Hunh," Sibley said.

She'd bent to examine an étagère. The shelves held an assortment of delicate objects in silver, ceramic, or crystal, adorned with Stars of David. Most of the items I could not identify. While Amy's father was born into a Jewish home, he and Theresa are staunch atheists, and he's retained very little of his upbringing, materially speaking. One notable exception is a sweeping silver menorah, inherited from his grandmother and occupying a place of prominence on the den mantel.

Gayle Boyarin and Richard Blumenfeld's menorah was humbler, webbed with tarnished filigree. Wax crusts around the cups indicated it still saw use.

I understood Sibley's bafflement: how to square the paraphernalia and symbols of Judaism with the tapestry of hatred that was Fritz Dormer's body of work.

"Maybe they're his," Sibley whispered. "The husband."

"Maybe."

"Boyarin? Is that a Jewish name?"

"Beats me."

Richard Blumenfeld returned, trailed by the lighter son. He'd grown up but not out, rangy and fox-like, chestnut hair cut in a high fade. Sockless canvas slip-ons exposed nubby ankles; black jeans rode low on his hips. Wu-Tang Clan tee.

"Hi Matthew," I said. "We need to speak to your mother."

"It's about the bear," Sibley said. "You got it back there somewhere?"

Richard Blumenfeld's lips parted. He re-donned his reading glasses, as if Sibley and I were a troublesome piece of syntax.

A bear? In my house? Stuff and nonsense!

Matthew said, "It's okay, Dad."

To us: "This way."

TWO MISMATCHED ORIENTAL runners stretched the length of the hall. The theme continued into the office itself, a cozy ten-by-twelve furnished with desk and divan and a flaking leather pouf. A patchwork of prayer rugs covered the parquet. Smooth walls and recessed lighting suggested a later addition, or a bedroom reclaimed in recent years as Professor Boyarin's personal sanctum. Hadn't she earned the right to a little peace and quiet?

Gayle Boyarin was slope-shouldered and pear-shaped, wearing linen drawstring pants and a drape front cardigan that fell open as she rose from her desk chair.

Just as Anita Giordano had, she thanked us for coming, her gaze steady and clear.

She shook our hands, rewrapped herself, and sat. "Please."

Sibley and I squeezed onto the divan.

Matthew hoisted the pouf, made as if to place it next to his mother.

Gayle stopped him with a kindly smile. "Go with Dad, please."

He frowned. He set the pouf down and glanced at us. "You don't have to talk to them."

She pulled him in to kiss his cheek. "I'll be fine."

He hesitated, then followed Richard out. The door shut softly.

"He's a sweet boy," she said. "His brother's the same. And Richard. Three wonderful men. I'm very fortunate."

I nodded. "We're hoping you might be able to clear some things up."

"That's what I want, too," Gayle Boyarin said.

She opened a desk drawer and brought out the bear.

Torn open along a seam, its structural integrity lost, it drooped when she set it on the desk, belching out a tuft of fluffy white viscera. The surviving eye hung from a single thread, pointing toward the ceiling, as if to consult the heavens.

Gayle Boyarin reached down for the wastebasket and handed it to me. At the bottom of the liner lay the smashed remains of the tracking device. From one piece curled a label: PROP. OF UCPD, along with a departmental inventory code.

"We didn't get to it fast enough, I guess," she said.

I told her I remembered her from the night of the panel.

She chided herself with a half smile. "I knew I shouldn't've gotten up there."

"The fact that you did tells me it still matters to you."

"Of course it does," she said.

She regarded the bear, its gashed blue belly leaking stuffing. "It's always mattered."

CHAPTER 30

He wasn't Fritz back then. He was Fred, and while he wasn't a flower child, neither was he the monster he'd become.

He was young. He rode a motorcycle and had hair down to his waist. That sufficed to put him on the right team.

Us versus Them.

Them: parents, cops, the university, anyone over thirty; Nixon and Westmoreland, all the architects of carnage; polluters and exploiters and those who failed to comprehend that change was in the air or, worse, had sniffed at its spicy perfume and proceeded to wrinkle their nose.

Us: everyone else. Who lived by their own rules; who understood that love was free; who believed there was more to life than a paycheck, two point five kids, and a white picket fence; who knew Mother Nature possessed infinitely more wisdom than an army of iron-eyed men in lab coats.

A simplistic way to divide the world. Yes. Was the alternative better? Look at us now, balkanized and so much the weaker for it. At least they only had one choice to make.

Us/Them.

Rough around the edges, Fred. Part of his appeal: the fringed jacket and the boots. Very *Easy Rider.* He called himself a nomad.

The white supremacist shtick—that was new. To her, anyway. Six months ago, after hearing about the park, she'd started searching for him. She checked Facebook. LinkedIn. In her mind he'd grown up and become a stockbroker.

A 2014 article in the *Chronicle* Sunday magazine marked the twentieth anniversary of the Anthony Wax murder. Fritz's portrait put him in his cell at San Quentin, ink-dark arms hanging through the bars. He hadn't aged well, in several respects, but the face belonged unmistakably to the same man.

It gutted her. She ran to the bathroom and threw up.

They'd met at a party. Nothing serious. Three or four nights. She shared a house on Derby Street with a bunch of girls. He'd pull up on his bike and gun the engine, and she'd run out and hop on behind him, and they'd zoom around the hills while she hugged his body, taking in the grubby lights of the East Bay, the water's black ellipsis, the San Francisco skyline, dazzling, unattainable. Afterward they'd return to her room. He had a surprisingly tender touch. Five nights at most. Once they pulled over by the side of the road, gravel under her bare feet. Maybe it had happened then.

The noise of the bike spared them having to make conversation. God knew they didn't have a lot to talk about. She allowed that he was intelligent after a fashion, albeit crude. He boasted about dropping out of high school, as if that was supposed to impress her. What did they have in common, really, except enthusiasm for psychedelics and disdain for the pigs? She had a BA in cell biology from Colorado State University, going to waste, if you asked her parents.

Fred told her he was thinking about joining up. Marines.

Why in the world would he do that, she demanded. Did he want to be a baby-killer?

Looking back, she felt bad about raining on his parade. He had limited options.

Still, she was frankly relieved when he stopped showing up. That was that. Fun while it lasted. Like the rest of her peers, she fancied herself a sailor on the seas of life. Why spoil nice memories with petty bourgeois resentment? She'd participated willingly. They'd never agreed to anything beyond the next morning.

By her second missed period, she had no means of contacting him. She didn't have his number. As far as she knew, he didn't own a phone. He might well be halfway to Da Nang.

She asked the friend who'd hosted the party about Fred with the bike.

The girl said *Who?*

Gayle couldn't even be certain he was the father. By the standards of the era, she was tame, but she had slept with another man in the preceding months, the drummer in a band that had rolled through town. The timing didn't seem to fit, unless she'd counted wrong. She couldn't contact that guy, either. Any decision was hers alone.

Roe v. Wade was over a year out. But this was California, not Alabama. Women always found ways. You went to the right doctors and said the right things. She made an appointment and rode the bus into the city. She went into a waiting room, made herself known, and sat down in a sticky chair. She leafed through a magazine but found she couldn't read anything. She tore out a subscription card, kneading it between her fingers, the paper breaking down till it felt as soft as lambskin. When at last the window squeaked open and they called her name, she stood up and walked out, as though the voice summoning her was judgment itself.

Weeks dragged. She carried on pretending, kept smoking and drinking and dropping acid. One morning she woke up sick as a dog. Drenched in sweat, hugging the toilet, she felt herself laid bare, not half-digested vegetables bobbing in the bowl but waterlogged tatters of her soul. She wanted it, this life striving inside her, wanted it with a desire that bled into madness. The primitive force of the emotion, its raw savagery, shamed her. *Mine* and *yours* had ruined the world. Yet she curled up on the floor, jealously cradling her midsection like it was a toy another child had tried to steal.

Speculation abounded about the culprit. Her friends expressed disbelief when she told them it was some biker guy she barely knew. They wouldn't have kept it. But none of them had experienced what she was experiencing.

Her parents she hadn't spoken to since leaving home. She couldn't bear the thought of coming to them on her knees, having proven their worst fears. Her sister was no better.

Go it alone. The seas of life got choppy. Part of the journey.

During her second trimester, circumstances began to deteriorate. She lost her job, waitressing at Spenger's, down by the train tracks. She was showing through her apron. The manager told her they couldn't have her serving families. He'd gotten comments. She could stay if she put on a wedding band, but she refused to do that.

Too sick and wiped out to job-hunt, she squandered time, napping, reading the funnies, observing with a peculiar indifference as the balance in her checkbook plummeted toward zero. The nurse at the clinic said it wasn't typical to have morning sickness that late in the game, but she continued to throw up much of what she ate.

While she'd stopped popping pills, she did continue to smoke the odd joint to take the edge off her nausea. She wept at the drop of a hat. Another reason the manager cited for letting her go: Her red eyes and red cheeks and tremulous voice bothered customers.

She hit her overdraft limit. Her housemates carried her for two more rent cycles. She could sense their growing discomfort, though. She packed up her few worldly possessions and left.

Her cousin Barry was a lecturer at the law school. Prior to that they'd never socialized. He was a Young Republican. Fifteen years down the line she would hold his hand while he lay in a San Francisco hospice, being eaten alive by AIDS. In 1971 he was closeted, fast-talking, *Them* in horn-rims and a tweed blazer. He frowned to find her on his doorstep, suitcase in hand, begging to pee. But he didn't phone her folks, and he moved to the couch, surrendering his bed to her. There she rode out the final weeks.

On the evening of September 5, Barry brought her to the hospital in a cab. He sat outside the delivery room, departing midmorning to teach a class. His departure elicited titters from the nurses. Not the first husband to flee right as things got hairy.

Six pounds, fourteen ounces. Twenty inches on the dot. He came out purple, sporting a fringe of black hair like some middle-aged accountant. He did not cry. She began to yell. Something was wrong, he was dead, she had killed him with her bad habits and her inadequacies. They suctioned him out and the doctor gave him a hard slap on the behind and he emitted a thin wet sound, like a thread drawn through milk, and she believed that he would live.

She named him Marc.

"With a 'c,' " she said.

She paused so I could write it down. I noticed her leaning toward the page, wanting to ensure I'd recorded the correct spelling.

"When they gave me the form for the birth certificate, I didn't know what to put down for the father. I was confident that it was Fred, because the other guy was African American, and the baby didn't look it, although I now know that pigmentation can take a while to change. They came back to collect the form and I still hadn't completed it. I could tell what they were thinking. *Loose woman. So many men, she can't say who knocked her up.* It gave me a taste of what was to come.

"I left the hospital without handing it in. I think I was supposed to finish it at home and mail it in, but I never got around to it. I didn't need a piece of paper from the state."

"Where did you go?" I asked.

"Back to Barry's. I was totally unprepared. I didn't own a crib or clothes. They'd discharged me with some diapers and formula samples. They didn't schedule a follow-up. 'Goodbye and good luck.' That's how it was. Right off the bat I had enormous trouble nursing. I had the baby sleeping in the bed next to me, and I was terrified I'd roll over and crush him, so I'd lie there until he started crying, and then I'd fumble around, helpless, while he got madder and madder, and louder and louder. You're supposed to just figure it out. It was ludicrous, but I didn't realize that. Every signal I'm getting is telling me it's my fault he won't eat. Meanwhile he's screaming and waking up the whole house, Barry's roommates are threatening to move out and leave him on the hook for the lease. He bought me a copy of the Dr. Spock book, and I stayed up till dawn, reading it cover to cover. The message was essentially the same: 'You know more than you think.' But I didn't."

Her voice had taken on a honed edge.

"I *didn't* know," she said, "and it demoralized me to be told I did, again and again. It's a message that shames women for asking for help. It discourages us from demanding the kind of minimal institutional support any sane, developed society should take for granted."

Maternal nutrition and perinatal health.

The sociology of mothering practices.

I said, "I can't imagine how you coped."

Gayle shook her head. "I was young. I had energy. After about two weeks I told Barry I was leaving so he wouldn't have to throw me out.

"I bounced from one friend to another. I was better off than many women, who don't have any safety net whatsoever, or have to contend with abusive partners.

"One night—it must have been November—I truly had no place to go. Everyone was full up or out of town for Thanksgiving. All night long, I sat at a bus stop with the baby in my lap. Luckily we had an Indian summer. But I could sense the weather starting to turn, I knew I had to get us indoors.

"Finding a new place to live turned out to be a lot more difficult than I expected. Barry had insisted on giving me three hundred dollars, but the problem wasn't money, it was that nobody would rent to me. I'd show up to answer the ad and the landlord would ask about my husband. I'd say, no, it's just the two of us. Wouldn't you know, he'd suddenly remember he'd promised the place to someone else. They probably assumed I was a prostitute who'd stiff them.

The parts of town I could afford and where they didn't have an issue with a single mother, I didn't think it was safe to be."

Overtones of race and class, hastily glossed over: "I was terrified of getting mugged. Walking around with newspaper stuffed in my bra, subsisting on Hershey's bars and milk, and nursing in public restrooms. Finally, I found a tiny room above a service station on San Pablo. The conditions were appalling. You accessed it by climbing up a ladder, through a trapdoor. I had to cradle the baby in one arm and climb with the other. The walls and floor were bare wood, with nails sticking out. It was meant for storage. The manager of the station would sleep there himself when he was fighting with his wife. He'd put in a cot and a cold-water sink, but there was no insulation. I bought a space heater. If I left it running for more than thirty minutes, the air got terribly stuffy, so I had to keep switching it on and off, opening and closing the window. During working hours the racket from the garage was deafening. Gasoline fumes leaking through cracks in the floorboards. I got migraines. I didn't want to think what it might be doing to the baby.

"That's what the manager said when I first approached him. 'This ain't no place for a baby.' But clearly he wanted the money more. He charged me twenty-five dollars a week—an outrageous amount, for what it was. I told myself it was temporary. I just needed some short-term stability to get back on my feet.

"I did my best to make it livable. I scavenged. I got a crib for three dollars at a yard sale. The stroller I picked up for free. It was one of those rickety aluminum contraptions, a plastic seat and a sunshade, and a wire basket underneath for groceries. The seat was yellow, with sunflowers. It was sitting out on the sidewalk, a sign taped to the handle. YOURS IF YOU NEED IT. The sunshade had a rip, it rattled like a jalopy, but the wheels worked.

"I was as frugal as humanly possible, short of stealing, but without a source of income I burned right through the money Barry had given me. I took a gamble and went to Mr. Brenk, my old boss at Spenger's. I said I didn't have to be on the floor, I could clean or wash dishes. I'm looking him in the eye, claiming this, and meanwhile I've got the baby in the stroller and I'm pushing him back and forth so he'll stay calm. Brenk stared at me like I was certifiable. But he said we could give it a try.

"I'd show up late, after hours. The baby had learned to sleep anywhere, under any conditions. I'd park him in the corner of the kitchen and do whatever they needed me to do: mop up, scrub toilets, fold linens, whatever. Eventually I started helping with light prep work for the next day. I got to be pretty good. Bear in mind, I'm the only woman in the kitchen. The things they'd say to me . . . It got so I stopped hearing them, I'd put my head down and chop, chop, chop."

Weary with the memory.

"Eventually, the sous chef realized I was competent with a knife. He asked if I wanted to start coming in before service, to help out with more of the involved tasks. He was a nice guy. Pablo. He had a crush on me, but he was shy about it, never pinched me or flicked water down my shirt like some of the cooks did. I'm amazed I didn't sever a finger. We were on completely opposite schedules, the baby and I. We got back from the restaurant at five in the morning, when he was waking up for the day. I had to wait for him to nap so I could close my own eyes. I never felt rested."

I must have betrayed something, because she said to me, "You have children."

"A daughter. Nine months."

"How's she sleeping?"

"Could be better."

A brief smile, decaying into sadness.

She said, "Your world contracts. All I did was go back and forth from the garage to the restaurant. Aside from the kitchen staff I didn't see much of people. My old friends couldn't relate. They got stoned, listened to music, talked politics. Socially I was useless. I'd glance at the headlines and none of them would make sense. I didn't hear about Nixon going to China until a week after the fact, and the only reason I did find out is . . ."

She shook her head in disbelief. "I used to change the baby in the women's lav. I'm crouched down, newspapers on the floor, trying to corral him, trying not to get baby shit on me. Lo and behold, there's the son of a bitch, waving from the tarmac, and a green glob lands smack in the middle of Pat's face . . . It was lonely. Very lonely. Every now and then, I went to visit Barry. He got a kick out of the baby. He'd buy him gifts. He . . ."

A beat.

"The teddy bear, and the blanket," she said. "Those were from Barry."

I glanced at the eviscerated doll.

Bright happy blue.

One eye dangling.

Gayle Boyarin cleared her throat. "It got hard to be around him. My issue, I guess. He'd put himself out for me, and I didn't like feeling beholden. Not until we both got older, and he got sick, was I able to think of myself as his peer. And he was forever trying to convince me to go home. The break came when he invited us over and handed me a bus ticket for Denver. He'd gone ahead and bought it without consulting me, and it made me so angry, because it felt like he was telling me to quit. Negating my noble struggle."

Briefly she sat back in her chair. Too relaxed. She drew in a sharp breath and bent forward over the desk, pushing out the words:

"It happened in June."

I calculated rapidly. Nine months old, give or take.

"We were still living above the garage. It was a Monday. The best day of the week. I didn't work Monday night. Fingers crossed the baby would sleep until four or five on Tuesday, and I could sleep, too. That was heaven. That morning, I took him to San Pablo Park and put him down on the grass. He was wearing a green shirt, and I remember thinking that he was like a little lizard, shimmying on his belly, babbling nonstop. Everyone thinks their child is a genius, but the way he took the things in, absorbing, studying the sky, my face . . . I'd talk to him about whatever came to mind. Old movies.

The Krebs cycle. When I was awake enough to appreciate it, everything about him was novel and wonderful.

"I nursed him, then we went back to the garage for a nap. The
plan was to wait for him to get up again and spend the remainder
of the day looking for FOR RENT signs. I put him in the crib, took an
aspirin, and got into my cot, listening to the banging below, wondering how I was going to get to sleep. I smoked a little dope to help
me relax. The next thing I knew I woke up and the sun was going
down."

The disorientation; the panic and self-loathing. I recognized all
of it, viscerally.

"I jumped out of bed, mad at myself for oversleeping, and screwing up the schedule. I thought we might still be able to squeeze in
some apartment hunting if I hurried. I was in such a rush that I
didn't notice he wasn't moving or making noise. I put on my shoes
and went to fetch him.

"He was bluish gray. My first thought was he was cold. It got so
chilly in the room, I was still drowsy. 'Let's go, honey, we have to go,
we're going to be late.' I gathered the blanket around him and
picked him up, and his body had a, a, a heaviness."

Beyond remembering, now; seeing and feeling, just as she had
seen and felt. She pressed against her shut eyes. Tears broke through
and streamed down her cheeks.

"His head rolled forward, against my neck, and his skin was like
ice. I almost dropped him. I still wasn't getting it. I climbed down
the ladder, going, 'Shhh, shhh,' like he was crying and I was trying
to pacify him, even though he wasn't making a sound. I wasn't getting it but I was. I knew. I knew.

"The garage was closed. Everyone was gone for the day. The
manager had a phone in his office, I wasn't allowed to use it. I
grabbed, I think it was a can of motor oil, or something else heavy.
I threw it through the glass on the office door and let myself in. I
dialed the operator and said it was an emergency. That was how it
worked, before 911, you had to wait for them to connect you to the

hospital. A woman picked up. I told her my baby isn't breathing. She started barking questions at me, does he have a pulse, what does he look like. She told me to take two fingers and press down on his heart, then breathe into his mouth. I put my mouth on his and he felt so cold. I was used to kissing him, or feeling him against me while he nursed, and, but . . . The coldness, it was totally repulsive, it made me physically ill. I kept wanting to pull away. I don't know what that says about me or the kind of person I am. I could feel his bones bending, his stomach was swollen up with air, but he wasn't responding or breathing. The phone kept slipping from my ear. I put it down on the desk and I could hear the nurse shouting for my address. I couldn't remember the number. I should've just said 'the service station on San Pablo and Virginia.' I didn't think of that. I started knocking the papers off the desk, opening drawers, trying to find something with the address written on it. I couldn't make heads or tails of any of it. The whole place stank of gas, and paint; there's grease stains on the floor, and I'm the one who brought us there. I'm the one who let him sleep in a room full of poison. *I* abused my body. *I* wouldn't put on a wedding ring, *I* wouldn't go to my parents, or back to Barry. Meanwhile, the nurse keeps screaming at me. 'Where are you?' I didn't know what to say. I was nowhere."

Sweat sheened her face.

"I put the phone back in the cradle.

"I wrapped him in the blanket and put him in the stroller. I buckled him in so he wouldn't fall out and left the garage and started walking.

"I went over to the tracks, behind the restaurant. They've turned the neighborhood into a mall now. It used to be industrial. I decided to throw myself in front of the next train that came through. But they're so slow. And they really slow down right at that spot, maybe to five miles per. There was no way it could end in anything other than farce. They'd stop the train, arrest me and put me on trial. Everyone would find out. That's what I was worried about. I didn't think I could bear it, everyone knowing about me, and thinking that that was the person I was.

"I turned around and started walking up University, trying to work up the courage to run into traffic. Each time a car went by, and I stayed on the sidewalk, I could feel my resolve fading. I remember seeing a policeman, he smiled at me and wished me a good evening . . . I ended up on Telegraph. I was thirsty and light-headed, and I went looking for someone who could give me a glass of water. Everything was closed, so I walked around the corner, to the park. I thought there might be a water fountain. But there wasn't any. I didn't know that. I didn't hang out in People's Park very much. It had never been my scene. The place was a bit of a shambles. People would leave tools lying around, and anyone could bring flowers or seeds and plant them wherever they pleased.

"I pushed the stroller over and sat down against a tree. Some people were having a bonfire, playing the guitar. A boy came over and invited me to join them. 'We've got wieners.' I told him, 'No thanks, I'm just resting my legs.' I asked him for water and he said they had beer. So he brought me some of that, and gave me some of his joint. He said they were building a stage. It would be a zone of total freedom. Anyone could get up and speak their minds. He asked, was I sure I didn't want a wiener, and then he went back to his friends.

"I got up to look at where they were building. They'd cut trenches for footings. The earth was broken up and it looked soft. It made you want to lie down in it. I went and found a shovel and dug down about three or four feet. It didn't take long, the soil was already loose. I took Marc out of the stroller. I kissed him on the forehead and bundled him up in the blanket. I tied the corners so it wouldn't come undone, laid him in the hole, and began replacing the dirt.

"The boy came over and asked what I was doing. I think he was worried I would mess up their project.

"I told him, 'My baby died, I'm burying him here.'

"I expected him to grab the shovel away. 'Are you crazy? You can't do that here. What's wrong with you?' He said, 'That's a bummer,' and left again."

She threw up her hands. "That's it."

Sibley looked at me.

I kept silent and she did the same.

Gayle Boyarin said, "It's never gone away completely. The pressure. But it did lessen. I kept moving. I went and had the rest of my life."

The evidence of that life surrounded us: her home, diplomas and awards and memorabilia, the husband, the living sons. All the trappings of fulfillment.

"Carl—my first husband—he was what you call spectrumy. We married never intending to have children. He had no interest, and I didn't think I could go through that again. When I found out I was pregnant with Adam, I started having panic attacks. Carl wanted me to get a prescription for a sedative. I blew up at him when he said that, and it all came out. His personality worked to my advantage: He could analyze what I was telling him without getting emotional. It had the effect of calming me down. Even so, I was on tenterhooks for the first year of Adam's life. I wasn't able to enjoy much. Things got a little easier with Matthew. But."

A long silence.

Gayle Boyarin said, "It's never really gone away."

She reached for a box of tissues, wiped her eyes, sponged her damp throat. The wastebasket wasn't in its customary spot—I had it by my feet—and she tossed the crumpled wad on the desktop, done with self-pity.

Her eyes passed from Sibley to me. "Just so you know, the bear was my idea, not Matthew's. He was following my instructions. Whatever the charges are, they're mine, not his."

Sibley said, "Professor, we came here to show you something."

She placed a copy of the toy company recall notice on the desk.

Gayle Boyarin picked it up, put on her reading glasses, scanned in silence.

"It's thoughtful of you to give me this," she said. "But ultimately, it's irrelevant."

She handed the page back to Sibley.

Some people hunger for absolution. Others cope by rejecting it.

I told Gayle Boyarin I'd issue a death certificate, listing her and Fritz Dormer as the child's parents.

"Does he know?" she asked.

"I was required to notify him. He wasn't interested in paying for burial, and I couldn't find anyone else, so by law the remains were cremated. They're in storage at one of our long-term facilities."

"I'd like to have them."

"Of course. I can help with that."

"Thank you. And I'd like to reimburse you, please."

Registering our confusion: "For the GPS thingy."

Sibley said, "That's not necessary."

"To me it is." Gayle took a checkbook and pen from the desk drawer. "I'll leave the amount blank. To whom shall I make it out?"

Sibley said, "You can just put 'University of California Police Department.'"

"I never thought I'd be giving you people money," Gayle Boyarin said.

With a choking honk she tore off the check, and a ferocious spasm took hold of her, leaving her jackknifed and shaking.

We waited till she regained her composure. Then Sibley took the check and we left.

CHAPTER 31

The autopsy of People's Park began on a sultry June morning, roughly six months since the onset of demolition.

Two weeks prior, the city council had voted, by a margin of five to four, to cordon off a corner of Bowditch and Haste for picketing. Councilmember for District 4 Jodi Davies sponsored the resolution. In a rare display of solidarity with Davies, Councilmember Leticia Stroh provided the swing vote, though she declined to endorse Davies's second resolution, condemning the University of California for imperialism.

A ragtag band of neo-hippies and Boomers took up positions inside the sawhorses, waving signs and chanting hoarsely as UC maintenance crews finished clearing the Free Speech Pit.

Siefkin Brothers, Builders, supplied a new perimeter fence. They also provided a small-scale front-end loader and a dump truck. A private security company was engaged to guard the equipment and ensure the personal safety of workers.

All in all, it was a modest showing compared with the legions of vehicles and personnel that had rolled up in December.

An unsettling sense of déjà vu prevailed nonetheless, and everyone stood at attention, bracing for fresh chaos. UCPD chief Vogel established a round-the-clock foot patrol. Our office got another memo putting the Sheriff's department into a state of readiness. Berkeley PD followed suit.

Defenders of the Park duumvirate Trevor Whitman and Sarah Whelan implored their supporters to exercise restraint, for the moment at least. Tweet after tweet went out: Do not interfere. Protest only within the designated zone. They understood it was difficult for people to sit on their hands. But if you truly cared about preserving the park, as opposed to grandstanding, this was the best way forward. They were confident that the evidence would vindicate them.

The bit about grandstanding was a shot at Chloe Bellara and the People's Park Alliance. Bellara—gone dark since her Molotov cocktail post—didn't respond. She'd failed to show for her academic standing hearing, and shortly thereafter, she deleted all her social media accounts.

The archaeologists arrived.

Professor Iliana Marquez Rosales was an angular woman who favored combat pants, military-style shirts with epaulets, and a sun-faded bandanna. By edict or osmosis, the dress code had spread to the rest of her team. They spent several days plotting out excavation sites with stakes and twine before commencing to dig.

That evening when I showed up for work, Brad Moffett beckoned me urgently to the coffee station.

He said, flatly, "They found more bones."

I said, "What."

Rex Jurow leaned over his cubicle wall. "At the park."

"Are we . . ." I looked back and forth between them. "Should we go out there?"

"B shift already got em," Jurow said.

A weighty silence.

"Please don't tell me it's another kid," I said.

Moffett's expression was inscrutable.

I dropped my bag and hurried down to the morgue.

Dani Botero was mopping up, about to depart for the day. She handed me a box of gloves, and I followed her into the freezer.

She took down a brown paper bag.

Bones don't typically smell much, and if they do it's more mineral than organic. The odor that puffed out at me when I opened the bag was of a wholly different variety.

Garlic.

I looked at Dani. "The fuck is this?"

"Dr. Bronson thinks they're chicken bones," she said.

The adrenaline began to drain out of me.

"They found them in the pit. They didn't want to take chances, so they called us."

As I climbed back up to the squad room, I tried to imagine how many picnics People's Park had hosted in recent months.

Jurow and Moffett leaned on each other, crying with laughter.

"Fuck you," I said.

"I mean," Jurow said. "Your face."

He mugged incredulity.

"Seriously, fuck the both of you. Dani, too."

"Oh now, respect your betters," Moffett said.

THE JOKE WAS on all of us.

In the ensuing days, the excavation stalled repeatedly, as every attempt to dig turned up bones.

First dozens.

Then hundreds.

Thousands.

The entire park, two point eight acres, had been studded with bones.

Pushed deep into the turf. Wrapped in burlap and buried. Broken into maddening fragments and scattered like seed. There were bones in the pit. Bones strewn around the former basketball courts. Bones in the urinals, in the toilet tanks, hidden in the bushes.

Now we knew why Chloe Bellara had been too busy for social media or school.

She must've known some hungry anarchists.

Mostly chicken, but also cow bones, cat bones, coyote bones, the bones of other birds, and a metric shit-ton of bones of indeterminate origin.

Every new discovery prompted a call to the Coroner's Bureau.

Every call required us to respond.

Every time we responded we had to take photographs. We had to bag the bones and bring them back to the bureau. We had to intake, open a report, and schedule an autopsy.

The pathologists had to study them and make a determination, which was getting harder and harder to do with the barest minimum of scientific rigor, because as soon as they'd finished with that bag, the techs brought in another bag, with more bones. Bags piled up in the freezer. It got so that everybody in the office knew Professor Marquez Rosales's phone number by heart, along with those of her graduate students. The sight of them on caller ID caused stomachs to bottom out.

And still they kept coming, and coming: a paralyzing tsunami of bones.

Brad Moffett wasn't laughing anymore. None of us were. At any given moment we were down two coroners, creating a state of permanent short-staffing. Legitimate calls went unanswered. We'd show up to a homicide three hours late and the detectives would chew us out. Paperwork went out the window. The county couldn't authorize enough overtime. The sergeants clamored to issue a blanket judgment of non-human origin. They took their request to the lieutenant, who took it to Captain Bakke, who took it to the sheriff, who consulted with the district attorney, who thought it over and said no.

Because what if, somewhere in there, there *was* a human bone?

Why not? It had happened once. It could happen again.

Lawyers for the university moved to have the park condemned.

These recent discoveries are nothing more than an act of mischief...

With the logjam mounting, a new policy directive came down. We would still respond to bone calls from People's Park but send only a single coroner.

Inevitably, the route became known as the KFC Run.

Independence Day fell on a Sunday. Rex Jurow and I drove to the scene of a bad accident at the 580/238 interchange. Kat Davenport stayed behind, waiting for someone to call in with more bones. It was midnight, but you could never tell.

Jurow and I removed three bodies, none of which belonged to the drunk driver who'd caused the wreck. He kept arguing with the EMTs, insisting he was fine, trying to sit up as they strapped him to the stretcher. Didn't they understand? He couldn't go to the hospital. He had somewhere to be. This pussy was waiting on him.

I ended up stuck at the bureau an extra hour, unpaid. Before leaving I knocked on Moffett's door. For a guy who liked to keep the mood light, he didn't take kindly to my crack about filing a grievance with our union rep.

THERE HAD BEEN a period when I would get home from work and notice Maryanne's bedroom lights on, her nervous shadow flitting in the predawn.

The windows were dark now as I walked up the driveway.

Outside the guest cottage I slipped off my boots.

Amy was asleep on the futon with her earplugs in and her eyeshade on. The monitor hissed white noise. I crept to the kitchenette to start coffee. While it brewed I thumbed through my inbox, stopping at the name *Elaine Shumway.*

Dear Deputy Edison—

I hope this finds you well. I apologize that it's taken me a little while to write to you.

I went down to the basement to check if my husband kept records of his old cases. Unfortunately, I wasn't able to find anything. I did a big housecleaning after he passed. You can imagine that it was hard having reminders of him around. I discarded a lot of paper. I don't remember noticing anything related to Phil's work, but if there was, I may have accidentally put it out with the trash. If so, I apologize.

However, I do have something that may be of minor interest to you. We have a vacation home on the Cape. I didn't think to check there because we only ever use it during the summer. I haven't had the occasion to go out in some time. Being there also reminds me of Phil. My daughter and her family are borrowing it for a few weeks, and yesterday I came out to spend the Fourth with them. There's an old postcard stuck up next to the kitchen window. Phil sent it to me when he went on that trip to California. He thought the picture resembled our view from that spot in the kitchen. It doesn't, much.

I'm sure it's a shoddy substitute, but since it's the best I can do I thought I'd pass it along regardless. I asked Hope to take some pictures and email them to you.

Warmest regards,
Elaine Shumway

I found Hope Morgan's email in my spam folder.
Hi there, from my mom. Thanks. —H
I tapped open the first photo, of the postcard's back side. Yellowed tabs of Scotch tape stuck out, top and bottom. No doubt the glue had long dried out, and it had come free with the merest pressure.

Smudgy postmark, some day in February 1988; six lines, written in Phil Shumway's strong cursive. Nice weather, but he missed her. He was tired and he looked forward to getting home.

The second photo showed the postcard's front. The colors had faded somewhat, but not enough to rob the image of its drama: a rugged coastline, waves flinging spray against a flawless sky.

Cheesy red lettering almost ruined it.

GREETINGS
from beautiful
Half Moon Bay

CHAPTER 32

t's a beach town. Thirty miles south of San Francisco, thirty miles west of Palo Alto.

Eleven thousand residents.

Four Klausens that I could find.

ON THE PHONE to Hayley Klausen, I introduced myself as a private investigator. It felt cleaner than misrepresenting myself as law enforcement. Not a total lie. I was investigating, and I was doing it privately.

The phrase elicited a sort of automatic candor, as though refusing to answer my questions would mar her permanent record. No, she didn't have any relatives named Chrissy. She did have a cousin Christopher who lived in New Hampshire. She was from Pittsburgh. Post-college she'd landed a job at a hot San Francisco start-up. The frat-boy culture got to her, and she'd quit before vesting a single share. She'd come down here to be closer to nature and for the last year had gotten by freelancing: web design, short-term coding gigs. With a defeated tone she told me she was mulling over moving back in with her parents.

Her story brought to mind Gayle Boyarin and Beverly Franchette née Rice and the countless others, men and women alike, who'd found their way to the Pacific, only to discover that it was not the golden bath they'd expected but a terrifying force of nature, immense and violent and indifferent.

I thanked her for her time.

JERRY AND VICKI Klausen owned Pillar Point Bait and Tackle. According to the store website—written in a fisherman's rambling, garrulous style—Captain Jerry had grown up in San Diego and been an avid saltwater angler since he was strong enough to hold a rod, working on ocean charter boats starting at sixteen. On one such trip he met Vicki Reyes, and it was love at first sight. In 1995 they bought the shop from the previous owner, establishing it as the premier supplier to the local sportfishing community. They ran charter trips for tuna, salmon, and rockfish on their fifty-three-footer, the *Sweet-n-Salty,* named for Jerry and Vicki (guess who was who!), as well as smaller charters and whale-watching trips on the forty-foot *Hard A's Night*.

The boy who answered the phone told me Captain Jerry was on the water till the afternoon. I left a message.

FRANCINE KLAUSEN WAS asleep when I called. This I got in broken English from her caretaker. She deflected questions about Chrissy: She didn't know, she was sorry, yes, she would ask the lady when she woke up, sorry.

MARIO KLAUSEN HUNG up on me.

A few minutes later I tried him again. He'd already blocked my number.

COULD BE ANY of them.

None of them.

Someone else.

Aside from his meeting with Janice Little, Phil Shumway's final report didn't go into detail about what he'd done or where he'd gone on his West Coast tour. If he'd headed down the Peninsula, I didn't know how, or even if, he'd settled on Half Moon Bay. His destination could have been another, more populous city nearby—San Mateo, Redwood City—and he'd taken a detour, picking up a postcard for his wife along the way. Maybe he'd driven out for no purpose other than to see the ocean one last time before he died.

But he had a beach house of his own for that. Nor did I see Phil Shumway as the kind of guy who indulged in spontaneous seaside jaunts to satisfy a squishy existential urge.

It is the belief of this agent that the investigation to the present moment has ignored the role of Ms. Klausen and that an effort should be made to ascertain her whereabouts with all possible expedience.

His time was limited. He knew he was dying.

He'd gone to Half Moon Bay for a reason.

THIRTY MILES SOUTH of San Francisco, thirty miles west of Palo Alto; forty minutes from either place with no traffic.

There's always traffic. Silicon Valley wealth manifests as multimillion-dollar shacks, a large luxury resort, and a quaintly preserved Main Street whose mom-and-pop stocks handcrafted cheese and presses fresh green juice.

I left before dawn, arriving into a morning that bloomed soft and cool. Along the coastal access road, banks of conifers alternated with grassy breaks, delivering me past the high school and through a determinedly ugly commercial strip where sandwich boards exhorted visitors to patronize Uncle Lou's World Famous Pumpkin Patch.

I crested the hill. The haze parted, and I pulled over to stand on the running board.

Same dramatic coastline, jagged rock and turgid waters. To the north jutted a spit of sand: Mavericks Beach, actually world famous for its big-wave surfing. Tiny black dots, like a handful of pepper strewn across the ocean's felted green, rose up and rocketed toward the shore, only to vanish in a burst of froth. Every so often, someone died there, chasing glory. Without really intending to, I began counting surfers' bodies, waiting for them to resurface; waiting for them to stay down.

Pillar Point Bait and Tackle was a cadet gray hut, harbor-adjacent. It shared a parking lot with several other businesses catering to the local trade—surf outfitter, seafood market—none of them yet open for the day. Captain Jerry's posted opening and closing hours were, respectively, TOO DANGED EARLY and WAY TOO LATE. I pressed my face to the glass, then headed down to the marina, walking the slips until I found the *Sweet-n-Salty*.

A leathery man with a stiff pewter-colored mustache was hosing off the deck. Everything about him appeared to have been left out in the rain. His shorts, once white, were virtually transparent; threads trickled from the hem of his T-shirt. His baseball cap declared that LIFE IS GOOD.

"Morning," he said affably.

"Morning."

He shut off the hose and came to the rail. "Can I help you?"

"Hope so," I said. "Are you Jerry Klausen?"

"So they say." He extended a barnacle of a hand.

I gave him my spiel: private investigator, hired to find Chrissy Klausen.

"Sorry, don't know her."

"What about a Francine Klausen?"

"I've never met another Klausen around here. Other than my wife, of course. And my cousin Mario."

"I found a number for him. I tried calling but he blocked me."

Jerry chuckled. "Sounds about right. Technically he's my first cousin once removed. He used to own the shop before Vicki and I bought him out."

"Is he married? Kids?"

"Mario? No. Lifelong bachelor."

"Do you think he'd know of any other Klausens?"

"I wouldn't bet on it." He paused. "What was that name you said before?"

"Francine."

"She lives in town?"

"I have an address for her on Miramontes Point Road."

"Know what," he said slowly, "I take it back. I have heard of her. I once got a package of hers by mistake. Sorry. Slipped my mind completely."

"Not at all. When was this?"

"Geez . . . While back. It came to the shop and I opened it without reading the label. We get about a million deliveries a week. I took one look and knew it wasn't anything I'd ordered."

"What was it?"

"Wine. I go to Vicki, 'Hey, did you order this?' and she goes, 'No, not me.' I checked the address and it's this woman named Klausen. I drove it on over."

"Nice of you."

"Well, I'm more of a beer guy. Anyway it looked expensive, like something a person'd want to have. The box had customs stamps on it."

"Coming from where?"

"Boy. I don't really remember. Europe? I don't know."

"Did you meet her?"

He shook his head. "Nobody answered. I left it on her doorstep. Hey, though, you think me and her might be related?"

You could imagine that the Sea Star Residential Park had seen better days.

Easier to believe that it hadn't, and that this was as good as it'd ever been.

The low-slung layout, pocked pink stucco, and scaly exterior railings wheezed neglect. A mile and a half inland, I could no longer

304 / JONATHAN KELLERMAN and JESSE KELLERMAN

see the ocean, but I could smell it: not the briny tang of summer beach days, but a penetrating iodine funk. Surrounding hills trapped the moisture, creating a clammy microclimate that slimed surfaces and ate paint. Seagull droppings stippled the walls and red roof tiles. It looked as though someone had attempted to freshen up, but they had a horrendous attention span and could only work in one-square-inch increments.

Mostly it was parking lot, an ameboid lake of asphalt relieved by curbed islets filled with brown mulch. Each of the sixty-eight units had its own numbered spot. The guidelines had worn away to specks, leaving vehicles crammed too close or spread too far apart or occupying careless angles.

Valuable real estate nonetheless; that it had escaped redevelopment seemed an errand Fate had forgotten to run. Eventually, the Sea Star would succumb. Until then it housed the remnants of a species nearing extinction: the local working class.

Francine Klausen lived in a ground-floor unit. A red midnineties Toyota Camry with a Tagalog bumper sticker and a bead cover on the driver's seat occupied her parking spot. Next to it, conspicuous among the pickups and 100K-milers, sat a black Tesla Roadster with tinted windows.

A tiny Filipina in Looney Tunes scrubs answered my knock. Stitched in red thread above her breast pocket were the words GOLDEN STATE IN-HOME CARE and the name ENNA F. She regarded with apathy my request to talk to Francine Klausen.

"She's sleeping."

I recognized her voice from the previous week's phone calls: She was the one who'd been putting me off, pretending to take my messages.

"Do you know when she'll be awake?"

Enna F. shrugged. "Maybe tomorrow."

"I drove down to see her."

She made a face. *Why's that my problem.*

"How about this," I said. "I'll hang around, and you call me when she wakes up."

"One second, sir," she said.

She shut the door and set the chain.

A moment later, a different woman came to the door.

Beverly Franchette.

CHAPTER 33

Beverly, and yet not.

Beverly's black hair, with modern layers and razor-cut bangs, smooth rather than windblown and nurtured to a healthy sheen.

Beverly's eyebrows, professionally sculpted.

Her nose was blade-thin and meandering, like a mountain ridgeline—Beverly's, right up until the very tip, where it bunched and became mildly bulbous, like some aftermarket adornment half a size too large.

That knob of flesh: It belonged to someone else.

Gene's genes.

The broad cheekbones tapering to a wedge were Beverly's. Beverly's large, dark, lozenge-shaped eyes, darting from point to point over my face, evaluating me as friend or foe. The corners of her mouth drew back, poised to turn up or drop down, depending on the results of the analysis.

The fog had begun to burn off. I could feel the apartment's stuffiness oozing out, carrying an aroma of witch hazel. The woman in the doorway wore a tailored blouse, black sateen with white piping, sleeves rolled to her elbows and buttoned in place with tabs; matching black slacks. She was barefoot. Somewhere inside that apartment was a matching pair of shoes, black sandals or ballet flats whose simplicity belied the quality of their construction. I knew as well that the sleek black car parked behind me was hers, too.

In the narrowness of her torso I saw Beverly's understructure with a touch more padding. This woman was not Beverly from the snapshot, Beverly at thirty. She was Beverly at fifty. Although people would say of her: *You have to admit she looks good.*

Her makeup was artful, taking advantage of the olives and umbers in her skin; accentuating her best features without making any vain attempt to hide her age. Along the way someone had taught her how to wield a brush. A stylist, or a skilled female relative.

Were she still alive, the real Beverly Franchette would be about eighty. No one had ever taught her how to do makeup. I had in my possession fifteen or so photos of her, and in every one she conveyed an unfinished aspect. To measure her against the woman in the doorway was unfair. Ask women what period of their lives they'd like preserved for the record. Few would pick high school or the months following childbirth.

Unfair to compare.

Impossible not to.

Beverly-not-Beverly folded her arms across her chest, and time folded, too. The nicked doorframe of the apartment was and was not the porch rail of the house on Vista Linda. The arrangement of her limbs became that of Beverly, holding a bundled, faceless infant, staggered by the weight of new responsibility, doing her best to look happy. She had no excuse to be anything but. She'd gotten what she wanted.

I was taking too long to speak, weaving in and out of the past.

Beverly-not-Beverly shifted her hip, blocking the doorway. Her fingers curled around the door's edge.

Definitely foe.

"We're not interested," she said.

I said, "I'm looking for Chrissy Klausen."

I said it because that's what I'd been prepared to say. I didn't need to say it. It was no longer true. I wasn't looking for Chrissy anymore. I had a single objective: to stall while I found the correct words, the phrase that wouldn't detonate in my face.

She reexamined me, rerunning her analysis. "Sorry, you are?"

"Clay Edison. I'm an investigator. A man named Peter Franchette asked me to find Chrissy. She used to work for his family."

"Doing what?"

"She was their nanny."

The idea appeared to amuse her. "Chrissy was?"

"In Berkeley. Late sixties." ·

"I guess everyone lived in Berkeley during the late sixties," the woman said. "I wasn't aware she ever held a job, though. Who did you say you work for?"

"Peter Franchette."

"Uh-huh. May I see some ID?"

I hesitated, then gave her my badge. If she thought it irregular for a Sheriff's deputy to be working for a private individual, she didn't give any indication of that. Nor had Peter's name elicited any reaction.

"What does this guy want with Chrissy?"

"To establish contact. She was an important part of his life."

"She must be, if he's hiring people to find her."

"I was able to narrow it down to this general area. I'm going around talking to every Klausen I can find."

Another amused smile. She returned the badge. "There's more than one?"

"Four, including Francine. You're the first person I've spoken to who knows Chrissy." I paused. "You do know her."

"She's my aunt," the woman said.

"Francine is your mother?"

"Grandmother. My mother's Carol. Chrissy's her sister."

"May I ask your name?"

"Audrey. Marsh."

"Nice to meet you, Ms. Marsh."

"You too. Well, I hate to disappoint you, but I'm not very close with my aunt."

"Does she live around here?"

"Oh no. She left years ago."

"Left for?"

"Italy. She married an Italian. You might want to inform the man who hired you."

"It's not a romantic interest, per se," I said.

"That'd be a first for Chrissy."

"When did you last see her?"

"Like I said, we're not close. I don't think my husband's ever met her. I doubt I have a working phone number. My mom probably does. I can ask, next time I talk to her."

"What about them? Are they close?"

Audrey Marsh shrugged. "Chrissy's lived abroad most of my life. To be honest, I never cared for her. She was always cold to me. It hurt my mom, though, to be cut out."

"Did they have a falling-out?"

"I don't think it happened at once. More an accumulation of little hurts. You know?"

"Sure."

"Her husband comes from some sort of aristocratic family. She became the Contessa de Something or Other when she got married. She might pass through, en route to someplace more glamorous, but other than that we barely saw her. I think it bothered my mom to see her putting on airs."

Suggesting the contessa's new life kept her too busy to maintain family ties.

I could come up with other reasons for her wanting to avoid California or acting awkwardly around her niece.

"Can I ask, is your mother older or younger than Chrissy?"

"Older. Four years? Five? Something like that."

"Do you take after her? In terms of appearance, I mean."

Too aggressive: The change of topic raised her antennae. She scanned me once more before saying, "Me? Not really. The story is my father had an ancestor who was black Irish, and that's where I come from. Anyway."

She shrugged again. Time to wrap it up. "Feel free to leave me your information and I'll pass it along."

"Thanks," I said. "If you don't mind—one more thing."

I knelt to unzip my bag. When I stood again, holding the snapshot of Beverly and the infant, she had shifted behind the door, as though I might come up waving a machete.

"Do you mind?" I asked.

Reluctantly, she took the photo.

Except for the most die-hard selfie addicts, most of us look at other people far more than at ourselves. What's true of one's life is true of one's physical appearance: We are often too close to see it clearly.

And I had my own biases. I wanted so much for this woman to be the girl in the photo.

Seconds ticked by. I felt my hopes starting to sink.

Audrey Marsh had a mother and a father. She had an explanation for why she did not look like either of them. She had a childhood and a set of memories to back it up. Why would she revise her autobiography, on the spot, on the basis of a snapshot?

She flipped it over to read the date.

Flipped to the front again.

"Who is this?" she said.

"Beverly Franchette," I said. "Peter Franchette's mother."

She nodded, gave a knowing smile.

She was the victim of a prank.

Only she'd gotten ahead of it. She was nobody's fool.

She gave the photo back.

"Take care," she said and shut the door.

· · ·

I STOOD IN the prickling heat, castigating myself. I could have stopped with her name, handed the reins to Peter, and let him make the first overture. Now I'd stoked her paranoia.

I peeled off two business cards, slipping one beneath the door and tucking a second on the Tesla's windshield.

I got in my car, backed out, and began heading for the exit.

Wait.

In the rearview mirror, Audrey Marsh strode shoeless across the asphalt, waving.

I lowered my window.

She said, "Give it to me, please."

I held out the snapshot. She snatched it away and took a long step back, as if I might try to drag her into the car.

"Where did you get this?" she said.

"From Peter." I paused. "I have a few others."

She gestured for them impatiently.

I gave her all the Beverly photos I had. She looked through them, lingeringly at first, but then in rapid cycles, like flash cards, cramming for an exam her life depended on.

Ribbons of heat rose up from the tar.

Seagulls circled and shrieked.

Her anger began to recede, replaced by an air of purpose. Curiosity, even. She'd lost her data and had to start over. A new problem to solve. No sense crying.

I'd seen this reaction before. It was Peter Franchette's reaction when I began to question his assumptions.

Audrey Marsh juggled the photos back into alignment and returned them to me—all except the snapshot, which she continued to hold against her chest, like a talisman.

She said, "Let's talk inside."

CHAPTER 34

We entered a living room/dining room/kitchen combination whose boundaries existed wholly in the imagination, the surfaces throughout being uniformly matted and soiled. Most of the space was taken up by a hospital bed and its accoutrements: drips, lines, monitors, over-bed table with an uneaten meal of white bread and pudding cup and foil-top orange juice.

Beneath layers of swaddling slept the oldest living human being I'd ever seen. Veins scribbled her waxy face; liver-spotted scalp, under fine white cloud cover, made a map of the world. Begrudgingly her chest rose and fell, as if she were debating the merits of each successive breath.

To accommodate the bed, everything else had been shunted up against the walls. Rolling stand with seventeen-inch television. Love seat, its itchy upholstery the same color as the carpet. Enna F. perched on an arm, browsing *Us Weekly*. A portable AC unit contributed vegetal humidity. The kitchen counter was a buffet of gauze, gloves, surgical tape, linens, and bedpans. The bin for dirties sat outside on a patio enclosed by a coarse plank fence and accessible via a sliding glass door.

From under the TV stand nosed a pair of smooth black ballet flats.

Two pilled samplers hung on the wall.

HOME IS NOT A PLACE IT IS THE PEOPLE YOU LOVE

FRIENDS ARE GOD'S WAY OF TAKING CARE OF US

Sandwiched between them was a wedding portrait.

The bride's gown was poofy and bejeweled, like an exploding soda can, the rhinestone and lace embodiment of a forgettable cultural juncture, the seventies belly flopping into the eighties.

A lot to overcome.

Chrissy Klausen had pulled it off with ease.

Her teeth were perfect. Her skin was perfect. Her bone structure was a miracle. Teased golden hair, against all odds, was perfect, with scores of dime-sized yellow sunflowers woven throughout.

One for each person whose hopes she'd crushed?

Which was Norman Franchette? Buddy Hopewell? Diane Olsen?

A closer look showed I was wrong. Her skin wasn't perfect. There were two faint scars, one by her chin and another above her right eyebrow, reminders of a brutal beating, a vicious fall. She'd healed well, and in a way the marks added to her appeal, humanizing her so that she seemed less doll-like and more a creature of flesh and blood.

Still, it was her wedding day. She could've asked the photographer to airbrush them out.

She'd kept them in.

The count wore a ruffled shirt and a mustard tuxedo with shark-fin lapels. He was not prototypically Italian, but sandy-haired and bucktoothed. Leaning against a tree trunk, dazed with dumb luck, he gripped Chrissy around the waist to prevent her from bolting.

Audrey Marsh high-stepped over clutter. "It's too hot in here."

I followed her out onto the patio, where she closed the door and we faced each other, crosshatched by the shadow of a latticework roof.

"Why are you here? Really," she said. "Why."

"Peter Franchette had a sister. Peggy. That's her as a baby, with her mother."

"And?" Without waiting for an answer, she held up the snapshot. "This could be anyone."

"Is that what you think?"

"*You* could be anyone. I don't know what you imagine this proves."

"It doesn't prove anything."

"Have you been following me?"

"No."

"How do I know that? This could be Photoshopped."

"It's not. But you're right. I don't have any way of proving that to you."

She rubbed at her upper arms, trying to free herself from an invisible rope.

"It's not my intention to upset you," I said.

"You didn't upset me. It's just a little surprising, is all."

I nodded.

"What do you expect me to say?" she asked.

"I don't expect anything."

"You brought this here to show me. You expect something."

"In my opinion, the resemblance is pretty striking."

She made a curt, dismissive noise.

"You don't see it."

"Are you actually asking? Or are you trying to get me to say something?"

"I'm asking."

"People look like people. It happens all the time. How many Elvis impersonators are there? How many celebrities have body doubles? Saddam Hussein had a whole stable of them, there was a story about it in *The New Yorker.*"

"All true."

"Okay," she said. "So?"

"You didn't have to invite me in. You did. I think there's something about that that bothers you, fundamentally."

"Yes, because it's surprising."

"Is that all?"

"Of course that's all. What else would there be?"

"I don't know. Otherwise I'm not sure why I'm not driving away right now."

"Good question."

"Say the word and I'll leave," I said.

Audrey Marsh didn't reply.

I said, "You implied that you don't look like either of your parents."

"That happens, too," she said, turning to grab a folding chair from against the fence.

She sat down clutching the snapshot. Her legs swept restless arcs until she noticed herself doing it and jammed her bare toes into the concrete. Tension radiated up through her body, as though she might catapult herself through the lattice and into the bleached sky.

"Whatever you're telling yourself this means," she said, "it's absurd."

"In your position I'd say the same thing."

"Completely absurd."

"Agreed. But it's enough that I'm standing here despite us both knowing it's absurd."

Silence.

I said, "Do you want to have another look at the rest of the photos?"

"No. I don't. I don't understand what any of this has to do with Chrissy, either."

To that point I hadn't mentioned the abduction. If Audrey Marsh were to draw any inference from the snapshot, adoption would have been the logical choice.

I hesitated. I didn't want to misstep again.

She sensed my dithering and immediately glanced up, alarmed. "What?"

"Peggy Franchette disappeared when she was eighteen months old. One of the FBI agents who was investigating believed Chrissy was involved."

Audrey Marsh stared. "Why in the world would they think that?"

"She was the sole eyewitness. That's why I wanted to talk to her."

"What does that mean, disappeared?"

"She was kidnapped. They never found her. They never recovered a body." I paused. "I can show you the file, if you'd like. I have it in my car."

Her chin vibrated, as if she might scream. What leaked out instead was a warble of laughter. "One thing at a time, please."

I nodded.

"This is all very entertaining," she said. "A lot better than watching Francine sleep."

Her tone was flip. A glassy sheath over serious distress.

"Anything else you'd like to share?" she said.

"How much do you want to know?"

"By all means, go ahead," she said. "I don't have anything till my three o'clock."

I TOLD HER everything. Gene and Bev and the affair; Norman and Claudia; Peggy and the house fire; Codornices Park; Buddy and Phil and a postcard of the Pacific Ocean. Now and again she broke in for clarification, but for the most part she sat attentive, taking slow, deep breaths, her agitation gathering into a dense ball, like a new, heavy element created from the collision of many lesser ones.

We'd been on the patio for some time when the nurse stuck her head out.

"Miss? You're okay?"

"Fine, Enna, thank you. Is Granny awake?"

"No, miss."

"I'll be in in a little bit."

The nurse nodded uncertainly and retreated inside.

Audrey Marsh said, "My first take is that they don't sound like people I'd want to spend time with."

"Peter's not a bad guy."

"He's paying you."

I decided not to put too fine a point on it. "I wouldn't've agreed to help him if I didn't think he was sincere."

"Sincerity's never in short supply. Terrorists are sincere." She squirmed in the chair. "What does he expect?"

"He wants to meet his sister."

"It's so important to him, what's taken him so long?"

"He's been searching for years. He just hasn't had much luck."

"Does he look like me, too?"

I smiled. "No. Like his father."

"Well that's good." She eyed the sliding glass door. "You're talking about my family. You realize that?"

"I'm not here to force the issue," I said. "And I'm not asking you to accept anything I'm saying on faith. There's a simple way to answer the question."

"I'm not taking a DNA test. Forget it."

I raised my hands in concession.

That established, she seemed to slough off a bit of her suspicion. An ironic smile played around her mouth. "I can't say this is how I planned my morning off."

"Honestly? Me neither."

"You're lucky you ran into me. Or—I don't know. Not lucky. But . . . I'm only here a couple of times a month. I used to come more often. It got to be too emotionally draining."

"I'm sure she appreciates your coming on some level."

"That's a nice idea. Let's go with that."

"May I ask, how old is she?"

"A hundred and three."

I whistled.

"It's not a cause for celebration," she said. "She hasn't spoken a word in five years. She rarely opens her eyes. I don't think anyone

318 / JONATHAN KELLERMAN and JESSE KELLERMAN

expected this to drag on as long as it has." She gnawed the tip of her thumb. "By the way, that's another bone of contention. My mom's always been the one to take care of her. She's seventy-six herself. She was coming every day till I convinced her to let me get the nurse. Meanwhile Chrissy's over there, living the life of Riley, contributing nothing."

"One of the other Klausens I met runs the bait and tackle in Pillar Point."

"No kidding. Who's that?"

"His name's Jerry. He told me he once got a box of wine misdelivered to him, addressed to Francine Klausen, from Europe."

She snorted. "That sounds like my aunt. Wine. For God's sake . . . My mom said Granny Fran always favored Chrissy, because she was so beautiful."

"When I talk to people about her, that's what they remember, her looks."

"My mother's an attractive woman in her own right. You can tell they're sisters. But Chrissy, everything about her was just . . . better. You know? It's a major source of insecurity for my mom."

"How'd Chrissy meet the count?"

"I don't know the story. I have to believe she had men proposing to her left and right."

"Do you remember when the wedding was?"

"Well, I was born in '68, and I was around eight or nine. So '76 or '77." Audrey blinked. "Wow. Saying that makes me feel so old."

Meaning Chrissy would have been long gone by 1988, when Phil Shumway came looking for her. "Did you go?"

"Oh sure. We all flew over. It was a big deal. I think it was the highlight of my grandmother's life, seeing her daughter marry this supposed count. I'd never left California, let alone the country. I assume Chrissy paid for our flights. Her husband, I mean. God knows we didn't have the money."

Designer clothes; luxury car. Yet that wasn't how she saw herself.

"The ceremony was in this village outside Naples, where his family's lived for ten thousand generations. All the crypts in the church had his surname on them. I was a flower girl. During the reception, they were passing out hors d'oeuvres, and I bit into a sandwich thinking it was peanut butter. It was liver," she said, laughing, "foie gras. I started gagging and spit it out. My mom got very embarrassed and yelled at me. She was afraid of looking stupid in front of these ritzy Italians."

"Does Chrissy have children of her own?"

"A son. I haven't seen him in forever, either. When I was in grad school I saved up some money to do the backpacking thing in Europe. Come to think, that's probably the last time I interacted with Chrissy in any real way. I'd ridden down from Rome to see Pompeii, and I called her from my hostel in Naples. I suppose I felt obliged to let her know I was in the vicinity. It ended up being this whole rigmarole. She invited me for dinner, but the nearest train station was fifteen kilometers from their villa. I asked if they could pick me up, and she began making excuses, saying I should take a cab. I told her I can't do that, I'm on a shoestring budget. She offered to send one for me, but then she said I had to come that night, because she had a party the next evening, and after that I was booked on the overnight to Zurich . . . It was starting to feel not worth the effort. I said forget it, never mind. Then she changed her tune and said she'd come meet me the next afternoon. She gave me the name of a café, on the main piazza.

"She was really late. The café was lovely, incredibly old and incredibly expensive. I had to order something because the waiters kept giving me dirty looks. When I asked for coffee, they brought me an espresso. I asked if I could please have some cream and they acted like that was the craziest thing in the world. They brought me an enormous carafe. In my mind it's around a gallon of cream. Not literally, but that's how it felt, they'd made me so self-conscious. I wanted to leave, but I couldn't, in case she did decide to show up, so I'm stalling, trying to stretch my drink as far as possible, hoping she'll appear and I won't have to pay for it.

"When she walked in, she had shopping bags on her arms. I couldn't believe it. She said, 'I'm sorry, I just never get in to the city, I have to seize the day.' She'd brought her son with her. That was the first time I'd met him. My mom had his baby picture, and now he was eleven or twelve. He was blond, like her. Chrissy spoke to him in English and he answered in Italian. 'Massimo, this is your cousin from America.' He was completely uninterested in me, throwing spitballs at the waitstaff, gobbling sugar cubes out of the bowl . . . Chrissy informs me that in Italy they don't drink coffee with milk or cream in the afternoon, only before ten a.m. I felt like I was a girl again, being scolded for spitting out my sandwich. Then she starts lecturing about how the café's from the eighteenth century. It had been destroyed in an earthquake, and her husband's family had given the owners money to rebuild. She said to her son, 'See? They have your great-great-grandfather's name on the wall.' He didn't care. She ordered him a slice of cake to occupy him and he took one bite. They lasted maybe twenty minutes in all before she stood up and announced they had to be going. I had to pay for their food, too."

"I'm not surprised you grew apart."

She nodded.

"What about your father?" I asked.

"He died when I was nineteen."

"Sorry to hear that."

"He was a heavy smoker, so that confounds the data."

"Can you tell me about him?"

"He was from Kentucky. Most of his family's still there. There's more of them, my cousins, uncles, and aunts. They're real country. We see them every few years. He came out here with the Merchant Marines and met my mom at a dance. She was a senior in high school. They got married right after graduation."

"What did he do?"

"He drove for Coca-Cola."

"Your mom? Did she work?"

"She was a housewife. Is. She draws his pensions."

"And you grew up in Half Moon Bay."

She nodded.

"Any siblings?"

"No. They wanted more but they couldn't."

"Where do you live now?"

"Atherton."

One of the area's wealthiest suburbs. The Tesla fit right in.

I asked what she did professionally.

"I used to be in med tech. Now I run a consultancy for women entrepreneurs, with a focus on high-leverage practices to address issues in public health."

"You said you went to graduate school."

"I have a PhD in bioinformatics."

People strike out along new paths. America relies on the promise of social mobility, and Silicon Valley fetishizes the scrappy, eccentric genius toiling in an unfinished garage. All the same, I couldn't help noticing the contrast between her upbringing and her outcome, as well as the parallels to Peter Franchette.

Perhaps she was thinking the same thing; perhaps it had always preyed on her mind. She had begun again to chew her thumb.

"Stephen—my husband—he used to call me an alien," she said. "It's a running joke, I came down from another planet and they found me in the backyard."

"Like Superman."

"Like Superman. Or I'm adopted. That's the other version of the joke. That's what I thought you were going to tell me, that she'd given the baby up. But," she said quickly, "everyone feels that way, growing up. 'I'm not like them.' It doesn't mean anything. It's how you figure out who *you* are. How much are you like your parents?"

"They're tall, too. But point taken."

"Right," she said. "So."

Silence.

She said, "I did ask her, once."

"About."

"Whether I was adopted. I wasn't serious. I was being a teenager. 'Ugh, you people are crazy, please tell me I'm not related to you.' My own daughters must've said something similar to me at one point or another."

"What prompted it?" I asked.

"I was going through old photo albums. It was for a school project, for my eighth-grade civics class. We were doing a unit on immigration. We were supposed to write about our family and where we came from. We had to assemble a family tree. I got out the albums to look for pictures to use. My parents at the county fair, when they were dating. Their wedding album. There's one of me, from right after I was born, in the hospital, and one or two more after that. Then there's a . . . sort of a gap."

"How big of a gap are we talking about?"

"I really don't . . . I don't remember. I'd have to look."

"You noticed it, though."

"Yes. There's no shortage of photos from when I got a little older. But if you're going through carefully, like I was, you'd think some must have fallen out or gotten lost. And . . . And, I thought it was weird, because my father took lots of pictures. He loved cameras, the latest technology. He was always bringing home things we couldn't afford, and my mother would make him return them. He had a camcorder before anyone else I knew."

"How did your mother respond when you asked?"

"She lost her temper. Not unusual, in and of itself. She got upset at me all the time, for all sorts of small reasons, or no reason. She said something along the lines of they were too tired to take pictures of me. Apparently I was an exhausting child. That may have also been when she told me about being black Irish. I'm not sure. I worked hard on that project. I got an A. I might have it lying around somewhere. Anyhow," she said, "we never talked about it again."

"And you never had any reason to doubt her."

"No."

"Did she or your father ever get a visit from the police or the FBI?"

"Not that I'm aware of."

"The agent, Phil Shumway," I said, "he came through this area in early 1988. Does that ring a bell?"

"I wasn't living here. I was away at college."

"Did you encounter anything else subsequently that made you wonder?"

"Such as."

"Do you have a birth certificate, for instance?"

"I think so. Stephen keeps all that stuff in a file."

"Social Security card?"

"Same thing," she said. "I'd have to check. But yes, I believe so. Yes."

But the last word faded on her lips, and her face grew newly troubled. She began to gulp air through her open mouth, the cadence no longer meditative but labored. Her neck and cheeks flushed; she arched, rubbing at her sternum.

"Ms. Marsh. Are you feeling okay?"

". . . fine."

"Would you like a glass of water?"

"I just need a moment, please."

To that point she had maintained a decidedly detached stance. With no real evidence, and nothing whatsoever that could be corroborated, she could, and should, disregard everything I'd said. Everything she said in return was likewise best written off as a thought experiment: a diversion to avoid having to sit in a cramped, depressing apartment with a woman unable to talk.

"Our house," Audrey said.

She sat up, plucking at her blouse. "Our first house, in Menlo Park. We lived there for fifteen years, it's where the girls grew up. We bought it in 1997, after Stephen made partner. I'd never owned a home before. I'd never owned anything. We were set to open escrow. The mortgage broker called me and said our application had been denied. I called the bank. They said there was a problem with my Social Security number."

"What kind of problem?"

"They wouldn't tell me anything else. They said I had to speak to Social Security directly. I called to ask what was going on, but they wouldn't answer me over the phone, either, I had to come to the office in person. I went down, and they looked up the number and said it belonged to Audrey Marsh, but that she was deceased. I said, 'That's impossible. I'm Audrey Marsh.' I had them check the birthday and it was the same as mine, June twenty-ninth. I said, 'Look, this is me, I'm sitting right here. I don't know what the source of the confusion is, but you need to fix it.'"

"You assumed it was a mistake."

"Of course. A bug, or a clerical error. I'm arguing with them and holding up the line. They sent me over to talk to a supervisor. He accused me of trying to perpetrate fraud."

"You'd never encountered any problems prior to then."

"Never."

"When you applied for a job, or a driver's license."

"No."

"Tax return. Passport."

"Nobody ever said a thing."

Throughout California—throughout the country—people live and work and drive and borrow and marry and divorce without government oversight. They rely on a system that's unwieldy, unco-ordinated, and opaque, providing civil servants no incentive to go chasing after even the most blatant of cheats. The IRS isn't in the habit of turning down money. Many of the automatic checks in place today didn't exist twenty or thirty or forty years ago, before modern computer networks, and when identity theft wasn't nearly as rampant. Time was you could obtain a birth certificate, over the counter, without ID. Even now it doesn't require much more than willingness to commit a little light perjury.

That the discrepancy had ever come to her attention was the real wonder.

I guess banks cared who they were giving money to, or did, once upon a time.

I asked what happened with the mortgage.

"We rewrote it in my husband's name. That was the least hassle. We didn't want to lose the house. Our cars are in his name, too. He's always managed our finances, it's part of our division of labor."

"Nothing's come up since."

"No."

"In your mind that incident wasn't connected to anything else."

"Connected to what?"

"The absence of photos of you as a child, say."

"But there are photos," she said. "It's just the one period that's . . ." She fell silent.

I opened the camera roll on my phone, finding the scallop-edged snapshot from the FBI file. "That's Peggy, around the time of her kidnapping."

Audrey slowly leaned forward. She stared at the screen for several beats, then sat back and moved her gaze to the ground once more. It was as if she had looked directly into the sun.

I asked, "Did your parents ever discuss why they didn't have more children?"

"They couldn't get pregnant."

"Did they say why?"

"My mother ruptured her uterus." She paused. "Giving birth to me. She had to have an emergency hysterectomy."

"So it was just you."

"Just me."

"Are there photos of your mother, pregnant with you?"

"I don't know," she said. "There must be. I don't know."

I believed that Audrey Marsh had a birth certificate and a Social Security card; I believed that they were real. I believed that there was a hospital photo of a newborn.

The question was if any of them were hers.

Her face was creased and wan. In that moment I saw what Beverly Franchette must have looked like for much of her life.

She stood up. "I've been out in the sun too long."

INSIDE THE APARTMENT Francine Klausen slept on. The nurse swung her knees aside, allowing Audrey a path to the bed. I expected her to take her grandmother's hand, but she leaned toward the wall with the samplers and Chrissy Klausen's wedding portrait to reach for another photograph.

I'd missed it on my way in. It was smaller, muddier, and less centrally placed. But the sobering heart of the matter was this: I'd missed it because I was too busy gawking at Chrissy in her bridal gown, sunflowers woven in her hair.

One for each fool.

"This is them," Audrey said, handing me the second picture.

It was a Sears-style family portrait, taken before a backdrop of periwinkle crushed velvet. Print quality and clothing suggested the midseventies.

The man was short, potbellied, with straw hair in retreat and dissolving features: a shallow scratch of smile, hairline eyes. His wife stood about five inches taller. As Audrey had said, Carol Marsh was an attractive woman—more so, absent her sister. But of course Chrissy wasn't absent. She never was, and her existence highlighted everything about Carol that was less than ideal.

Ears too wide. Brow a degree too shallow. The blond, washed-out rather than sun-kissed.

Carol wore her height without confidence, caving at the upper back so as not to tower over her husband. Her hand rested on the shoulder of a girl about nine years old. The girl's greenish complexion and somber mien clashed with a flouncy white floral dress and matching bonnet tied over a helmet of dark, straight hair.

This is them.

You could read aloofness in her choice of words, an attempt to exclude herself: *them,* rather than *us.* But I heard a plea. I had thrown a slew of photos at her, and now she was offering one of her own as a form of rebuttal. The people Audrey Marsh knew as her mother and father were not a figment of her imagination. They'd fed her, and clothed her, and taken her to Sears for portraits.

This is my family. They are human beings.

There was another way, besides a DNA test, to begin answering questions.

Carol Marsh was still alive, and I had a badge.

Francine Klausen's chest went up and down.

I handed Audrey the photo. "Thanks for showing it to me."

The frame was old, starting to pull apart at the corners, its wire corroded and rough. When she put it back on the wall, it didn't want to sit straight. It listed this way, then that, and she fussed with it until at last she achieved a semblance of balance.

THE SAN MATEO County Office of Vital Statistics was part of the health department, located in a bland, flat-roofed building shared by animal control. At the counter in room eleven, I spoke to a genial man named Felipe. He told me that as long as a death certificate had been issued after 1966, they could access it on-site. Otherwise I'd have to go to the office of the assessor–county clerk–recorder in Redwood City, and they'd have to call the document up from storage, which could take a couple of weeks.

I told him it was probably 1969 I needed, although it might be 1968 or 1970. I apologized that I didn't have exact dates of birth or death.

No worries. Fill out the form to the best of my ability.

He did need to ask: What was my relationship to the decedent? Close relatives like a spouse, child, or parent were entitled to an official copy. Everyone else had to settle for an informational copy. Some sections would be redacted, and it would be labeled as such, making it useless for many types of transactions.

I said an informational copy would be fine.

In that case, they accepted credit, debit, checks, money orders, or cash. Give him five or ten minutes to complete the search.

I went down the hall to the vending machine.

I bought a bag of Fritos, two packages of beef jerky, and a Diet Coke. I ate them standing. I texted Amy that I hoped to be home by four, stuffed the wrappers in the trash, and went back to room eleven.

Felipe had it waiting for me in a plain white envelope. He wished me a nice day.

Outside the building, I sat on a low concrete bench to read.

STATE OF CALIFORNIA
CERTIFICATION OF VITAL RECORD

COUNTY OF SAN MATEO
SAN MATEO, CALIFORNIA

INFORMATIONAL — NOT A VALID DOCUMENT TO ESTABLISH IDENTITY

CERTIFICATE OF DEATH
STATE OF CALIFORNIA — DEPARTMENT OF PUBLIC HEALTH

1A. NAME OF DECEASED—FIRST NAME	1B. MIDDLE NAME	1C. LAST NAME
AUDREY	ROSANNE	MARSH

2A. DATE OF DEATH—MONTH, DAY, YEAR	2B. HOUR	3. SEX	4. COLOR OR RACE
NOVEMBER 6, 1968	8:47 PM	FEMALE	CAUC.

5. BIRTHPLACE (STATE OR FOREIGN COUNTRY)	6. DATE OF BIRTH
CALIFORNIA	JUNE 29, 1968

7. AGE	IF UNDER 1 YEAR	IF UNDER 24 HOURS	
YEARS	4 MONTHS 8 DAYS	HOURS	MINUTES

8. NAME AND BIRTHPLACE OF FATHER	9. MAIDEN NAME AND BIRTHPLACE OF MOTHER
FLOYD NEELEY MARSH KY.	CAROL ROBERTA KLAUSEN CALIF.

10. CITIZEN OF WHAT COUNTRY	11. SOCIAL SECURITY NUMBER
USA	[REMOVED]

12. MARRIED, NEVER MARRIED, WIDOWED, DIVORCED (SPECIFY)	13. NAME OF SURVIVING SPOUSE
NEVER MARRIED	——

14. LAST OCCUPATION	15. NUMBER OF YEARS IN THIS OCCUPATION	16. NAME OF LAST EMPLOYER
INFANT		——

17A. PLACE OF DEATH SAN MATEO CNTY GEN HOSP	17B. STREET ADDRESS 222 W 39ᵀᴴ ST.	17C. CITY OR TOWN SAN MATEO	17D. COUNTY SAN MATEO

17E. LENGTH OF STAY IN COUNTY OF DEATH LIFE	17F. LENGTH OF STAY IN CALIFORNIA LIFE

18A. USUAL RESIDENCE—STREET ADDRESS 261 HARBOUR COVE DR.	18B. CITY OR TOWN HALF MOON BAY	18C. COUNTY SAN MATEO	18D. STATE CALIF.

19. NAME AND MAILING ADDRESS OF INFORMANT
FLOYD NEELEY MARSH (SEE 18A)

20A. CORONER: I HEREBY CERTIFY THAT DEATH OCCURRED AT THE HOUR DATE AND PLACE STATED ABOVE FROM THE CAUSES STATED BELOW AND THAT I HAVE HELD ON THE REMAINS OF THE DECEASED AS REQUIRED BY LAW AN:

(INVESTIGATION OR INQUEST)

20B. PHYSICIAN: I HEREBY CERTIFY THAT DEATH OCCURRED AT THE HOUR DATE AND PLACE STATED ABOVE FROM THE CAUSES STATED BELOW AND THAT I ATTENDED THE DECEASED:
FROM: 6-29-68   TO: 11-6-68 AND I LAST SAW THE DECEASED ALIVE
ON: 11-6-68

21A. SPECIFY BURIAL, ENTOMBMENT, OR CREMATION BURIAL	21B. DATE 11-10-68	22. NAME OF CEMETERY OR CREMATORY SKYLAWN MEMORIAL PARK

23. IF NOT CERTIFIED BY CORONER, WAS THIS DEATH REPORTED TO CORONER?
(SPECIFY YES OR NO)
NO

24. DEATH WAS CAUSED BY

(A) IMMEDIATE CAUSE

ASPIRATION OF EMESIS

(B) DUE TO, OR AS A CONSEQUENCE OF

HEPATITIS

(C) DUE TO, OR AS A CONSEQUENCE OF

MULTIPLE BLOOD TRANSFUSIONS

I didn't know when Chrissy had started nannying for the Franchettes. The earliest it could have been was February 9, 1969, the day their daughter, Peggy, was born.

By then, Audrey Rosanne Marsh, daughter of Carol and Floyd Neeley Marsh of Half Moon Bay, had been dead for three months.

How long did they grieve?

How long before they began to get desperate?

What other options did they consider?

Did they ask Chrissy outright? Or was it her idea, watching them suffer? Did she feel guilty for being the favorite? Everything came easily to her. She was nineteen and perfect.

Visiting sister for weekend, confirmed telephonically.

Did the three of them discuss it over dinner? Did they debate the mechanics? The morality? How did the turbulence of the Franchettes' marriage factor in? Gene's work on the bomb? Did they cobble together an argument from the greater good?

Who gave Chrissy her injuries? Her sister? Her brother-in-law? The tibia is the second largest bone in the human body. It's built to take a beating. Breaking it would have been a gruesome process. Did they use a baseball bat? A hammer? Did they shrink back? Pull punches? Did she have to tell them to keep going? Do it again. Harder, this time.

The man walking his dog, witness to a dark sedan fleeing: His name was Floyd Neeley.

The mute woman in a hospital bed: What intelligence lay in her dormant brain?

Questions, with teeth and claws.

I wondered what I was going to say to Peter. Having met Audrey Marsh, it was hard for me to tell myself that my sole obligation was to him.

I put the death certificate back in the envelope.

Approaching the bay, I could once again smell the ocean, brackish and choked with diesel and exhaust. The road ahead ran like a needle into oblivion. Traffic was already beginning to stack up over the bridge.

CHAPTER 35

I sat in a booth at a sushi restaurant in downtown Palo Alto.

Outside the sky bellied low. Intermittent rain pricked the pavement.

Peter Franchette glanced at his phone again.

"She'll be here," I said.

He frowned dubiously and reached for his green tea.

I understood his pessimism. Every element of this meeting—its timing, location, the terms under which it could occur—was the product of a lengthy and fragile dance. It had been moved, postponed, called off. This wasn't the first booth Peter and I had shared.

Since leaving Half Moon Bay, some five months prior, I had not spoken with Audrey Marsh face-to-face. At her insistence, I hadn't attempted to contact Carol Marsh. Nor had I spoken to Buddy Hopewell or anyone currently at the FBI.

I did return the case file to Special Agent Tracy Golden, saying it contained some interesting stuff. I'd follow up if and when I had anything worth pursuing. She dumped the box in the trunk of her car and raced out of the Coroner's Bureau lot, bumper scraping.

In her emails, Audrey continued to refer to Carol and Floyd Marsh as her parents. She did not bear them any ill will. She saw no upside to having her mother prosecuted, and she made clear she would not cooperate with an investigation. Her willingness to connect with Peter was in direct proportion to my willingness to look the other way.

I had either an immense amount of leverage or none.

I worked that through for a while. Was the goal to punish past injustices? Or was it to bring two people together, so that they might be able to build a future?

I could scarcely imagine the level of cognitive dissonance Audrey was grappling with, love and lies, mixed in equal measure.

Twice more I had raised the possibility of a DNA test. Twice she had declined, calling it *putting the cart before the horse.*

Her attitude baffled Peter. Establishing a genetic link *was* the horse.

I counseled patience. Pestering her risked driving her away for good.

The real reason for her reluctance, I guessed, was that she agreed with Peter. A match tied them to each other—permanently. Audrey Marsh didn't know anything about the Franchettes except what I'd told her, and based on my description, they didn't sound like people she wanted to spend time with.

We don't usually get to choose our blood relatives. By refusing the test, she was leaving herself an exit ramp.

It hadn't helped matters when she'd called Gene, only to have him hang up on her.

"We should probably order something," Peter said.

He flagged down a server and asked for an Asahi. "Anything?"

I shook my head.

The server smiled obligingly and went to fetch the beer.

Peter rubbed gently at his overturned phone, as if coaxing it to ring. "I meant to ask you how the party went."

One of our previous meetings had to be scrapped after I realized Amy had scheduled Charlotte's first birthday party on the same day.

"It was fun, thanks. The baby got her first taste of chocolate."

"I bet that went over well."

I took out my own phone and showed him the video: Sitting in my mother's lap, on Paul and Theresa's back patio, with a crowd cheering her on, Charlotte opened her mouth to accept a forkful of devil's food cake. The novelty of texture and taste caused her to shudder. Then a new kind of confusion set in, and she began swiveling her head, at Amy; at me; at the tines of the fork, smudged with frosting. Her little face etched with betrayal.

Why the fuck have you people been keeping this from me?

Peter chuckled.

The server brought his beer. He took a sip and moved it aside. "The party's really for you and your wife, making it through a year. Listen, I hope you don't mind: I got your daughter something. You don't need to say it," he said. "You're not allowed to accept gifts."

"I'm not."

"It's for her, not you."

"That doesn't make a difference."

"Well, you can think about it and do what you want."

I started to object, but he was no longer listening, his attention riveted to a point over my shoulder. Palms to the tabletop, he rose partway, eagerness checked by nerves. The light moved, occasioned by the opening of the restaurant door, and above the swell of street noise, above the soft tap of chopsticks, a woman's voice said *I'm with them.*

FOR FIVE-PLUS MONTHS I'd given Audrey Marsh and her mother a respectful distance.

I hadn't stopped looking for Chrissy Klausen.

Of the many old, chichi cafés in Naples, none was older or chichier than Pasticceria L'oca D'oro. Travel review sites praised its "authentic atmosphere" and ranted about the "outrageous prices," with one user warning "their very snobby."

I browsed a gallery of mouthwatering confections. A single shot of espresso cost eight euros. The history tab stated that the café had been in its present location, on the Piazza del Plebiscito, since its founding in 1857. The main dining room, with its numerous mirrors, abundant marble, and sumptuous floral motifs, was regarded as Italy's premier example of art nouveau design. It had been installed later, following earthquake damage.

I reached a manager who spoke serviceable English. He confirmed that a plaque behind the bar, dated 1909, lauded the generosity of Umberto Calvatti, sixteenth conte dei Barboni di Napoli, in aiding with the refurbishment.

Wikipedia had a stub on the current title holder, the nineteenth conte dei Barboni di Napoli, Giorgio Calvatti. What minuscule noteworthiness he possessed came from having sired Massimo Calvatti, a race-car driver, also of exceedingly minor importance.

It was Chrissy's full married name that at last yielded a hit: her charitable foundation, Benessere dei Bambini Transnazionale.

I ran their website through translation.

Contessa Christine and her husband had created Children's Welfare Transnational in 1998, after traveling to Eritrea and witnessing the challenges faced by younger people. The foundation supported a number of projects, including one aimed at combating child labor and another to increase literacy among girls.

I sent a carefully worded email, claiming to be a reporter.

A woman named Noemi wrote back. She would be happy to arrange an interview. First, however, she would like to understand the nature of my interest. How had I come to learn of the foundation? What questions did I have? As a rule, the contessa preferred to avoid the limelight and to keep the focus on the work.

With each exchange, Noemi's tone grew warier, until she wrote: *This is you?*

She had linked to an article naming me as a deputy coroner and discussing my role in solving an old murder.

It's hard to hide these days.

I called the number listed on the foundation website.

It rang and rang.

I sent several more unanswered emails before receiving a final response.

Thank you for your interest in Benessere dei Bambini Transnazionale (BBT, Children's Welfare Transnational). Due to the large volume of correspondence we receive, we cannot reply to individual inquiries, however we are grateful for your support in empowering children to lead lives of greater health, education, and dignity, thereby fostering new opportunities for the future of our global community.

Noemi Tedesco
Assistente Direttore
Benessere dei Bambini Transnazionale
"Migliorare la vita dei bambini"

ON THE FLIP side, someone unexpected had contacted me: Dr. Darren Aldrich, widower of the late Dr. Claudia Aldrich née Franchette.

He was sorry for the long delay. He'd had my name and number on a Post-it, stuck to his monitor, staring at him, for quite a while now. He appreciated my kind note. He'd meant to contact me sooner, he just hadn't found the wherewithal. It had been a hard year; a hard few years. He didn't know if I was familiar with ALS as a disease.

Claudia Aldrich had died at the same age as her mother. I'd assumed the same cause. "Reasonably familiar."

"Then you know, it's a terrible way to go. Even since we got the diagnosis I've been pretty much living in the Twilight Zone."

"What I read makes her sound like a remarkable woman."

"She was. She was. Intellectually she was in a class by herself. To lose the ability to write, or to speak—it was devastating for her. It devastated me to watch it."

"How long were you married?"

"Thirty-nine years."

"My condolences. And there's no need to apologize. Thank you for reaching out."

"It's really at Claudia's behest that I'm calling. If it were up to me . . . But it's what she wanted."

According to Darren Aldrich, toward the end, his wife had begun to take stock.

"On the one hand I was glad for her, because as wonderful as she was, as sharp and insightful as she could be when it came to others, she kept a lot of her own emotions bottled up. I thought it was healthy for her to work through some of that. I won't lie: It was hard to listen to, at times. I'd never heard her express regrets."

"About what?"

"The rift with Norman, for one."

"I got that they were estranged but not how it happened."

"It started when Helen died. Norman wanted to have her cremated, which went against her express wishes. One thing led to another . . . He's not a small personality."

"I know. I've met him."

"For the record, neither was Claudia. Losing him caused her a great deal of pain."

"She never tried to reconnect."

"Too much pride, I think. Over the years she brooded on it, until it became a matter of principle: *I shouldn't have to be the one to apologize.* Then she got sick and didn't have the energy for a confrontation."

"He's still around," I said. "I could put you in touch with him."

"Well, maybe. Maybe. I don't know that I want to start dealing with that. I was on the fence about whether to invite him for the funeral. In the end I decided against it. I didn't want him causing a scene, and frankly I didn't want to share the mourning process with him. He'd been out of her life for so long, I didn't think he had the right. Though in retrospect I have to ask if that was a mistake, for me as much as him. I didn't . . . But you're saying she has another brother."

"Half brother, yes."

"Well. Unfortunately, it's the same thing: too little, too late."

"Not for your kids. He's their uncle."

"The last thing we need is more complications," he said.

I figured the conversation was over. I didn't know why else he'd call, if not to reach Peter. But in the ensuing silence I heard him clicking his teeth.

He said, "What you need to realize is the impact it had on her when her father walked out. It wasn't something she talked about a lot. When we first met she didn't want to discuss her family at all. But obviously it scarred her."

"I don't know how it couldn't," I said.

"She never forgave him. It led her to develop strong ideas about loyalty. When our daughter Alexis was young, she had a best friend whose parents got divorced. After that Claudia wouldn't let them play together. I realize that probably sounds extreme. She had tremendous contempt for couples who couldn't work it out, or who she thought weren't making an effort. She did soften up, eventually. She had to, or else we wouldn't have had any friends at all. Practically everyone we know is divorced. And I don't mean to say we didn't have our own ups and downs, in thirty-nine years. You see what I'm saying."

"I think so."

"The bust-up with Norman was especially bruising, because he was the last remaining link to her childhood. They shared those memories, even though the memories were bad."

"Mutual witnesses," I said.

"Yes. She felt indebted to him."

"For what?"

"So far as anyone tried to take care of her back then, it was Norman. He wasn't much of a protector. He was only a few years older than her, and in terms of emotional maturity . . . but. He wanted them to reconcile."

"Him and Claudia."

"Everyone. Him, Claudia, Helen, Gene. He tried to convince Claudia it was better for everyone to get along."

"He didn't seem to feel that way when I spoke to him."

"Well, but you only met him recently. I'm talking about years ago. Claudia didn't want to have anything to do with her father, but Norman had this idea—naïve, if you ask me—that they could sit down together and talk it out. He bugged her until she caved in and agreed to go along with him."

"To see Gene."

"That's right."

"When was this, exactly?"

After a beat, Darren Aldrich said, "It's important to me not to sully her memory. She wasn't proud of everything she'd done. And," he said, "she's gone. There's nothing to be done. My daughters don't know. I want to keep it that way. Certainly I don't want to cause problems for them."

"I can't make you any promises. But it's hard to think how it could."

"What I'm asking is that you take what I'm about to say in strict confidence."

"I'm listening," I said.

Darren Aldrich sighed. "Shit."

On a warm summer afternoon, a young Norman Franchette and his sister Claudia rode their bikes up to the house in the Berkeley hills where their father was living with his new family.

"The woman who answered wouldn't let them inside. She said she'd never heard of them and threatened to call the police."

Norman Franchette, sweating on the front porch of 1028 Vista Linda Way, asking to see his baby sister.

He never claimed to have gone alone.

Me, I'm cursed with the fatal flaw of a warm, beating heart.

"You can imagine how it made Claudia feel, to be treated that way. It's not as though she'd gotten over Gene abandoning them. She didn't want to be there in the first place; she let herself be dragged along. And then to have this person treat her as if she didn't exist . . . It reopened every wound."

"Correct me if I'm wrong," I said. "Summer of 1969."

"That sounds about right. It made her furious."

"What did she do, feeling furious?"

"Nothing. At first she didn't do anything. She stewed on it for a while and then wrote Gene a letter. He didn't answer her. He wouldn't take her calls, either, so she wrote another letter to hand to him in person. She got to the house—she went by herself this time—but she was afraid to knock. She didn't want him to scream at her or hit her."

"Had he done that?"

"What I can tell you is that she was scared of him. She'd already given him a letter. What difference would a second one make? So she left and went home."

I said, "But she came back again."

"Yes."

"Alone?"

"Yes."

"When?"

"A few months later. She went at night. I don't know that she had a plan," he said. "She was angry, she needed to express that. How it occurred was happenstance. She peeked inside the garage and saw his workshop. He had one in their old house, too. He was refinishing a table."

Dr. Franchette told us he'd leave the windows open at night on occasion, air it out from the stink of varnish.

"All she wanted was to show him how she felt."

Lumber, a soldering iron, wood stain, paint thinner, the works.

"How he'd hurt her. She didn't mean for it to get out of hand."

Once it caught, it went hell-for-leather.

Darren Aldrich said, "She was sixteen years old."

It's a miracle the whole place didn't burn down to the foundation.

"Was she aware that there was a baby in the house?" I asked.

"She didn't say so to me. She wanted to make a clean breast of it. She had me write it all down. But. I don't know. Maybe that was too much for her to face, even now."

"Does anyone else know?"

"Norman," he said. "She told him, right after it happened. She didn't know what to do. She had no one else to turn to. She was terrified they were going to cart her off to prison."

Matter of fact he came to us.

He was practically begging us to arrest him.

He liked to bluster.

Maybe he thought it'd get him laid.

Darren Aldrich said, "You can't judge someone by what they do when they're young. It's the ratio of good to bad that matters. She was a loving mother, and an accomplished scholar. That doesn't happen overnight. You spend a lifetime becoming the person that you are. She never forgave herself, she carried it around for fifty years. Don't you think that has to be worth something?"

I DROVE TO Forty-Seventh Street in Temescal.

On the sidewalk outside the shuttered bank, a guy in a white button-down shirt and slacks and another in a black polo shirt and jeans stood conferring over a piece of paper.

I started toward the back of the building.

The man in the white shirt called, "Excuse me. Sorry. This is private property."

"I'm going to the record store."

"It's closed."

"I'll leave him a note."

"No no no. *Closed* closed."

I came toward the men. "As of when?"

"Couple months."

"Did he relocate?"

The man in the white shirt shrugged. "No idea."

I saw now that he was holding an architectural sketch. "You're tearing it down?"

"Not if we can help it," the man in jeans said.

"The goal is to preserve as much of the original structure as possible," the man in the white shirt said.

I scanned the block, a redoubt of shittiness amid the rising tide of gentrification. "What's the plan?"

"We're still in beta. Do you live around here?"

"Not far."

"Escabeche bar or beer garden," he said. "What sounds better to you?"

THE DELUGE OF calls to our office from People's Park tapered off throughout the summer, and two days before the semester opened, the site was officially declared bone-free. But the cleanup process had chewed through Professor Iliana Marquez Rosales's allotted time, leaving none at all for the excavation. She had classes of her own to teach. She and her team returned to Seattle without having completed a single full day of digging.

Lawyers for the University of California appeared before Alameda County Superior Court judge Sharon Feeley to argue that the school had done its due diligence.

Lawyers for the Defenders of the Park countered that nine weeks remained before the deadline.

The university countered that it had taken nearly that long to agree on an archaeologist in the first place, never mind the time necessary to excavate.

The Defenders countered that the deadline should be reset.

The university countered: Did the word "deadline" mean anything or not?

The Defenders countered: They had repeatedly urged their members and affiliated groups to exercise restraint. Why should they be penalized for third-party bad actors?

A tired-looking Judge Feeley listened to the arguments on the Friday before Labor Day. She announced that she intended to issue a ruling when court reconvened on Tuesday.

On Sunday evening, the judge and her husband attended a barbecue at the home of friends. During the ride home to Walnut Creek, she complained of feeling nauseated and dizzy. She thought it might be food poisoning. The shrimp Louie, maybe.

Her husband pulled into the driveway. He went around to open the car door for her. She unbuckled her seat belt, tried to stand, and collapsed onto the flagstone.

She was taken to John Muir Medical Center.

MRI revealed a massive cerebral hemorrhage.

The hospital held a press conference. A spokesperson confirmed that the judge remained in a medically induced coma, alive but unresponsive. He declined to speculate if the stress had been a contributing factor.

AN EMAIL CAME to Tom Nieminen, CCing me, from Blake Tipton, the correctional sergeant who'd chaperoned us during our visit to San Quentin. Fritz Dormer had recently gotten another visitor. That alone was unusual; what happened next surprised Tipton enough that he thought we might want to know about it.

He'd attached a recording from the visitation booth phones.

Hi Fred.

The audio was poor, marred by a piercing, electronic whine. Nevertheless I had no trouble identifying the speaker as Gayle Boyarin.

Thirteen seconds of silence followed.

A new sound filled the line, like a motor straining to start. It lasted for twenty-one seconds. Then the file cut off.

At that point, Tipton wrote, Fritz had dropped the receiver and exited the booth.

For what it was worth, Tipton had never seen Dormer show any emotion, let alone cry. He figured it might be a useful lever to get additional information, if we still wanted that.

I didn't have a chance to write back before Tom Nieminen's account autoreplied. He was on vacation. Persons needing immediate assistance could contact Sgt. Lon Haack at the University of California Police Department, extension two oh seven.

"I'M WITH THEM."

I joined Peter in standing, and we watched Audrey Marsh make her way past the hostess stand. Her expression was placid, in contrast with Peter's; he kept wiping his palms down his pant legs, and as she drew near I heard his breath catch.

She showed up in image searches, and I'd described for him what it was like to see her for the first time. Theoretically, at least, he knew what to expect. But pixels on a screen did not touch the heart of it, the irreducible kernel of identity that in real life presented with astonishing force and clarity. I could see his mind fighting to integrate her into the world of the possible: his mother in black slacks and a quilted blazer, a crocodile-skin bag slung in the crook of her elbow.

"Sorry I'm late," she said. "I got stuck on a call."

"No no, please," Peter said. "I'm so glad you're here."

For a moment nobody spoke.

Peter said, "Do you prefer . . . uh . . . You can have the inside, if you'd like."

"This is fine."

"Great. Great."

Nobody moved.

"I'm going to sit down now," Audrey said.

Peter laughed. "Good. Great. Yes."

The server came to take Audrey's drink order. She asked for a Diet Coke, then changed her mind, pointing to Peter's beer.

"You know what, alcohol's a better idea," she said. "Glass of Pinot, please."

The server asked if I wanted anything yet.

"I'm not sure I'm staying," I said. "Am I staying?"

They glanced at each other.

"Maybe for a little," Audrey said.

Cautiously they waded in, leaning on subjects of mutual interest: raising teenagers, the tech world.

It emerged that they knew several people in common. Small tech world.

By the time miso soup had come out, they were talking directly to each other, and I had begun to feel vestigial.

I said, "If it's okay with you, I think I'll be going."

Audrey nodded.

Peter reached for his coat to tug out a white greeting card envelope. "Thank you."

I couldn't accept it.

I also didn't want to embarrass him in front of Audrey.

I took it and wished them luck.

Exiting the restaurant, I walked into a stiff wind. The conversation inside had resumed, Peter gesturing excitedly while Audrey cradled her wineglass.

I still had forty minutes left on the meter. Not knowing how long I'd be, I'd paid the maximum. For a second I considered taking a walk, just to get my money's worth. But it was cold out, and whatever I'd paid was a sunk cost.

CHAPTER 36

usually work Christmas. Someone has to; people never stop dying. In fact, they tend to die in greater numbers on holidays, of both natural and unnatural causes. Too much food or booze. Too many relatives for too many days packed into too few bedrooms. The relentless demand for happiness that often leads to its opposite.

Thankfully, Amy's not one to stand on ceremony. She'd rather I earn the overtime and cache the time off for when we truly need it.

When the main line rang, at eleven thirty-one p.m., on Friday, December 24, I was standing by the coffee station, topping up my mug, browsing a picked-over box of pastries dropped off by a former coroner who now ran a bakery. It was my second to last weekend before new shift assignments took effect and I left graveyard behind.

Enrolling Charlotte in daycare had put a serious dent in our savings plan. But she'd been there for four months, and so far, she was happy. They'd normalized her nap schedule. At night she was going nine hours.

I hadn't bothered writing that down in her baby book, afraid I'd jinx it.

I selected an old-fashioned.

The phone continued to ring.

Brad Moffett yelled, "Someone want to answer that?"

On another night, under other circumstances, I never would have taken the call.

Kat Davenport was in the bathroom.

Rex Jurow was on another line.

"Fuck, never mind," Moffett said. He jabbed the speakerphone. "Coroner's Bureau."

I overheard the information roll in.

Deputy Blanchard, ACSO badge 1440, apparent homicide, one victim, GSW, address 10206 Carlos Canyon Road.

I started across the squad room.

Blanchard was saying, "It's called Rip's Gulch."

"I don't know where the hell that is," Moffett said.

"About eight miles southeast of Livermore," I said.

"Right on," Blanchard said.

Moffett looked at me funny.

"I got it," I said, putting down my donut and reaching for an intake sheet.

Moffett shrugged. He snatched up the donut, broke it in two, stuffed half in his mouth, and strolled away.

"You've got Deputy Edison on the line," I said. "Decedent's last name?"

"Dormer."

"First name."

"Gunnar. With an A."

I KNEW THE route well enough. I ought to. It was my third visit.

Kat Davenport gazed out the passenger-side window at the black, sloping terrain.

"Who lives here?" she said.

As we approached the final turn, a red corona appeared over the hilltop, and then, in the distance, we saw them: emergency vehicles, their flashers the sole source of illumination for miles, a malign throb surging unimpeded over the earth like a scarlet flash flood.

Davenport's phone began to count down.

Five hundred feet, two hundred, one, we had arrived at our destination.

"Whoa, hang on," she said.

"The entrance is up there."

She looked at me the same way Moffett had.

The gate hung open. I took it slow, inching along the cratered road while in back the gurneys clattered and banged around. Gradually the homestead came into view, its cairns of garbage and appliances in disrepair.

"Seriously, what is this place?" Davenport said.

"White Trash Disneyland."

Of the six trailers, three were dark. A group of uniformed deputies idled at the center of the semicircle, occupying the same spot I had, except that there were no women and children hemming them in, no twitchy shotguns aimed at their kidneys. I couldn't see Dale or Kelly anywhere. I guessed everyone had been shepherded inside and ordered to stay put. Dogs, too.

I parked off to the side, near two squad cars, an unmarked, and the ambulance. We climbed out amid the eerie soundless pulse of the flashers.

Deputy Blanchard was a doughy twenty-something. He told us the call to 911 had gone out at around seven thirty p.m. EMTs coming from Tracy ran into problems trying to access the property. In the dark it took them thirty minutes to locate the gate. Not that they could've done anything, anyway.

"He's in there," Blanchard said, pointing to the trailer with the satellite dish.

"What's the story?" I asked.

Blanchard waved vaguely. "Idiots arguing."

One of the other deputies spoke up: "There's two other brothers."

"They separated them for questioning," Blanchard said.

"Do you know who pulled the trigger?" I asked.

Blanchard shrugged. Why should I care? My business was the body, not the suspects.

The trailer's interior was smaller than I remembered. I was sharing space with Kat Davenport, as opposed to all three Dormers, and you'd think I'd feel the extra elbow room, but the effect was similar to stripping a home of furniture, the sudden lack of reference points causing space to deflate.

Compounding the illusion was blood, lacquering the cabinetry and the vinyl flooring and flattening the visual field. Blood dripped from the light fixture; blood caulked the nooks of the acoustical baffling.

Gunnar Dormer sat in his comfy chair, swiveled toward the door, boots kicked out, body stapled in place by sheer bulk. More blood pooled beneath him. His belly was a glistening void. From within poked a white tuber of spine.

The size of the wound, along with peripheral holes in his chest and groin, suggested two barrels of buckshot. The blast had sheared off the bottom half of his beard. He'd raised his hands to try to stop it: Three fingers were missing. Cracks webbed the laptop screen, shot speckled the wall. Perhaps more than two barrels; perhaps a reload. Aside from the damage to his beard, his face was relatively unscathed. His headphones had been knocked off and hung down his back, the forked wire catching against his throat like a bolo tie. He'd been in the middle of recording. Someone had come in, called his name, and waited for him to turn around.

They didn't want to shoot him in the back.

They wanted him to see it coming.

Davenport started taking flicks.

Knowing the decedent firsthand did not stop me from searching for ID. That he'd clearly been shot did not stop me from examining the body for other trauma.

We have a system.

I found his wallet in a drawer.

Gunnar Frederick Dormer. DOB October 11, 1984. He required corrective lenses to drive. He was not an organ donor. A moot point.

I headed outside to talk to Blanchard. The tight confines were making it tough for us to operate without disturbing the scene. We'd done our best not to touch the wrong things, and we'd taken pictures. If they wanted, though, we could wait to remove until the crime scene unit had done its thing.

He entered one of the lit trailers to ask the detective, returning shortly.

"He says go for it."

Movement stirred behind a darkened curtain. A small face peered out.

"Probably best for the kids to stay inside," I said.

"They are inside."

"I mean away from the windows, so they don't have to see it."

"I told their mamas to put them to bed," Blanchard said. "What do you want me to do, tie them down?"

"You might want to remind them," I said.

I prefer the give of sheets to a plastic body bag, but in this case a waterproof barrier was necessary to contain the remains. Davenport and I eased Gunnar Dormer to the floor and zipped him up. When carrying a long, heavy, sagging object down the stairs, it's a good idea for the taller person to lead. Kat Davenport took the shoulders, I took the legs, and at a silent three-count we stood, grunting. Even with the loss of tissue and fluid, he must've weighed two fifty.

We waddled toward the door, huffing and puffing and trying to steady the bag as it sloshed from side to side.

"Goddamn it," Davenport muttered.

She halted abruptly, yanking back on the bag like the reins of a horse so that I lost my grip on the plastic. I barely managed to catch hold of it again before it hit the floor.

She said, "Excuse me."

I craned around.

In the doorway, framed by darkness, stood a boy.

He looked to be about fifteen or sixteen, soft around the middle, with pimples clustered at the corners of his mouth and patchy facial hair. I recognized him as one of the twins, though I could not at a glance say which of the Dormers had fathered him.

The space around him blazed red, black, red.

"You can't be here," Davenport said.

She sounded a little irate, which was not ideal, but understandable, given how he'd sneaked up on us. His arms hung down at his sides, and he wiggled his fingers, swaying on locked knees, dreamy and halfway satisfied, as though he saw not us and the body bag and the blood-covered trailer but beyond, to some future moment when all this horror dovetailed with his fantasies. He radiated the patience of school shooters. And though I knew he was a child, and I knew what we ought to do—set the body down, talk to him, and bring him to his mother—I felt afraid, not for myself but for what had been put out into the world.

I gripped the slippery bag, my forearms starting to burn.

"Hey. Hey." Deputy Blanchard came bounding up the trailer steps. "What you doing out here. Come on, son. Let's go. Come on."

Blanchard pulled, not gently, at the boy's shoulder. There was brief resistance. Then he let himself be led away.

WE PLACED GUNNAR onto the gurney and began fastening the straps.

A door opened, and Dale Dormer emerged in handcuffs, followed by a uniformed deputy and a third man wearing slacks and an ACSO windbreaker. Despite Dale's bloody clothes and face, he appeared at ease, docile as the deputy walked him to a squad car.

"Be right back," I said to Davenport.

The detective was named Nelson O'Dwyer. He was in his fifties, sunburnt, with jostling teeth and a wattle of flesh below a thin face. He told me it wasn't any big mystery what had happened.

"He got tired of taking his brother's shit and shot him."

I said, "He confessed."

"More like bragged."

"What about the younger brother?"

"They're both saying he had nothing to do with it. How do you know these guys, anyway?"

"I've run into them before."

"Lucky you."

"Yeah. You believe them, though."

"About?"

"Kelly not being involved."

O'Dwyer frowned. "Is there a reason I shouldn't?"

I always wanted someone littler'n me to kick around.

"No reason," I said. "Monday or Tuesday for the autopsy."

"Pretty sure I don't need to see that again."

"You mind I say a quick hi to Dale?"

"Knock yourself out."

Dale Dormer sat rigidly in the backseat of the squad car.

I came up and he turned his head, blinking at me through the window bars.

He spoke to the deputy at the wheel, who stopped typing on his MDT to peer at me, then lowered the rear window.

"How's it going, Dale?" I said.

"You're lookin at it."

"Do you feel any better now?"

"Shit, I feel pretty fuckin good."

"What did it for you?"

"Ah, shit, I dunno." He paused. "He wouldn't let me sing."

"Sing what."

"On the show. I thought it'd be fun to sing something." There was blood crusted in his braids. "It's fuckin Christmas."

"Like a carol?"

"I'm not saying gimme the whole two hours. It's one fuckin song we're talking about. Gunnar, he's, 'Shut the fuck up, what do you think this is, *American Idol*.' Always taking shit too serious, you know? Pokin and proddin. What about you? You doin all right?"

"I'm fine, thanks."

"Get your window fixed yet?"

I felt breathless with anger.

My wife. My daughter.

"Little on the nose," I said, "a swastika."

"You got the message, didn't you?"

I said, "Be thankful for those bars."

Dale laughed. "See you round, dickwad."

As I WAS backing the van out, a bowlegged Kelly Dormer stepped from his trailer. He came down and stood in the dirt with his hands on his hips, surveying the homestead that now belonged to him—all of it, along with all of its people. Drowned in red brake light, a woman and child watched him with faces full of expectancy and hatred, waiting on him like a fallen god.

CHAPTER 37

Three hours later, I sat in my car in the bureau parking lot, beneath a pinkening sky.

I reached for the glove box, took out the envelope Peter Franchette had given me, and broke open the flap.

Inside was a birthday card. A whale spouted sequins from its blowhole, and an elephant with a sequined trunk held up a "1."

I opened the card. A folded check fell out into my lap.

The card's message read *It's a Big, Big Day!*

Peter had scribbled *congratulations*.

I unfolded the check.

It was made out to Charlotte Edison in the amount of two hundred fifty thousand dollars.

I did some math.

Amy and I might not be able to touch the money, but we could borrow knowing that future expenses would be offset.

Braces. First car. College fund.

What did a two-hundred-fifty-thousand-dollar down payment get you in the East Bay?

We'd still have to move.

It was five fifty-eight in the morning.

At or about that very moment, Dale Dormer was getting booked for murder.

At or about that very moment, my daughter was waking up for the day.

Her mother was rolling over, heaving off inertia. She was looking at the clock and telling herself that it could be worse; could be in the fours.

Swinging her legs over the side of the futon, she shuffles to the kitchenette and takes a bottle from the drying rack. The baby cries, and she glances at the microwave clock, wondering where I am, if I am safe, when I will walk in the door.

I put the check in the card.

I put the card in the envelope.

I put the envelope in the glove box and drove home to see my family.

ACKNOWLEDGMENTS

Frances Dinkelspiel (*Berkeleyside*), Jef Findley (Berkeley Public Library), Anthony Bruce (Berkeley Architectural Heritage Association), Wanda Williams and Roger Miller (Berkeley Parks and Rec).

Benjamin Mantell.

Clea Koff.

Sergeant Patricia Wilson and all the members of the Alameda County Coroner's Bureau.

ABOUT THE AUTHORS

JONATHAN KELLERMAN is the #1 *New York Times* bestselling author of more than forty crime novels, including the Alex Delaware series, *The Butcher's Theater, Billy Straight, The Conspiracy Club, Twisted, True Detectives,* and *The Murderer's Daughter.* With his wife, bestselling novelist Faye Kellerman, he co-authored *Double Homicide* and *Capital Crimes.* With his son, award-winning playwright and bestselling novelist Jesse Kellerman, he co-authored *A Measure of Darkness, Crime Scene, The Golem of Hollywood,* and *The Golem of Paris.* He is also the author of two children's books and numerous nonfiction works, including *Savage Spawn: Reflections on Violent Children* and *With Strings Attached: The Art and Beauty of Vintage Guitars.* He has won the Goldwyn, Edgar, and Anthony awards and the Lifetime Achievement Award from the American Psychological Association, and has been nominated for a Shamus Award. Jonathan and Faye Kellerman live in California and New Mexico.

jonathankellerman.com
Facebook.com/jonathankellerman

JESSE KELLERMAN won the Princess Grace Award for best young American playwright and is the author of *Sunstroke, Trouble* (nominated for the ITW Thriller Award for Best Novel), *The Genius* (winner of the 2010 Grand Prix des Lectrices de *Elle*), *The Executor,* and *Potboiler* (nominated for the Edgar Award for Best Novel). He lives in California.

jessekellerman.com
Facebook.com/JesseKellermanAuthor